By
Gretchen S.B.

Copyright © 2020 by Gretchen S.B. on Dreame.com
Copyright © 2021 by Gretchen S.B. on Kindle Vella
Copyright © 2023 by Gretchen S.B.

All rights reserved. Without limiting the rights under copyright reserved above. No part of this publication may be reproduced, stored in, or introduced into a retrieval system, or transmitted,
in any manner whatsoever without written permission, except in the case of brief quotations embodied in critical articles or reviews.

This book is a work of fiction. Names, characters, businesses, organizations, places, events, and incidents either are the product of the author's imagination or are used fictitiously. Any resemblance to actual persons, living or dead, events, or locales is entirely coincidental.

For information contact:
GretchenS.B.author@gmail.com
http://www.GretchenSB.com

Cover Design by Gombar Cover Designs

Works by Gretchen S.B.

Night World Series:
Lady of the Dead
Viking Sensitivity
A Wolf in Cop's Clothing
Hidden Shifter
Visions Across the Veil

Berman's Wolves Trilogy:
Berman's Wolves
Berman's Chosen
Berman's Secrets
Berman's Origin (Companion Novella)

Anthony Hollownton Series:
Hollownton Homicide
Hollownton Outsiders
Hollownton Legacy
Hollownton Case File

Lantern Lake Series:
Pizza Pockets & Puppy Love
A Flurry of Feelings
Teacher's Crush
Pugs & Peppermint Sticks
Moving Home for the Holidays
Mayor May Not
Building a Holiday Miracle
Founder's Day Festival (November 2023)

Jas Bond Series:
Green Goo Goblin
Spectacle Stealing Supernatural
Book Burgling Blood-Magic
Antique Absconding Arsonist
Property Pilfering Pariah

Stand Alone Stories:
The Tongue-Tied Hunter
Poker in Portland
Big City Bachelor
Lone Wolf
Witchy Inheritance

Scent of Home Series (Coming 2024)
Alpha's Magical Mate
Girl Meets Wolf

Acknowledgments

Thank you to my editor, Rose David. You made this book readable for everyone.

Thank you to Gombar Cover Design for giving this book such a beautiful cover.

Thank you to all the readers that followed this story as it was written. You drove me to finish this story.

As always, thank you to my friends and family who cheer me on as I work toward my dream of being a full-time author.

Last of all, but not least, is the Hubster. Although he hates to be mentioned, he deserves credit for all his support.

Chapter 1:
Five Weeks Ago

Emma

Emma and Richard had been together since she was an undergrad. Emma hadn't believed her luck when the Alpha's son paid attention to her. She never saw his interest coming, as her parents had no real standing in the Central Washington pack she grew up in. They were not at the bottom of the pack hierarchy, but they were not Alpha or Beta standings either. So, that the son of the Alpha, who would most likely become Alpha himself one day, would come sniffing around Emma, made her feel as if she lived in a fairy tale.

Emma wasn't unattractive. Her wavy light auburn hair hit mid back, and she had been told multiple times that her large emerald eyes were compelling. The downside to being a redhead, she was rather pale. She was also somewhat petite for a werewolf. It wasn't entirely unheard of for a werewolf to have her size and stature, but it was by no way common.

Richard was everything you would want in a male werewolf. He was six foot two and brawny, every inch an Alpha wolf. Their courtship hadn't taken long as Richard pursued her with a single-mindedness that had Emma smitten almost right off the bat.

It had only been natural that once she finished her master's degree and got a job working at a local university that they moved in together. Richard had a lot of pack business to do, so between that and her less than steady teaching schedule, they saw each other less than either of them liked. But what time they had, they made the most of. It was a dream relationship, and Emma couldn't think of any way her life could improve.

But they'd been living together for two years. Her mom and several of her friends asked if Emma had any inkling of when Richard was going to pop the question. He'd never been with any female as long as he had been with her, so their assumptions were not totally unfounded. At first, she waved it off and smiled, saying it would happen when they were both ready.

But lately, Richard had been acting a little antsy, with more of a temper. She wondered if he was getting the same pushes to enter an engagement. It made her wonder whether he would get cranky and lash out, or if he would succumb to peer pressure and propose.

A proposal would not be totally out of hand. They had been together almost five years, and an engagement was the next logical step. They had, of course, discussed the long-term. But Emma pushed those thoughts from her mind. She didn't need to be adding pressure to the relationship on top of what they were probably both feeling from outside the two of them.

She knew Richard and his father had been having some stressful meetings with several other packs in Washington State. The last of which was early this afternoon. So, she cut her afternoon class short; they were working on projects anyway, so it wouldn't affect the schedule too much, and surprised him by coming home early and getting takeout from their favorite Chinese restaurant. It wouldn't be as good as a home-cooked meal, but it would be one less thing they would have to worry about. She knew Richard well enough to know he'd appreciate it.

Smiling to herself, Emma snatched the bag from her passenger seat and slammed the car door behind her. She could hear her heels clacking up the driveway that led to their apartment building. They echoed louder as she made her way up the three flights of stairs to their apartment. She had a big grin plastered on her face when she put her key in the door, only to realize the door was unlocked. Adrenaline and fear spiked through her. She wasn't the best fighter. She could hold her own well enough, but she was nothing compared to some of the big beefy enforcers they had in their pack. She opened the door slowly in case something happened and tried to force herself to stay calm.

She told herself Richard would leave the door unlocked if he was expecting other wolves to show up at the apartment. It was easier to have them walk in than to have them interrupt any kind of meeting or phone call he might be occupied with. Most pack homes had an open-door policy, and he told her when they moved in together that their home would be no different. That thought went out the window as the door opened to their modest living room and she saw no one there.

Silently, she laid the food bag down on the floor by the door and shut it as quietly as possible. Her heart began beating faster and harder. It wasn't until the door clicked back into place that she heard the first moan. She felt her wolf twitching as it drew her attention to the back of the apartment where the bedrooms were. It'd been a female noise, not one Richard would've made.

Warning bells went off in Emma's head. *Surely, I'm just imagining things. The walls in this complex are thin.*

Slowly, so as not to hit any of the creaky parts of the floor, Emma made her way to the only closed door in the apartment. It was the door to the bedroom she shared with Richard. And the door wasn't entirely closed either. It was open enough she could've put her arm through. Her heart dropped into her stomach as Emma stuck her eye to the crack in the door and saw her worst nightmare.

Long raven hair cascaded over a woman's shoulders as she sat on top of Richard, who was lying on his back. There was no mistaking what activity was being done in there. And as if to remove the last of her suspicions, she heard Richard growl. Panic, hurt, and anger shot through her in waves, as if her body couldn't settle on how it was feeling.

Her wolf growled loudly and bounded to the forefront.

"Are you freaking kidding me?" Emma stammered as she slammed the door all the way open. She knew her eyes widened with panic as the door hit the wall. Emma was cool and levelheaded; she was a submissive wolf through and through. Outbursts of anger were not her thing.

Both heads swiveled toward her at the sounds she made. The woman was Cecily, one of the more popular she-wolves in the pack. She was the daughter of one of the

Beta wolves, which gave her a higher standing just by being herself than Emma had when she wasn't attached to Richard. The smirk she gave Emma showed she wasn't embarrassed at being caught and merely thought it was funny, as if this were some elaborate prank they were playing on Emma.

Her wolf growled inside of her head. *That woman is on top of our mate.* Her wolf wanted to act, but Emma was glued to her spot as Richard looked at her, surprised. There was no genuine remorse on his face, just shock.

"Emma, what are you doing home so early?"

Her jaw dropped at his words. "Are you... What?" Her eyes stung, and the world grew watery.

Growling again, her wolf kicked into action, and Emma turned and rushed from the apartment. Her eyes grew more and more bleary as she went. Her only thought was to get to her car and away from the embarrassment of what she'd seen in her own apartment, in her own bed.

Wrenching open the door to her beloved Honda Fit, Emma heard Richard thundering down the stairs after her.

"Emma! Emma, I am so sorry you had to see that. It was a stupid mistake. You must forgive me. Please Emma, come back upstairs so we can talk about this."

Her wolf growled in her head. *We have to do no such thing. If you will not scratch his eyes out, get in the car and get away.*

Her wolf had always been much more assertive than Emma had the right to be. Emma wasn't a dominant wolf, her parents' lower standing in the pack aside. It wasn't in her to be violent. That didn't stop her wolf from trying, though.

"N–no Richard, I need to not be here. I don't know what I could have done to make you think what you were doing was okay."

Nothing. Her wolf hissed in her head, but Emma ignored her.

"Emma." It was the croon he always used when she was upset. It worked every time to soothe her nerves, but not this time. This time it was adding fuel to the fire of her fears, and Emma felt herself shake.

He grabbed the driver's door.

"Let, let go of the door, Richard." Her voice was so quiet she knew no one without supernatural hearing would've caught her words, as her legs collapsed and she dropped into the driver's seat. She couldn't make eye contact with him.

Not that it would've mattered if she was looking at him, as she could barely see the windshield in front of her. When Emma blinked several times, she saw Cecily standing at the top of the stairs, still with that smirk on her face and her arms tucked under her ample breasts.

"No, Emma, we need to go inside and talk about this. There's no reason to make a scene."

Her wolf growled at his words, and that only made Emma's nerves fray further. She tried to yank the door away from him, but he wouldn't budge.

"Please, please let me go." She sobbed quietly as her world shattered into little pieces around her.

This time, remorse wasn't in his voice when he spoke. This time, it was more of a growl. "Emma, you belong to me. You are mine, and you will do what I say." He was using an intimidating Alpha voice he only used when someone challenged his place among the pack. It was a dangerous voice and Emma went stock still as he used it. Panic set in like butterflies in her stomach.

Just then, a car blasting music Emma couldn't identify came screeching into the parking lot. Adrenaline shot through her, and she used the momentary distraction to rip the door from Richard's hands and shut it. She locked it immediately and jammed her keys into the ignition.

Richard regained his focus and began banging on the window. Adrenaline shot through her veins faster as she yanked the car into reverse and burst out of the parking lot.

She kept watching her rearview mirror, hoping Richard would not follow her. The last thing she wanted was to continue that scene somewhere else. She didn't know what to do or where to go. Everyone she knew, except for her coworkers, was in the pack. Their lives were so intertwined. There was nowhere she could go to hide from Richard. He knew more about her than anyone else on the planet. Emma began crying in earnest as she forced herself to continue driving, hoping to lose Richard. Should he have decided to follow her. She weaved on and off the main roads, stalling until she could figure out where to go.

Chapter 2:
A Dog in Wolf's Clothing

Emma

In the end, after driving for forty-five minutes, Emma knew there was only one place she could go. One place she would feel safe to hide from the world while she processed that Richard hadn't thought enough of her.

Why wouldn't he have just broken up with me? I thought we were so happy.

Turning the car around, she got back on I-90 and headed to her parents' house. Checking the time, she knew at least her mother would be home by the time she got there. Needing comfort now instead of waiting for the fifteen minutes it would take her to drive to her parents' house, Emma told her Bluetooth to call one of her two best childhood friends, Bess. If anyone could share her pain and shock, it would be Bess. Her other best friend, Raelene, moved to the western side of the state years ago, and she and Emma only kept in contact once every couple of months. Whereas Bess had a standing Sunday brunch with Emma every week.

Bess picked up after three rings. "Hun, shouldn't you be in class?

Emma's eyes flooded with fresh tears, and she let out a sob before she even knew she was doing it.

"Emma? Emma, what happened?" Worry threaded her friend's voice.

The words tumbled out of her before she could get more than two thoughts together. "I came home early to surprise Richard, because I know he's been stressed lately. He was in bed with Cecily when I got there. He was cheating on me... and the look she gave me, the smirk. Like she was bragging." Saying that last thought out loud made her want to puke. It'd been niggling at the back of her mind, but saying it out loud somehow made it so much worse.

"Oh," was all Bess responded.

Suspicion snaked through her mind, and Emma blinked back her tears as a wariness filled her. "What do you mean, oh?" Emma asked, though she wasn't entirely sure she wanted the answer.

"I thought you knew." Bess' words were so quiet, Emma swore she must have been hearing things.

"What?" Her heart was beating so hard it felt like it was going to rip itself from her chest.

Bess cleared her throat and took several heavy breaths. "It's been happening for years, different women. I just figured you knew and didn't want to talk about it. It wasn't like he was secretive about it. I just figured you were ignoring it, so I never brought it up. I'm so sorry Emma. If I had known you didn't know, I would've told you when it started. Or at least when I found out it was going on." She could tell from her friend's voice Bess was crying.

That brought a fresh sheen to Emma's vision. Not only had Richard been cheating on her, but everyone knew. Everyone knew he was making a fool of her, and no one said a thing.

Did they all think I wasn't worthy of a monogamous commitment? Did I not warrant loyalty simply because of my lower status in the pack? I thought I was well liked. How could everyone have kept this from me? How could I be so stupid? So blind?

Panic zinged through her as she tried to force herself to stop crying so she could keep driving safely.

"I didn't know," she sobbed.

"Oh Emma, honey, where are you? I'm leaving the office now. Wherever you are, I'm coming to you." There was rustling in the background, and Emma knew her friend was collecting her belongings from her desk.

"I'm headed to my parents' house."

"All right, I'll be there in twenty minutes. I'll grab booze on my way there." Then there was a click as Bess hung up.

He's been cheating on us for years? We should turn around and ruin his manhood until it is no use to him. Her wolf growled through clenched teeth.

"Everyone knew. If Bess knew, everyone knew. Nobody cared." Swallowing back a sob, Emma clenched her hands around the steering wheel and put all of her attention on getting to her parents' house safely. Forcing the thoughts from her head was harder than she thought it would be.

I'm almost there. I can fall apart once I get there. Just hang on.

When she was in her childhood home where safety and love were ever present, then she could fall apart, not before.

Chapter 3:
Home is Where the Wine is

Emma

It took three tries to get her parents' door unlocked through her blurry vision. But once the door swung open, Emma ripped out her keys and called out to her mother. "Mom? Mom, are you here?"

A moment later, the older brunette woman appeared around the corner, her hair in a messy bun, slightly askew on her head with her glasses firmly in place, letting Emma know she caught her mother working on the computer in her office. Her mother gave one look at her and concern filled her face.

"Emma? Sweetie, what happened?" Her mother came rushing toward her, arms outstretched.

It was then she fell apart. As soon as her mother touched her, held her close, Emma felt the last of her resolve collapse and she lost it. She couldn't form words, just cried on her mother shoulder. Her mother, bless her heart, rubbed Emma's back and made reassuring shushing noises. They were still standing like that when Bess arrived. The purple-haired woman placed the bag she was holding on the ground behind her before walking over to them.

"Do you know what's happened?" her mother whispered over Emma's shoulder as she continued to sob.

"She walked in on Richard sleeping with another woman in their bed," Bess explained, both sad and matter-of-fact.

Emma felt her mother stiffen and tighten her embrace. There was a slight growl in the older woman's chest, and it soothed Emma's spirit to hear her mother upset on her behalf.

"Sweetie, let's sit down." Emma's mother commanded in a solid, take charge voice as she slowly moved Emma toward the couch where they both collapsed, still mid hug.

Emma felt the couch move behind her and knew Bess had taken up the third seat. A moment later, a hand began rubbing her back. Emma didn't know how long she sat there letting herself break into pieces, but it seemed like forever and yet no time at all.

She didn't know what she was going to do. She had no place to live. She didn't want to live with Richard anymore, knowing he had been sleeping with other women for years in their bed. And yet she had nowhere else to go. She'd gone from her parents' house, to dorm rooms, then home again, to living with Richard. Emma never stood on her own two feet. A fact that had never been so painfully clear as it was in this moment.

It only made things worse that it appeared the whole pack knew. They knew and didn't tell her.

What did people think of me? That I was ignoring it? Just how many know that my supposed mate didn't think I was worthy of commitment?

Her wolf growled angrily at those thoughts, but Emma ignored it, too absorbed in her emotions.

Once the sobs slowed, Emma slowly pushed herself from her mother. The older woman let her. A Kleenex appeared over her shoulder, and Emma took it. "Thank you," her voice quaking as she spoke. She began dabbing at her face.

"Maybe, maybe it's just a onetime thing." Her mother said in a voice that reassured Emma, but it didn't even seem to work on her mother.

"It's been going on for years. Most of the pack, at least the younger generation, knew about it," Bess interjected.

Her mother growled. "And no one thought to tell her?" The look her mother gave Bess was murderous, and Emma heard her friend gasp. Her mother's eyes flashed to the yellow/gold color of her wolf's. All werewolf's wolf eyes fit in the yellow/gold range. While in human form, they only flash or appear in times of great negative emotion.

"I thought she knew. If I had known she didn't, I would have said something, I swear." There was a tremble to her friend's voice Emma knew was sorrow, not fear.

Bess' family was higher, barely, up the pack hierarchy than Emma and her parents. That hierarchy was too firmly engrained for her mother to do more than snarl.

Her mother continued to stare before she pushed herself off the couch and left the room. "I'm getting glasses for that wine," she called over her shoulder at them, a growl still threading her voice.

"I promise, I would have Emma. I wouldn't have let you live in ignorance if I had known you weren't aware of it. I just, I just figured you knew. He practically paraded them around. I'm so, so sorry. Please forgive me." The sorrow in her friend's voice gave Emma a pain in her chest as she turned to face her friend.

"I know you didn't mean to hurt me, but I still wish someone said something," Emma whispered.

The two of them sat in silence, neither sure what should come next.

I feel so hollow inside. My private life has been a lie... for years. Emma's stomach started rolling, and for a second, she contemplated a run to the bathroom.

Several minutes later, her mom came back with three very large glasses and popped open two matching bottles before pouring an indecent amount of wine into a glass and pushing it into Emma's hands. "Drink," her mother commanded.

Luckily, she passed her love of wine on to Emma. Even though her stomach rolled a bit at holding the light red liquid, the familiarity of drinking wine with her mother was enough to ease the knots and soothe some of Emma's nerves.

The three of them sat in silence through two bottles. Then her mother stood and headed back into the kitchen to make dinner. At which time Emma took the corner of the couch and curled up under the blanket her maternal grandmother knitted years ago. All she could do was sit and stare off into space. Feeling as if she was hollow, just a shell of embarrassment and unworthiness.

Emma was never under any delusion that her relationship with Richard gave her a higher status among the pack. That would only happen if they took part in a formal mating ceremony. But she felt her lack of status shouldn't matter in this situation. Sure, it was practically unheard of that the Alpha's son would want to be with the likes of her, but that shouldn't excuse this kind of behavior.

Surely our years together meant something? We even talked about performing the mating ceremony. It was all but official. Sure, werewolves are promiscuous, but weren't they also loyal?

Her parents never cheated on each other.

That I know of anyway. Was this an Alpha male thing? Do Alpha wolves not believe in monogamy? Richard would have told me that was the case from the get go if it was, right?

He's trash, end of story. Her wolf interjected flippantly. *Do not give him any excuse. Mates have each other's backs. He did not have yours.*

Emma's thoughts swirled uninterrupted until her father stepped into the house. His initial response at seeing her was to beam. Then he took in the situation at hand and frowned before her mother called him into the kitchen. He gave Emma one last look of concern before heeding his wife's call.

A few seconds later, a loud growl rumbled from the kitchen before her father stormed to the back of the house, ripping his cell phone out of his pocket as he did so. A door slammed and even with Emma's fantastic hearing, she couldn't make out more than a growly muttering. When silence followed, Emma went back to staring at the wall until her mother called her and Bess in to the kitchen for dinner.

Chapter 4:
Indecent Proposal

Emma

Dinner was silent and tense. No one tried to start a conversation with Emma, which she appreciated. It was a comfort to have her parents and Bess with her. She gained some strength from being near them. But that didn't mean she was ready to talk about the matters at hand.

The only time anyone spoke was when her father slid into his chair and looked at her very matter-of-factly. "Your old bedroom is made up. You're going to be staying here as long as you need to. We will take care of moving out your things."

It was comforting, but it also solidified her sadness. The happiest time in her life was now over, officially. She didn't think she could take Richard back. If it had been a onetime incident, maybe she could have overlooked it in time, *but years? Bess says this has been happening for years.*

Emma choked back a sob. It was getting easier to stop herself from breaking down. She supposed that was something.

They were most of the way through dinner when there was a banging at the front door. Everyone at the table stiffened and exchanged glances before Emma's father stood and walked into the living room to the front door. The smell hit Emma before she recognized the voices. It was Richard and his father, the Alpha. They were keeping their voices low. But she could hear the growl in her father's tone.

Bess reached over and gripped Emma's hands. There were several minutes of what sounded like arguing before her father stuck his head around the corner and looked straight at her. "Emma, will you join us in the living room, please?"

What could they possibly want with me? It isn't to apologize, that is for sure.

Just stay calm. Do not give the Alpha a reason to be angry at us or our family. Her wolf responded warily.

Emma exchanged concerned glances with both Bess and her mother. Bess was chewing on her lower lip, while Emma's mother gave a stoic expression. Emma took one large shuddering breath before pushing herself up from the table and slowly making her way into the living room, taking in the group.

Her father stood, arms crossed over his chest, frowning over their Alpha's left shoulder. No one in the pack looked the Alpha in the eyes except his mate, and possibly his children. There were exceptions in informal settings, but as a general rule, it wasn't done. Since her father wasn't anywhere near the inner circle, eye contact was always a no-no. Alpha Peters stood a yard and a half away from her father. His hands clasped in front of him, with a serious, concerned expression on his face. Next to him, only about a foot away, stood Richard, his expression smug.

What does that expression mean? What does he have to be smug about? He cheated on me.

Rip him a new one. Her wolf growled.

"Ah, Emma, thank you for joining us. As I said to your father, I apologize for interrupting your evening meal." The Alpha's smooth, deep voice was cordial, as if they were discussing clothing options for a formal event. He was an older, slightly taller version of Richard. There was never any doubt the two were related.

"Of course, Alpha," Emma replied automatically as she came to stand only a few inches from her father. The anger vibrating off of him was comforting. And she took a deep breath before looking at the Alpha's chin, waiting for the older man to speak. Her nerves winding tighter now that she was close enough to smell Alpha Peters' annoyance.

"Your father informed me of the situation you and Richard find yourselves in. I, like several others, thought you were aware of his dalliances and had no problem with them. Honestly, I figured you were having a few yourself and were more discreet than my son." There was some disgust in his voice as he mentioned his son's lack of discretion.

Emma felt her wolf bristle with insult, but Emma forced herself to remain calm. It wouldn't do anyone any good for her to show any anger or aggression toward the Alpha. So instead, she said nothing and waited.

The Alpha sighed heavily. "I have come in an attempt to make amends with your family. Although you are not a Beta family in my pack or an Alpha in another, Richard and I have come here so he can discuss a solution with you." The older man turned to his son and motioned for him to step forward. "Richard?"

What the heck is going on and why do I think things are about to get worse?

Because they are. That sorry excuse for a wolf is hiding something. I can smell it on him. The growl was so thick Emma had trouble making out her wolf's words.

Richard took a step forward. Then he hesitated, but only for a moment, before a cocky smile reformed on his face. "I am sorry you had to find out about my dalliances in this way. I promise you, I planned to stop once our union was solidified. That is until our first child is conceived."

Union? What union? Does that mean he'd planned to cheat on me for as long as possible?

Of course he did. He would see no reason to stop. Her wolf snorted. Emma could feel her furry counterpart pacing with agitation.

"I see how my actions have affected you. Because of that, my father and I think it would be best to move up our timeline. Emma, I would like to ask for your hand in marriage. We can put this all behind us and start fresh as husband and wife." He stepped forward again, opening a small box to show off a rather large, gaudy diamond ring.

You hate diamonds, snorted her wolf.

I told Richard several times that when it comes to jewelry, diamonds are the last thing I want. They are so overpriced, and the industry is so flawed. Is he mocking me? Or was he never actually listening? Either way, it hurts.

Before she could respond, she heard the soft growl coming from her father. "You insult my daughter." Her father's voice was so menacing it snapped Emma's attention to him. Her father was an easy-going, lovable man. This was a side of him she never saw.

"Do not snap at my son. Know your place, wolf." The Alpha growled back. It was a warning, and everyone in the room knew it.

"He does not apologize for repeatedly cheating on my daughter but apologizes that she found out. Then insists he will stop, but only for a time, and only if they are mated. How would you feel if that same proposal was given to your daughter?" Her father snarled, but this time he kept his eyes on the ground as he spoke. Proving he was not completely out of control.

There was silence in the tension filled room, and Emma waited to see what the Alpha was going to do. Her father was challenging the Alpha on her behalf. No one had ever done that for her in her entire life. She loved her father dearly, and the idea of him being in the Alpha's crosshairs because of what Richard had done made her heart hurt.

I don't want to be the reason dad gets in trouble.

It also made her hate Richard. The kernel that formed when she'd seen him with Cecily was growing. Her father was right, he wasn't apologizing for cheating on her. He was just sorry he was caught. He wasn't even promising to stop, not really. Rage swirled through both her and her wolf, and Emma fought to keep her face blank. She fought even harder to keep the growl from escaping her lips.

"It is not a request. Your family's ranking in the pack is low middle at best. It is foolish to assume an Alpha wolf like Richard would not have a wandering eye. He can, after all, have anyone he wishes. You should also consider that in all likelihood he will be Alpha one day, which would make you his Luna. That increases both yours and your parents' rank exponentially. You should count your lucky stars that Richard would pick you." Alpha Peters paused in his speech and turned his focus from her back to her father. "We will give the young lady some time to decide." The Alpha's tone was icy and made it clear he would take no argument from either of them.

There was a beat where they all stood in silence before she heard the Alpha turn and leave. Richard smiled at her in a seductive manner that used to make her heart patter but now made her a little queasy, before he turned and followed his father out.

"And if I refuse?" The words passed her lips before Emma could stop them.

Alpha Peters appeared in the half-open doorway. "You will not like the outcome of that decision." He watched her for two full seconds, letting his meaning hang in the air before he shut the door and left.

Several seconds passed as Emma and her father stood in continued silence. Emma could feel herself shaking. It would have been within the Alpha's right to strike her father, and yet he hadn't. It was a blessing, yet Emma couldn't help but feel insulted by the older man's actions.

"You should take him up on it." Came her mother's voice from the kitchen doorway.

Both Emma and her father pivoted in shock, but it was Bess who spoke from behind her mother.

"What? No, she shouldn't." Bess walked around her mother and stood behind Emma, wrapping her arms around Emma in a hug. "The man is garbage, and you deserve way better than that."

Emma moved her hand to squeeze her friend's arm as a thank you, but she continued to stare at her mother.

Her mother sighed and focused on Emma. "Think of it like this. Your father just endangered himself by questioning the Alpha about his son's behavior. He is lucky to have not been struck down. As Richard's mate you're standing in the pack will rise, it's true. Eventually you will be Luna. You will be the most powerful female in our pack. No one would challenge you. And eventually you could intimidate lesser women out of sleeping with him. I'm not naïve. I know he won't stop sleeping with other women, but eventually you will amass enough power to greatly limit his options. You will have the power to speak your mind in a way that your father and I do not when it comes to pack politics. I know you grew up in this pack, but the strong hierarchy here isn't entirely normal. And you could change that from a position of power. Plus, Peters will not make it easy for you if you say no. At least this way it would be your choice..."

Emma watched her mother with dread as the older woman spoke. She was at a loss for words. Her own mother wanted her to enter a loveless marriage with a man who thought nothing of cheating on her. That she should let that man have access to her body, not knowing where he had been the night before. Her stomach rolled at the thought, and tears pricked her eyes again.

"You want her to give up a chance at happiness for power?" Bess whispered in disbelief.

They all stood there staring at her mother for several seconds before a growl over her shoulder reminded Emma her father was still there.

He took two large steps before he stood in front of Emma and grasped her shoulders tightly, so tight it almost hurt, and he looked straight into her eyes. "You will do no such thing as long as I breathe. That man is not worthy of you and no amount of power in the universe is worth having him humiliate you repeatedly. Do you understand me?" He was growling deeply and his eyes were golden, but Emma knew the anger was not pointed at her.

Love for her father bloomed within her, and she nodded once as tears dripped down her face.

Her father looked away, and Emma knew he was looking at his wife. "You and I both know Richard would never give her enough power to make that kind of mating union worth it, even if she decided it was worth putting up with him for power." His voice was angry, but mostly flat.

"For whatever reason, Richard and his father have fixated on Emma. Their attention will not be easy to shake," her mother countered, her tone wary and tired.

Her father turned his attention back to Emma and moved his hands until they were on either side of her face. "You're going to have to leave. You can't stay in the pack territory anymore. We have to find you somewhere else to live. If the Alpha has this idea and is set on it, he won't take no for an answer. But if you're not here, there's no one to give him that negative answer."

Her tears came even faster. *Leave home? Leave my family? I have lived in the pack territory my entire life.*

Bess clutched her tighter, and Emma felt wetness spread through the cotton covering her shoulder. The horror of the situation she found herself in came crashing around her. Her father was right. Arranged marriages weren't unheard of in wolf packs. The Alpha decided his son would marry a lowly woman, no matter what Richard, or she wanted. Richard made it clear he didn't particularly care if they were married or not.

Because he thinks you are a sure thing. Her wolf snapped.

How were we together so long and I didn't see this side of him?

Love blinds humans. It's nonsense and rarely useful, her wolf quipped.

Emma blinked away the tears and looked at her father again. "Okay, what's our next step?" He kissed her forehead before letting go of her face and taking a step back.

"While I reach out to some of my contacts, you reach out to that friend of yours who lives in Western Washington. Maybe the other side of the mountains will be far enough to deter Richard. But whatever happens, your mother and I can't know your exact location. If we have any proof of where you've gone the Alpha and his men can use that to find you and drag you back." He made eye contact with her as he spoke, his gaze heavy. Then he waited one long second before leaving the room.

    The world was spinning so fast. Slamming her eyes shut, Emma forced herself to breathe. Not only was she now going to leave her home, but her parents wouldn't know where she was. For the foreseeable future, she couldn't see them, couldn't contact them. She'd started the day on such a high note, how could everything have spun so out of control so fast.

Chapter 5:
Covert Agenda

Emma
One Week Later

"Wait, wait, walk me through this again. No, I take it back, let me make sure I got this right. Richard's been cheating on you for years. Everyone knew about it and no one told you. When you find out, he and his father's response is the two of you should go through an official wedding and mating ceremony and that you should just buck up and deal with the fact that he will probably be unfaithful the entire time. Do I have that part right?" Raelene's voice dripped with disdain through the phone.

Emma bit her lip while taking a deep breath and closing her eyes. She had just marched through the story without pausing or letting Raelene interrupt. She was worried about what her reaction might be. Raelene had never been a fan of Richard from the get go so she couldn't imagine her childhood friend's opinion would change with this story.

"Yeah, that's right," Emma responded on an exhale.

"And this was basically an ultimatum given to you. And you, like any reasonable person, want to remove yourself from that situation. So, you've been applying for jobs in my neck of the woods and hoping that since I'm already here, I can help you find the right apartment. Do I have that right?"

Out of habit Emma nodded before she rolled her eyes, realizing Raelene couldn't see her. "Yeah, if you wouldn't mind."

Her friend snorted. "Your request is ridiculous. Forget that it's kind of hard to find an affordable apartment. But that crazy dick might come find you, or send thugs after you, I'm certainly not okay with you staying by yourself. I have a spare bedroom in my condo and if you're headed out here, you're going to be staying with me. It's better if you have somebody with you in case something should happen."

Love for her friend bloomed in Emma's chest and her eyes stung. Raelene was fiercely loyal and had never been one to put much stock in pack hierarchy, it was why she moved out of the pack territory as soon as she turned eighteen.

"You don't have to do that, Raelene. I can stand on my own two feet."

There was another snort. "Of course you can. But I would feel better if you had someone with you and I don't feel like interviewing strangers. So, you are going to stay with me. The room is furnished, but it is big enough that if you have some furniture, you could bring it. Not a lot of stuff, but some."

Emma was so grateful for how quickly Raelene volunteered to help her that she needed to take a moment to swallow her tears before speaking again. "What's the local pack dynamic like? I know that the Seattle area pack is much larger than the others in the state. Will I be stepping from the frying pan into the fire on this one?"

"No," Raelene answered without hesitation. "There are too many members and so many loose associations, because of how big the territory is. It's pretty easy for wolves to get lost in the shuffle. So, don't worry about that. Granted, you will still have to petition the pack, but I can't imagine they would turn you down."

That was what worried Emma, she didn't know how close the Alpha of Seattle and Alpha Peters were. She knew Richard's father was rather combative with the two packs in Eastern Washington, the one in Bellingham, and another in Southern Canada. But she couldn't imagine Peters would want to be combative with the Seattle pack. It was twice the size, and then some, of the Central Washington pack. But even if they weren't friends, she was worried about her applying tipping off Richard on her location. She didn't want to go through the trouble of moving and changing jobs only to be found right away.

"Actually, I've been thinking about going lone wolf, at least for a little while.

Until the heat dies down with Richard and his father."

This time there was silence. Raelene was rarely speechless which meant she was weighing her words carefully. "You can do that... But I don't think you can manage it for very long. Unless you stay completely off grid, someone will notice you. And you'll either have to make an agreement with the pack to live in their territory or join. It is a delicate dynamic when the pack territory is as big as it is over here. I'll support you no matter what it is you want to do, just know that is a much more difficult road."

Emma had been afraid of that. Going lone wolf was easier if you weren't living in a pack's territory. If you moved around a lot or were on the fringes, it was something that could be easily done. But if you were in the heart of the pack's territory it wasn't an easy feat. Some packs, like the Central Washington one, would scare lone wolves out of their territory. Emma heard that packs in larger cities had more leeway for lone wolves as there were just too many people to keep track of. She hoped the population difference would benefit her.

You are stronger than you realize, her Wolf crooned quietly. *Do not waver from this path. It's the right thing to do.*

Emma sat in silence a moment and was genuinely surprised Raelene didn't interrupt her thoughts for several minutes.

"When are you and your parents going to be moving you over here?"

The tears pricking her eyes fell now as a heavy weight cemented in Emma's heart. "They won't be moving me. We've discussed it and decided it is best if they and Bess don't know where to find me. That way should Richard or his father try to question them they're not lying to him. The last thing I want is to endanger them more than I already am by leaving."

"Oh Emma," Raelene whispered, "do you need me to drive over there and help you? Help you bring stuff over or help you pack?"

Steady yourself. We will get through this. Her wolf repeated.

"No, the way I see it, once I get my clothes and everything of mine from the apartment, all my belongings will probably fit into my car. Anything that can't fit will get tucked into the back of my parents' storage unit. But considering I am leaving most of the furniture behind I don't think there will be anything too big."

"All right, I'll send you my street address and you just head on over when you're ready. Text me when you are on your way so I can make sure I am home."

"Thank you, Raelene. I can't express to you how much I appreciate this."

"Don't mention it. It gets you away from Tricky Dick and ultimately that's what matters in this scenario. I'll talk to you soon."

"Bye Raelene, see you soon."

After hanging up, Emma tossed her phone onto the twin sized bed in her childhood room. She faced straight ahead, simply staring out of the window into her parents small but jam-packed backyard. Several of the flowerbeds were blooming and the first pops of color were appearing. Emma had been staring for several minutes when she realized she was rubbing at the necklace she always wore under her shirt.

She forced herself to pull her hand away from the pendant necklace Richard had given her for their one-year anniversary. Knowing her love of history and ancient cultures, the pendant was a replica of an old Greek coin with a square hole in the middle that the chain wound through. It was simple and yet meant the world to her. Knowing he put the effort into getting to know her and applied it to that gift. It'd become a touchstone, something she played with when she was nervous.

But I have to stop that now. The necklace has to go. I can't depend on anything related to Richard. Even the necklace that's become part of my daily wardrobe. With shaking hands, Emma tugged at the chain until it and the pendant came out from under her shirt then she lifted it over her head and tossed it. It landed in the plush mint green carpet across the small room. The coin was barely visible, the weight pushing down several strands. Tears pricked her eyes as she looked at the necklace across the room. She knew she couldn't take it with her.

I love that necklace. But it represents him, and I can't have anything in my life that represents him if I'm going to have a clean break. I have to depend on myself and not Richard. Even if it's just a simple token, he gave me.

You are better than him. Her Wolf's voice somehow sounded stronger, louder in her head. *You should remove everything from our life that has to do with him. You need to gather up your strength and keep packing. Decide what it is we're taking with us. The sooner you can leave here the better.* Her wolf's words strengthened Emma's resolve in a way she hadn't felt since the decision to leave was solidified.

I can do this; it's just putting one foot in front of the other.

That a girl, her Wolf growled. It wasn't threatening but filled with pride.

Forcing herself to stand up, Emma went back to the stack of boxes she was putting together and mentally began the list of things she would somehow have to get from the apartment she'd shared with Richard. She knew if he was home there was no way he'd let her leave with all those items.

Don't worry, we'll think of something, her wolf responded, soothing Emma's nerves.

We need to wait until at least the end of next week. There's a pack meeting on Friday and if I'm not in attendance that would definitely be suspicious. I just have to lie low and figure out a way to attend the meeting without being cornered by Richard or his father.

"That's easier said than done," Emma muttered under her breath as she went back to building box lids.

Chapter 6:
Lying Low

Emma
Four Days Later

"Brothers and Sisters, that concludes this month's official pack business. Is there anything anyone would like to bring up before we disperse?" Alpha Peters scanned the crowd, his eyes lingering on Emma a beat longer than was necessary, causing a few glances in her direction.

People rarely spoke when given the invitation at monthly pack meetings. Alpha Peters went into a bit of a rage if someone dared bring up new business without running it by him first. He felt as Alpha everything should go through him and then get filtered and dispersed as he saw necessary. Because of this, a lot of news would be outdated by the time it reached the pack at large because no one dared to bring anything up without running it by him first. The only exceptions were mating and birth announcements. Emma could feel Richard's eyes boring into her from where he stood on the dais next to his father. She purposely didn't look at him, gripping her father's hand tighter so as not to show any of her emotions. She was finding her impulse control not a strong as it usually was. She couldn't help but wonder if it was because of her distressed emotional state or if it was because her wolf was suddenly louder in her head. It was probably a combination of both, not that she asked anyone about it. She felt foolish being in her mid-20s and still having questions about the affects her wolf had on her mental state.

There is nothing wrong with us. Her wolf commented on her train of thought.

Emma turned her attention back to Alpha Peters as he finished his scan of the pack members in attendance. "Very well then. This meeting is adjourned. There are refreshments as always and everyone is welcome to stay as long as they see fit." He banged the gavel on the long tall bench in front of where he stood. The noise of wood hitting wood rang through the large well-manicured backyard on the Peters' estate.

The house itself would get a little crowded if all one hundred plus members of the pack attended a meeting, so when the weather allowed, meetings were held in the very large veranda that led out into the backyard and the ten acres beyond.

Remember the plan, her wolf whispered to her before there was a feeling like a brush of fur against the inside of her mind. Her wolf clearly meant it as a reassuring gesture, but Emma was so unused to the sensation she jolted a little, causing her father to glance at her suspiciously.

Knowing the pack meeting would take at least two hours, Bess faked a head cold to get out of attending. Emma passed along her apartment key so that while Richard and his father were busy schmoozing and lording their authority over the pack, Bess could clear out all of Emma's belongings from the apartment. Emma had given her a list with the exact locations of all the things she wanted. She unfortunately couldn't take everything, but she wanted to make sure that anything of any importance didn't end up in Richard's hands. She was sure once she fled Richard would burn or destroy anything that belonged to her and Emma had several family heirlooms, mostly pieces of jewelry, that she wouldn't be able to live with herself if she left them to his mercy. Bess asked for as much time as possible. Emma and her father's job was to monitor Richard and text Bess if he appeared to be leaving so she could get out of there within the fifteen minutes it would take Richard to drive to the apartment.

  It wasn't the best of plans, since it hinged on Richard not hunting her down as soon as he realized her stuff was missing from the apartment. The only saving grace they had was much of Emma's stuff was kept in the guest bedroom, since between them they had more clothing than what could fit in the small master closet. Emma hoped that was enough of a head start. The plan was for her to leave first thing in the morning, she had already put in notice at work. When she explained the situation to the chair of her department, in as non-werewolf terms as possible, the older woman had been incredibly understanding. It helped the week she put in notice was finals week. Emma scrambled to put in grades early. The department would still have to find someone to teach her class next quarter. It wasn't an ideal situation, but it didn't leave the department scrambling to find someone mid-quarter. It was some comfort, though not much.

Emma had been lucky the chair gave her a recommendation for the satellite campus in Seattle she was interviewing with two days from now. The pay would be less than she was making now but there was room for growth and it would still be enough for her to live off of. Still, the thought of having to start over in her career made her angry, but she knew it wasn't an anger she could show in such a public setting.

As pack members began milling about the backyard, Emma was aware of Richard's eyes on her from across the crowd. He wasn't headed her direction yet, he still had some schmoozing to do. But if his continued glances said anything, it was that Emma needed to steel herself for his attention.

I just want to leave. I want to get out of here and have nothing to do with him.

You can't do that and you know it. Stick it out just a little longer, for Bess. Her wolf chastised. Though she didn't need to, Emma already knew what was at stake.

"Do you want any food?" whispered her father in her ear.

Emma simply shook her head, her stomach had been rolling all day. She'd only been able to get down yogurt and some fruit midmorning. She was fairly certain, now that the rolling had picked up to roller coaster levels, she would not be able to keep anything down.

He squeezed her hand in reply. "Stay strong, kiddo."

Emma could see eyes drawing in her direction. It was weird for her not to beeline straight to Richard, or in his general direction once the meeting got out. Though if Emma had to put money on it, she would bet word got out about her walking in on

Richard and Cecily. Based on the different looks she was getting, the more dominant female wolf had put her own spin on that tidbit of information. A lot of the more dominant female wolves her age were giving Emma amused glances, and it made her want to shrink down so she could disappear in the grass.

Shifting her gaze away from all the piteous, and amused expressions, Emma stared at the ground in front of her, but only for a few seconds until a pair of shiny wingtips appeared in front of her. Shoes that would only belong to one person. Emma felt her shoulders slump as she exhaled. Her eyes trailed up to meet those of the sadly smiling Morris Wilkinson.

Once he had her attention, he slipped his hand in her empty one and turned to Emma's father. "I got her Mr. S, grab some food." He squeezed Emma's hand as he spoke.

Emma's father looked at her for reassurance and when she gave him a weak smile, he nodded once before letting go of her hand and heading over to grab himself some dinner.

"I'm so sorry, honey." Morris' voice was so low and so quiet Emma was sure no one around them could make out his exact words.

She squeezed his hand in response as she rolled her gaze back to him.

"For what it's worth, I didn't know it was happening. I'm not necessarily in any of the inner circles, thankfully." He exhaled loudly with that last word.

Morris worked for the same university Emma did, though he taught in the computer science department. He was a transplant from California five years ago and only joined the pack when it became clear Alpha Peters wouldn't let him be a lone wolf in their territory. Morris went out of his way not to attend any pack functions he didn't have to. But for whatever reason he'd taken to Emma, Bess, and a handful of other wolves. Something Emma had always been very grateful for. Morris spoke his mind and was a lot more straightforward than a werewolf usually was. It was a trait she'd always appreciated, in the tall leanly built man.

"So, are we avoiding him as much as possible? What's the game plan?" Morris asked quietly under his breath.

Emma glanced around, and while they weren't exactly in the middle of the fray, they were close enough that if ears really wanted to listen to their conversation, they could. Without seeming to be, Emma gripped Morris his hand before weaving him through the crowd. He didn't fight her, but she could feel the curiosity rolling off of him. They slid their way to the drinks table where she stopped, grabbed two water bottles, and kept walking. Morris took one without saying anything and followed behind her until they were mostly out of earshot of the pack.

Emma knew they couldn't go too far into the yard, as that would be too suspicious, so instead she aimed for a small sitting area near the furthest of the three fire pits the Peters had in their yard. There might be a handful of people who walked past them, but the majority would head into the wooded area to shift and run as wolves. They would be too preoccupied to listen closely. It also gave them a good view of the rest of the pack. They could see if anyone came walking their way. Morris cracked open his bottle and sipped without breaking eye contact with Emma. He simply waited for her to speak.

Emma gave one last look around, making sure she knew exactly where Richard was. She didn't want to forget her mission especially since Bess was doing her a huge favor. When she was sure no one was around, she quietly and quickly launched into the entire situation for Morris.

To his credit, he didn't interrupt her. There was a lot of frowning and scowling as she spoke. Morris was a very dominant werewolf in his own right. He just simply stayed outside of the pack hierarchy as much as possible. He told her after several drinks, years ago, that his uncle was in fact the Alpha of the pack he had come from.

When she got to the point in the story where Richard's father offered her his ultimatum, Morris was growling. There were several beats after she finished speaking that the only noise that could be heard was his growl. Once he pulled himself together, Morris stopped growling and took a long swig from his water bottle. He then let out several choice curse words before smiling tight-lipped at her.

"Please tell me you did something other than take the Alpha up on his... offer." The last word was drawn out and packed with disgust.

There's a reason we like him, her wolf chuffed happily.

I know, I only wish we had him where we were going.

Chin up, we'll get through this.

"I'm leaving tomorrow." It was the first time Emma said it out loud. She spoke so quietly that if Morris had not been sitting directly next to her, he wouldn't have heard her.

Emma knew he had because he stiffened next to her and she felt a twinge of sorrow hit him. There wasn't even a second before he spoke. "Good."

The two of them went silent and stared at the small fire in the pit in front of them. They unfortunately didn't stay like that long. Two chestnut, brunette, gamma wolves, twins in fact, slinked over and sat across from Morris and Emma.

Twits, her wolf muttered.

If she was honest with herself, Emma wasn't a fan of the Johnson twins either. Megan and Mary liked to pretend they were both dumb as stumps but in actuality they were quite conniving and cutting when they needed to be. Both of them, like many of the single female wolves in the pack, had their eyes on Morris ever since he arrived. Originally, many of them overtly vied for his attention but when he gave none of them the time of day, their contest for his affection became more covert.

Little did they know, Morris preferred the company of human women romantically. He didn't like all the politics that came with dating another werewolf, so he stayed away from them. It was a little fact Emma never felt she needed to share with the female population of the pack. She rather enjoyed watching them making fools of themselves trying to get Morris. Though if he asked her to intervene, Emma certainly would have. But since he said nothing she never felt the need.

"Morris," Megan crooned, batting her eyes at him and giving him a coy smile before diverting her attention momentarily to Emma, amusement on her face, before switching back to Morris. "Emma, what are we discussing so privately over here?"

Emma had never been one to be quick-witted, so when her mind drew a blank it wasn't a surprise but it made threads of panic spread across her chest.

"There's a tenure-track position open at the University. Emma can't decide whether it's worth switching departments to get it. Technically, she's qualified for it since she has an interdisciplinary degree so we're weighing the pros and cons of going to a department you don't know versus waiting for a position to come up in the department you're already in, where you have a proven track record," Morris responded dryly.

The twin's expressions went comically confused. Apparently, that was the last thing they expected and now weren't sure how to proceed. In that moment she could've kissed Morris to show the appreciation and relief she felt. But she knew better, it would give away the lie. Displaying any relief would be strong enough the smell would've wafted across the fire and hit the twins' noses, also giving away the lie.

"What does Richard think?" Mary responded when she recovered, a haughty smirk curling her lips as she focused on Emma.

Bless his heart. Before she could speak, Morris answered for her. "They haven't discussed it yet. It's only rumors at this point and since I know the political climate Emma asked my opinion first. Richard's got enough on his plate dealing with the Eastern Washington packs. Emma doesn't want to bother him with it until it becomes something worth worrying about." His nonchalant tone left no room for argument and no place for the twins to dig in a sharp poke in what Emma was sure they knew was a sore subject.

The four of them sat in front of the fire, the twins glancing between her and Morris.

Look at them, they can't decide whether they want to flirt with Morris or antagonize you. Pathetic creatures. Her wolf snarled.

Don't make me laugh, Emma retorted to her furry companion as she tried to tamp down her lips twitching into a smile.

Her emotions must've changed in some way because she could feel Morris' wolf shift his attention from the twins to her in curiosity. It was something more dominant werewolves could do, their wolf half and their human half didn't have to pay attention to the same thing at the same time. It helped make them better hunters and more aware of their surroundings than less dominant wolves.

It was a weird feeling, Emma usually wasn't aware of other's wolves. Short of when she and Richard were physically very close, she was pretty much oblivious to that kind of thing. That she could sense Morris' wolf was a bit of a shock. If they'd been alone, she would've asked about it. She and Morris weren't really ones to beat around the bush with each other, but it wasn't the thing she wanted to admit in front of the twins, just in case it was something they would've been able to do that she should've been able to if she had a stronger wolf.

"May I borrow Emma, please?" Richard's slick voice sounded near Emma's ears from the side of the fire pit closest to the tall hedges that lined the fence.

His presence made her jump, she didn't know how he could've gotten the drop on her like that. He had clearly done it intentionally, as that was the only way she would've missed him. *Dang it, why did you let the twins steal your attention,* she chastised herself.

Never mind that. Just stay on guard now that he's here. Her wolf warned, the wolf's undivided attention was on Richard.

His body language appeared calm and poised, his expression amused as if this was any other day. But there was a burning to his eyes that Emma didn't like. For whatever reason he intentionally snuck up on them and no good would come from that.

She could feel Morris' wolf next to her tensing, baring its teeth at Richard. It was quite disorienting since from what she could see Morris' expression never changed. He simply moved his eyes from the twins to Richard. This was all so strange. It had never happened to her before. Was this the sort of thing that happened when werewolves let their emotions get the better of them? She heard stories of overly emotional werewolves losing control, but nothing like this.

"I promised her father I would give Emma my full attention." Morris' voice was like silk over a blade. There was nothing ominous on the surface but there was definitely a sharp point hidden underneath.

From the corner of her eye, Emma could see the twins' exchanged looks of surprise. "We can keep Morris company until you bring her back," Mary crooned.

I don't want to be alone with him. Please don't make me be alone with him.

Don't worry, you won't be.

Emma stiffened at the voice. It came from the same place in her mind her wolf's voice always did, but this was quieter than her wolf's voice and deeper. Definitely male. When she forced her attention to where that voice had come from she realized with a start it was Morris' wolf. It was terrifying, when she searched with her mind's eye for her own wolf. It was as if she could see through her own head into Morris'. His yellow-eyed wolf stared directly at her and the energy he sent was that of a protective sibling. She knew in that instant, somehow, she was speaking directly to Morris' wolf. It was something completely unheard of.

Werewolves could only talk wolf to wolf if both were in wolf form, the wolves already being in control made that barrier easier. But being able to communicate to a wolf as a human was impossible. Emma fought to keep her fear tamped down. The last thing she wanted was to give off scent signals to the other wolves nearby. She wasn't frightened of Morris, she could never be, but the situation was impossible.

Just relax, I'll take care of this and later we can talk, Morris' wolf promised. This time in a soothing voice, much like the tone one used to comfort a child who had a nightmare, before withdrawing back to his own head. As if he closed the doorway that opened between the two of them. Emma waited for a moment, but it seemed her wolf was as dumbstruck as she was.

"What possible threat could I be to my own girlfriend?" Richard's voice held amusement, but it was only on the surface.

Much like Morris, the undertone was clearly threatening.

As Emma switched her attention back to Richard, she saw the twins exchanging confused and worried glances as if the two women were just now getting the hint that perhaps they shouldn't be there.

"As per lineage laws, her father physically handed Emma over to me. This makes her well-being and safety my responsibility. This means I forfeit my life and my honor should harm come to her under my watch. With all due respect, to you as the Alpha's son, your few moments alone with Emma are not worth either of those things. So unless you hunt down her father and get him to give me expressed permission to let her leave with you, you're stuck with me."

Emma knew her mouth hung open as she stared at Morris. Morris never engaged in any kind of dominance fights, ever. It didn't matter how many people challenged him, he simply walked passed them as if they were a piece of laundry on the floor. Now he was all but outright challenging the Alpha's son.

Not to mention lineage laws were a set of rules no one invoked anymore, unless it was regarding small children. The original set of laws were put into place to protect unmarried women in an aggressive male society. It also extended to protect children. Since women had more autonomy these days, it was something rarely invoked. It meant a woman's parents had the right to control where she was and who she was alone with. It was, most likely originally, supposed to protect unwanted mixing of lineages but over the course of history had been used to prevent women from doing many things. As human society gave women more freedom, werewolf society had done the same thing.

Richard let out a bark of a laugh, though there was no amusement in it. At that sound, both of the twins stood up and at a quick clip headed straight back to the crowd where they'd be a safe distance away from whatever happened next. Emma couldn't blame them, this was unheard of territory and she didn't want to be here either.

"Lineage law? Really, that's what you're going to resort to?" He let out a dark laugh again, this time louder, gaining the attention of several groups nearby. Emma watched as many of them exchanged glances before most of them decided it was in their best interest to go to the other side of the lawn and watch from a safer distance. "Those laws are antiquated and out of date. I very much doubt Emma appreciates being compared to children. She is in her 20s which makes her passed the age of maidenhood." There was a snide level of confidence to Richard's voice as he changed his attention dismissively from Morris to Emma. He reached out to grab her arm but before his hand could clasp around her flesh, Morris moved and grabbed Richard's wrist.

"I state again that under lineage law you should back off." His voice was a growl now, not as much a threat as a promise.

The surprise on Richard's face quickly flashed to anger.

Chapter 7:
Between a Wolf & a Hard Place

Emma

Emma drew her gaze away from where the two men's hands were to the surrounding crowd. There were a multitude people staring openly now, though not within hearing distance. She scanned the crowd looking for her father and he was nowhere to be seen. That concerned her. Made her wonder whether Richard delayed her father in some way, as if he was trying to wean her away from the people he knew she'd feel safe around. That made anger flash within her and her wolf. Only one person strode toward the fight, Alpha Peters.

This is bad, really, terrible. Emma knew it was the panic speaking, but even knowing that didn't make her heart stop racing.

Before anyone could react in any other fashion, Alpha Peters reached them and stood two feet behind Richard. "I would appreciate it if you would release my son's wrist." It was a command plain and simple even though the wording was polite.

Without looking away from Richard, Morris answered the Alpha. "With all due respect, Alpha, I invoked lineage law by taking physical custody of Emma away from her father. Since her father is not here, I am his proxy. Richard is trying to drag Emma away against her will. That makes it my responsibility to prevent that from happening."

While he was hotheaded, Alpha Peters thought things through quicker than Richard did. She saw the Alpha take in the entire scene before frowning and pivoting so Richard could see his face. "Are you trying to interfere with lineage law?" His tone was more neutral now as he looked at his son, his face a mask.

Emma could feel his emotions anyway, there was a tumultuous storm within the Alpha. He was angry and disgusted, but that disgust was aimed surprisingly at Richard. It wasn't as if the emotions were strong enough she could smell or sense them like a normal wolf. He had them bottled up so deep inside that she shouldn't be able to know they were there, and yet she did.

"Lineage law is outdated. He has no grounds to invoke it." Richard was snarling, his attention still on Morris. Which meant he wasn't directly challenging the Alpha. If he'd been anyone else, Emma was fairly certain Alpha Peters would've backhanded him across the face.

Alpha Peters cursed several times under his breath, so quiet Emma could only guess at what the words were. "Lineage law is still technically on the books. That means as long as her father did physically hand Emma off to Morris as an unmated woman, he is within his rights to claim lineage law." For the first time Alpha Peters' attention turned to Emma.

She felt a new emotion spin within him as he looked at her. It was lust, not sexual but a lust for power. As if he thought to possess her in some way. There was nothing sexual or domineering about it, but it frightened her anyway.

"Emma? Did your father physically hand you off to Morris?"

At first, all she could do in the shock of the situation was nod, the confusion and fear at the different sensation she was picking up was too much for her to form words. But then her wolf stepped into the light, stepped into the forefront of her brain and somehow, not took over, but gave her the strength. She mirrored the wolf's words as the wolf spoke. As if they really were as one mind.

"Yes, I was holding my father's hand when Morris came up and held my other one. He then told my father he would look after me while my father went to get food. My father agreed then walked away. He hasn't returned since." Her tone was more even and assertive than it should've been, than it had ever been in her wildest dreams of speaking to the Alpha.

Alpha Peters simply lifted one eyebrow in curiosity before he turned around and scanned the crowd before frowning and turning back to them. "Where is Emma's father?" Those words didn't indicate a specific person answer but by the time he finished speaking his eyes were pinned to his son.

Emma watched as Morris slowly let go of Richard's hand and Richard took a step back. It moved him away from her, not completely out of arm's length but far enough to settle a few of her nerves.

"Tony and Sheppard are discussing a possible business opportunity with him." Though Richard's voice was blank, he was purposely keeping his head down, it was as close to admitting guilt as Emma had ever seen from him.

"And did you orchestrate that conversation hoping to keep her father away from her?" his father questioned, a slight growl threading through his voice.

"I did not know he had invoked lineage law. I had no reason to believe talking to my girlfriend would be a problem."

"Not your girlfriend," her wolf snapped, but this time the words were not confined to the inside of Emma's head. This time her wolf spoke out loud, using Emma's mouth.

She felt herself shrink as the Alpha's attention swiveled to her. She could feel the rage at her comment streaming from both him and Richard.

"Sit," Alpha Peters hissed as he pointed from Richard to the seat the twins had vacated.

Richard didn't question it. Instead, he stepped around his father and sat. The Alpha sat on the bench to Emma's right but at the far end of the square to not be next to her, but not next to Richard either.

"I thought I made myself clear. A mating between the two of you is mutually beneficial to both parties. But I can see that in his anxiousness my son seems to do the opposite of winning you over to our side." The Alpha's voice was a whisper but still managed to be somewhere between a growl and a hiss as he looked between Richard and Emma. He was dismissing Morris completely as if the other man wasn't there.

"Infidelity is not an unforgivable infraction. I myself have not always stayed the course. Neither has my Luna. It is not the end of the world as long as the offspring produced are only from the mated pair. I think it is childish for Richard's wandering eye to be the driving force behind the breakup of a perfectly matched union."

Emma swore she heard Morris snort but since no one else reacted she couldn't help but wonder if it had been his wolf instead of the man.

What is going on here?

If I'm not mistaken, the Alpha is trying to pigeonhole us. Her wolf growled, clearly not buying what the Alpha was selling.

Peters was using the magic that came with being a dominant wolf to lay an oppressive air on their little group. It was to encourage them to agree with him. She knew from experience when she was younger that when a dominant wolf, especially an Alpha, impressed their will on others it would feel like an increasingly heavy weight until the other individual agreed. It was baffling to her that the Alpha would use such measures in this circumstance.

What could be so interesting about me that he would push this? There are much more suitable mates for his son for him to force his will down on.

"That being said, I think it has become blatantly clear that Richard is taking your acceptance for granted. He needs to be putting in an effort to convince you that infidelity is forgivable." It was as if his voice dripped with venom as he turned his attention to Richard with the last few words.

Richard looked taken aback as he watched his father. He hadn't expected to have some of his father's outrage pointed at him.

"You have one week to convince young Emma that you're worth mating. At the end of that week, I will announce your engagement to the pack. I don't want anyone to have any reason to denounce the union. Do you hear me?" He was outright growling at Richard now.

She couldn't believe what she was hearing. Emma would not be given a choice, this wasn't even going to appear like she had a choice. It was simply decided for her and she had no way out unless a third party in the pack decided Richard wasn't worth Emma. Given their individual statuses, chances of that happening were slim. The only people who could go against it would be her family, Morris, and maybe Bess. There were one or two others, if they had enough cause might say something, but it would have to be pretty strong evidence to the pack to go against the Alpha's wishes like that.

When an engagement was announced, the pack could denounce the union and give evidence why the couple wouldn't be a good match. If the evidence was strong enough, the engagement would be dissolved. It was rare, usually only used in arranged marriages, or when the couple involved were too young to be getting married. But if the facts weren't strong enough, she had seen the Alpha take out his frustration on someone for wasting the pack's time. She couldn't think of anything strong enough, since infidelity was apparently not a problem for the Alpha, that would be worth someone taking that risk. That the Alpha was telling Richard to make it appear as if they were a worthy couple made her sick.

We're leaving tomorrow. Just remember we're leaving tomorrow, he won't have a chance and with you not available the Alpha won't be able to announce your engagement. Your lack of appearance will make announcing the engagement all but nullified.

She knew her wolf was right, but that didn't help damp down the panic swirling around her.

"Yes sir," was Richard's only response.

"Good. Now leave them the hell alone," the Alpha responded before pointing across the lawn.

Once Richard stood and began stalking away, Alpha Peters stood and stared directly at Morris, whom much to Emma's surprise stared directly back.

"I have my eye on you. I don't want you impeding my plans for my son." He stared Morris down for several more seconds before looking away dismissively and walking away himself.

Though Emma couldn't hear any of the conversations, she watched the chattering stop as the Alpha walked by individual groups before storming into the house. Once he was inside the lawn was abuzz again and both Morris and Emma got more than their fair share of wary and curious glances.

"What the hell is going on?" Emma knew her voice was threaded with the fear shaking through her.

Now that the Alpha and Richard were gone, it was as if all the emotions hit her in one wave. She yanked out her phone to text Bess that she didn't know where Richard was, but relief flooded her when the screen lit with a text from Bess saying she packed up and left about ten minutes earlier. As she relaxed, Emma felt her body grow tired from the stress of the situation she found herself in.

"Honestly," Morris responded warily, "I don't know. But I have an inkling of an idea. I'm not comfortable discussing it until I have more information." She felt him shift slightly so he could look at her face.

Emma followed suit. It was almost as if she could see the wolf's eyes behind his own. It was a weird double vision, and she had to blink several times before her brain could accept the image without her wanting to cross her eyes.

"Are you keeping the same phone number?" he whispered.

"Probably, for a little while at least. Unless it becomes a liability to."

Morris nodded once. "Okay, I need to check some things out. If I don't text or call you by the time you change your number, text me the new one. I think there's a bigger problem at play here then Richard or the Alpha are letting on."

You think, her wolf muttered.

"You will not tell me any part of the idea?" Emma knew the frustration she felt was displayed in her voice. She didn't like secrets. While she trusted Morris, she was at her wits end with not knowing what was happening in her own life.

Morris reached out and cupped her hands in his. "I promise you I will tell you the entire thing. But just in case I'm wrong I don't want to worry you more. I've been hearing rumors that Alpha Peters has been picking fights with the Alphas in Eastern Washington and Idaho. For some reason he wants to pick up more territory, and he thinks he has a shot at doing it. I don't know why he thinks he does but his actions today give me a sinking feeling something is afoot here. I am going home for the remainder of spring break and will have a talk with my grandmother." Morris trailed off.

    Emma didn't have to ask which grandmother he was talking about. His maternal grandmother was an Omega wolf. Omega wolves were rare in the werewolf world. They could do a wide range of things that basically came down to the fact that they were witches as well as wolves. There was no rhyme or reason to when an Omega wolf was born, at least not that anyone knew. It didn't follow down family lines or follow any kind of pattern. They would just appear and that was it. Having an Omega wolf was a coveted addition to any pack. Omega wolves were outside of the pack hierarchy because they could easily take over any pack they wanted with the level of magic they possessed, but it only happened a handful of times throughout history, at least as far as Emma knew.

Morris' grandmother specialized in psychometry and seeing the future. Emma didn't know enough about Omega wolves to know how often certain gifts popped up but she knew, from Morris, that his grandmother had about an eighty percent accuracy rate. He told Emma his grandmother met with his home Alpha regularly and she had her ears to the ground about almost everything related to the werewolf world. He made it sound as if there was a network of all Omega wolves who communicated with each other, but she didn't know how realistic that was since it was only conjecture on his part. But if he was going home to talk to his grandmother about what was happening in their pack, whatever he was thinking must've been serious.

"It's going to be okay," he said quickly, squeezing her hands.

"You don't know that." Emma sighed.

Letting out a laugh, Morris let go of her hands. "No, I suppose I don't. But I'm glad you have a plan to get out of here."

Before he could say anything else, her father came jogging up to them, a frown on his face. "What the hell happened? I was talking shop with several other wolves when the Alpha stormed into the room and tells me to check on my daughter. Are you all right, Emma?" Her father's gaze bounced between Morris and Emma before landing on her, his expression full of worry.

Morris turned to face her father and motioned for him to sit down across from them. Her father sat on the bench closest to her instead before folding his arms and giving Morris his attention. Morris then, quietly so the people milling about couldn't hear, retold the events to her father. The older man frowned more and more as the story went on. When Morris finished her father's eyes had a panic to them and he shifted his gaze to Emma.

"You're leaving tonight. Your mother and Bess have probably unloaded her car by now. We're going to load you up and you're leaving right away. I'm not giving this any kind of chance to escalate further."

It was not what she expected from her father and she blinked at him in surprise for a full minute.

Does he think Richard's going to do something tonight, or that the Alpha will?

He's right, her wolf responded. *It's not worth taking the chance.*

"I agree. I'll follow you back to the house. I would feel better if you let me follow you across the pass to make sure you get to your destination safely," Morris added, his gaze heavy as he watched Emma.

Emma looked from Morris to her father and saw relief and appreciation on her father's face. "I would actually feel much better about this whole thing if you let him travel with you."

"Plus, it's a second car," Morris added, forcing a lightness to his voice.

Honestly, I would feel better if he was with me.

"Okay, we should probably head out now then," Emma agreed quietly.

The three of them stood, and as they moved through the yard and the various groups in the house and outside of it, most would go silent as they walked by. There was curiosity in the air, almost like a physical scent. It made Emma itch a little. People desperately wanted to know what the exchange had been about but no one was about to ask what happened. For once she appreciated the more backstabbing nature of the pack's rumor mill. No one wanted to appear nosy by outwardly asking. Emma didn't breathe easier until she was sitting in the passenger seat of her father's SUV.

Her father reached over after starting the car and gave her knee a squeeze. "Don't worry, Emma. I won't let the Alpha force you into anything." His voice was so resolute and Emma desperately wanted to believe him, but she knew his standing in the pack wasn't high enough for him to make that kind of guarantee.

Still, while it made her a little sad, it warmed her heart to have people with her. People who had her back and saw how insane this situation was. That camaraderie calmed her a little. If Morris was right and this was related to Alpha Peters trying to gain more territory, or if he was throwing his anger out at something he could control because the procurement wasn't going the way he wanted, maybe once things settle down with Eastern Washington the Alpha would look elsewhere and Emma could let down her guard. But who knew how long that would be.

Either way, Emma had a long night ahead of her. She made a mental note to visit the nearest drive-thru coffee stand open this time of night. She would buy something for both her and Morris. She would also have to put in a call to Raelene and let her know she was bringing a man with her as well. She knew Raelene would feel the same way Emma did; they'd put Morris up on the couch instead of letting him drive back that late at night. If she couldn't spend the night at home, she'd at least be surrounded by people who cared for her. Even though it was only a small comfort, it was something.

Chapter 8:
Teacher Gonna Teach

Emma
About Three Weeks Later

Emma sat in her Honda Fit staring at the building in front of her.

Is it weird that part of me doesn't want to go in? she asked her wolf.

In the last few weeks, Emma had grown accustom to checking in and communicating with her now much stronger wolf. It was weird her wolf was so much stronger. The only idea she had about it was that maybe her wolf hated Richard more than Emma initially thought and had been lying low while they were together.

Yes, teaching is your passion. Buck up, Once you start class everything will fall into place.

Half of the building was dark, but what did she expect, she was teaching a night class. Emma never pictured herself teaching night school. In the interview, the committee mentioned evening classes four nights a week would be her trial run. If she did well this quarter, they would start her with a year-long contract and a regular schedule in summer.

Breathing deeply Emma steeled herself to go in. *I can do this. No one here knew me as Richard's girlfriend. No one here will whisper behind my back about how I couldn't maintain the attentions of the Alpha's son.* Other than Raelene, and Morris the first day, Emma had been without werewolf contact for three blissful weeks. She understood now why Morris swore off dating other werewolves.

Emma pushed open her car door and grabbed her backpack out of the passenger seat, blowing the small curls out of her face as she walked toward the building. Yanking the door harder than necessary, she took several steps into the hallway before she stopped and her eyes rounded.

Werewolf. I smell werewolf. Male and definitely dominant. Please be a student in a different class. Please don't be in mine. Emma pleaded as she bee-lined for the room she knew her class was in. Hopefully, if she moved fast enough, the other wolf would never know she was there.

It was another skill she'd picked up since the night she left home. Her senses were sharper, and she was better at reading other wolves, though it had only been Raelene and Morris so far. Emma could feel their wolves and read their moods. As of now, she had not been able to communicate with Raelene's wolf the way she could Morris', but she had not tried all that hard. The idea of poking around in other people's heads made Emma feel dirty.

Emma all but dove into the classroom. It was smallish with thirty-five single person chairs with individual desks attached to the arm. There were about half a dozen students already seated, though there were still fifteen minutes until class started. Emma put on a calm face and smiled at them before setting her backpack on the desk and turning to face the white board. She concentrated on writing her name and her email address for the students when she felt a tingle on the back of her neck.

A split-second later, she smelled werewolf again. This time it was different. This time there were two of them and neither were dominant. But she could feel their wary curiosity. Keeping her face as blank as she could, Emma looked over her shoulder to see two younger people taking seats in the back of the room. They were clearly a couple, and both smelled her already as they were watching her wide-eyed.

Against Raelene's better judgment, Emma still had done no kind of check-in with the Seattle pack. She hadn't let the Alpha know she was in their territory, which considering she was living with Raelene who was in fact a pack wolf, was unorthodox. After the first week, Raelene stopped pushing and both of them had been careful when they went places together. If these two students were pack wolves, her days of being an unknown could be limited. If they were both lone wolves, she had a fifty/fifty shot of them either jumping her in the parking lot or being left alone completely. Without drawing attention to them and asking outright, Emma couldn't know for sure.

They do not feel like a threat, her wolf chimed in. Though Emma wasn't sure what her wolf's threat level was, as Emma couldn't fight against two wolves of any kind. She would lose hands down.

She watched them with a blank expression that didn't show the interest both of their faces conveyed. Emma knew it was key to show dominance with these two, even if she didn't feel dominant. Neither of them were dominant wolves and the last thing she needed was them going to their pack and mentioning her, if they were pack. If she didn't show any weakness or worry she might be fine. As Emma turned back to the whiteboard, she heard a man clear his throat from the doorway and she jumped slightly before turning.

The man before her was about forty, if she had to guess. His hair was slicked back, and he had one of those smiles that made her think of an oil spill. Clearly this man was a predator in his own right, and as he shifted into the classroom, Emma realized this was the werewolf she smelled earlier. She couldn't help the snarl that twitched on her lips, but the man didn't seem remotely fazed by it.

"Well hello there. I don't believe I've seen you around here before. My name is Wilson, Wilson Rawlings. I teach the business ethics class four rooms down. I'm actually a broker, but a buddy of mine is the chair of the department and was in a bind, so I teach for him from time to time to help out. May I pull you from your class a moment? Since we still have about ten minutes before we owe students their education." He was arrogant enough that he just smiled at her and turned out of the room, assuming she would follow.

Arrogance at that level would get him killed if he didn't have the skill to back it up. Be careful. Her wolf warned.

Not wanting to make a scene, especially in front of those two young werewolves, Emma followed him out of the room. When she stood in the doorway, she saw him several feet to the right of her door, clearly trying to get out of hearing range of the two young wolves in her classroom.

Interesting, I wonder if that means they are not acquainted with each other. Raelene said there was a lively lone wolf population here, Emma mused.

As she came to stand in front of him, she crossed her arms, trying to portray the same dominance she showed with the two students. The last thing she wanted was anyone thinking they could walk all over her like those in her home pack. It didn't come natural but with her wolf's encouragement it was getting easier. "And what can I do for you, Mr. Rawlings?"

His smile never faltered. In fact, it seemed to increase. "I haven't even gotten your name yet."

Emma felt her jaw clench and her eyes narrow as she looked upon the stranger who reminded her of a shark. If he was one of the dominant wolves, or the Alpha, of the local pack she might be screwed.

"Emma Stanton. Now Mr. Rawlings, what can I do for you?"

His eyes grew sharp, but the smile didn't change. "Miss Stanton, I merely wish to welcome you to the territory. As I am pretty sure you are new to the Seattle area. I certainly would've remembered a she-wolf that looked like you. I also wanted to give you a heads up about the local pack. As I myself am a lone wolf in the territory."

What, a dominant lone wolf? That's a little weird. Normally they get pushed out of the territory. Unless they were on some boundary line she didn't know about. But she kept her thoughts to herself and her face an uninviting blank.

"They are a bit out of sorts. The leadership is not exactly as it should be; the hierarchy is a bit of a mess. There are dominant wolves who are power-hungry. I feel it's only polite to warn you. In this area, there are a decent number of lone wolves and there is a network of us that work together. That way, there is someone backing us should the pack cause one of us trouble. I'm willing to bet you haven't met with the pack and told them you were here. A gamble on my part, of course, but I think a safe one. I would like to speak to you about it after class. As I think it is in your best interest to work with our little network. I am the point man, but there are more than a dozen others involved and we are openly recruiting anyone who wishes to leave the confusion and craziness of the pack. May I call on you after class? Maybe we can grab some food in a diner or something."

I don't trust him as far as I could thrash him. Her wolf growled.

Unfortunately, I agree. Something about this man set her teeth on edge. It was a relief her wolf felt the same way.

She also wanted nothing to do with werewolf politics whatsoever. But a loose network of lone wolves might indeed be in her best interest if she wanted to avoid being part of the pack.

Against her better judgment, Emma nodded. "Sure, I'll meet you after class. Assuming we're out at the same time. I'm out at seven-thirty."

His smile grew larger and somewhat slimier. "As is mine. I will meet you outside in the parking lot. Have a good class, Miss Stanton." With that, he sauntered around her and to his room.

Waiting a beat, Emma turned and headed to her own, trying to ignore the growling she heard in her head. *I don't trust him either but any information that will help me navigate the werewolf politics around here is worth listening to. If it makes you feel any better, I plan on talking to him in the parking lot, not going anywhere else.*

The growling quieted. *Check his wolf, see what he is hiding.*

Emma frowned as she reentered the classroom. *I'm not doing that. It's weird and invasive.*

What happened to any information that would help you navigate?

Inwardly sighing, she turned her attention away from her wolf and began prepping for class.

Chapter 9: Nothing Good Comes from Dominant Wolves

Emma

Her class was pleasantly uneventful. Most of the people in her Introductory Lit course truly wanted to learn the material. Sure, there were a handful taking it simply as a requirement, but Emma could work around that. She felt silly for having been so nervous.

When the last of her students filed out of the room and there was nothing left to do for class, she strode out of the door and into the parking lot. She frowned when not only did she not see Wilson, but there was a rather attractive inky-haired man leaning against her car.

That's a dominant wolf if I ever saw one, Emma commented to her wolf.

At least this one is attractive, her wolf responded.

That made Emma miss a step. Her wolf rarely commented on the attractiveness of anyone, outside of television or movies. Schooling her face, Emma slowed her steps to make her walk more deliberate.

The man ran his hand through his thick jaw length hair and pushed off of her car. He was muscular without being bulky and if Emma hadn't been so concerned about what he was doing there, she would have agreed with her wolf.

"I'm guessing you're Ms. Stanton. My nephew gave me a brief description of you on a call to me when you gave your class a break. He was pretty sure he didn't recognize you, which is why he called me. My name is Keegan. I am a Lieutenant of the Seattle pack. I don't remember seeing a petition for a Stanton to come into our territory. I'm assuming that was an oversight, not on purpose. Our territory is in a bit of turmoil at the moment and I'll save you the details, but I think it's in your best interest to join our pack. There are some lone wolves in the area that are not to be trusted."

Her heartbeat faster and her adrenaline swirled. *I do not want to be forced into pack politics.* Before Emma could respond out loud, a growl wafted over her shoulder.

"Now, now Keegan, you couldn't possibly mean little me, could you?" came Wilson's voice from behind her.

Emma could feel him walking up beside her and she shifted so she could face both of them at once. Her wolf growled her approval. They didn't trust either of these men. Emma didn't stop moving until she was out of lunging range of both of them.

Now if that Keegan person would just back away from my car.

The attractive man in front of her frowned. "I was told you were skulking around, Wilson."

Wilson smiled before turning to Emma. "Don't believe a single word he tells you, Ms. Stanton. They are losing members of their pack left and right so they're trying to recruit as much as possible without giving people the whole situation."

Keegan snorted before taking a step toward the other man. "You mean the unrest you caused when you challenged the Alpha. A challenge, by the way, you lost but started enough discontent with your rumors and setting things in motion that we still haven't been able to clean out the rat's nest you created. Is that what you mean, Wilson?"

For the first time Emma saw Wilson frown. "They aren't rats. They are merely people who saw the problem with your Alpha's brand of management."

At that point, Emma stopped listening. This sort of pack politics and trivial drama was what she was hoping to avoid. Trying to be as nonchalant as possible, she shifted toward her drivers' side door. Once she was in the car, she was home free. She knew she could trust her wolf to keep tabs on the two men in case one made a move toward her.

If what she was putting together was true and Wilson was trying to start his own network, he could convert into a pack because he lost the bid for Alpha, she certainly didn't want any part of it. Something about Wilson made Emma think he would turn her over to Richard's father without hesitation if he thought it would gain him something.

Emma turned back to see both men were a foot apart, clenching their fists. Clearly if she didn't intervene, there was going to be a fight. They were snarling at each other and Emma scanned the lot. She was relieved to see there were a couple of people still lurking, but they were far enough away that they wouldn't hear the inhuman noises coming from the throats of the two men on the other side of her car.

Ignore them, her wolf interjected. *It will be the perfect time for you to escape as they won't have enough time to scramble to their cars and chase after you.*

It isn't as if they don't already know where to find me. They know where I work.

Yes, but at least we know a bit of what we have to deal with. The key is to get out of here in one piece and regroup.

Even though her instincts were to stop the fight, to placate the two angry dominant wolves in front of her, Emma knew her wolf was right. She hadn't been prepared for this in your face first interaction with other wolves in the territory. Raelene told her there'd been problems. She hadn't specified what they were, and Emma hadn't asked. Something she could now see was a mistake. It was definitely going to be a discussion they would have when she got back to the apartment.

"You are nothing but a mangy rabid dog." Keegan growled down at the man who was several inches shorter than he was.

Yeah, I don't actually want to be around if they get into a fist fight in the middle of the parking lot. If the cops arrive I don't need to be questioned and be in any official reports.

That was enough to jumpstart her into action. She unlocked her driver's door and had it slammed shut and relocked before the two men even realized what she was doing. They both looked at her, inches apart, in comical shock as she started her car and drove away. Neither of them moved into action until she was turning out of the lot.

By then it would be too late for either of them to catch her unless they were going to speed. Just to be safe, Emma took the long way home, entering the apartment address into her GPS to make sure she wouldn't get lost in the streets of North Seattle. When she was sure no one was following her, she buckled down and followed the GPS instructions in earnest.

She didn't take a deep breath until she parked in the underground garage which held the assigned tenant parking. As she took the elevator up to the fourth floor, Emma forced herself to take several deep breaths.

What am I going to do if one of them shows up tomorrow?

We'll just keep avoiding any kind of confrontation as long as we can. But realistically, for all they know this is your only class. They don't know you are teaching Tuesdays and Thursdays as well. Emma knew her wolf was trying to soothe her, but she also knew the class schedule was public record and if anyone was feeling intrepid enough, they could look up the schedule to see her other class.

As Emma walked through the door into the apartment, Raelene called her from the kitchen. "Hey Em, you're later than I thought you would be. How was the first day?"

Emma locked the door before sliding her backpack off her shoulder and onto the floor, propping it up next to the door frame before giving Raelene her undivided attention. "We have some pack related things to discuss."

Chapter 10:
Girl Talk

Emma

Raelene tilted her head before setting down the spoon that had been halfway to her mouth, her expression worried. "Okay, what exactly happened?"

Emma gave Raelene a brief rundown about what happened earlier in the evening, starting with the two young wolves walking into her classroom and ending with her leaving the parking lot. Raelene didn't interrupt but her frown increased as the story went on. When she finished Emma stared at her friend, waiting for the other woman to say something.

"Well, um…" Raelene started and trailed off. She blinked several times as if she was trying to arrange the words she wanted to say in her head. "I heard rumors that there had been a challenge to the Alpha. I hadn't been there as I guess it happened during a strategy meeting, where those close to the Alpha, higher up in the pack were discussing some pack issues. It wasn't a full pack meeting, but the day before. So I only heard rumblings about what happened. It was played off as if somebody made a challenge from outside the pack, and the Alpha quickly subdued the man and that was that. I did not know there was another level to this whole situation."

She's not lying, her wolf tentatively stated. *And it isn't as if someone vying for the role of the Alpha is necessarily abnormal in most packs.*

But it never happened in our home pack. Each time Alpha Peters had them executed when their bid for Alpha wasn't successful. Why wouldn't they do that here?

When her wolf didn't respond, she drew her attention back to Raelene. "So where does Keegan fit in to all this?" Emma had a fear that if he was high enough on the food chain it would show just how big of a problem Wilson and his little group were. If he was some mid-level Beta wolf, she could relax and hope to get lost in the bureaucracy.

She knew as soon as Raelene bit her lip that she would not like the answer. "The Seattle pack hierarchy is the Alpha, then his second, then three Beta wolves that serve as his lieutenants, for lack of a better word. Keegan is one of the lieutenants. Has been for about two years when the last one retired to have a quieter existence. There were a few weeks of struggles and fights for the position. Keegan ended up on top. Each of those lieutenants has two Betas below them then after that you get into gamma and delta wolves. Then everybody else."

Great, so he wasn't some mid-level bureaucrat. While he wasn't at the very top he was high enough to be a problem for her. She did not want the attention of people who were high enough to know Richard or his father.

"Maybe it's time for you to reach out to them, let them know you're in the territory and that you don't wish them ill will. I know you don't want to join the pack and that's fine, but that, well, that this

Wilson is putting people together hoping to build some kind of alliance is worrisome. If you chose to help overthrow the pack that could be terrible. The Seattle pack is the largest one in the region and pretty stable for their size. If they get overthrown, it would be bad for everyone. Even if you decide not to talk to them, which I encourage you to do, I need to go to them and tell them about Wilson's plan." Raelene looked stressed as she spoke and wouldn't make eye contact with Emma.

Emma understood Raelene felt a certain level of loyalty to the pack she was a part of for the last eight years, but there was still a sense of stinging betrayal that she was going to run to the pack with the information Emma was giving her.

When Emma spoke she knew there was agitation in her voice. "I get it and you should do what you have to do, but leave me out of it as much as you can. I don't want to be any part of this scenario. I just want to be left alone by everyone, at least for a little while. Just until Richard and his dad decide I'm not worth the effort."

I still say there's more at play there than we think, her wolf commented. *I don't understand why they're so eager for you to join their family. There's no reason for them to be so hung up on you when he could just as easily mate a more dominant female wolf. Someone with a more appropriate status.*

Emma felt the sting at her wolf's words. Her wolf didn't mean it to be insulting but she couldn't help the little prod that she wasn't somehow good enough for Richard.

You're too good for him but that's beside the point. Something else is going on here.

Her wolf's aggressive defense of her soothed the sting a little, but didn't completely make it go away. But the more her wolf talked about it over the last month or so the more Emma was thinking there might be something to it. She didn't understand why Richard and his dad would push like this. Unless Richard absolutely loved her, which she was doubting if he ever had, as painful as that realization was. He seemed more smug and appeared more goaded into mating with her. If he loved her... Emma ended that train of thought before it could finish. It was only going to center on a downward spiral she didn't want to be on.

It just felt as if she didn't have an ally in the world, minus her father and Morris. Everyone else seemed to have ulterior motives but those two. Morris texted her earlier in the day and wished her a good first day of class. He told her he'd be coming over to visit at the end of the week to check on her.

"Emma, Emma!" Raelene said sharply as she waved her hand in front of Emma's face.

"Sorry, just lost in my own thoughts there for a second."

Raelene frowned at her as she dropped her hand. "I won't make you try to join the pack. While I think it's your best bet, you need to do what's best for you. I have to tell them what's happening with Wilson though. I couldn't live with myself if he made some kind of ambush and I could've given the pack a heads up and didn't." Raelene reached out and gave her arm an apologetic squeeze before heading back to the kitchen and continuing to eat whatever she had sitting in a bowl on the counter.

Emma knew she should eat something. But she couldn't rise above the anxiety building around her to consume anything. It'd been a problem since moving. The anxiety she'd been feeling since the whole Richard being forced to propose thing threw Emma off eating. She'd lost about fifteen pounds in the last month. And while Emma wasn't exactly chubby, she knew if she continued on this track she would probably end up losing more weight than her body really should be losing. Especially since werewolves needed to eat more than the average human.

"Good night, Raelene." She didn't even glance over to see Raelene's reaction to her words. Emma simply picked her backpack off the floor and waved over her shoulder as she headed to the back of the apartment before shutting the door to her room. Once she was in there, she kicked off her shoes and slid on to her bed, sitting cross-legged and closing her eyes.

Meditating had been something her wolf had always encouraged her to do, but it had never been something Emma was good at. Up until recently, her wolf had been pretty quiet, so she had never been compelled to try. But now that her wolf was getting louder, meditating and checking in with her wolf seemed more vital to Emma's sanity.

Closing her eyes and putting her hands over her knees, Emma concentrated on taking deep breaths. She would count to four slowly as she inhaled then repeated as she exhaled. When she started, it would take her over ten minutes just to get into a relaxed state, now it would only take maybe two.

Feeling the anxiety and stress melt away Emma concentrated on the dark inner world where her wolf lived inside her head.

Chapter 11: You're only as good as your Concentration

Emma

The place in Emma's mind where she imagined her wolf resided was almost pitch black. There were no set walls or ceiling and yet she got the distinct impression of being in a cave. It was weird because while she couldn't see, Emma knew that if she simply took several steps forward, deeper into the darkness, she would run into her wolf making those same steps toward her. She could see her wolf perfectly, as she was seeing it now. The wolf somehow in the darkness glowed, was the only way Emma could put it into words. She could see it as if they stood in a field at high noon, and yet everything around them was swallowed by darkness.

Smiling, she tried not to think too much about the fact that she was somehow inside her own mind, and that she seemed almost instantly comforted every time she was here. She worried that if she spent too much time thinking about it, it would unravel around her and the broader peace it brought her would dissolve and Emma couldn't chance it.

As she sat, the wolf padded toward her and walked a circle around Emma's seated form, as if checking her for injuries.

When Emma turned into her wolf form, she was only slightly larger than an average timber wolf. Though there were werewolves that could be almost twice the size of a wild wolf, Emma was not one of those. But here, inside her head, Emma and her wolf were almost the same height when they stood next to each other. And even though the massive creature look deadly with its menacing jaws, Emma never feared something could happen to her. Not just because she was inside her own head but she could feel no ill will coming from her wolf. So she sat and waited until her wolf finished her inspection and came back around to the front of Emma before sitting, then sliding down until it lay on the ground in front of her. Those massive paws, inches from the front of Emma's crossed legs.

The first time they'd sat like this it had been eerie for Emma as the wolf's giant head was less than a yard away and almost at her eye level. Though she never felt panic as they walked close to each other, the first time they sat she couldn't help the spike of panic that ran through her at the sheer proximity to a creature that could rip her to shreds before Emma could defend herself. While she no longer felt that pang of fear it was still a little disconcerting.

You get here faster each time, her wolf commented. Even here in Emma's head the wolf's voice was an echoing sound around them versus a sound coming directly from the creature's vocal chords.

Practice makes perfect I guess, Emma responded.

Her wolf nodded sagely before tilting her head to the side as if listening. *Can you hear that?* she asked Emma from where she looked over Emma's shoulder.

Refraining from looking to see what was behind her in the blackness, as Emma knew firsthand she wouldn't see anything, she instead closed her eyes and listened.

I understand where she's coming from, she heard a foreign voice say in the distance. It was a wolf's voice. Emma had gotten to where she could identify the difference between somebody's inner monologue and a wolf. Not that she heard inner monologues all that often. She'd only ever heard Morris' once, the morning after he spent the night on their couch.

She does not know where anyone's loyalty lies. She's trying to escape a terrible situation and doesn't want to be thrown back into it if somebody thinks being on Alpha Peters' good side will benefit them.

Is that Raelene's wolf? Emma asked her large furry companion.

Her wolf nodded again. *Yes, I believe she is making her presence known to Raelene and letting her know she might agree with you over whatever it is Raelene is contemplating.*

It was weird to hear somebody else's wolf. As far as Emma knew, that was not a gift anyone had. Anyone she'd ever come across bragged about what gifts having their wolf brought them. But she wasn't about to ask anyone about it, just in case that was something she should've been able to do for years. She had a sneaking suspicion, both she and her wolf did, that it wasn't as common of a gift as they first suspected.

Focus, concentrate on her wolf's voice. Pretend that there is nothing else in the world, her wolf instructed.

Emma stopped questioning her wolf's instruction several weeks ago. Nothing bad happened, her wolf never steered her wrong. It seemed as if her bond with her wolf got closer and stronger the more she practiced. Right now the closeness to her wolf was exactly what she craved. Her wolf always had her best interest at heart and in a time when the world didn't seem safe, her wolf's steady confident presence was a rock to grip in the storm for Emma.

Slowly, making sure she didn't distance herself from her own wolf, Emma concentrated on the quiet voice of Raelene's wolf. It was like tuning into a radio station. If she worked too hard she'd get a headache and lose concentration and would lose the voice altogether. It wasn't until she made herself take the breaths and focus in a meditative state, much like her actual body was outside her mind that Raelene's wolf snapped into focus. With that focus came so much information and clarity.

Raelene's wolf wasn't as assertive as Emma's wolf. The wolf was more of a timid voice of reason in Raelene's head. It wasn't as pushy as hers. It made Emma curious why, since Raelene was slightly more dominant in their old pack's hierarchy, than Emma was. As her thoughts wandered, the voice got quiet again and Emma forced all other thoughts from her head.

As she focused on nothing but the foreign wolf's voice something strange happened; she could hear Raelene's inner dialogue with her wolf loud and clear, louder than she could hear Raelene's wolf's voice. It was weird and felt as if she was eavesdropping, and yet Emma continued on. She would feel guilty about it later.

Shouldn't I be loyal to my pack? They took me in when I left the Central Washington pack. They're kinder to me and treat people better than Alpha Peters ever did. Shouldn't I be loyal to them? Shouldn't I help them when it looks like somebody is out to get the pack? Raelene sounded frustrated and worried. If Emma wasn't mistaken, there was a bit of guilt thrown in there.

Put yourself in her shoes, really think about it. She's running from Alpha Peters. She doesn't want attention drawn to her. If you can think of a way to tell them you heard these rumors without bringing Emma into it then yes, your loyalty should mean you say something. But if endangering her is the only way to get this done, I don't think you could live with yourself if the consequences threw her back into the situation she's trying to escape.

You're right. I know you're right. I will think about it and if I can think of a way to broach it without factoring Emma into it I'll call headquarters tomorrow and let them know. I just feel sick. I don't know whether I did the right thing giving Emma a place to stay.

Emma felt nauseous and hurt hit her in swirls. For a second her connection to Raelene's mind broke, but she forced her way past the pain to concentrate once again.

What if I am endangering her by bringing her here? The pack is big here, there aren't as many places to hide. What if I put her in more danger because of these lone wolf problems we're having?

The emotions swirling through Emma forcibly broke her connection to Raelene's wolf. It was all she could do to stay in the concentrated meditative state with her own wolf. Luckily, her connection to her wolf was so much stronger than it was Raelene's. She felt guilt, love, and fear swirling through her.

What if moving here was a mistake? I'm putting Raelene in an impossible position. She's picking between me and her pack. A pack she actually feels loyalty to.

You need to calm down. If you let your emotions control you, you're going to spiral out of concentration, her wolf warned.

I don't want to go back. I don't want to be stuck in that marriage. Not to mention I have this feeling his father will be angry with me for running. I don't know how I know. I just get the feeling they'll make things worse for me if I turn tail or was forced to return now.

Calm down Emma! her wolf called, but this time it seemed like it was farther away.

Her wolf disappeared, the world shifted, as if she was looking at a watercolor painting and the image swirled and moved until Emma gasped and opened her eyes to stare at the closed bedroom door. Tears dripped down her face before she cried in earnest.

The emotions and stress were too much for her. She didn't want to return to Richard and be stuck in a loveless marriage that she was sure would be even worse for her now. Emma was sure Alpha Peters would punish her for trying to escape it. He was not a forgiving man and was big on retaliation. She also didn't want to be part of some war. With the idea that someone could return her to Richard looming over her head, she didn't know what to do. She didn't want to put Raelene in a position where she had to pick between her and her pack. And what if they found out about Richard? What if someone used that as blackmail to get her to do something? There was no way out for Emma. Her situation was inescapable. Unless she moved to some distant place where there was no pack.

That thought calmed her some. Maybe that was the only answer. Maybe she had to go somewhere where no pack was strong and there was no connection to the Central Washington pack. She needed to go somewhere like Alaska where there were no defined packs and it was a land of lone wolves. Life for a werewolf was supposed to be hard up there but Emma could manage it. She might not be the strongest person in the world, but she and her wolf would at least be safe from Richard and his father's wrath. She'd seen Alpha Peters do many things when he got angry or sought revenge. She didn't want to be on that list. It hadn't even occurred to her that she would be until now.

Standing up, she shook out her body, trying to relieve some of the tension. The stress and emotions made it impossible for her to hear her wolf. She could hear mutters as if her wolf was trying to get through to her but there was too much else going on in her head for Emma to make out the words. Instead, she grabbed her laptop and hopped onto the Internet. She would see what job prospects look like in Alaska. If there was anything promising, she would apply in the morning, or bare minimum at the end of the week. If she could make it through the quarter safely, so she didn't have a bad reference from the community college she was currently working for, maybe then she could move to isolation and safety.

Chapter 12:
Girl's Got Skills

Morris
Two and a half weeks earlier

"All right, darling, tell me about this friend of yours you think might need my help." Mormor, Morris's Swedish grandmother, and Omega wolf to the Northern California pack crooned as she patted the large burgundy leather armchair across the dark wooden end table from where she sat.

Morris called his family to let them know he was coming for an impromptu trip. He texted Mormor separately to let her know a friend of his was having some issues and he thought she was the only one that might be able to help. Her only response had been telling him to let her know when he wanted to sit down to talk about it.

So here he was, at his grandparents' house. After a nice lunch with both his grandmother and grandfather, Mormor and Morris made their way into the study where she shut the door behind them and tottered over to the two large, matching burgundy armchairs near the fireplace. It was too warm for there to be a fire but Morris knew that in the fall and winter months, logs would burn almost constantly.

Taking a deep breath, Morris launched into the situation Emma found herself in. And because he was talking to his grandmother, he added in every thought he had not said out loud at the time and didn't hide the disgust from his voice when talking about Richard. He knew strong emotions could help trigger visions for his grandmother, so he didn't hold back. He didn't slow down until he got to the morning after they had driven to Western Washington.

"It was weird. My wolf spoke to her. And I know that is just a holdover from my being related to you. But she understood him. She understood the words he was using and not just impressions like most people get. While I understand that I'm a little more sensitive than the average wolf, this was more than that. I chalked it up to a fluke until the next morning when I woke up and thought to myself that I should hit the road as soon as possible and wondered where the nearest drive-thru coffee place was so that I could stop and get sustenance on my way home. My wolf commented we had had little for dinner last night and that he would appreciate a large breakfast so maybe a diner would be more appropriate.

"It was at that moment I heard a clank of metal hitting metal in the small kitchen area and realized Emma was in their cooking. But that wasn't the weird part, the weird part was when I turned, she smiled at me shaking her head. She told me it was ridiculous for me to eat elsewhere when they had perfectly good coffee sitting in the pot in the kitchen and she was making a large breakfast as a thank you to both me and Raelene.

"It through me so off guard that I just blinked at her several times. It took her a minute to realize I was looking at her funny because she frowned at me and asked what was wrong. I told her I hadn't spoken. What she heard was a conversation internally. She looked at me baffled, as if she didn't really believe me. I tested it again by speaking to my wolf and she heard me. I had already planned to come see you and talk to you about her, since she had heard my wolf so clearly before, but this solidified my trip. She not only heard my wolf's voice but my inner monologue as well. I played it down. I brushed it off as if it wasn't that big of a deal as I could see her panicking, could smell it coming off of her, and I knew with how stressed she was that was the last thing she needed."

Mormor leaned back in her chair, curling her fingers around the armrests and playing with the small brass buttons that held the seam together on the arms. She stared off into space straight at the mantle for several minutes.

Morris was used to the silence. He knew it was part of her process; she was searching for the answers. They didn't simply snap into place, even when they wanted them to.

Eventually his grandmother let out a breath then turned her neck to smile at him lovingly. "I imagine this isn't a surprise for you to hear, but I'm guessing this friend of yours is probably an Omega wolf. Being able to hear a wolf, when that dominant and sensitive wolf is talking to you just means that you are probably sensitive yourself. But if she can hear your inner monologue, I'm willing to put money on her being an Omega. But this is not a set of skills that I'm familiar with. I'm going to have to do some digging around to see if any of the ladies I know has those abilities, or knows about them. But being able to connect with the other wolves in your pack could be quite useful. Especially if a youth was struggling to change or communicate with their wolf. It would also help with trauma if a werewolf might've regressed. It's a fascinating skill set. First, I'm going to give you some equipment so you can test her to see if in fact she is an Omega and not just a very sensitive wolf."

His grandmother stopped for a second, turning away from him, furrowing her brows. He could tell she was mentally scanning the house as if she was checking off where she would need to go to find the items she was talking about.

"I'll rummage around a bit. But I think I have an old brooch that should still work. It's a beautiful green stone that looks completely benign. But it is tuned to the same wavelengths of magic that Omegas use. If she's holding it and uses her ability to listen to your inner thoughts, the gemstone will glow warmly. Depending on how strong the glow it could mean she's more powerful or using more magic to do it. There are a lot of variables there.

"I will also give you a bracelet made of gold and several other metals. It has several spells and protections weaved through it. If she is in fact an Omega give her the bracelet and tell her to wear it. It will help anchor her power so it isn't as difficult for her to access it when she needs it and it won't shoot off half-cocked when she doesn't mean to use it. Omega's need to have a stronger control over their emotions and considering the state you tell me she's in, she could do with one of these bracelets. It'll be hers to keep even after she's learned to control her power. I have several just in case I come across young Omegas in situations such as this. You say the two of you are about the same age?" Mormor's voice filled with disbelief as she turned back to him and asked her question.

At first Morris nodded but then he thought about his answer. "Honestly I don't know exactly how old she is. But I know she's at least in her middle 20s."

His grandmother let out a noise in the back of her throat and frowned. "It is highly unusual and practically unheard-of that she would only now be developing these powers. If she is an Omega wolf, you should've noticed it before this. Without meeting her in person I have no way of knowing whether this is some kind of transference, where maybe she's reflecting someone else's power, which is a complicated process, or if something stunted her growth." She patted his knee with her hand. "Once you've tested her and given her the bracelet, explain to her what it means to be an Omega wolf. Then let me know how the test goes one way or the other. If she is in fact Omega, either I or one of my counterparts in the western region will go to her. We are the closest and probably the best ones to help. If she's an Omega, it might help and hinder with this Richard problem. Either way, I think perhaps you should leave that pack's territory as well, if you can. If the Alpha is the kind that would force someone into a marriage..." His grandmother trailed off as her eyes lit and her hand stopped patting his knee. "Do you think the Alpha or his son know Emma could be an Omega wolf?"

Dread filled Morris' stomach. His gut reaction was to say no, that if he didn't know how would they? He had more experience with an Omega wolf than either of them did. But he paused, it would explain the marriage between Richard and Emma. It made no sense that Peters would want his, someday Alpha son to mate with a subordinate wolf. If it had been a love match that would've been something, but this was not the situation. But if he knew she was an Omega wolf, or suspected she was, Alpha Peters would definitely see it in his best interest to keep her connected to his son. Morris' stomach rolled with disgust.

"I honestly don't know. But it would explain some things."

His grandmother frowned and her eyes grew worried. "It goes against everything it is to be an Omega wolf. We are outside of the pack hierarchy so that we can move and operate without sanction or worry regarding pack politics. Our purpose is for the good of the pack, not the good of the Alpha. Morris, you need to leave this territory. If the Alpha is so manipulative that he is trying to force an Omega wolf into a mating with his son purely for power reasons you don't want to be anywhere near that."

Morris was not about to argue with his grandmother. She was completely right. He'd also been thinking along those lines when he found out Emma was leaving. He only had a handful of friends in the pack, and job opportunities would probably be more plentiful in Western Washington.

His grandmother's hand started patting again and she let out another sigh. This one seemed to release the stress she held before. "Did I ever tell you about the vision I had when you were younger. About you being a Guardian wolf?" she asked quietly.

That brought Morris' full attention back to his grandmother. Guardian wolves were dominant wolves paired with Omega wolves. They were drawn to an Omega as it was their innate responsibility to protect them until the Omega wolf came into their full power. They were never mated to an Omega wolf, as it was never that kind of relationship. Guardian wolves were there for the uphill battle that it took for an Omega wolf to complete their training. A Guardian wolf rarely worked with more than one or two Omega wolves in their entire lifetime. They, in some cases, stayed with an Omega wolf for decades. Usually when the Omega was not connected to any one pack. The Guardian or Guardians and the Omega would serve as their own mini pack and hold the same position and authority as any other pack.

Out of the three guardian wolves who surrounded his grandmother, only one was still alive. One died in a fight when they were much younger, when someone tried to kidnap his grandmother. The other passed away two years ago. It had been a blow for his grandmother and the remaining Guardian wolf. They were like siblings and mourned his death as such.

But she had said nothing to Morris about him possibly being a Guardian wolf.

"I see from your expression I probably said nothing. That your wolf can sometimes talk to others, or bring his impressions to others is not simply because you're related to an Omega but it is how Guardian wolf power works. It gives you an extra edge, another way to communicate with an Omega wolf in difficult situations. There might also be a few things you can do that either you or I don't know about that cater more toward whatever abilities she might have. But your wolf being able to communicate with her is definitely a sign of a guardianship. It also explains how you and Emma became such fast friends compared to the other wolves in the pack. Since your allegiance is naturally going to be to her over all of them. It helps that you're a good man." She rubbed his knee a few times, smiling lovingly at him again. "I'm going to schedule you to have coffee with Samuel tomorrow morning. The two of you can sit down and discuss what is involved in guardianship. Samuel worked with another Omega for a few years before me, so he'll have a good chunk of experience to tell you about. Now let's go find that broach and bracelet." His grandmother heaved herself out of the chair before stretching slightly and turning toward him, a smile still on her face.

"Wait Mormor, what was your vision of?" Curiosity burned in him but he wasn't surprised. His grandmother would sometimes reference her visions but not give them in detail.

Her smile widened as he stood. "You were standing hand in hand with a woman with white-blonde hair in a braid halfway down her back. There was no romance in the way you stood, as both of you frowned and power whipped around you both. You seemed aware of but immune to the power. Normally if you stood that close to an Omega that visually agitated the power would affect you in some way. It would feel like static electricity along your skin. But since you were clearly her guardian wolf it washed off you like water. It was just a glimpse, but it was so vivid and strong I knew what it meant. I guess I decided not to let you know until the subject brought itself up." Mormor closed her mouth but continued to smile up at him kindly. He had almost a foot on her when the two of them stood next to each other.

They stood staring at each other for almost a full minute. Morris in a slight shock that slowly grew to an excepted understanding and his grandmother simply waiting for him to process what she told him. But she mentioned white-blonde hair, Emma's was auburn. It made him curious what that meant because she might be an Omega, but not his Omega. Or whether he was just sensitive to her as a Guardian. It all left him with so many questions and several answers but he was unsure which paired with which.

Eventually, his grandmother patted his arm before heading out of the room, knowing he would follow her. She said nothing as they walked, giving him time to process as they traveled throughout the house collecting the items she decided he would need to test Emma and her abilities.

Chapter 13:
What She Doesn't Know Won't Hurt Her

Richard

"I can't believe you let yourself become so careless." Richard's father snarled as he banged his fist on his worn wooden desk.

Richard stood at attention, fighting to keep his expression impassable in the face of his father's disgust, disappointment, and anger. But he could feel his mouth twitching. It wasn't his fault that Emma ran. It had been his father's idea to give her time to sort things out. Sure, Richard had been a little lax in his affections for Emma the last few months. But she had gotten her first full-time job since graduating and he didn't want to stress her out by demanding too much of her time. Not that he needed much of it, since he'd been seeing other women the entire time he and Emma had been together, which meant he never hurt for female affection.

He had been careful over the years, with a couple of near misses, to make sure that Emma didn't know about his dalliances. He always suspected that she would not approve of his affairs, even though none of them were anything serious compared to his long-term relationship with her. He honestly figured by the time she figured it out, if she ever did, they would've been together so long that it would've been easier for her to live with it. Having her under his thumb was the whole point. He clearly miscalculated how strong her will had been. He never in a million years would've thought running away from him would've been an option for her.

"It's only a matter of time before we figure out where she went. I can't imagine there are a lot of options for her, considering she's lived here her entire life," Richard responded, concentrating on keeping his own snarl down to a minimum.

He liked Emma fine, but he would've never fancied himself in love with her. He dated her on a whim and enjoyed her company well enough. But once he stumbled upon her well-kept secret, he knew he had to hold on to her. When he'd explain that secret to his father, the older man practically foamed at the mouth with excitement at bringing Emma into the family and adding her to their bloodline.

"You damn well better find her. I have reached out to all the Alphas I am on speaking terms with and none of them mentioned a new wolf in their territory that goes by her name or fits her appearance. Why didn't you introduce her to your other relationships slowly? Ease her into the idea. Because I find it hard to believe that you were unaware that she knew nothing about them." His father raised an eyebrow and curled his lips.

Richard's father cheated on his mother as far back as Richard could remember. He didn't remember his mother doing the same thing until after his youngest brother was born. He hadn't asked his father about it until he was in his 20s. The Alpha and Luna had an understanding that once they were done providing offspring, they were free to have whatever carnal relationships they wanted. As long as no extramarital children came from those affairs neither had a problem with it.

It wasn't the type of marriage Richard would've wanted. But that was mainly because he didn't particularly want to have a wife who would sleep with other men. He figured, as future Alpha, it wouldn't be an issue for him to stray. But he didn't think that his wife should be allowed the same thing.

Both his parents were discrete about their affairs, there were only whispers and murmurs, usually after the fact. Richard didn't keep the women he slept with secret. He saw no reason to. He didn't announce it or parade the women in front of Emma but he figured it was a well-known secret. If he was honest with himself, he was surprised they went this long without Emma noticing.

"You better find her and win her back, boy. You will not get so lucky as to find another woman with that kind of power willing to let you be in the driver seat of the relationship. You had a good thing with Emma because she doesn't know the power she holds. It meant we could keep her weak and controllable. Without you there to keep her in line who knows if her power will grow into something less manageable." His father banged his fist on the desk again, rattling everything on top of it.

    Richard snarled at his father's words and rolled his eyes. "Don't be ridiculous, father. I told you years ago, once I figured out the sort of power Emma had I did some investigating. Once I realized she didn't know the power she has, I bought her a pendant to keep her abilities in check. So that instead of them growing, as they should have, she was stunted, meaning her power would never grow to full strength. I also bought several others, varying in strength with the idea that once we were married, I would slowly wean her from the power blockers until she no longer needed them but had fully entwined her life with mine. By then we would be a mated pair and it wouldn't be an option to break away. She hasn't given me the necklace back so we have no reason to believe her power will grow out of control."

"You have been with her for years. You should have had this completely under control. If you were not so stupidly open with these women you're sleeping with perhaps you could've held onto her long enough for your plan to come to fruition." His father's eyes flashed the orange gold of his Wolf.

Once the Wolf's eyes flashed, Richard carefully drew his eyes to his father's shoulder. Now was not the time to challenge his father's Wolf. Richard never expected his father to step down as Alpha and he knew one day he would probably take on his father and beat him in a fight. But as of now, his father was angry and still strong enough to take Richard should the challenge be brought. No, he needed to bide his time. He would placate his father for now, because he knew it was in his best interest.

With Emma by his side, other Alphas would think twice before challenging his pack for their territory. It would also mean the acquisition of Eastern Washington land, that his father was currently trying to accomplish, would be easier once Emma trained enough to display some of her powers.

"I will find her. I promise. I will find her and bring her back, even if it needs to be kicking and screaming. I know her, I know how to convince her to stay put." Richard could feel the slight growl in his chest as he spoke. He fought with what little control he had left to maintain the calm exterior he displayed to his father. Even though neither of them would be fooled.

"You better, don't make me do your work for you. If you can't convince her to mate you, I will give her and her family no other option. I know her parents knew she was leaving. That neither of them has any idea where she went is infuriating. I am tempted to contact the Omega in Eastern Montana and ask for use of her services to see if she can find out what the parents know about her leaving. I can smell they aren't lying when they say they do not know but that doesn't mean there isn't more information they could give us." His father waved his arm in a dismissive gesture and gave a heavy sigh. "Leave me. I'm sick of discussing this and dislike having to rearrange my plans of announcing your engagement simply because you could not hold on to the girl, a submissive wolf at that. I'm now having to scramble to rearrange meetings and plans because of you. If you do not find her within two weeks, I am taking out my frustration and broken plans out on your hide." With that, his father looked away from Richard dismissively and picked up the landline on his desk.

As his father dialed, Richard bowed his head before pivoting and striding out of the office, shutting the door a little stronger than was necessary behind him. He let out a loud growly roar as soon as he walked out of the nearest exit. Startling the group of three guards standing a few feet away. But smartly none of them gave him more than a cursory glance.

Though Richard wished they said something because it would've given him an excuse to take out his frustration on them. It wasn't just his father's plans Emma ruined. Now Richard had to deal with his father's wrath and inconvenience himself in order to save face and get her to come back. The last thing he wanted was to put effort into wooing her. But he knew it was his only option right now. She wasn't stupid, and that meant any sort of wooing, as disingenuous as it would be, she would probably see right through. But he wasn't entirely sure force would be the way to get her to respond in the manner he wanted. He was going to have to spend just as much time calculating his plan as he was reaching out to any wolves he knew to find out if they had seen her.

Yanking his phone out of his pocket, he dialed Amber's number, a daughter of a high-ranking Beta wolf, one of a handful he occasionally slept with. He needed to get out this frustration and clear his mind before he could move forward on his pursuit and Amber would be exactly what he needed to get the job done. Richard knew his smile was all teeth as she answered and he did not hide the growl from his voice.

"Hello Amber, what are you doing right now?"

Chapter 14:
Just Here to Learn

Emma

Emma felt much better as she got out of her car for class on Wednesday. She needed a change, so that morning she made an appointment at Gene Juarez to get her hair trimmed and dyed. Now it was no longer the dark auburn it had been most of her life, but a pale silver blonde. It was much lighter, which took some getting used to, but overall she liked it. It was just a small change in appearance, but it gave her more confidence. Maybe it was because from afar she would no longer be recognizable to anyone as the she-wolf Richard dated. Or maybe it was because she wanted to feel different from the Emma that had been with

Richard. Either way when she walked into the building she had a huge smile on her face.

Striding down the hall, she was grateful she didn't smell Wilson yet. She'd purposely come in early today to prevent any kind of run-in with him. While she didn't want any part of the pack, she certainly didn't want to be part of any kind of outside group who had its eyes on replacing the current pack. Which she was fairly certain was Wilson's plan, whether or not he admitted to it. She just wanted to be left alone, and she suspected Wilson wasn't about to do so. Until she could come up with a better plan, avoidance was key.

She headed into her classroom with that big smile on her face. That was until she turned to the other occupants of the classroom and dread hit the bottom of her stomach. There, in the back row, with the two young werewolves sat Keegan. His beautiful dark hair was brushed back from his face as he focused all his attention on her. If she wasn't mistaken, there was a look of attraction in his eyes for a split second before he blinked it away and gave her a neutral, more pleasant, less predatory smile. Emma didn't smile back. In fact, she snarled a second before she whirled around when other students walked into the room. The three wolves had been the only students and while she could've confronted him in front of the other wolves, she certainly couldn't do it in front of human students. Werewolves were not 'out' to the public, and she was not about to be the person who made that happen.

She smelled the dominant wolf a second before she felt Keegan standing behind her. Her wolf growled within her, standing at attention, clearly watching him even though Emma's head was not turned in his direction.

"I didn't mean to startle you," came his smooth deep voice from over her shoulder.

Part of Emma could listen to that voice say just about anything. He would've been a great voice actor. He had the perfect cadence and speed. His voice was liquid chocolate.

Blinking twice, Emma chastised herself. *Get a grip.* She turned and gave him an appraising but put upon look. "I believe I made myself clear when I left on Monday that I have absolutely no interest in joining your pack, or any pack for that matter. I wish to be left alone and I in turn will leave others alone."

Keegan actually blinked at her for a beat. That clearly hadn't been what he'd expected her to say, but he recovered and that benign smile returned. "While I appreciate your candor, that isn't really an option, at the moment. We need all the wolves we can get to prepare for the little uprising Wilson and his ilk are causing. But you don't need to decide now. I may grow on you, eventually." His smile broadened and while it was completely gorgeous and would normally be disarming, Emma had enough of men informing her what she would or wouldn't do.

Emma leaned in so they were practically nose to nose and she watched as his eyes widened a touch. It was a very dominate move that no submissive wolf should make, given his position. "I decide how I feel on things. No amount of male intervention is going to change my mind. If anything, your words convince me further than with an attitude like that your pack is something I want no part of, ever."

Where is this coming from? Emma asked her wolf. Normally, she didn't have this amount of confidence with anyone but her close friends and family. But here she was standing nose to nose with a very dominant wolf and making direct eye contact as if it was nothing. It wasn't as if he could know she was a submissive wolf in her previous pack, but she did. Emma knew this was out of character for herself.

You and I are getting a stronger bond. We won't be letting someone control us like Richard did.

She seemed to have stunned Keegan to silence as his eyes were a little wide and his smile had all but disappeared. As surprisingly exhilarating as it was to stand up to a dominant wolf, she had a class she desperately needed to prepare for. Taking a step back she flicked her long braid over her shoulder.

"Now leave my classroom so I can get ready for my students." Her voice was even and though it came from her own lungs

Emma had to fight to keep the surprise off her face at her own words.

Keegan took a step back and held his hands up in front of him, palms out. "I meant no disrespect, and I certainly didn't mean to anger you."

His words shocked her. She could not remember the last time she'd seen a wolf as dominant as him apologize for anything, even when it was their fault. This was just a minor mix-up compared to some of the other things she'd seen over the years.

"I've actually enrolled in your class. I do occasionally do that. I'm one of those strange people that enjoys learning new things occasionally. So, for the rest of the quarter I'll be here to learn. But should you need to talk to me, or choose to talk to me about the pack or anything in the related region, I am at your disposal." He then pulled a card from one of his back pockets and slowly slid it onto the desk to her left. He gave her a second look, as one would when they were respectfully moving away from a dominant wolf. He inclined his head slightly as he backed away, not turning until he reached the first row of desks.

It was weird to be on the receiving end of that gesture. No one ever backed away from Emma as if she could pose a threat. The idea thrilled part of her. Another part of her was terrified of what would happen when he found out that she wasn't as dominant as she was propping herself up to be. In this case, appearances were definitely deceiving, and she didn't want to get railroaded when they realized how submissive a wolf she was.

Don't let yourself fall into old habits. It may not seem like it but you let Richard control your life and it suppressed our connection and your growth. I'm strong enough now that I won't let that happen again and I don't think you will either. You have nothing to worry about should this wolf decide to come for us.

Her wolf spoke with such confidence that Emma knew the words were true. She did not know how on earth she and her wolf could stop anyone from trying to control them but in that moment the words rang with so much truth it took Emma's breath away. The wolf was right, she hadn't noticed until she been away from Richard for weeks how his whims and desires controlled much of her life. She rarely changed into her wolf form, and when she did, Richard was always with her. Being able to change on her own had been novel and exciting. Her connection to her wolf had grown stronger, and she ended up depending on the wolf's words of wisdom much more than she had prior in her life. She wouldn't let someone separate the two of them, not again. But worry still niggled at her. Werewolves rarely moved from the bottom half of the pack. Growing up Emma had only seen it maybe twice. They never made it so high up the food chain that the submissive wolf had a position of power.

How is timid me supposed to manage it?

Forcing those thoughts from her mind, Emma returned to the blackboard and began writing the outline for that day's lesson. Most of her lesson was on PowerPoint but there was something about writing it out with chalk that filled Emma with a warm joy each time she did it.

When she finished the outline, she looked up to see there were about ten minutes before class and the room was about two-thirds filled. That was when she saw Wilson standing in the doorway. His sudden appearance startled her, as she hadn't sensed him standing there. Her wolf growled slightly, letting Emma know the wolf had not sensed him either.

When he knew he held her attention, he smiled and crooked his finger as he backed away from the door. It wasn't a come-hither gesture, there was no hidden agenda behind it. That was the only reason she went. She had to fight the urge to turn and look at Keegan and the other two wolves to see what their expressions were as she walked out of the room. She knew if she looked for that level of approval, or disapproval, it would show her cards as a submissive wolf. Dominant wolves didn't answer to people, and that was what she needed to practice being. Even if it didn't come naturally. So instead of turning and looking she balled her hands into fists and dug her fingernails into her palms to stop her from giving in to the urge to turn.

Once she was down the hall, about halfway between her classroom and

Wilson's, Emma slowed her pace. She stopped three feet away and waited for him to speak.

He smiled at her. It was that same oily, predatory smile that set her wolf on edge. "We were interrupted last time, though I know both you and I have class to teach I wanted to check in with you and see what your thoughts were about joining our local pack now that you've had a run in with their dear Keegan." Wilson lifted his eyebrows as he finished speaking and though Emma could sense his genuine interest in what her answer would be, there was something else there she couldn't quite put her finger on.

So when she spoke she chose her words carefully. "I have tried to make it clear to Keegan that I have no interest in joining his pack. I have had enough of werewolf politics to last a lifetime and I have no interest in jumping right back in to that nonsense." She watched as a satisfied smile slithered onto his face.

Emma kept her voice cool because she knew her next words would strip that smile. "For that same reason I have no interest in joining your loose collective of lone wolves. Both that and the pack have more structure than I wish to be a part of. I do not wish to help overthrow a pack nor do I wish to be a part of one. I also don't want to answer to a loose collective of any kind. I am trying to clarify that all I want is to be left alone. I will bother no one if they do not bother me. Therefor I am not picking sides in whatever fight is happening here." She kept her tone cool and calculated, trying to keep up the facade that she was in fact the dominant wolf she was pretending to be because there's no way a submissive wolf could speak the way she was speaking to both Keegan and Wilson. Emma got the impression that out of the two, Wilson would probably be angrier at the audacity than Keegan would.

Sure enough, Wilson frowned at her and folded his arms over his chest. He waited a beat before he said anything as if he too was weighing each individual word in his head before he spoke. "While I'm glad you have no interest in joining the pack, I can't say I'm thrilled that you want to go it alone. The pack, as you can imagine, will not appreciate a lone wolf like you wandering around its territory. I can't imagine they won't want to at least watch your movements to see if you're a threat. It would be better for you to have us at your back should this happen. But I can't decide for you. Obviously, if you feel alone is the way to go that's what you should do, but you should know that the offer to join us is always open. I would like to offer to take you out to dinner before class on Monday. Just to get to know each other better, no hidden agenda. As we will work with each other this quarter in proximity, it seems only polite that I help you find interesting places to eat about town. Feel free to say no, as it's obviously your choice, but I would more than enjoy your company."

He's much more polite than I thought he would be, Emma commented to her wolf.

He is, but I'm still not sure I trust him. her wolf responded.

But I'm not sure I want to be on his bad side as well as the pack's. One dinner will not hurt anything. And it'll give me insight into his side of this disagreement. Then I can ask Raelene for the rest. I can fill in the gaps and I'll get a fuller picture of what exactly I've walked into by moving to this territory.

As long as you stay on your guard it's not a bad idea, her wolf responded begrudgingly.

"All right, I will meet you somewhere." She emphasized meet, as she didn't want him getting any idea that they would drive together. She certainly didn't want him knowing where she lived. "You can just tell me where at the end of class and I'll meet you at say, five?" She deliberately gave a short timeline so that it would keep them close to campus and it would mean they had little time to dally before class. She may be interested in what he had to say but Emma certainly didn't trust him enough to give him more than an hour of her time.

Her meaning didn't seem lost on him because his smile quirked up as he pushed off the wall. "Very good. I suggest Dick's Drive-in in Lake City. We can sit on the hoods of our cars and talk since there is not an abundance of seating." He waited a beat, just smiling before he turned and headed to his class, walking away like any other dominant wolf who wasn't trying to stop a challenge. It was the attitude she was used to, though perhaps he was more polite.

Emma knew she had to fight to appear as a dominant wolf, even though it didn't come naturally, if she planned on keeping a more neutral stance in this. She didn't want to pick sides, and she didn't want someone to pick sides for her because they realized she wasn't as calm and collected or powerful as she initially seemed. She was honestly surprised she managed to pull it off during the two encounters she had with Wilson and Keegan.

As she walked back into the classroom, she scanned the students out of the corner of her eye. She saw Keegan frowning deeply at her. He was definitely not pleased that Emma went out into the hall to talk to Wilson and she could practically see his mind trying to calculate what his next move would be.

Part of Emma wanted to go to him, and say she had no interest in joining Wilson's little group, reiterating her earlier statement, but she forced herself not to and instead turned on her computer and hooked it up to the AV system

If I was truly a dominant wolf, I wouldn't answer to him. Especially since I'm not in his pack. I just have to keep reminding myself of that so he's not tempted to use dominance magic to make me join the pack.

Dominance magic was just a powerful extension of a dominant wolf's will. The more dominant a wolf the more of their will they could exert on others. Even an Alpha couldn't make somebody do something completely out of character. But it could, much like Alpha Peters preferred use, create a weight on a person who was so heavy you would rather give into the Alpha's will then continue to feel it. Emma had been on the receiving end of that will several times and she didn't want to put herself in that position again.

So she continued to go against her instincts as she smiled at the class like she would any other class and taught. She needed to set all this aside. She couldn't let herself get distracted from doing the job she loved. Teaching was the time where pack politics didn't enter the picture. It was just her and her students' world and she wouldn't let a little thing like a wolf dominance fight stop her from enjoying it, even if she had to stop herself from glancing at the incredibly sexy Keegan several times during class. He was incredibly beautiful and even if he wasn't a wolf, that would've been distracting enough. But the dominance that came off of him felt like a calming blanket. That it was appealing bothered her. She had never found Richard, or his father's dominance attractive. So she didn't know why it was pleasant on Keegan. The only reason she could think was because he wore his more like a mantle, as if it was part of him instead of something he lorded over people the way Richard or his father did.

Just stop, Emma. Concentrate on teaching. Teaching is why you're here not checking out men, she chastised herself before she focused on the computer screen and changed slides, forcing herself to not look at him for the rest of class.

Chapter 15:
Wine and Dine

Emma

Dick's Drive-in was not what Emma expected. She heard of the Western Washington burger chain but in the handful of times she visited Raelene they had never gone. But she liked it. It had an upbeat character to it that made her understand why there was such a line to get food. When she'd driven up, she had luckily found a parking spot in the opposite end of the lot. She didn't wait for Wilson, as she got there ten minutes early, but headed straight to one of the lines of people in front of the glass windows. She could give the menu a long look before she got to the window to place her order.

Emma chatted with Raelene the night before about what she should try. At the front of the line, Emma smiled back at the teenager speaking to her and ordered two deluxe, a fry, and a chocolate shake. As per Raelene's instructions, she also ordered a side of onion and two tartars. Raelene'd specifically instructed how she was supposed to eat these burgers that Emma was going to find a little hard to do since there was no particular place to actually sit down.

As she waited off to the side, she watched as the efficient staff got her food ready and she was impressed with how quickly her order was filled. She grabbed the bag and shake, thanking the teenager as he turned to the person in line behind her.

As she headed back to her car, she saw Wilson's BMW parked next to her car. She assumed it was his anyway since he was leaning against the trunk. His arms and ankles crossed, and he was smiling at her with a friendly expression on his face.

But Emma wasn't fooled. It was more difficult to read regular people than it was wolves, but they had been to Green Lake and practiced on regular people over the weekend, so reading Wilson had become much easier than it had been last Wednesday. He was cocky. He firmly believed he could convince Emma to join his little group. But he was prepared to go slow and let her think they were friends first and he would slowly pepper their conversations with stories of how ill the pack was run. He hadn't even been actively thinking all of that, at least not in those exact words, but Emma picked up on it all the same.

Smile, her wolf warned her.

I know, we'll be fine, she responded.

"Good evening, Emma. I'm glad you already got your food. If you don't mind, I'm going to go stand in line and will be back probably within the next ten minutes." Wilson waited for her to nod in understanding before pushing off of his car and striding over to the nearest window. She stood in silence, waiting for him to get back. She only did that for about five seconds before shaking her head and opening the bag of food. She was not about to wait to eat simply because the more dominant wolf had not gotten his yet.

Stupid. I need to not be obvious about being a submissive wolf, Emma chastised herself.

Just relax, you're eating now and that's fine. Don't worry about what he thinks. Her wolf responded in a calm and soothing tone.

Her wolf was right of course. Wilson hadn't seen her hesitation, and that was what was important. Calmly she ate her fries and drank the fabulous shake.

I'll have to remember to tell Raelene how much I enjoyed eating here. We should eat here more often, Emma commented as she watched Wilson finally get to the window.

By the time he got back to her Emma had already added tartar sauce and onions to her burger and was eating the first one.

"They are good, aren't they," Wilson remarked smugly as he put his own bag on the hood of his car and turned toward her before taking a sip of whatever liquid he had in his cup.

"They are. I also enjoy how happy the employees seem to be," she added just to see how he would respond.

Wilson smiled before putting down the cup and grabbing his own container of fries out of the bag. He seemed content to stand there and eat for several minutes. Emma waited, as she'd set an alarm on her phone to go off when she needed to leave to get to class. She didn't want to give herself or Wilson any excuse to stick around longer than was necessary. Emma finished her food in silence and finally gave up waiting.

"So, what was it you wanted to tell me?" she asked, wanting to cut to the chase instead of having this drawn out into a second meal, which she wasn't entirely sure wasn't his plan.

Wilson gave a sigh before setting aside his burger and making eye contact with her again.

"I know you said you have no interest in joining the pack, and for that I'm grateful. As you probably could figure out, I'm not their biggest fan. At the same time, the reason I developed this little group I belong to of lone wolves was to protect those of us who didn't want to join the pack. It's something similar to a union in that when they come for one of us they come for all of us. While that means you are available should something happen, the group of us are available to you should you need it. It comes in handy should the pack ever try to give you trouble."

How is that different from a regular pack? her wolf mumbled quietly, though the low tone wasn't necessary as Emma was fairly certain Wilson couldn't hear her wolf.

"I know what you may be thinking. But we don't have meetings and obligations the way a pack does. We occasionally have dinner together as a group to sort of check in but other than that, the occasional text message is really the only communication we have. We all simply want to not have to have all the rigmarole that goes with being part of a pack and we want the option to stay that way. I appreciate you want to do it yourself. But I also understand just how difficult that could be. Which is why I don't want you to feel forced or backed into a corner, but I don't want you to feel that this is a onetime offer either."

Why do I get the impression there's more here than he's letting on?

Because there is, her wolf purred.

Emma really wanted to read his mind; to see what exactly it was he was planning on doing. Emma had a theory that he wanted to use this little network of wolves to overthrow the pack as a solid group instead of just challenging the Alpha. If that was the case, she definitely wanted no part of it. But she also didn't know why he was not selling it that way. Why would he try to hide the whole thing? Part of Emma wanted to ask but another part of her didn't want to show that much interest in whatever it was he had planned.

When she spoke Emma tried to keep her voice as diplomatic as she could. "I appreciate that you're willing to keep the offer open for me. I'm not ready to join anything formal or informal. I get that if an Alpha is strict about not having lone wolves in his territory that it would be in your best interest to band together. While the idea is interesting, I don't want to join at this time." She picked each word deliberately. She didn't want to show him she suspected he had ulterior motives.

She got the impression that Wilson wasn't as calm and collected for his dominance as Keegan might be. And while Keegan could hide his feelings from her, he seemed less likely to have an outburst when not getting his way than Wilson did. She could feel his displeasure coming off of him in waves though there was only a disappointed frown for a split second before he nodded in understanding. But on the inside he seethed. If she had only been using regular werewolf senses, she might not have caught it.

"That is all I ask. We're not looking to control you or your actions. We believe everyone should get to live their own life as they see fit, within reason of course. But should you need to reach out to me for help…" He then, much like Keegan had, pulled of business card out of his wallet and handed it to her.

Emma took it because she didn't want to be outwardly rude and inclined her head. She sensed some of his anger and frustration abate when she took the card. She certainly had no intention of calling on him for help but he didn't need to know that. She would simply put it in the part of her backpack where Keegan's card was and leave it there. She had no intention of using either card, so it made sense to just keep them together.

Before either of them could say anything else, her alarm buzzed in her pocket, letting her know she needed to leave now if she was going to get to class on time.

Wilson let out a laugh Emma was fairly certain he didn't feel. "Well, duty calls." He smiled jovially and if Emma hadn't been paying close attention to what was going on in his mind, she would've thought he meant it.

"Yep, time to head to class and get all the last-minute prep work done," she responded as she balled up her garbage before heading to the nearest trashcan and tossing it in.

Wilson followed her and tossed in his own trash behind her, getting closer to her than she would've preferred. Not a threatening distance, just close enough to be in her personal space.

"I'll see you at work then. And please by all means, remember that you can call that number any time you require assistance. If I can't come, I can send one of my colleagues. Don't feel you have to do this alone, even if your first inclination is to do so." He then gave her a reassuring smile before climbing into his car and starting it up.

Emma waited until he backed out before turning on her own car. For whatever reason she didn't want to drive to work with him. She wanted the little time that arriving at a different moment would give her. She didn't want to walk in together, make it appear to the wolves in her class as if she was siding with him over them. Part of her wondered whether Wilson would wait for her in the parking lot to do just that. She wouldn't put it past him. He seemed sneaky to her and she could see him trying to make it appear as if they were closer than they were so that Keegan would think she allied with Wilson. It wouldn't matter what she said as long as it appeared she was siding with the lone wolves. It was going to be a delicate dance moving between the two groups. She didn't particularly want to spend time with either dominant wolf. But if Wilson was going to be grabbing bits of her time like this, Emma needed to give time to Keegan as well to even the playing field. She couldn't let it appear as if she was picking one over the other.

I don't want to spend time with either of them, Emma commented to her wolf as she drove from the parking lot.

You have the right idea though. You spend time with both. Then you're picking neither. It might be your best-case scenario at this point. Emma didn't know how she found herself in this position. All she wanted was to escape Richard and his father who were trying to control her as if she were a child. She didn't want to be controlled, and she didn't want to be in a marriage where her spouse didn't feel he needed to be faithful to her. All she wanted was to be left alone. But if the only way to do that was to play nice with both the pack and these lone wolves then so be it. She could straddle the middle, as long as she could maintain her independence. As long as she could make it look like she was the dominant wolf she pretended to be she could do this.

But I don't know how long I can do this for, she admitted to herself.

As long as it takes for them to get the hint that you're not picking sides. Eventually they'll lose interest. You just have to hold out that long. Her wolf was trying to comfort her, Emma knew that. But knowing it didn't make it any better than not knowing it would have.

Moving to Alaska is looking better and better.

Her wolf only snorted before going quiet as Emma drove the rest of the way to campus.

Chapter 16:
Friendly Faces

Emma

It had been a huge relief to Emma when she opened the door Friday evening, about five minutes after the pizza arrived, to see Morris' beaming face at the door. He had a duffel bag slung over his shoulder, and his laptop bag in his hand. She missed him more than she'd expected and had to fight the urge to launch at him for a hug. The last thing they needed was toppling down the hall and crushing his laptop. So dutifully, she moved aside to let him in. Once he dropped his bags on the ground, she flung herself at him for a hug.

I missed you more than I thought I would. I needed your biting sarcastic comments more than once during the last few weeks, she said in her head but pointed it in his direction.

She had been practicing trying to direct her thoughts. Though she hadn't directed them at anyone yet, as giving no one a heads up, it felt a little intrusive. Morris was the only one who knew she could do it.

From the look of shock on his face when she read his thoughts last time, she bet it wasn't a normal gift. So, she refrained from telling Raelene about it, though she felt guilty keeping such a large secret.

We missed you too, his wolf responded. Its deep voice resonated in her head.

She hugged him tighter, and he did the same. She heard him without them talking. It sent her head buzzing. It wasn't something she'd ever heard of, or something she'd seen in the limited research she'd done on her own in the last week. And although she had a slight headache from the effort, she was amazed it worked.

"You have a room. The two of you could use it," Raelene hollered from the kitchen where she had been when Emma answered the door.

A feeling of indignant revulsion spiked through her and she felt an answering revulsion zinging through Morris.

"She is like my sister and that is disgusting," he responded out loud, his disgust clear in his voice as he gave one more quick squeeze before backing up a step to face Raelene.

Having heard that argument before, Raelene rolled her eyes and motioned to the three extra-large pizzas that sat in front of her. "Whatever. We ordered extra food since we knew there'd be three wolves eating tonight. So help yourself. We also have the latest *Star Wars* movie queued up so whether you're a fan or not you're stuck watching it with us." She gave them both a huge grin before sliding one last piece of pizza on her large plate and brushing past the counter to go sit in the large recliner that faced the television.

"Oh pizza. You ladies sure know how to show a guy a good time," Morris commented gleefully as he headed into the kitchen and picked up his own plate.

Emma laughed, feeling the tension in her shoulders ease. It had been building up all week as her interactions between Wilson and Keegan continued. She tried to go out of her way to speak pleasantly to Keegan the one time she did so. Unlike Wilson, Keegan did not put himself in positions for them to talk alone which made it hard for her to look as if she was walking the line between the two groups. She was getting frustrated with how often Wilson would stop by her classroom. Though she arrived early on Wednesday, Wilson had already been there and stopped her in the hall before she reached her classroom. It made her wonder whether it was intentional on his part or was a coincidence.

Either way, she was grateful to have a weekend with two of her closest friends. Raelene had an event to go to on Saturday morning for a charity she volunteered with. That meant she would have Morris all to herself until the afternoon. Emma was grateful Raelene and Morris got along. She didn't know what she would do if the two of them hated each other.

She gave one last glance to both of them before smiling and turning to the movie as the opening credits rolled across the screen.

Chapter 17:
Beware Friends Baring Gifts

Emma

Raelene wandered off to bed soon after they finished their second movie, which the three of them joked their way through. It had hands down been the best evening Emma had in a very long time. It wasn't even until she had that thought, halfway through the second movie, that she realized how true it was. Part of her was sad with that realization, that she had spent so many years without moments like this. But that was quickly brushed aside when her wolf commented that at least she got to have them now.

Once Raelene went to sleep, Emma turned off the TV and turned to Morris, giving him her undivided attention. When he told her he was coming to visit this weekend, after having to cancel last weekend because of a problem with the test he'd given his class, he said they needed to talk. He hadn't had a joking tone, which concerned her. When she'd asked if it meant Richard found her he was quick to douse that fire, letting her know that as far as he was aware Richard and his father still did not know where she'd been. But beyond that he had not given her any information.

Now he looked at her with a mixed expression on his face. Emma couldn't quite tell what emotions he was feeling, and she didn't feel like prying. Whatever he wanted to say clearly was making him nervous or uncomfortable and it felt almost rude to intrude on his thoughts in this moment. So, she would wait until he vocalized, either verbally or in her head, what it was he was thinking.

He kept glancing between her face, his hands in his lap, and her hair. She didn't think her hair looked bad but she couldn't help but self-consciously touch it for a second before returning her own hands to her lap. The gesture seemed to draw his attention to the fact that he was staring because Morris blanked his face before shifting his own position so he faced her.

He bit his lip a moment before speaking. "I like your hair. It caught me off guard when I saw it. I've never seen your hair this light, but it's pretty, and flattering.

"Thanks." Emma responded with forced lightness to her tone. He was putting off whatever it was he came to talk about and it made her itch a little. But she would respect his privacy, as long as her patience would let her.

"Do you trust me?" Morris asked sheepishly, not quite making eye contact as he asked.

His lack of eye contact didn't hold any deviousness or secrets. It was as if he was embarrassed of the question.

"Of course." Emma didn't even have to give it a second thought. She trusted Morris implicitly, as did her wolf. She had since they first met, though she couldn't say why.

He actually looked relieved when she answered, he then pushed himself off the couch before heading over to his duffel bag and began rooting around in one of the small side pockets. When he came back, he was holding two cloth, cinched bags. He sat back down and set one of the bags in his lap and opened the second, pulling out an elegant, Victorian looking brooch. It had what appeared to be an emerald the size of a quarter in the lower middle and a mixed metal ornate circular design around it.

He held it out to her, hesitantly. "This isn't for you to keep. I'm going to need it back. It's just for you to hold on to for a couple minutes." He held the pendant out, hovering just above her hands. She turned her hands palms up so that she could hold it and he placed it gently against her skin.

As it made contact, she felt a zing of magic in it. It was less unpleasant than static electricity. It didn't hurt, just surprised her and she knew she jumped. When she looked up at him questioningly he was eyeing her, as if he was taking in her reaction and making notes.

"Now close your hands over it, hold tightly, and concentrate on talking to my wolf. Once the two of you have spoken a bit, open your hands." His explanation came quickly in one breath, his voice quiet, almost as if he didn't want to say the words out loud.

Emma frowned at him before looking down at the brooch. Frowning deeper, she looked back into Morris' eyes. There was an eagerness and hesitancy that she could see there. He was curious about something but there was also an internal debate on what he hoped the outcome would be. But she trusted him so instead of asking about it, she closed her hands over the brooch, made direct eye contact, and concentrated on communicating with his wolf.

Unlike with Raelene, Emma found she didn't need to touch base with her wolf before reaching out into Morris' mind. She didn't know whether that was because her connection to her wolf was stronger, because it was, or if it was because he was more dominant, or something else. She hadn't spent too much time thinking about it because she knew she would not get an answer. So she focused on his beautiful blue eyes and reached out to the wolf behind them.

Have you avoided any pack events since I've been gone? It was the first thing that occurred to her to ask.

Morris hated pack events, always avoided them like the plague. Though he'd gone to several when he was younger, since moving to Central Washington he'd gone to required pack meetings and that was it.

She felt his wolf slowly step out of the shadows of his mind. *No, though we've had our ear to the ground and rumor has it the Alpha is at odds with his son. He talks to him and treats him differently than he did a few weeks ago. There was something about a change of plans for giving the ultimatum to the Eastern Washington packs but we could not get details.*

The twins came to my office though. This time it was Morris' internal voice that answered her instead of the wolf. Though it was just as loud as the wolf's voice had been in her head, there was a definite tonal difference that let Emma know she was talking not to the wolf but the man. *They came by, offering to make me dinner. But it became clear after a few minutes they were in fact trying to get information about your whereabouts. Whether that was because Richard asked them to or because they were trying to get on his good side, I don't know. I didn't give them anything other than saying I didn't know where you'd wandered off to and I was mad about me not knowing. After it became clear I would not give them anything, they rather quickly lost interest on having a meal together. They didn't give up the pretense entirely, but it became relatively obvious. Check the brooch now.*

That last part was almost tacked on as if an afterthought.

Emma broke eye contact, blinking a few times. It was almost as if his eyes disappeared and she'd been able to see Morris' inner self and the wolf through them. She could also feel that her eyes were dry, letting her know she probably hadn't blinked in the few moments they'd been talking. She then opened her hands and looked down at the pretty brooch she held.

The emerald in the middle glowed like a nightlight; warm, soft, and bright. It wasn't blinding like a flashlight but there was no mistaking that it was emanating a light from within itself.

Emma had to force herself not to drop it. The brooch itself didn't feel any different to the touch, and she didn't feel magic coming from it like she had that initial zing, but she knew jewels didn't glow from inside like that. Not unless there was some sort of electronic device in it, which it didn't feel heavy enough to have. She quickly flipped it over to see that it looked like any other brooch, with a pin on the back.

She then looked up at Morris with a worried curiosity. "Um, it's glowing."

He looked relieved and a little resigned, as he looked down at the brooch in her hand. After a beat he reached out and covered her hands in his and squeezed them before looking up and making eye contact with her again. He gave a sad smile, and she felt affection pour out from him.

"I got it from my grandmother. She said it was a magic detector of sorts. She told me the same instructions I gave you. She said if the gem within it glowed when you did something that required Omega magic it meant you are in fact an Omega wolf. If you had just been a sensitive regular wolf nothing would've happened.

Panic filled Emma. There was no way she was an Omega wolf. Omegas were powerful and dominant in their own right. No one controlled them. No one could force them to do anything. They moved as unique members connected to a pack but not of it. They did things for the good of groups of people. They had miraculous powers that were helpful. And most of all, they came into their powers in their late teens.

"There's no way that's possible. There has to be another answer for this. Maybe there's a fluke. Maybe it's because you touched it and it's your magic it's picking up. You have a grandmother who is an Omega wolf. There's no way *I'm* an Omega wolf, I don't have power. I'm in the middle of my 20s. if I was I should've started displaying years ago." Her words came out in one breath, fast and shaky.

Her heart pounded in her chest. Morris' words rang with truth. Deep down her wolf knew what he said made sense and knew it was true. But she couldn't believe it. She would've known. Richard would've noticed. Richard would've told her. That was if he knew it was Omega power. Which he wouldn't. Because he never actually met one in more than passing.

She forced down the panic, squeezing Morris' hands out of habit, pushing the brooch to bite into her skin a bit.

"There's no questioning it. It's the definite test. I asked my grandmother about it. She said there's no way to fake it." He gave her hands another squeeze before letting go and reaching for the second pouch he held with his left hand, grabbing the brooch from her hands with his right. Deliberately he placed the brooch back in its bag, re-cinching it before dropping it in his lap and opening the other.

This time he pulled out an intricate bracelet with different intertwined colored metals. They were weaved in and around each other with an almost copper looking vine that appeared to be holding them all in place as it wrapped around the entire piece. It wasn't a complete circle, it was one of those bands that you would push over your wrist and turn. It was a beautiful piece. Reaching out, Morris put it in her hands where the brooch had been, since she hadn't moved since he'd taken it.

"This, this one's for you. This one is for you to keep. My grandmother said if you turned out to be an Omega, wearing this would help control and focus your power. It would help prevent accidental slippages and displays of power. And when you need to focus your power, it will help you do so."

Still shaking, Emma looked down at the bracelet she held in her hand. Her urge was to throw it across the room and pretend she'd never seen it. But when someone was gifted something from an Omega wolf, it was absurd to toss it away. Especially if it did what Morris' grandmother said it did. Even before she started practicing reading people's thoughts and emotions, she felt the occasional strong emotions wafting off of others. But even with her practicing, nothing happened that would require her to wear this level of magic to stop it.

"Thank her for me. It was habit more than anything else that had her speaking.

She continued to stare down at the bracelet but didn't put it on. Instead, she slowly picked it up with her right hand and daintily put it on the coffee table to her right. She then stared at it. When it just lay there, she moved her attention back to Morris.

When Emma reached out to her wolf, the wolf was there, sitting quietly absorbing everything being said. There was no shock, no denial, just pure acceptance this was their reality.

Not quite willing to accept it, Emma pulled back from her wolf. "Omegas they... They develop the power younger than this. Sure, I was a late bloomer for being able to change into my wolf form and all of that but this is ridiculous. There should've been some inkling before this.

Morris simply shrugged, "I don't have an answer for you. But the brooch doesn't lie. You are clearly an Omega wolf." If Emma wasn't mistaken, there was a thread of nervousness in his voice.

Emma felt her own panic notch up, there was something else he was thinking, something else he was keeping from her that he didn't want to say. She couldn't imagine what would be bigger than his last information drop. Part of her wanted him to just not say it so she had nothing else to tip her over the edge into a full-blown panic attack.

When he looked back at her his expression was sad. "I discussed it with my grandmother and while we don't know why your abilities would only just be developing now, but they are developing quickly. Almost as if you're making up for lost time. Do you think there's a chance Richard would know you're an Omega wolf?" His question was so quiet and so hesitant Emma felt herself leaning in as he spoke.

"I doubt it. He'd only ever met Omega wolves in passing. I didn't know. I don't know how he would."

Morris' expression didn't change as he continued on. "My grandmother and I were talking about it and we have a sneaking suspicion that the reason Alpha Peters is so dead set on you marrying Richard is because they somehow stumbled upon the fact that you're an Omega wolf. It was the only explanation we could see that would make him so hell-bent on it happening. No offense, Emma, but Richard didn't seem that broken up about you leaving him and the fact that Alpha Peters is pushing it so hard means he has to have some other agenda. Saving face wouldn't come into account since you and your parents have such submissive positions in the pack. The only alternative is that they know or suspect that you are an Omega and want to use that power to their advantage." He went quiet as if waiting for her to get mad at him.

But as she absorbed it, it made sense, in an insane way. If he said this two months ago, she would've denied it adamantly. Sure, Alpha Peters was manipulative and cruel at times, but Richard was nothing like that. Richard was kind and caring and sometimes a little aloof. But now, now she wasn't so sure. The layers she'd seen since finding out he'd been cheating on her made her think he was capable of this kind of thing because Morris was right, Richard hadn't seemed that upset about the break up. He seemed more angry that she wouldn't just do what he said. And her gut told her that was a weird reaction but she dismissed it.

I don't know how he would know, she muttered to herself, trying to get her train of thought to focus on something in the whirlwind happening in her brain.

It could've been a slip? It could've been anything. Maybe you commented on something he didn't say out loud. Who knows? Morris' wolf crooned in her head. It was trying to soothe her.

Emma tried to put aside the anxiety that came with the fact that his wolf could so easily enter her train of thought. What had been exhilarating moments ago now made her panic. But she pushed that aside as she couldn't afford to lose herself in a panic attack. She needed to focus. Emma tried to think back, think back on any time when anything like that could've happened. But nothing came to the forefront from her memory. And her wolf had nothing to contribute.

Then a truly strange thing happened. Her wolf stepped forward out of the shadows and she could feel that absent brush of fur against the inside of her head. A comforting gesture that though felt strange Emma had known instinctively was her wolf's way of showing affection. *He wouldn't have shown any surprise. He would've played it off as if it was nothing. Richard likes power. Power that is his and not his father's. If it was clear, you didn't know you were an Omega wolf he wouldn't have done anything to tell you.*

I don't understand how you wouldn't have noticed abilities out of the ordinary, Morris' wolf responded to Emma's wolf.

It was such a strange sensation having Morris' wolf and hers communicating with each other while both of them were in human form. It went against everything Emma learned while growing up, and yet it felt as natural as breathing.

She needed to be allowed to learn the lesson herself. Not to mention I did not have as loud of a voice as I do now. There was frustrated confusion in her wolf's voice as she said that last part. *I don't know what it was but while she was with him it was as if I was tethered, staked in a yard and unable to reach out and warn her about his deceptions.*

That is what we feared. Morse's wolf growled before he turned his attention from the other wolf to Emma. Emma didn't know how she knew his attention shifted but she did. *Other than the breakup did anything change when you left Central Washington? Did you leave anything behind or feel any kind of difference when you crossed the mountains?* The wolf's words were patient and calm like a wise man asking a question he already knew the answer to.

But it wasn't until he asked that Emma remembered the necklace she had thrown across her room at her parents' house. She never picked it up, just left it in the lush carpet in the corner. Her voice, the voice of her wolf, had been louder since then. *But there's no way the two things could be related, could they?*

Richard gave me a necklace for our one-year anniversary. It was a beautiful necklace that I loved, and I wore it every single day after he gave it to me. Until I left. I took it off and threw it across my bedroom at my parents' house and never picked it up again.

She got the distinct impression that both Morris and his wolf frowned

Are you okay if I go pick it up and send it to my grandmother? I don't want to believe it, but I think there was some sort of magic hindering your abilities. Not having those abilities would make you more... Malleable, Morris interjected into their internal conversation.

Do it, her wolf growled in response. *We need to know if this was purposely being kept from us. If he has that kind of knowledge, that kind of access to power, that's information we need on our side.*

"What the hell are you guys doing?" Raelene's sharp voice startled both Morris and Emma out of their heads and they both jumped.

Chapter 18:
The Truth Comes Out

Emma

They turned to Raelene who was frowning at both of them, arms crossed under her chest.

"I woke up, had to use the restroom, and figured I'd get some water. I come out here in the two of you are staring at each other, staring right in each other's eyes. Neither of you realized I was standing here and neither of you spoke. I know you're not having a staring contest because one of you would've started making faces. So, I repeat, what the hell are you doing?"

You can't keep it from her any longer.

She doesn't know?

Both wolves spoke at the same time.

Emma gave a heavy sigh and rubbed her fingertips over her eyebrows. "Raelene you need to sit down. There is a complicated secret I have to share with you." When she opened her eyes again, Emma could see Raelene frowning at her but there was concern in her eyes.

"What did Richard do?" Raelene moved to the recliner she'd been sitting in earlier, her gaze shifting between Morris and Emma.

Emma sighed again as she turned to give Raelene her undivided attention. It meant giving her back to Morris, but she trusted him and knew that wasn't an issue.

"We don't know for sure yet but let me walk you through the theory." She then spent the next half an hour walking Raelene through everything that happened since she broke up with Richard.

Raelene made her stop and go into great detail every time she tried to use her power. There was a slight whiff of offense when she got to where she heard Raelene's inner thoughts. But after that Raelene brushed it aside and kept listening. Asking attentive questions as they went along as if trying to get the best visual she could. When Emma finished, Raelene was frowning again but her arms were no longer crossed and there wasn't anger or frustration, just surprise and disbelief. Emma half expected her to question the whole thing.

"And Richard hid this from you? For what, four years?" Emma felt Raelene's anger spike, not directed at either of them but the Alpha son several hours drive away. "That mangy worthless dog." Raelene growled and Emma swore she heard Raelene's wolf growling along with her friend. "This is a big deal, Emma. If he knew, he knew, and he's been hiding it from you, stunting your growth. That's a huge deal. Omegas are treasured members of our society. They help the greater good. That Richard and Alpha Peters, would unsurprisingly, put themselves and their power base first is a huge violation of that. If the other Alphas in the area knew he planned that kind of thing they would probably take him out. There's no way they'd let an Alpha be in power who would abuse the old Omega laws like that."

When they were teenagers, Raelene had an obsessive curiosity to study all the laws put in place for pack hierarchy. She didn't understand why some wolves thought they were better than others simply because they were more dominant. So, she'd thrown herself into studying every single pack law she could get her hands on. The first time she'd tried to assert her knowledge in a full pack meeting Alpha Peters slapped her so hard she'd skidded across the room. After that Raelene only muttered law violations to either Bess or Emma before leaving.

"If you can prove it," Raelene was talking to Morris now. "If you can prove that he did that with that necklace. We can take it to the Seattle pack or other area packs as proof. We can get that toxic environment cleaned out." There was a zealousness to her voice.

Emma's initial response was to back up and deny it. She didn't want to be responsible for the downfall of anyone, even though she wasn't a fan of Alpha Peters either. But she didn't want to get involved with the Seattle pack, even if it meant offering this evidence.

"And what are we going to do if they decide to side with him? How do we know that the Alpha here would react any differently than Peters would?" Emma countered.

Not all packs are like what you're used to, Morris' wolf whispered to Emma in her head. *The pack where my grandmother is Omega is more representative of everyone in it. There's less infighting for power struggles, they are more cooperative. I think that is more the norm than Alpha Peters' megalomania.*

Even if Morris' wolf was right that didn't mean Emma wanted to get involved. She didn't want them to do it, to make a move and then fail. Then she would be stuck under Peters again.

"I can't get involved. I can't put myself in a position where they'll know where I am. And if you go to the Seattle pack with that information that's exactly what will happen."

Raelene looked like she was going to argue with Emma's words.

But Morris beat her to it. "We won't go to the Seattle pack. I'll bring it to my grandmother and give her all this information and she can decide who to go to with it. Everyone knows my grandmother is an Omega wolf, so it won't be any kind of giveaway or surprise if it's my home pack that steps forward. If anything, it will move them away from your location and focus them on a different one."

Emma bit her lip. She knew Morris had a good point. She wanted to know is much as they did if Richard actually betrayed her in this way. Part of her still cared about him, despite everything else and she wanted to believe he wouldn't use her like that. But it explained Alpha Peters' push that the two of them become a mated pair.

"Okay fine. Just... I don't want to be involved... Just let me know what your grandmother finds." Emma knew her voice sounded defeated and tired.

Up until now, her night had been fantastic, the best. Now there was so much more at play here than she thought there was. She wasn't just a submissive wolf trying to get away from some dominant wolf wanting to mate her. Now she was supposedly an Omega wolf, struggling with late blooming powers that couldn't really get her anywhere or help her do anything, from a manipulative Alpha who was determined to use her and her powers for himself. Emma closed her eyes and leaned back on the couch. She felt queasy on top of tired.

"I feel as if I'm never going to be safe again." She didn't mean to say it out loud, for the others to hear that thought. But as soon as she realized she said it out loud she also realized it wouldn't have mattered. If Morris and his wolf were listening to her inner thoughts as intently as she thought they were they would've heard it, anyway.

She felt his hand reach out and squeeze her shoulder. "I will not let him do that kind of thing again. If this turns out to be what we think it is, I won't let them get away with it. I'll help you stay independent, whatever that means to you. Do you hear me?" The question was almost desperate. As if he was trying to will her to accept his comfort.

Emma simply nodded, too exhausted and drained to do anything else.

The three of them sat there in silence for a long time. Emma with her eyes closed and her brain floating, stray thoughts whispering by as if on a breeze. Her wolf stayed nearby, a comforting presence but said nothing. She didn't feel Morris or his wolf which made her wonder whether they were giving her space to process. Finally, when it seemed as if exhaustion was going to overtake her, Emma opened her eyes and saw Raelene watching her.

"Let's get you to bed. It's late and we all need sleep." She then stood and held her hand out to Emma.

Without the energy to protest, Emma simply lifted her hand and put it in Raelene's and let her friend pull her up.

"Good night, Morris. Sweet dreams," she murmured over her shoulder sleepily as she let Raelene guide her to the back of the apartment where the bedrooms were.

It's going to be okay. You're stronger now and you have friends at your back. It's going to be okay. Her wolf's murmurs of reassurance were the last thing Emma heard as she drifted off to sleep.

Chapter 19:
What an Interesting Development

Emma
Four Years Earlier

"Oh, I forgot to tell you that my father is requesting our presence for dinner this coming Saturday. There are two out-of-town Alphas visiting and it's a special celebration for them. I of course have to go but I would appreciate having you on my arm. Mostly I think it would be great to have your company. Someone to make comments with about all the silly political things that will be sure to happen throughout the meal," Richard called out from where he sat propped up against the pillows on his bed.

Emma was spending the night at his apartment, since she had two roommates in her on-campus apartment. Staying with Richard meant they had a bit more privacy. He also had a nice bathtub she could bathe in whenever she wanted. She'd only taken advantage a handful of times, tonight being one of them. She'd come over and Richard had unexpected business so she'd pulled out some bubble bath and relaxed, eyes closed, and listened to the murder mystery audiobook she was in the middle of.

She hadn't realized she'd been dozing off until she heard Richard come into the bedroom looking for her. It snapped her awake and Emma drained the tub, turned off her audiobook, and was drying off.

"I'm flattered you want me to go. But are you sure my presence would work in your father's favor? My family are submissive wolves and it might not help give your father any clout to have me there, seeing as how I will probably be the only submissive wolf in attendance." Emma hadn't been to any political dinners yet, since she and Richard hadn't been dating for even a year so it made little sense for her to go. But now he was asking her. She almost couldn't believe it. Part of her was so excited, the other part was anxious.

I think this means were a long-term thing. I mean why else would he ask? He wants to show me off, that makes it official in the eyes of the other packs, doesn't it? she asked herself, trying not to get too excited about the prospect of one dinner.

Just be careful in case he has some other agenda, her wolf commented quietly from somewhere in the deepest shadows of the back of her mind.

Her wolf had never been strong, not that she expected it to be since she was so submissive. It would occasionally chime in but that was about it. Unless she changed into wolf form, it stayed back and kept to itself. It had never been a fan of Richard's.

"Don't worry about that. You'll be with me so you won't be in any danger. And no one cares that you're submissive. You're beautiful and you're my date. It also helps that you're very smart. It'll look good to have you there," Richard replied comfortingly.

Not to mention we'll look like a more accepting pack having the Alpha's son dating a low submissive wolf. That will definitely play to the sensibilities of the Eastern Oregon Alpha.

Emma was surprised by that last comment. Richard didn't seem like much of a social climber most of the time. She almost forgot that he would probably take over the pack when his father stepped down. She supposed he needed to think like a political shark. It was just when he was with her, he didn't usually say those thoughts out loud. With the towel scrunching her hair dry, she stepped into the doorway between the main bathroom and the bedroom so she could look him in the face.

"Does the Eastern Oregon Alpha think so little of pack hierarchy that my presence would appeal to him?"

Her curiosity got the better of her. The hierarchy in their pack was so stringent, minus her own baffling relationship with Richard. Occasionally there would be dominance fights but usually it was pretty quiet. Emma couldn't imagine being in a pack where hierarchy wasn't important.

Richard blinked at her a second and Emma couldn't help but wonder whether she'd stepped out of line by asking. She went over his words and then her own but couldn't see where the offense could have been. The surprised blink was only on his face for a split second before he smiled at her, a little predatory. "He himself married one of the more submissive wolves in his pack about fifteen years ago. Since then, the lines are a bit blurred between the different levels of wolves in their pack. He appreciates more progressive packs where the hierarchy isn't as strict. Which means he doesn't approve of a lot of packs."

Emma nodded before stepping back into the bathroom and putting the towel back on the rack.

"Are you okay attending then?" he called from the bedroom.

Emma was nodding before she realized he couldn't see her. "Yeah, sure. I'll come over here mid-afternoon so we can get ready and leave together."

"Fantastic. I am so pleased you agreed. I of course didn't want to force you, but it's a relief that you're coming. I am going to pop out to the den and call my father and let him know that the two of us will be there. I'll be right back."

Emma heard rustling in the bedroom and knew it was Richard sliding off his king-sized bed and heading out of the room. Taking her time, she pulled on her pajamas before sliding into his comfortable giant bed. She restarted her audiobook as she didn't see a reason not to listen to it until Richard got back. Much like the first time she turned it on, she slowly lolled herself into a doze.

Chapter 20: Good Things Come to Those Who Wait

Richard
Four years ago

"Why are you calling me this late, Richard?" His father's gruff voice answered the phone.

Richard forced himself to swallow the first and second remarks that came to mind. It wouldn't do to challenge his father even though he itched to do so. He would have to wait until the time was right, when his chances at besting the older man were highest. So instead he breathed and forced his voice to be calm.

"I'm calling to let you know Emma will accompany me to the dinner on Saturday."

There was a pause on the other end before his father responded, "I thought you were going to break up with her. You said she wasn't really Luna material. Although, I am grateful that you've decided to wait until after our dinner with Eastern Oregon. Having her there will definitely win us in ally. But I don't know why this couldn't have waited until the morning."

It was true, he'd been toying with breaking up with Emma for the last two weeks. It was fun and enjoyable as a relatively short-term fling. But they were approaching a year together, and that was longer than Richard had ever been with anyone. He was at an age now where he needed to think about who he would pick for his packs future Luna and it wouldn't do to have someone as submissive and people pleasing as Emma. Richard needed a Luna who could stand up and challenge others. It was why all the women he slept with on the side were Beta wolves in their own right or in their parentage. They gave him that feisty challenge that he so craved. It had gotten to a point where he'd rather be in their company than Emma's. That was what made up his mind that they needed to break up. Then his father mentioned having dinner with the Eastern Washington Alpha and he knew he needed to stick it out a few more weeks so they would look good in front of the other man.

That was until just a few minutes ago. Emma had done the most remarkable thing. She'd always been a relatively intuitive person, and Richard always just chalk that up to being a submissive wolf. They were more at the whim of dominant wolves than anyone he was used to dealing with, so he figured that was part of who she was. He'd never been one to spend a lot of time with submissive wolves so he had no real comparison to compare her to. But a few minutes ago she had actually read his mind.

It wasn't like when they were in wolf form in her wolf and his wolf could communicate. This was different. He had been thinking about how having her at that dinner was to his advantage and she'd responded to that out loud, as if hearing his inner monologue was nothing. He wasn't even sure she knew she'd done it. Which made it even more interesting. It made him do a quick run through of their time together and there were bits and pieces of things she would pick up on that he didn't say out loud. Nothing as obvious as this time but enough for him to form a theory.

"I think she might be of more use if I keep her around," he said, not entirely sure he wanted to share his theory with his father. It had not been his first instinct but then he thought about it and if she started displaying abilities in front of his father and the older man found out Richard already knew about it, the older man would be livid.

"Oh? And how exactly is a submissive wolf of use to you? Other than as a pawn to use in our dinner with Eastern Oregon?" His father's voice held disdain and disbelief. Not that Richard blamed him, as on the surface he thought it sounded ridiculous.

"I believe she is in fact an Omega wolf. It's only a recent theory. But if that's what she truly is, then having one by my side, especially as she comes into power, will make our pack virtually unchallengeable to others."

There was silence on the other end of the phone. Richard could practically hear the wheels in his father's head whirling.

"How sure are you of this?" A predatory tone was in his father's voice.

"I'm fairly certain but I don't have concrete proof yet. I think she must be some kind of late bloomer since she's already twenty-three and her powers haven't displayed obviously enough to hit anyone's radar yet. The key here is to see if I can get something to tamp down her power. Put it on pause until the two of us are so entwined that it wouldn't occur to her to strike out on her own."

There was silence again, though not as long this time. "And how do you presume to do that?" The tone in his father's voice stated he clearly didn't believe Richard could pull that off.

He knew there were some black-market items to help slow the young wolves change if they were changing too early or too swiftly to control their wolf half. There were also a few wolves that dabbled in magic, and one or two questionable Omega wolves who might help him, for the right price. He couldn't do it through official channels but he was fairly certain he had a few of the right friends in the wrong places that could get this done for him.

"Let me worry about that. I think this means Emma and I are definitely destined for the long haul." Richard chuckled at his own words. Having an Omega wolf by his side, one that was tied to him, would all but guarantee that he was the strongest Alpha in the western United States. It would make his father's dream of expanding a reality, for Richard, probably not his father. All he had to do was convince Emma to stick around and ignore her fledgling powers. That would be easy enough, since she didn't seem to register they were happening. All he would have to do is keep his cool whenever the powers popped up and she probably, as oblivious as she was, wouldn't even notice the magic she was displaying. It would also mean he would have to tone down his extracurricular activities some. He couldn't have her knowing about the other women he was sleeping with. That wouldn't do the best job of tying her to him. He would at least have to attempt to hide them.

"If you think you can pull that off, our pack would definitely have the strongest power base in the state if not the region. You need to get this taken care of and quickly."

Richard rolled his eyes. He could already hear his father taking credit and possession of Richard's findings. That was fine. Emma would be tied to him and not his father. When it came down to it, she'd side with Richard over their Alpha and if he bided his time well enough, she would guarantee success when he decided to overthrow his father and take the Alpha position for himself.

He knew the smile that grew on his face was predatory and unpleasant, more of a showing of teeth than of emotion. "I'll see you tomorrow. I'll set the ball in motion tomorrow morning." With that he hung up the phone, tapping it against his hand as he thought.

It was quick mental work going through the list and web of people he would need to speak to in order to get an item that would dampen Emma's powers, at least until he was sure of her loyalty. If he really was right, and she was an Omega, he had just stumbled upon the jackpot. It was a gift from the universe and Richard planned on taking full advantage of it. With one last laugh he walked out of his den, turning the light off as he went and headed to bed, curling up behind a sleeping Emma with images of his future dancing through his head.

Chapter 21:
What Dreams May Come

Emma

He's right, you know, her wolf stated almost as if she was chastising Emma for not believing Morris.

This was only the second time she and her wolf met while she was asleep. Unlike when she was awake, they weren't meeting in a dark dimensionless cave. Instead, it was a grass filled, hilly beach alongside of a lake. It looked vaguely familiar to Emma but she couldn't quite put her finger on whether this was just some place she had created or if it was a place she had been. Emma stood at the base of one of the smaller hills while her wolf stood at the top, making its already giant form appear to tower over Emma. Though Emma was still not intimidated by her wolf, their size difference was not lost on her. That wherever they were appeared to be on the dark side of dusk made the wolf's looming figure appear more than it would have in daylight.

Emma forced herself to concentrate on the wolf's words. *It's just all too much. Not only the fact that I may be an Omega wolf, but that Richard knew and hid it from me. I don't think I'm all that powerful and I don't think Richard is terrible enough to do such a thing. I think he loved me, in his own way, at least at some point.* She felt her eyes sting as tears formed. *I can't believe that I wasted almost five years of my life on someone who was just using me. That such a long time to do something like that. I don't want to believe Richard is capable of that.* The last part she said quietly as if that would stop it from being true. But even as she said it, Emma knew she was wrong. It made her sick to her stomach but maybe she wasn't as important to Richard as she thought she was.

The tears fell freely now and Emma didn't bother swiping at her face. She could feel herself believing everything. That she had power that other wolves didn't have. That it was an Omega wolf's power. And that Richard the man she loved, had been betraying her all this time. She already knew he had been doing it physically. So really, not that big of a step to assume there'd been more to it.

Emma pushed all the turmoil aside, as hard as she figuratively could. She couldn't process that betrayal now. It wouldn't help her to dwell on it, not when there were all these other issues at hand. Maybe if she could push it aside, she could concentrate on everything else first and heal later.

What good could my power possibly do others? she asked her wolf demandingly. She knew her voice was harsh, but she also knew her wolf wouldn't take offense so she didn't tame it in.

Her wolf's tail flicked slightly. *I don't know. I don't think we will know until we know exactly what your power can do. Right now you can hear inside people's heads. You and I can both think of several extensions of power that could build from there. Who knows if your ability will be to heal minds or to help control emotions. Maybe you'll be able to help those who can't control their wolves. We won't know for a while. All we can do is develop the gifts as they come. Concentrate on stretching your abilities. While you get a headache pushing the boundaries now eventually those will go away. And now that Raelene knows what you can do, maybe she'll let you practice on her.*

Emma didn't like the idea that maybe she could control people's thoughts, or sway them one direction or another. It wasn't something she wanted to do. And it certainly wasn't something she thought Richard or Alpha Peters should get a hold of. Who knew in what nefarious ways they would want her to use her skills. Already she could imagine them asking her to listen in on other people's thoughts, to listen for them to get some kind of advantage. Thinking about that made her queasy. Maybe, just maybe if she got strong enough, she could fight off whatever it was they wanted her to do. But it would mean practicing, almost constant practicing.

She turned her attention back to her wolf. She hadn't even realized she'd been staring past it at the rolling hills beyond. *I'll tell you what. We'll practice this weekend with Morris here. And if things are easier after all that practice, even a smidge, then I'll throw myself into training, to get better at this. But if it continues to be hard and painful, I'm just going to let it do what it does naturally. We have a deal?*

She watched as the wolf's tail flicked again. It was more irritated this time. She could tell her wolf didn't like the idea of not training her gift. But it wasn't as if the wolf could make her use it either.

Deal.

A few moments after her wolf agreed the world around them grew watery, much like a watercolor painting, and then before she knew it, Emma was in just another run-of-the-mill dream.

Chapter 22:
Pump up the Volume

Emma

Come Monday evening Emma regretted making her deal with her wolf. But what she regretted more was telling Raelene and Morris about it. The two of them had gone gung-ho about helping her practice all weekend. There'd been everything from pop quizzes about their thoughts to taking her to crowded restaurants, parks, and coffee shops to quiz her on what people were thinking. The downside to this entire process was twofold. The first was that Emma is a terrible liar. When she tried to fake listen in on people's thoughts to prevent from actually doing it, because it was a violation of privacy, either Raelene or Morris always knew she was lying. So after the first two false thoughts she'd given up and gotten more serious about it.

All of Saturday she had a low-grade headache that would intensify when she actively tried to use her abilities. She ended up taking several painkillers just to concentrate by late afternoon. And as it turned out, physical painkillers only help to dull the magically caused pain, instead of eliminating it as if it was a physical headache. That was a lesson Emma wasn't too thrilled to learn. By Sunday, when the three of them went to brunch at a small local breakfast place the pain was tolerable. It was something she could ignore, and it only spiked to an annoyance level when she tried to use her gift. It was still unpleasant, but it wasn't a blinding migraine like it had been the day before. That her power was moving along that swiftly scared Emma. Everything she knew about Omegas said their powers moved in stops and starts. They gain one ability and then nothing new for weeks or months before taking a leap in power. That she was moving so swiftly in a stream was scary.

Her wolf insisted it was because her power had always been there, just tamped down, hindered. Her wolf's theory was that it continued to grow even though she hadn't been using it and now she just had to build the habit of accessing it. Emma wasn't sure how she felt about that theory so she didn't really argue.

When Morris left on Sunday night, he made Raelene promise to go out for coffee or breakfast with Emma this morning to test things out after working her gifts all weekend.

Emma had been looking forward to a bit of a break but Raelene lived up to her promise and the two of them had gone to the coffee shop three blocks from their house. The place had been packed. They'd gotten the last seats, up on stools facing the windows. Emma found her headache was more of an unpleasant feeling and when she used her abilities, it wasn't as much pain as discomfort. She was so surprised that she made the mistake of telling Raelene as much, and of course her friend then pushed her harder.

After Raelene left for work, Emma went grocery shopping before settling in to grade the assignments that had been due over the weekend. And she found it was almost as if she couldn't turn her power off. She was hearing snippets from other people's heads almost constantly in varying degrees of noise. It was loudest when she was close to people, such as behind them in line, or when they were extremely emotional.

The loudest had been another werewolf in the store parking lot. She'd been so caught off guard when she heard someone's inner wolf complaining that Emma actually stopped walking with her cart. The wolf was far enough away that she couldn't smell him to identify for sure, but from the voices she was hearing she would've bet money on it. Emma didn't make herself known. She didn't know who the wolf was or how they played into the territorial politics of the Seattle area, so once she got a hold of herself she kept walking to her car, trying not to draw attention to herself.

Chapter 23:
TMI Exhaustion

Emma

By the time she got to work she was exhausted. The normal excitement that went with teaching was muted with how tired she was. She also was hungrier than she would usually be on a day where she had exercised. It was as if using the magic somehow used calories. It made little sense so Emma wasn't entirely sure how she was supposed to fix the problem. So instead she snacked throughout the day on various vegetables she bought and made a mental note that she was going to have to get something more substantial if she was going to continue to burn through this much energy.

As she walked in to the building, Emma forced herself to take a deep breath. She knew if any of the four werewolves were in her vicinity they were going to come in loud and clear and there wasn't anything she could do about it. She only hoped that they'd be quiet enough so as not to distract her from class. She was incredibly grateful that most of the lecture today would be people presenting their initial research on their term long projects. She would only lecture for the first forty minutes, then there'd be a break, and after the class presenting their work thus far. So all she had to do was make it through the next hour with full concentration and she would be okay.

I smell the she-wolf. It was a nasally wolf's voice that sounded like a Hollywood version of a snake.

"Crap," Emma mumbled under her breath. She was walking past Wilson's room. She very much doubted Keegan or the two other students would be milling about this far down the hall. That left only one person.

Sure enough, Wilson's head popped out of the room and he grinned at her wide, showing more teeth than was strictly necessary.

"Emma, how are you doing today? How was your weekend?" he asked before pushing off the door and entering the hall.

Give him minimal answers. Nothing that could identify you as an Omega wolf or someone from Central Washington, her wolf hissed.

I'm not stupid, Emma clapped back.

"Good, an old friend of mine came in from out of town so I was showing them around the area and reminiscing about old times."

She watched Wilson's eyebrow quirk up.

Out of town. It's not terribly helpful, but it confirms my suspicion that she hasn't always lived in the territory, Wilson's inner voice mused.

"How about you, Wilson?" Emma turned her body as she spoke, still facing him but making it clear she was about to move farther down the hall.

"Nothing much. Just catching up on work. Met with a few other lone wolves for lunch yesterday. Overall pretty slow. I mentioned to them that I met a female lone wolf since the last time we got together.

Since, as I told you, we're not together very often. There was a lot of curiosity about you. Mainly because a female lone wolf is very rare in this neck of the woods. You should come with us to brunch one time. Even if you don't intend on joining us, it will give you the company of other wolves."

Good, this'll tell us whether she just doesn't enjoy being around wolves or whether her hesitancy to join us is more pointed, Wilson's wolf commented eagerly.

Did I mention I don't like him? her wolf muttered.

Emma forced her smile, small as it was, to remain on her face. "That's a very kind offer but the company of werewolves is not something that's important to me. No offense to you or the other wolves you have made an agreement with, but I have no interest in being around groups of wolves of any kind. Now if you'll excuse me, I need to get to class." She gave one quick flash of a bigger smile before she pivoted and began striding the rest of the way down the hall.

There's something else going on there. No wolf, unless traumatized or crazy, truly doesn't like to be around the company of other wolves. They will do it by necessity but not necessarily by choice, Wilson's wolf mused before Emma walked far enough away to be out of hearing range.

There's nothing I can do about it right now. I just need to teach class and get out of here. Maybe if we end a little early, I won't have to run in to him again today, Emma thought more to herself than her wolf.

Her wolf seemed to understand that because it didn't respond.

When she walked into the classroom, she was relieved to see none of the other wolves were there. It would give her a few minutes of peace, unless one of the students came up and spoke to her. The desks were far enough away from the front of the classroom that unless someone was overly emotional or loud, she would have some blessed silence.

Taking a deep breath in that silence, Emma began getting her laptop out, connecting it to the room's system, and putting up the course outline for the day. She almost finished the outline when she smelled the three wolves enter the room.

She is so unbelievably beautiful. I wish there was a way to get around the pack politics and take her out like a normal person. I don't understand why she is so hell-bent on being a lone wolf. It was Keegan's inner monologue.

It surprised her so much that she spun around, chalk still in hand to watch the three wolves walk to the back of the classroom where they normally sat. Keegan was turning his gaze away from her as she turned.

He thinks I'm beautiful? That's so... I don't know how I feel about that, Emma said to her wolf as she felt herself blush.

Try focusing on the others. See what the other two are thinking. Maybe they can give you a better idea on what's happening with the pack then Lover Boy can, her wolf responded.

Oh please don't start calling him that, Emma pleaded with her wolf.

Nope, it's done now. Set in stone, her wolf countered.

Great, Emma muttered as she focused her attention on the young man who claimed to be Keegan's nephew. She focused on his voice, his inner voice, and she really had to work to reach him as his inner voice was awfully quiet. She turned to face the board, so she wasn't caught staring at the three of them. The last thing she needed was to draw attention to what she was doing. She made herself copy what was in her notes, but her mind wasn't in it, her concentration on that young wolf.

He should just let her be. If she doesn't want to be part of the pack, she should be allowed. She's clearly not a fan of Wilson's either. I get it. She wants to be left alone. The young man's soft voice was so quiet Emma had to strain, causing a slight headache to form but she pushed through it. She didn't know why he was so much quieter. Maybe he wasn't as dominant of a wolf as his uncle was.

I have a sneaking suspicion his attention isn't simply because she's a lone wolf. The young man's wolf chuckled at his own words.

Okay, well that was completely unhelpful, Emma thought as she broke her concentration from the young man's mind and turned back to her computer screen.

She did not need to hear how obvious Keegan's affection for her was or wasn't. He didn't even know her. Surely his being in her class had nothing to do with him finding her pretty and everything to do with the fact that she wanted to be a lone wolf. Maybe he even wanted to monitor Wilson.

You're protesting too much, her wolf countered.

Shut up, Emma responded a little sharply.

She found Keegan extremely attractive, but she certainly wasn't in a place where she could do anything about it. Even if he was perfectly human, she wasn't sure she would've done anything. That he was basically an Alpha wolf made it completely out of the question. She couldn't get involved with him and not get involved in pack politics.

As the rest of the students filtered in, she got more snippets of different peoples thoughts. By the time class started it was all Emma could do to force out the words for her lecture that day.

Chapter 24:
Hungry for the Wolf

Emma

When she finally finished her lecture, Emma forced herself to wait several beats in the classroom to answer the questions students had. As they came close, she could hear snippets of their minds. As soon as the last one wandered away Emma made a break for it. She headed out of the exit closest to her room to not pass Wilson's room again. She was sure her lecture was more on edge than usual, probably not as interesting or entertaining, but she couldn't help it. She heard stray thoughts of what people thought of her lecture as well as stray thoughts from the wolves for the entire hour. She needed a break, she needed fresh air.

Once she'd taken several ragged breaths, she pulled out her phone and called Morris. Luckily, he picked up after two rings.

"Hey Emma. Shouldn't you be in class? His tone was cheery but questioning.

"I'm on a break. But I'm having a problem I need you to talk to your grandmother about."

"Oh?" The playful tone was gone, replaced by something more serious and concerned.

"I can't shut it off now. You know those werewolves I have in my class. I'm hearing their thoughts. Not a lot since they're across the room from me but I'm also getting stray thoughts throughout the lecture from my students, my human students. I need some way to put up a wall or some way to block it."

There was a long pause before Morris' voice came hesitantly over the line. "Are you wearing the bracelet?"

Emma clinched her jaw together. "No." She knew she sounded like a teenager who'd been caught coming in after curfew.

"I'll tell you what," Morris gave a heavy sigh, "try wearing the bracelet tomorrow and see if that makes a difference. Let me know if it does, but if it doesn't I'll call my grandmother. I'm due to have a phone conference with her tomorrow evening anyway. But try the bracelet first, this is one of the reasons she gave it to you." He was a little chastising at the end and it set Emma on edge. She felt weird wearing it but he was right, he told her it would help.

"Okay, deal," she responded resigned.

There was a chuckle through the phone. "It's just a bracelet, Emma. It's not the end of the world. Good luck getting through the rest of your class. I'll talk to you tomorrow." He hung up and Emma slid the phone back in her pocket. But not before checking the time. Two more minutes before she had to walk back into the room and queue up the students' presentations. Then she could sit at her desk and breathe. Attention wouldn't be on her so when she caught stray thoughts, which she was sure she would do when people came to the front of the room to present, she wouldn't have to worry as much about keeping her train of thought going.

"Are you okay?" Keegan's voice rumbled from behind her.

Emma jumped. She hadn't heard, sensed, or smelled him coming.

She spun to look at him in surprise.

He had a small, lopsided smile on his face from where he stood about ten feet away. "Sorry about that. I figured you would've heard the door shutting."

"No, you're fine," Emma responded a little too fast.

When he took a step toward her, Emma unconsciously took a step back. He seemed to notice and hesitated before pushing his foot back again and remaining where he was. His face was confused, but he said nothing.

She truly appreciated that he was keeping his distance. He was far enough away that unless she tried, or he was loud about it, she couldn't hear him or his wolf. If he had been Morris, she could've still communicated with him, but Morris was different. Maybe it was because they're friends, she didn't know.

"You just seemed a little more distracted than normal so I figured I would check in," Keegan said, looking a little sheepish.

She felt bad about snapping at him and she softened her features some before responding. "No, I'm fine. I had a good friend over this weekend and some of our conversations just rubbed me the wrong way."

I want to run with her wolf. I want to know what she's like to run with. Keegan's wolf sounded eager and loud with his demand. It caught her off guard. They were far enough away that the wolf must have said it fairly loudly for her to register it.

Yeah, well I would love to run my hands through her hair. But we can't always get what we want, Keegan snapped in response.

Emma absently lifted her hands and pulled the back half of her hair, which wasn't tied back, over her shoulder so it wasn't as in view.

"I hope it wasn't all bad news," Keegan said, his voice soothing.

Emma blinked at him a second as she tried to remember what their actual conversation had been.

"No, no it wasn't. Just a lot to chew on." She tacked the last part on as an afterthought. She thought the last comment had been something about conversations.

But she couldn't quite remember in her surprise at hearing both him and his wolf. At hearing the yearning in both of their voices. She barely knew the man in front of her, yet his interest was so strong. To be fair, she never heard inside the head of her suitors so who knew what the inside of the heads of people she actually dated sounded like.

That's a terrifying thought.

Her wolf chuffed in response.

Keegan hesitated another moment before he took one step back and pivoted. "All right, well I'll see you in class in a few minutes." He hesitated, but only for a second.

Without even thinking about it, she reached out with her power to see what he could hesitate for.

Oh, just ask her out. His wolf sounded exasperated.

No, she wants to be a lone wolf. That means she doesn't want to be involved in the pack at all. I am a pack wolf through and through and though she might not know how high up the food chain I am, once she found out she'd want nothing to do with me. It's best to just leave it alone and be around in case she changes her mind, or in case she continues leaning toward joining Wilson.

You're being a coward. And he's a useless mutt Ethan should've dealt with when Wilson challenged him.

That's not our place. I told you his word was final and we leave it at that.

She didn't hear the next words, just the wolf grumbling as she pulled back into her own head and watched him walk back into the building.

It's sweet of him trying not to be overpowering. Though I don't like the fact that he thinks I'm leaning toward Wilson.

Just keep straddling the line the best you can. Who knows what he'll do if he's convinced you've actually picked a side. He is clearly actively watching for it. The best you can do is not make it obvious you've gone one way or the other.

"I've got to get back to class," Emma whispered out loud before taking one last deep breath and heading back into the building.

Chapter 25: Where Did She Come From?

Keegan

"So Keegan, tell me about this she wolf my niece has been raving about?"

Darian's voice coming from over his shoulder made Keegan jump. Keegan had been pouring over the accounting paperwork for all the packs finances. One of the three individuals in charge of the pack funds had brought it to his attention that the numbers weren't adding up as they should the last three months. He had been spending the better part of a week wrapping his head around how to understand the numbers and reconciling the books being kept by the three individuals. He chastised himself for concentrating so hard that he didn't even notice his superior walking into Keegan's office. The space wasn't exactly large and with how little attention Keegan was apparently paying, the older man could have jumped him and attacked if he'd wanted before Keegan could've even lifted an arm.

While the Seattle packs hierarchy was not as violent as other packs in the area, such as the one in Central Washington, it still was unwise of someone in Keegan's position to have his back to a doorway, an open one at that. Let alone to not be paying at least some attention to said doorway. But he found it hard to concentrate on just about anything since Emma entered the picture.

He'd half dismissed his nephew's comment about not recognizing the she-wolf teaching his class. If he hadn't been in the area already the first night he met Emma, he wouldn't have driven over to the parking lot and waited for her. Once he was there and smelled a unique blend to her scent, he knew he had to wait it out and see her for himself.

There was something to that base smell of hers that was different and he couldn't quite put his finger on what it was. Then he laid eyes on the gorgeous woman and his wolf growled. His wolf wanted her instantly, and the man agreed but had enough sense to maintain a sensible distance and talk to her first.

  She had been all fire and vinegar and all but out right challenged him, letting him know that this was someone who was not used to any kind of pack hierarchy or simply didn't care about it. That made her dangerous. Wolves didn't stay in territorial areas without joining a pack unless they were hiding. And since she showed a good amount of dominance to him, a very dominant werewolf, he bet she was someone with the disdain for pack hierarchy. This kind of lone wolf rarely stayed in pack territories. That she was there was a bit of a conundrum. She was so dominant, stubborn, and absolutely beautiful. It was a combination he found heady and confusing. Keegan found it hard to keep his attention on just about anything else, which was to his detriment at just this second.

Cringing, he turned to face Darian is the older man shut Keegan's office door. Since Keegan was on the opposite side of the desk, instead of in the large chair he usually sat at, Darian leaned against the closed door instead of moving closer. He must've sensed that Keegan was a little off and decided it was wiser to keep at least some distance.

You need to answer his question, Keegan's wolf growled insistently.

"Sorry Darian, would you ask that again please?" He didn't like admitting that he hadn't caught the question. It was stupid that his wolf paid more attention than he had. If it had been anyone other than Darian or Ethan it could've been a dire mistake.

He was lucky that his superior, and their Alpha for that matter, were pretty laid back in general, unless it was an outright challenge to their authority. And since Keegan had made it clear that he had no interest on moving any farther up the food chain than he already was, the two of them settled in to a camaraderie that turned into a friendship.

Darian frowned before giving him a small lopsided smile that almost turned his upper lip into a snarl, thanks to a scar the older man had from his nose through his upper lip from a dominance fight he'd been in a decade earlier. "My niece, Soraya, your nephew's girlfriend. She tells me she and your nephew are taking a night course from a she-wolf who is not a member of the pack. Soraya tells me the woman is quite attractive and intelligent. She's rather observant about this kind of thing, quite the dominant wolf. My niece loves this woman. She says that she is one of her favorite teachers thus far. So it makes me curious since she tells me you're taking the course as well. Want to fill me in on this situation?" Darian's expression was outright amused now. He knew Keegan well enough to know that if Soraya said the woman was attractive, that was at least a partial factor in Keegan's attendance.

"There isn't much to tell. She seems very smart. And while my instinct is to say she is rather dominant, I don't know if that's simply because she makes eye contact when she speaks to me. She speaks with a certain level of authority in her tone. Or, if that is just a side effect of the fact that she doesn't particularly like other werewolves.

Remember Wilson, that lone Wolf who challenged Ethan a few months back? It turns out he's teaching in a classroom in the same building as her at the same time. I'm sure it's purely coincidence, but he has had an eye on her as well. She doesn't particularly seem to like him but she holds conversations with him more than she does me. Which makes me think either he's pushy, or she's more apt to join him than the pack. She's made it quite clear that she has no interest in any sort of organized werewolf group. Which I think is why Wilson is so interested. A dominant female wolf alone within another pack's territory is rare and I think he is just as curious about her as I am."

Darian's eyes narrowed slightly. "And she's attractive?"

Unsure whether that was a statement or question, Keegan nodded. "Very."

"Interesting," Darian muttered as he pushed off the door. "You are right, a lone female wolf wandering into a fairly stable territory is rare, rarer if she's a dominant wolf. When Soraya was telling me about her, I searched what I could remember about dominant lone wolves in this country and in

Canada, since the truly powerful ones everybody seems to know by name as an occupational hazard and she didn't ring a bell with any of those.

"I want you to look into her. See where she comes from. I don't want to bother Ethan with this yet, but if she really is a lone wolf trying to avoid wolf society in general, it makes me wonder if she's running from something. And if so, is it something that we should be concerned about? Also, do what you can to make sure she doesn't side with Wilson. He is enough of a nuisance on his own with his little network. I don't want this unknown dominant wolf joining him as well. Let me know about anything interesting you find." Darian waited a beat for Keegan to give one swift nod before he yanked the office door open and strode out, leaving the door ajar behind him.

Keegan let out a loud breath as he leaned back against his desk. He had been debating looking into the she-wolf himself but for whatever reason he hadn't so far. It was silly, because if she had been any other lone wolf he would've done so, but he hadn't with Emma.

Don't be stupid. You know why you haven't looked her up, his wolf chastised before snorting. *You're interested in her and therefore want to let her maintain her privacy, whether it's in the best interest of the pack or not.*

Keegan cringed. His wolf was right. His interest in Emma had overshadowed his need to protect the pack from a possible threat. No part of him thought Emma was a threat, but that didn't mean that she wouldn't be, or that a threat wouldn't come looking for her.

Darian was right. He needed to find out exactly where she had come from and why she was in Washington. He had gone as far as looking at her profile on the school website and it stated she was an adjunct professor, so it was clear she wasn't a full-time employee. For all he knew, she was a dominant wolf that went from territory to territory, never settling in anyone place. It would explain why nobody knew about her, if she moved often enough, as in every quarter or two, there'd be no reason for any of the packs they associate with to come in contact with her.

Feeling immensely guilty about invading her privacy, Keegan shoved off his desk and moved around it until he was in front of his laptop again. Then he typed in Emma's name and searched through her history in earnest.

Chapter 26:
It's Gotta Be Her

Wilson

"I told you to let me handle it," Wilson hissed at the taller bulkier man with a shaved head who lumbered up to his car as Wilson got out.

Mario snarled at him, and to an outside observer it would look as if the bulkier man was prepping for a fight. But Wilson knew better. Mario, much to his own chagrin, was not as dominant of a wolf as Wilson was. He may challenge Wilson's authority, push back when he thought he could get away with it. But when push came to shove, Mario almost always step down for Wilson. It was why Wilson had been the one to challenge Ethan, the Alpha of the Seattle area pack and not Mario.

"She's been here two months, Wilson, and you have yet to bring her to any of our gatherings. The others are getting nervous that maybe you don't have as much authority and dominance over her as we need you to have in order to bring her to our side. If you can't dominate one lone she-wolf, how on earth are you going to handle the pack once we take it over?" The other man was full on snarling.

Idiot, Wilson's wolf growled.

"Keep your voice down, Mario. There are pack wolves in her class and the last thing we need is for them to overhear you talking about our plans." As he finished speaking, Wilson looked around to make sure Keegan and the young wolves weren't around to hear Mario's outburst. He breathed a sigh of relief when the coast appeared to be clear but he didn't remove the frown from his face. He would not let Mario off the hook that easily.

When he looked back at the larger man, Mario was visibly scenting the air to see if he could smell the other wolves.

"With a dominant pack wolf in her class, I have to show some restraint with the she-wolf. She's clearly cagey for some reason. Though I'm not sure why she has such a distaste for other werewolves. I know that if I try to make a move too quickly, it's only going to convince her that Keegan and the pack are the right direction for her. As it stands, she talks more to me than she does him, which helps us. She is an incredibly dominant wolf and there's something about her that smells off. I haven't figured out what it is yet. But that doesn't mean that I won't. And the last thing I need is for it to appear as if I'm trying to ambush her by having members of our alliance waiting in the parking lot for her. Nothing says you're a threat more than that."

As he finished speaking, he heard the rumble of a car entering the far side of the parking lot. He turned his head just enough to see it and cursed.

She *might not have seen you two. You can hide him behind the car, or in your backseat. She might not smell him if she doesn't get too close,* Wilson's wolf chimed in as both the wolf and Wilson's attention zeroed in on Emma's car entering the parking lot.

"Get in my backseat. She can't know you're here," Wilson growled as he clicked his car unlocked.

Mario stared between him and the car entering the parking lot and his eyes widened when Emma was close enough for Mario to see the driver. "Is that her? She's much more attractive than you let on."

"Get in the back seat," Wilson hissed, pulling open the door and shoving Mario toward the open door.

The bigger man ducked down and crawled in. It wasn't the sneakiest of things since Mario was six-foot-four and built like a football player. If Emma looked too close at Wilson's car it would be obvious someone large was hiding in the backseat. Their only hope at her missing the large man was if she tried to avoid Wilson as much as she had earlier in the week.

Emma exited her car, yanking out a backpack as her long white braids slid over her shoulders. Mario was right, the younger woman was very attractive. And not simply because she was so dominant. For some wolves, a dominant female was irresistible. It wasn't Wilson's cup of tea though. Wilson preferred the company of less dominant women, or human females. He didn't particularly want a challenge for his love life, plus he preferred his women more petite than Emma. While he toyed originally with the idea of flirting with her in getting close to her that way, both he and his wolf quickly dismissed the idea. The idea of faking affection left a bad taste in his mouth and while both he and his wolf wanted to be the new Alpha of the Seattle pack, that level of dishonesty disgusted him.

Emma turned, smiling at him as she shut her car door and threw the backpack over her shoulder. "Evening, Wilson."

He was letting out a relieved breath when she turned her back to him. He watched as she stopped.

Dammit, his wolf cursed.

She pivoted, raising her eyebrows at Wilson, staring directly into his car curiously. "Wilson, why is there a large man hiding in your car? Let me rephrase, why is there a large werewolf hiding in your car?"

Wilson knew his lips twitched as he fought off the snarl. Then he banged on the back window and motioned for Mario to get out of the car without looking away from Emma. He forced himself to plaster on a polite smile as he stepped away from the door so that Mario could slowly swing it open.

"This is my associate. He is one of the lone wolves I have been trying to introduce you to. He and I grabbed dinner before class and we carpooled. But since my front seat doesn't quite have enough legroom for Mario's thicker frame he sat in back." He spoke slowly and loud enough that Mario could hear the entire scenario so he could back the story.

He watched, inwardly cursing as Emma frowned deeply at the large man as he got out of the car. And if he wasn't mistaken her eyes flashed wide at Mario's size as the larger man stood fully.

Wilson glanced over to see Mario trying his best to look sheepish. He looked disingenuous at best and Wilson fought not to roll his eyes. The larger man knew the size and power that came with his stature, yet never perfected how to make himself look less looming.

Mario stepped forward, his hand outstretched, but he quickly stopped as Emma matched his movements, only in the opposite direction. Mario let his hand dangle in the air for a second but when it became clear Emma had no intention of touching him, he slowly dropped it, his smile tightening.

"It's nice to finally meet you, Emma. Wilson has told me about you. It's nice to have a face to go with all the lovely things he said."

Dammit, his wolf cursed louder this time as they watched Emma's eyes widen and her attention circle back to Wilson. They weren't widening in surprise or fear but it was almost as if they widened to accommodate the eye roll she did in order to move her attention from one wolf to the other.

"Has he now? I was under the impression he only just mentioned me. And he and I have not had nearly enough conversations for either of us to have any information about the other that would be lovely." Her voice dripped with disdain as she made eye contact with Wilson.

Something that wrangled his wolf a little but Wilson didn't show it. He didn't know how dominant or strong she was, or her wolf. It would do neither of them any good to challenge her in a parking lot, especially in front of Mario.

Her eyes rolled back to Mario. "Did he also tell you I have no intention of joining your little group?"

This will not end well. End the interaction now, Wilson's wolf growled at him moving its anger and frustration away from Mario and toward Wilson.

Forcing his smile, fake as it was, to widen, Wilson took a step forward so that he was clearly between Emma and Mario. "Of course. I told them of your disdain for organized wolf groups. We all share that dislike. And while none of us wish to join any kind of organized groups such as the pack, many of us have lived here long enough to know having allies can be helpful at certain points. But I have let those in our group know I have left the door open to you should you change your mind and want other wolves to back you up. I know you feel strongly about it now, but you may change your mind once the pack realizes you and interferes in your life in a way that most of us would appreciate they didn't." It was the most diplomatic way Wilson could think to diffuse the situation. He didn't want Mario latching on to Emma's denial and causing problems for him within their little organization.

When he lost his bid fight to Ethan a few months ago, it almost tore their little network of twenty lone wolves apart. Wilson, and his two closest compatriots only kept the group together by the skin of their teeth. They had convinced the others that more subversive ways would be the only way of getting what all of them wanted. That had been enough for now but if Mario gave the group an excuse to think Wilson was weak, it could create a fissure in the group. Just like having Emma join them, a dominant, female wolf, would show Wilson was a dominant enough Alpha wolf that continuing to back him would be in everyone's best interest.

Emma looked around and he could see there was a running monologue in her head, either by herself or with her wolf until her eyes settled back on Wilson. "I appreciate your persistence. But I think I've been clear in my disinterest." There was clearly more she wanted to say, but he watched as she bit her lower lip as if fighting the words from exiting her mouth. After a long moment, she gave him her own forced smile. "Have a good class." She gave one more dismissive look at Mario before pivoting and heading into the building.

Thankfully, Mario waited until the door to the building shut behind Emma before whirling on Wilson. "She clearly has no interest in joining us. You made it sound as if she was indifferent when she's clearly not." The man was fighting the growl in his voice.

Think fast. Mario might not be the quickest of the wolves in the alliance, but he will barrel through things until he gets what he wants. And there is a sizable minority in our group who appreciate that approach.

"Of course she is," Wilson said smoothly, slowly bringing his gaze back to Mario as if he was unfazed by the events that just unfolded. "She thinks you're here to ambush her. Just like I told you she would. She thinks that were trying to force her into joining and with her distaste of organized groups I can't say I blame her. But it is as I said. Just give it time, once Ethan and his meddling wolves take one step in her direction, she'll come running in ours. Because as much pushback as she gives me it will be twofold for the bureaucratic nature that is a pack."

Wilson couldn't afford to have any of them questioning him while they were trying to make a bid to overthrow the current Seattle pack. They already had two spies within the pack hierarchy, one of which had fought his way into a position that rivaled Keegan's. The other was more low-level, but still valuable within the bureaucratic hierarchy. They couldn't afford for their plan to go sideways now because Mario couldn't see the bigger picture.

He could see the larger man processing and when he opened his mouth to protest, Wilson cut him off. "Think about it. You left the pack when they started dictating how much you could lift during your bodybuilding challenges. They didn't want you to give away how strong you were. You didn't want them to be in charge of your life, so you left. She's going to run up against the same thing. We have to be patient until the pack makes their move and then be there to sweep her up when her attention is elsewhere."

Mario closed his mouth again and frowned in thought. It was long enough that Wilson fought himself not to look down at his watch.

"How much time are you thinking of giving her?" Mario asked, a wariness to his voice.

This time, Wilson didn't hide rolling his eyes. "I don't know. I don't know how long it will take the pack to make a move. The pack wolves have been in her class for two months now. My guess is by the time the quarter ends, Keegan will somehow misstep since he won't be seeing her every week and will still somehow want to keep tabs on her. So, we wait for that."

Mario didn't seem sold, but he thankfully kept his mouth shut and nodded once.

"Now, unless there is something urgent we need to discuss I need to go get ready for my class," Wilson responded dismissively.

Mario snarled at him, an aggressive and angry gesture. And if Wilson wasn't mistaken, he saw the wolf behind the bigger man's eyes. But it was fleeting before Mario growled a quick good night, pivoted on his heels, and headed back toward the direction of his truck at the back corner of the parking lot.

He's going to be a problem, Wilson's wolf commented as they watched the larger man walk away.

I'm aware. But it was a chance we took when we brought him into our fold.

She is key to our plan. Especially if she gets close to Keegan. You see the way he looks at her. He is interested. If you can get her to join our side that could work to our advantage.

Wilson thought on what his wolf was saying as he walked into the building. He found his wolf was right. The handful of times he'd seen both Keegan and Emma in the same place over the last two months the other man's attention for the she-wolf was more than just curiosity on why she was there and why she was choosing to be a lone wolf.

Interesting. I think it's time I did a little digging about our little she-wolf. I think there's more to her than meets the eye and if there's something to push her along our side of the path, that would be even better.

Be careful. You don't want anyone to know you're looking into her. If you draw too much attention to her, the pack will pay more attention to her, if they're not already and they might beat you to whatever it is you find.

Let me worry about that. You try to figure out how we can get in the she-wolf's good graces.

He heard his wolf snort and recede farther back in his mind as Wilson stepped into the classroom and went into teaching mode.

Chapter 27:
Wham, Bam, What the Hell was That?

Emma

"Back off, Barry. I'm not interested. I've never been interested. Not to mention I've been with Peter for six months," Emma heard Soraya's worried plea as she exited the building.

The younger woman's voice was enough to concern Emma. Without worry for what she was about to step into, Emma bee-lined around the building to where she'd heard the younger woman's voice. She went into teacher mode, that voice in her head that claimed responsibility for her students learning and their safety, even if Soraya was a werewolf and probably capable of taking care of herself. When Emma made it around the corner and observed the scene in front of her, she heard her wolf growl protectively in her head.

There was a young male, somewhere around the same age as her two students. None of them could be older than twenty in Emma's estimation. Peter, Keegan's nephew, was squared off against another male werewolf who had several inches on him, in both height and width. Soraya, worried expression on her face, stood just behind Peter's right shoulder, staring up at the taller male.

"You heard her, Barry. Back off," Peter growled up at the taller man.

Emma could hear the low growl emanating from the kid she didn't know. Even though the three werewolves in front of her were less than ten years her junior, she couldn't help but see them as kids.

Be careful about that, her wolf warned. *They may be younger than you but that doesn't mean none of the wolves are strong or dominant.*

That made Emma slow her step, and she brought her right hand around the bracelet Morris had given her that rested on her left wrist. She used it to amplify her power, focusing on the unknown male's inner monologue and his wolf. She had little practice with it. She found if she concentrated on pushing her energy through it and toward a target, it worked like a laser beam.

She is ours. She belongs to us. Do not let the weaker male take her from us. The younger man's wolf growled in a sort of crazed frenzy. She could feel the lack of control the boy had over his wolf or its impulses. That was bad, terrible.

It wasn't unheard of for a young werewolf to struggle in their more formative years for impulse control and emotions. It was harder for them to wrangle their own teenage hormones as well is the werewolf within and all the changes that come along with that. She'd known at least one male wolf, when she was younger, who had gone crazy for almost a full year and had to remain heavily sedated in order to keep him from hurting anyone else in the pack.

"Barry, I need you to step back," came Keegan's voice from behind her, smooth and even but his authority rang clearly throughout his words.

The younger man's attention diverted from Soraya so he could snarl menacingly at Keegan.

Take him out. Take anyone who stands in your way out. The wolf snarled within the younger man's head a split second. The words had barely entered Emma's head before the young man tackled Peter to the ground, inadvertently taking Soraya with them.

The three of them hit the ground with a hard thud, the young petite woman ending up on the bottom. Emma winced. If she hadn't been a werewolf, the girl would've had several broken bones. As it was, she would have a good number of bruises if not a sprain.

Keegan shot past Emma, diving into the action and pulling Soraya out from under the two fighting werewolves. Luckily, both boys were still in human form. As changing would've drawn some unwanted attention.

Emma slowly stepped forward, keeping her hand around her wrist as fists flew and the two young men rolled across the pavement. She had to do something, she was a teacher for goodness sake. An adult. But those born instincts to be a submissive wolf told her to hightail it out of there and run. She didn't want to get involved in whatever mess this was.

But I'm their teacher. I'm responsible for their safety, she thought to herself.

Use your power. Her wolf's voice was so quiet and so steady it made Emma pause.

What do you mean?

Her wolf stepped forward into the spotlight in her mind. *Try getting involved in the young man's thoughts. You can hear him clearly, the frenzied state he's in. See if you can stop it.*

The idea seemed ludicrous. Being able to control someone's mind was something out of a sci-fi movie and a violation of all sorts. But it wouldn't hurt anything to try. Emma might do nothing, in which case there would be no harm no foul. But if she continued to stand there and watch as Keegan tried to separate the two boys someone was going to get more hurt than they already were. She could already see blood trickling down Peter's shirt as Keegan got a hard grip around one of Peter's arms before yanking the younger man back.

It did nothing to stop Barry's anger, that was fueled by some crazed rage. All it did was change the target to Keegan. And while the boy got some punches in, it looked like Keegan might hold his own. But Emma didn't know how long it would take to bring the boy down to a point where he could be put in one of the training cells she was sure the Seattle pack had.

She could hear Soraya crying on the phone with someone, pleading with them to hurry, as she squatted above Peter who was struggling to sit up.

A crazed werewolf was dangerous. They didn't pull their punches, and they seemed stronger than their levelheaded counterparts. Somehow that angry crazed state made them almost impossible to deal with, especially if the werewolf was full grown which she didn't know if the boy in front of her was or not.

Do something, her wolf growled angrily.

Panic spiked through Emma and she slammed her eyes shut, concentrating on where she heard the young man's inner voice. It was almost as if each time she heard someone's thoughts her mind remembered the path it took to get to them and the more often she reached into one person's head the easier it was to get there. She pulled as much power into the bracelet as she could and aimed it at the young man. She could feel the pounding headache throbbing in her head but forced herself past it. She wasn't used to concentrating this hard, throwing this much power into one place. When she felt herself connect with the young man's head, her eyes flew open and she felt a weird power, a sort of echo, enter her voice. She didn't know how to speak to him mentally in the state he was in. Which meant all the power seemed to concentrate in her words as well as the stream that came from the bracelet straight to the boy's mind.

"You will cease fighting now." Her weird power filled voice made their area of the parking lot go utterly silent.

All four heads swiveled to her, eyes wide, but she ignored them and continued, all of her concentration on the young man they were calling Barry. She concentrated less on the human, instead focusing on the barely contained creature inside him.

"You, wolf, are out of line. You will stop this immediately. No woman belongs to you. You will cease fighting and relinquish yourself to whatever punishment is deemed necessary by those you consider in charge of you." She was very careful not to mention the Alpha of the pack as she didn't know if the boy in front of her belongs to the pack or was one of Wilson's lone wolves. Either option seemed equally possible to Emma.

It took an extra push but the young man went slack in Keegan's embrace. Keegan held the younger man's arms behind him to stop him from using his fists. A hold that if Barry was really concentrating, he could break, but he didn't.

"Are you able to act like a normal wolf again or do we need to repeat the process?" Emma talked directly to the boy's wolf. Using less power behind her voice, she wanted to see if the wolf would comply once she released him.

An all black wolf peered at her from behind Barry's eyes. It was disconcerting to see the wolf in her head when she knew the young man hadn't changed, but there it was, clear as day. Her wolf stood beside her as the two of them looked at the midnight wolf in front of them.

The all black wolf bowed his head and pushed its front legs forward as if bowing. *Yes, Omega. You have cleared most of the fury state from our mind. You have my word we will remain calm and accept whatever punishment our Alpha gives us.*

Though gravelly, the wolf's voice seemed calm. She decided to take the wolf at its word and Emma retrieved most of her power. Leaving just an inkling of awareness in his head in case it was a lie, or he changed his mind and went back to that fury state. It didn't feel as if she'd forced her will on him as much as she had put out the fire blazing in his mind.

Emma fought to keep her face entirely blank, as if she wasn't as amazed or frightened as the others looking at her were with what she'd done. Instead, she let go of the bracelet and hiked her backpack up on her shoulder before stepping back, climbing onto the sidewalk. On the inside she was shaking from the whole encounter. But she knew she had to hide that. Hide the fact that she was so submissive and make them all think this was an everyday occurrence for her.

"I'll stick around until whoever you called shows up. Just to make sure he stays under control." Her voice was so calm Emma herself was impressed.

Barry seems somewhat dejected and exhausted. But the other three looked at her with varying degrees of awe. Soraya was practically beaming at her with gratitude. Peter looked more shocked than anything else. While Keegan had a more calculated expression. He wasn't fooled. What she had done was not normal werewolf abilities. She had just played her hand right in the pack's face. There was no way Keegan wouldn't go back to his Alpha and tell him Emma was an Omega wolf. If there was any doubt in her mind of what she was, she couldn't afford to hold on to it now. She couldn't pretend that what she had just done was normal. Only an Omega would have the ability to control another wolf's psyche.

"Thank you. Seriously, thank you!" Soraya let out breathlessly.

Emma smiled down at her, her exterior cracking. She gave one nod before turning her gaze back to Keegan and Barry.

Keegan tugged at Barry's shoulders. "You're sitting in the back of my car until the padded wagon shows up." There was a command to his voice that held no question but the younger man nodded.

Keegan looked at his nephew and Soraya, his brows creased with worry as he seemed to take in his nephew's injuries. He then looked back at Emma, his face more blank and unreadable. "I'll be right back," he said quietly as he turned both himself and Barry toward the main part of the parking lot. He then paused and looked at the car several spaces away. "Barry, is that your car?" When the boy only nodded, Keegan held out one of his hands, freeing one of Barry's. "Give me your keys." The boy complied with a heavy sigh, pulling the keys from one of his front pockets before handing them to Keegan. Keegan then grabbed him and moved the boy toward his own car.

As Keegan unlocked the vehicle and put the boy in the backseat, Emma reached out in front of her and put her hand back on the bracelet. Her brain was pounding now. She would have a full-fledged migraine by the time she got home that would stop her from being able to sleep, at least until heavy painkillers kicked in. While she normally would've been able to reach out and hear Keegan from the distance he was, there's no way she could fight through the headache without using the bracelet. And both she and her wolf agreed that they needed to know what exactly Keegan was thinking about her newly discovered powers.

Chapter 28:
Secret's Out

Emma

An Omega wolf. She's a lone Omega wolf in our territory. There's no way she's not running from something, she heard Keegan's wolf say, clearly in the middle of whatever monologue it had been giving when she tuned in.

There's no way she'll be able to keep hidden now. She was clearly hiding from someone. I don't think it was us, Keegan commented to his wolf.

I doubt it. It must be someone in the Central Washington pack she came from.

All of Emma's veins ran cold. Fear spiked through her and she lost the connection for a second.

They know where we're from. Her wolf's voice was chilled.

There's no way this will be good, Emma responded quietly to her wolf.

I wonder how long they've known, her wolf asked in a cold tone. *They're not on good terms with Central Washington. But that doesn't mean there isn't some sense of loyalty among them. Keegan doesn't strike me as terribly deceptive. I think your best bet is to plea to his sense of honor and ask that they not report you to Central Washington.*

I don't want to grovel. That's what a submissive wolf does and I don't want him or his Alpha to think they can control me.

We don't have a lot of choice right now. In case they haven't contacted Alpha Peters, you want to get ahead of it.

Emma knew her wolf was right, but the idea of pleading left a sour taste in her mouth.

Keegan walked back over to his nephew and began checking the younger man out. Emma watched with as blank of an expression as she could manage, though she wasn't entirely sure how convincing she was.

After several minutes, Keegan strode over to Emma. She felt her entire body tense as he walked past her only to pivot and lean against the wall on the far side of her so that his nephew and Soraya couldn't make out his words.

"So, you're an Omega?" His voice was so quiet Emma barely heard it.

She knew what he was doing. He was trying to keep as much privacy between them as possible. She also knew his effort was practically useless. Wolf hearing was extraordinary and if either of the other two were actually paying attention, they be able to make out some of the words if they tried. So instead, she figured she would confirm him in the quickest way possible. Running her thumb along the bracelet, she concentrated on his face, on his eyes. It took Keegan a second to realize she was concentrating on them. Then he looked at her puzzled.

His wolf was very dominant. Having that dominant of a wolf meant it was easier for her to reach out to the creature, to hear the wolf's thoughts. But she had to give a little extra effort to get into his head to plant her own words there. He had some defenses that made it harder than it did for her to speak to Morris this way, and she knew that pounding headache wouldn't be going away soon because this was probably going to add to it. After several long seconds, she could see Keegan's salt-and-pepper wolf and she directed her comments at both the man and the wolf.

Yes, I'm an Omega wolf.

Keegan's eyes widened, but that was the only outward tell that he was surprised.

You hear us, Keegan's wolf responded quietly and calmly. There was a deadly edge to it as if the wolf couldn't decide whether he was curious or offended.

Yes, she responded, feeling her own wolf come and stand beside her mentally where Keegan and his wolf could see her. Though her wolf didn't say so, Emma could feel that this was a sort of gesture of trust. A way to even the playing field since she could see inside of his head. It would give him the merest glimpse inside hers.

You cannot alert Central Washington that we are here, her wolf commented firmly. Cutting right to the chase.

Emma was sure her own eyes widened a smidge at her wolf's bluntness.

She could almost see Keegan's wolf's head tilt slightly in curiosity. *We have not mentioned it to anyone, yet. But why should we not tell Central Washington their Omega wolf is here? Surely they are concerned for you.*

Emma fought to find the right words, she struggled and floundered as the whole thing felt so overwhelming.

Show them, her wolf nudged her in the side.

Emma looked over at the wolf who could've easily toppled her. *What?*

Her wolf gave a put-upon sigh. *Show them. Share your memories with them. It will be faster than the explanation.*

How on earth do I do that? Emma asked incredulously, forgetting Keegan and his wolf could probably hear the entire exchange.

Her wolf gave another put-upon sigh and chuffed as if the answer to Emma's question was the most obvious thing in the world. *Take the human's hand and think of Richard. Follow your mind through all the events and focus the memories into the bracelet.*

The idea was absurd but part of Emma ran cold again. Sharing her memories with someone seemed horrifying and embarrassing. But after that was fear. If memories could be plucked from her head, it could be used against those in her memories. It meant she had an even stronger reason not to end up at the hands of Richard and Alpha Peters.

Breaking her focus on the man and his wolf, Emma reached out with the hand that wore the bracelet and much to her surprise Keegan cupped her hand gently, proving he heard the conversation between her and her wolf.

As the two of them touched, she felt a zing go through Keegan system. If she hadn't already known he was attracted to her that would've given it away. She felt a blush sneak onto her face but tried her best to ignore it and concentrate on the memories of Richard. She put all of her focus into the bracelet, but concentrated on not breaking her connection to Keegan and his wolf.

Her head began throbbing mercilessly and her stomach rolled with queasiness from the pain but she kept pushing through it. She knew that as soon as she finished what she was doing her head would soften to a dull roar. She knew the moment it started working because the bracelet warmed and she watched as memories of Richard, mainly over the last few months, played like a movie inside Keegan's head. She could feel his and his wolf's surprise and feel his wolf was impressed at her skill. Only becoming more so when it became clear these were skills she only developed recently. The projection ended with her and Morris driving in their cars to Seattle.

Emma broke the skin to skin contact. That seemed to surprise Keegan as he twitched slightly when she let go, as if he wasn't expecting the contact to break so quickly. But as soon as they were no longer touching the nausea rolling in her stomach ceased and her head went back to a migraine throb. She was glad it was nighttime because daylight would've made this agony. She stretched her fledgling power too far and now she was going to be paying for it.

Though their mental connection was still there, she ignored Keegan for a moment. His wolf seemed to be hanging on to it more than Emma was. She let her legs slowly slide out from under her, taking her to the ground. Keegan followed making it appear as if they had sat down, not as if he was following her collapse onto the concrete.

Are you all right? Keegan's voice rumbled through her head.

In response she shook hers. *Not really. That was a new trick for me and between that and helping with Barry I think I've made myself sick.*

Darian, the second in command for the pack will be here soon with two others to help take care of Barry and my nephew. Peter's injuries will heal in a few days and I will bet you don't have any kind of healing powers considering most of what you've done is mental. I don't pretend to know a lot about Omega wolves, but what I know is their abilities, whatever they are, run in just one vein and not a wide variety. Plus, even if you could heal him, I'm not sure you'd be able to in your current state. Do you need me to drive you home once help is here and everyone is secured? I don't think you should be driving.

The worry and guilt she could hear in his mental voice struck a chord with her. He actually cared what happened to her and that meant more to her than she'd like to admit. Sure, Richard had put up a good show but in the end it turned out he didn't care for her as much as he pretended. Keegan actually seems to

No, I'm okay. Her inner voice was weak even to her own ears. The mental image of herself was almost propped up on her wolf. The wolf made it look as if she was still standing, but the wolf was carrying the brunt of her weight. *I'm going to call my roommate to come get me.*

Keegan was eyeing her warily but before he could say anything else two large SUVs pulled into the parking lot and his attention was diverted.

"That's them, are you okay sitting here by yourself?" he asked calmly and quietly.

"Yep," Emma responded.

He eyed her for another second before leaping up to his feet and making quick time to the closest of the two vehicles.

Exhausted and in pain, Emma closed her eyes and rummaged by feel through the front pocket of her backpack until she found her phone. Once she pulled it out, she pulled it close to her face and hissed at the light. Closing one eye, she entered her passcode and went to her contacts. The light emanating from the screen was making her stomach roll again. Once she hit the screen to call Raelene, she put it to her ear and closed her eyes again. There were enough dominant wolves here that if Barry got out of control they should be able to handle him. They didn't need her help.

Plus, if she wasn't mistaken her wolf was still eyeing the scenario warily. Which Emma wasn't entirely sure how she could do since Emma's eyes were closed, but she didn't have the mental wherewithal to concentrate on that too much.

"Hun? Shouldn't you've been out of class twenty minutes ago?" Raelene answered by way of greeting.

"Long story. But I'm going to need you to pick me up."

"What happened?" Raelene's demand was sharp and Emma could hear rustling in the background but knew her roommate was gathering stuff up to bolt out the door.

"Long story. I'll tell you when you get here. I overused my new talent and now I have a migraine the size of Texas. I'm just not sure I can drive myself home." She spoke as quietly as she could but she was fairly certain if any of the werewolves were listening to her they'd know what she said.

There was cursing at the other end of the phone. "Is there anyone there with you?"

"Yeah, Keegan, someone named Darian. The other two pack students from my class and a handful of other people."

There was silence a moment, but the shuffling continued. "You're in it deep if Darian showed up. I'm on my way. I'll see you in about fifteen minutes." Then the phone went quiet.

Emma glanced at the phone with one eye to make sure Raelene had in fact hung up. Then slid the phone back into her backpack and shut it. Leaning her head against the cold brick building, Emma sat there with her eyes closed just breathing.

She could hear the wolves talking and though she knew she could make out words, she didn't focus enough to comprehend them. Whatever it was it didn't matter. She didn't want to be part of pack politics and nothing would come from having whatever information she would glean from listening to them.

"Someone coming for you?" a voice several octaves deeper than Keegan's wafted from somewhere in front of her. It startled Emma enough that she was grateful her head had already been plastered to the brick, because otherwise it would've knocked her into next Tuesday.

She opened one eye to see a tall, muscular werewolf standing in front of her. He had close cropped dark blond hair and was looking down at her with authority, concern, and more than a little suspicion.

"Yeah, my ride will be here within the next fifteen minutes."

There was silence as the larger man appraised her and Emma was almost grateful she was in so much pain because it meant she didn't squirm under the dominant wolf's scrutiny like she would normally be prone to do.

"Do you require medical attention? We have a medic with us."

Emma fought not to shake her head, knowing the gesture would only bring more pain. "No, what's bothering me can't be cured by a medic, unless he has some decent painkillers to help a migraine." Emma closed her eyes as she finished speaking. She hoped by doing so she could will him to accept the dismissal and not make her talk anymore.

She felt a breeze as the man walked away a few seconds later and relief flooded her. Having her eyes open was difficult and holding a conversation didn't help the migraine. Much to her chagrin, a few moments later there was another breeze, and she felt someone squat down in front of her. She couldn't help the growl that came up from her throat. But was surprised when that growl was met with a chuckle.

"You don't have to open your eyes. Hold out your hands, I'll put these two nice strong painkillers in one and a small water bottle in the other." This man's voice was lighter, and not as deep as the last. He wreaked of friendliness, which she supposed was something that came in handy as a medic, since she assumed that was who she was talking to.

She held out her hands and sure enough pills went in one and he moved slightly to put a small water bottle in the other.

"Thank you. I appreciate it."

There was another chuckle. "No, thank you. The last time Barry had one of these fits he injured two people worse than Peter is. Peter is going to recover in the next couple days and doesn't have any broken bones. You made my job easier. A couple pain pills are the least I can do. Don't take any other meds once you get home. They're pretty strong and will last you about twelve hours. Now let me see you take them." The last was a little firmer, though the friendly tone didn't disappear entirely.

Emma juggled the pills in her hand so she could open the bottle and took the pills accordingly.

"Awesome, now I'm going to put a card in your hand. It has my cell phone on the back of it. If things get to where you find yourself in need of help, of the medical variety, call me. And if I can't show up, I will send one of the other two medical personnel we have in the pack. I know you're not pack but we owe you one for taking care of this." As he finished speaking, Emma felt a small piece of paper press into her palm. Instinctively, she curled her fingers around it.

"Thank you, that is very kind of you."

There was a snort this time. "Don't mention it. You don't strike me as the type of person who calls wolf when it comes to needing help. And I'm going to stick around until your ride gets here. I would just like to give them instructions to check on you and give them my card as well."

Emma's heart clinched a little. While she didn't want people to know she lived with a pack wolf, it seemed unavoidable at this point. Not to mention the kindness this man was showing touched her. She couldn't remember the last time anyone, other than Morris or Bess in her home pack, showed such compassion for her.

"I'm sure she already has it." Emma whispered it so quietly she wasn't entirely sure the other wolf heard her.

But he must've because Emma felt him leaning in only inches away from her face. "Oh, and why would that be?" he whispered equally as quiet

"She belongs to the pack. And you strike me as someone who doesn't keep those cards to themselves or a select few people." The last part was more her wolf speaking than her, but Emma didn't disagree with it.

There was another pause before the man chuckled again, leaning back. "Oh I think I'm going to like you. We haven't officially met, you haven't seen my face, yet you've already got me down pat. Are you going to need help standing when your roommate shows?" The last part was more serious.

Emma thought about it. Raelene was a werewolf, and could lift her fine. But Raelene would appreciate someone who could balance out the weight on the other side of Emma.

"Maybe."

She felt a breeze again as the man stood up. "All right, we'll see when she gets here. I am going to check in with the powers that be and tell them we don't have to worry about you being terribly injured." He stood still for a second, as if appraising her to make sure his statement was valid before she heard him walk away.

She didn't know how long she was sitting there by herself before she heard a car pulling into the parking lot. A door slammed, and she heard Raelene calling and knew from that second forward there was no way she could hide from the Seattle pack. She was at their mercy, whether or not she was one of them.

"Emma!" Came Raelene's frantic voice as she heard the woman running toward the building. "Emma, where the hell are you?"

"This side of the parking lot," came the voice of the large dominant wolf Emma didn't know.

There was the sound of boots clicking on the sidewalk as Raelene jogged around the building.

"Oh Emma, what the hell did you all do to her?" Raelene growled as she stepped beside Emma and knelt next to her, reaching out to grab one arm and put her other hand to Emma's forehead.

I can't believe she's speaking to dominant wolves that way, Emma commented to her wolf.

I think the lines are a little blurred in this pack when it comes to dominance, her wolf commented quietly from where she sat back in the shadows of Emma's mind, since she didn't have the strength to pull her forward.

"From what Keegan tells me," the deep dominant wolf's voice responded, coming closer with each word and Emma could hear thick-soled shoes moving toward them at the same time. "One of our younger wolves who is having a difficult time with his change was attacking one of Emma's students, another young wolf. Emma somehow stepped in and calmed Barry's wolf. But the effort seems to of taken quite a toll on her." He wisely kept more of a distance than he had the first time he approached Emma. "You are one of our wolves, aren't you?

The silence this time was tense and longer than the silence before. "I am." As she spoke, Raelene kept one hand on Emma shoulder and stood to face the man in front of them.

"You harbored an Omega wolf in our territory for months without mentioning it to myself or Ethan."

If Emma wasn't mistaken, there was a growl bubbling up from Raelene's throat before she responded. "No, I gave haven to a childhood friend of mine in distress. It has nothing to do with you." There was such a sharpness to her voice that Emma was surprised.

Raelene was a fierce friend but the fact that she was standing up to what Emma was believing was the second in command for the pack could be a horrible mistake on Raelene's part. And yet Emma adored her for it.

There was that tense silence again. "Very well. Take her home. CJ has some instructions for you before you go."

Emma heard the larger man pivot and walk away. She was so surprised that she was sure her mouth gaped open. She then heard the shorter footfalls of who she assumed was CJ, probably the medic, walking toward Raelene. The two of them took several steps away from Emma and spoke in whispers. They were purposefully staying out of hearing range from wherever the rest of the wolves stood. It made Emma like this CJ more than even her initial estimation. She didn't know how dominant of a wolf he was, but he was clearly someone who cared for those around him.

After a few moments, footsteps came back toward her and she felt Raelene's hand on her shoulder again. "All right, hun, CJ is going to be on your other side and we will lift you up and plop you into my car. Don't worry, I'll grab your backpack on the way up. You ready?"

Emma opened her eyes and felt the world swim a little. But she forced herself to keep them open so she could see what was in front of her. She knew very well that either of them could've probably firefighter carried her to the car but she appreciated they were letting her keep her dignity and walk herself.

"All right, here we go," Raelene called.

As soon as she finished speaking, Emma pushed herself off the ground and though she had very little weight since the two people were propping her up, she felt the world swim with the motion and her stomach rolled again. Emma forced herself to grit her teeth as she stood. Once she was standing, CJ and Raelene gave her a couple moments to steady herself and her stomach. When she put out her first leg to start moving, the two of them took most of her weight and they made the slow trek to where Raelene parked, next to Emma's vehicle in the front part of the parking lot. No one said much as Raelene unlocked her car doors and threw in Emma's backpack, before they slowly set Emma into the seat.

When she was seated, Raelene went around to the driver side of the car. CJ reached around Emma and put on her seatbelt. Once that was done, he smiled at Emma.

"You were right. She does have several of my cards. You take care of yourself, okay? Since I know how to get a hold of your roommate I might come by and check on you in a day or so just to make sure." He spoke quietly, though no other wolves, other than Raelene, were close enough to hear him. "The pack I grew up in, in Northern California, has an Omega wolf. I know that what ails you probably can't be helped by me, other than some painkillers. But even if that's all I can do I would rather be safe than sorry." He gave her right hand a squeeze before patting it and shutting the car door behind him. He stood on the other side of the window and gave one wave to both her and Raelene before heading back to the rest of the wolves.

Northern California? What are the odds he's from the same pack Morris grew up in? her wolf chimed in from the darkness in the back of Emma's mind.

I can't imagine their high. But I'll ask Morris next time I talk to him.

Closing her eyes again, Emma settled into the seat. All she could do was wait for the pain pills to kick in. She hoped, since they were prescribed by a werewolf in the medical field, that they would be stronger than the run-of-the-mill painkillers she'd been taking until this point when she exhausted her abilities. Because she knew for a fact the stuff she had in her medicine cabinet at home would barely put a dent in what she was feeling.

That didn't even account for the dread she felt now that she was outed to the Seattle pack. At their mercy. She didn't know what Keegan was going to do with the information about her. He hadn't made any kind of agreement not to sell her out to Richard. If she wasn't already sick to her stomach that would've done it. Maybe she would end up having to move sooner than she thought after all. She couldn't risk the Seattle pack telling Richard about her. But she still had another three weeks of class left. A lot could happen in three weeks. She might have to move even if that meant getting a job outside of academia. A thought that didn't appeal to her at all.

We can worry about this later. Rest now, recoup. I think we're going to have to be at full strength to deal with the storm that's coming.

Knowing her wolf was right, Emma focused on the classical music Raelene had playing on the radio and felt herself drift somewhere between sleep and awake. She was sure she wouldn't be able to sleep until her head stopped pounding, but she could feel the nausea subsiding. At least there was something positive.

Chapter 29:
Explain Yourself

Keegan

"Let me get this straight," Ethan interrupted while running his hand through his thick auburn hair. "Not only is there a female lone wolf in our territory, which is an anomaly, but not a big deal. But she is a dominant wolf and an Omega wolf with the ability to take down a crazed young wolf without even touching him. Do I have that right? Oh, and Keegan has been a student in her class for two months and didn't notice half of this?"

The Alpha's tone was angry but Keegan knew that frustration and anger wasn't really pointed at him as much as the situation in general. Even if Keegan hadn't been somewhat smitten with the beautiful Emma, he wouldn't have noticed her Omega abilities unless she displayed them. She had been careful not to.

"Darian and I discussed her. I was doing research on her background and was going to bring it up the next time we had a meeting about something else. This just happened first," Keegan said, keeping his tone as flat as possible.

Though the only people in the room were Ethan, Darian, Dante, and Jesse, who had the same authority level as Keegan. Keegan wasn't particularly friends with Dante. He knew the other wolf well enough to know that he wasn't one to stand on ceremony any more than Ethan or Darian did in private. Jesse, the third Lieutenant though, was all about rules and regulations. Keegan felt bad for the wolves under him.

Blinking, Keegan set those thoughts aside. He needed to keep to the subject at hand. Even though his brain kept swimming with the images Emma had somehow trusted him enough to show him. He understood why she was running now. Though he could tell from her thoughts, she hadn't put two and two together yet. But Keegan was fairly certain that this Richard from the Central Washington pack was only with Emma to use her for her abilities. It was a little too convenient for him that her abilities started showing up as soon as Richard wasn't in the picture. It could be he had a more suspicious nature than Emma did or she was just too close to the other wolf to see the truth. That thought prickled him and his wolf.

He's not good enough for her, growled Keegan's wolf. Who over the course of the last few hours seem to develop more of a possessiveness for Emma where there had been more indifference before. It was as if her displaying her abilities and then the subsequent vulnerability made Keegan's wolf want to protect her and hold her close, defend her against the world.

"Well, don't leave us in suspense, Keegan. What exactly did you learn about the young woman's past?" Ethan asked raising an eyebrow, a little sharpness to his tone.

Keegan picked his words carefully. He knew there was part of this he needed to get out before he continued. "I want to start by saying that even though Wilson, yes *that* Wilson, teaches down the hall from her and has approached her several times she doesn't seem thrilled with his attention. She seemed polite and though he is making quite the effort, I don't see her joining him and his band of lone wolves soon."

Ethan's eyebrow quirked up at the information but other than that his body seemed to relax with that news, which was of course why Keegan opened with it. He didn't know why he wanted to defend her and look out for her but he did. And knowing that she was not about to join Wilson and his gang would go a long way to do that.

Keegan didn't look to see the expressions of anyone else in the room at his words. Even though Ethan could be fairly democratic, Keegan knew that if he could get the Alpha on his side with a strong enough argument the others' opinions wouldn't matter. "I don't know if he's going to try to push her any harder to get her to join them. But for the foreseeable future, I don't think she will. I don't know if he has other tactics in mind other than being polite."

He wasn't sure how to phrase this next part, because part of him felt as if he was betraying Emma's trust, but if she was having trouble with a different pack Ethan had every right to know if the Alpha of that other pack would come looking for her.

"It seems that she grew up in the Central Washington pack, and that she didn't leave under good terms. From the information I've gathered, it would appear as if the Alpha and his son wanted to use her for political gains and that wasn't something she wanted any part of. So I believe the reason we haven't heard about her before this is because she's keeping a low profile so they don't find her."

The silence in the room was thick with tension. Though there was no love between them and the Central Washington pack, no one was looking for a fight either.

"Huh," Ethan grunted before wrapping his fingers along his desk that he stood beside. When all attention swiveled to him he stared off into space a moment before continuing, "It's interesting you would say that. I received a phone call a little over a week ago from Alpha Peters. He stated he was reaching out to those packs in neighboring territories because his son's fiancée had gone missing. Though he didn't out right say it, he heavily implied that he expected there was some foul play involved. As if she might've been taken against her will. I remember thinking it was odd because if kidnapping was really what was on his mind he seemed fairly calm. I'm guessing this Omega wolf is the missing fiancée? Not that I would trust Alpha Peters with a ten foot pole but what do you think the odds are that his version of events is correct and what research you gained is wrong?"

There was a split second when Keegan's wolf took offense but Keegan calmed the creature down. Ethan hadn't meant any offense. He didn't know Keegan plucked his information straight from Emma's mind, so it was perfectly reasonable for him to wonder how accurate the information could be.

"I'm fairly certain that the version of events I have is correct. Alpha Peters and his son wanted to use this Omega wolf to their advantage and were, for lack of a better term, grooming her. That way she wouldn't realize they were trapping her in a bit of a cage."

Ethan frowned and Keegan knew the Alpha was switching through several unpleasant remarks. Omegas were rare and something to be treasured. Having one associated with your pack did bring a certain level of power in and of itself. If Alpha Peters was indeed trying to trap an Omega wolf into doing his bidding, it went against a number of the rules werewolves lived by. If there was proof, he should be sanctioned and be forced to step down as an Alpha. That kind of sanction was rare, because it led to a destabilization of a pack's hierarchy.

"So you are of the mind that we should assist this Omega in hiding from her home pack?" Ethan's words were measured and careful.

Jesse stepped forward, folding his arms over his chest and frowning. "I'm not thrilled that this puts us in the middle of an argument with Alpha Peters and his pack's Omega. While I understand an Omega is free to move about from territory to territory as they see fit, they rarely move alone, or under the radar, which until tonight this

Omega was. But I've been hearing rumors of Alpha Peters trying to consolidate his power and I think a fight with him is something we should avoid just in case my intel is old and he's already managed to make some sort of agreement with other packs in the area."

"Personally," Darian interrupted, "I think it's a little despicable that we would even consider using this woman as a bargaining chip. As much as I don't like her hiding in our territory and causing problems for us by being here, the idea of putting any wolf, especially an Omega, in a situation to be used like that makes me sick to my stomach, even if it put us in Peters' good graces."

Darian's words went a long way to soothe Keegan's wolf. Both Keegan and his wolf had no interest in letting Emma be thrown back into the situation she was in with Richard. While arranged marriages weren't unheard of in the werewolf world, no one should be forced into one against their will. That would be exactly what they were doing if they tipped Alpha Peters off to Emma's location.

You cannot let them give her away, Keegan's wolf growled.

"With all due respect, Jesse," Dante chimed in, "I think we can avoid the confrontation and let the young woman stay put. Since Alpha Peters never mentioned the young woman was an Omega wolf, you can easily feign ignorance that the two are related. Plus, as an Omega wolf we can say that we didn't question where she came from since she seemed to be here of her own free will. We can say we were following the rules set out for having an Omega wolf in your territory and let her live her own life in exchange for the occasional favor to the pack, such as with Barry this evening. That way should he come angrily out here saying that we were hiding or kidnapped his Omega you can plausibly deny any interference. She's not asking for permission into the pack, or she would've done so already. So, I say we tell her that if she doesn't cause problems for us, we don't cause problems for her."

Blackmail? We're resorting to blackmail? Keegan's wolf growled in disgust.

"I need to think about this. While I agree that forcing the young woman to be involved in whatever scheme Peters had is horrible, his pack territory is the closest to ours and our relationship is already tenuous at best. Give me a few days to think about how best to attack this problem then I'll get back to all of you." When he finished speaking, Ethan waved his hand dismissively at the room at large.

All the occupants nodded with varying degrees of respect and walked out. Keegan was debating whether to go to his own office or to head straight home when Darian put his hand on Keegan shoulder. Once the other man was sure he had Keegan's attention, he motioned his chin toward his own office. When it became clear Keegan got his meaning, Darian let go of Keegan's shoulder and began striding to his closed office door.

It wasn't until Keegan had followed him in and shut the door behind him that Darian spoke in a hushed tone, since he shared an office wall with Ethan.

"On how good of terms are you with this she-wolf?" The older man's tone was bland, intentionally so. Making Keegan feel a little wary.

"Not close. But not hostile either. Why?"

"One of our young wolves change hit early and fast. She is struggling to maintain one form or the other. She's only fifteen and while most of our wolves at her age are just beginning to get the itch to shift, she's been shifting for several months and is struggling heavily. All the side effects of those initial changes and the intense hormones of puberty are making her life hell. She's close friends with my youngest niece and if there's any way you could convince this Omega wolf to come in and try to help her it would make a world of difference. As it is, the young woman sometimes spends nights in one of the padded rooms downstairs to prevent her from hurting herself or others. Would you be willing to ask her for assistance? Tell her she would gain a favor from the pack as a gesture of goodwill."

Her powers are still weak. She was exhausted from helping Barry. We shouldn't have her exhausting her abilities when she's still possibly in danger, his wolf muttered.

"I'll ask her, but I cannot make a guarantee as I do not know exactly what her abilities entail. I'll let you know when I hear from her."

Darian nodded solemnly, clearly not thrilled with Keegan's response but not willing to push it. "Understood, thank you for putting in the request."

Keegan stood there a moment and when it became clear Darian was finished he nodded once before turning and leaving the other man's office. Not wanting to get caught by anyone else, Keegan headed straight outside to the parking lot where he parked his car. Luckily, no one else stopped him on the way to his vehicle. Which simply left his own thoughts swirling in his head for the ride home.

He wanted to get to know Emma better. The beautiful she-wolf was interesting, smart, and clearly powerful. Asking her this favor would mean he would get to spend more time with her outside of the classroom. But he also didn't want to take advantage of the fragile connection they had. He didn't want her to think he'd only communicate with her if he needed something. He wanted more of a relationship than that but considering the situation they found themselves in, Keegan didn't know the right way to navigate to his desired outcome. It irritated both the man and the wolf that there was no clear path going forward.

We will think of something, his wolf commented agitatedly at Keegan's thoughts.

While his wolf seemed to feel surer than Keegan, he didn't take comfort in the wolf's words. He honestly wasn't sure if there was any hope for him and Emma, especially when he considered the strong feelings he sensed for the dominant wolf he had seen in her memories that drove with her to Seattle. There was a bond between them that was strong and permanent. From what he felt, there was no way he could come between them, no matter how much his wolf wanted to.

Chapter 30:

Out With It

Emma

"Okay, out with it!" barked Raelene as Emma walked out of the bathroom the next morning.

It took a second for the words to sink in. Emma stood there blinking at her roommate who sat, fully dressed for work, on their loveseat. Emma hadn't even changed out of her PJs yet, so she was still in the matching red plaid boxers and camisole. Raelene hadn't even waited until Emma had consumed some coffee to ambush her.

"Shouldn't you be on your way to work or something?" Emma mumbled through the hangover she felt as she stumbled into the kitchen and filled a mug with the coffee left in the pot.

Her head felt like it was full of cotton and the world seemed kind of foggy. While she didn't feel sick to her stomach like an alcohol hangover, there was still a thick pounding in her head from the overuse of power last night. Emma had been extremely grateful that the pain meds CJ gave her eased the migraine enough that she slept. But, she supposed, it was too much to hope that those little pills would've made the morning after better, too.

Emma could practically feel Raelene's impatience wafting across the room but she took her time dressing her coffee and made her way over to the couch before making, somewhat blinky, eye contact with her childhood friend.

"Long story short, and before you ask no, I don't know how my wolf knew I could do certain things when I didn't know I could do them. But I'm not sure I could explain to you how things worked even with hindsight." Emma then took a deep breath and launched into a full account from when she exited the building until Raelene arrived.

Though Raelene didn't interrupt, there was a lot of frowning and face making as Emma went into as much detail as possible while still maintaining a clipped pace. It wasn't easy considering how fuzzy her brain was. But she didn't want to have to go back over things and re-describe them because she hadn't done a well enough job the first time.

When she finished, Raelene squinted for several seconds over her own coffee mug. "That's an insane amount of power you have." There wasn't any disbelief in her voice. Raelene took the entire thing in as truth and didn't seem to have even a minute doubt that Emma could do what she said she did.

It gave a certain amount of relief to Emma that her friend wasn't questioning her or suspicious. She felt her shoulders slump, and she exhaled a breath she hadn't really noticed she was holding.

"That is an insane ability. You could do all kinds of things with that. Can you imagine? The ramifications of being able to rummage around in someone's head and possibly control what they're doing? Did you control what Barry was doing? Or did you just sort of... soothe his soul?" Raelene screwed up her face at her own wording. She frowned deeply. "Do you think Richard and his dad knew you could do that kind of thing? That would really come in handy if you're trying to control the surrounding territories, which Peters has been talking about on and off for years. It would be a dangerous ability for them to get their hands on." The frown turned to outright worry now.

Part of Emma wanted to shove aside Raelene's worries. To say that Richard would never use her like that. But there was a little kernel in her mind that stopped her and it wasn't just her wolf that believed the worst in Richard. Emma was finding it hard not to believe the worst of him as well.

"Honestly, I don't know. I don't think I ever displayed any kind of ability like that. But I don't think I displayed any abilities at all. But there had to of been something, I had to of done something. Why else would Richard's dad push so hard for us to be together? I can't believe I'm that consequential to him just being me." Saying the words out loud hurt more than Emma thought they would. It felt as if it was the first time she was truly admitting to herself that Richard hadn't wanted her for her. Pieces were starting to fall into place.

Was I really just a pawn for them all? Emma asked her wolf.

Her wolf stepped forward hesitantly and bowed as if trying not to make eye contact. *Honestly, I don't know. I would assume there was some sort of attraction in the beginning. But I have long suspected his motives were less than decent. Though I'm not sure I can pinpoint to you the event or events that made me change my mind.*

Feeling her eyes sting, Emma concentrated on her roommate.

Raelene's eyes held sadness and compassion as she reached out with one hand to pat Emma's bare knee. "For what it's worth, Richard is a dick." Her friend's lip twitched as she said it. "You always deserved better. And if he and his dad can't see how fantastic you are, beyond being a holder of some intense magic, then there's more of you for the rest of us."

Emma felt anxiety swirl through her. Her world was twisting and turning and she had no way to control it. These insane powers of hers were valuable, but she had no control and didn't know what was going to pop up next.

"Having these powers scares me. I don't know what I'm supposed to do with them."

Raelene scrunched her mouth together in thought. "I'm not sure how to help you train with those abilities. I mean, no offense, but I really don't want you rooting around in my head and trying to control my thoughts."

"None taken. I don't particularly want to do that either."

Before either of them could say anything else, there was a loud brisk knock at the door.

Chapter 31:
The First is a Favor, the Second is an Obligation

CJ

Normally, CJ wasn't phase by not being 'in the know' as far as pack politics went. He had enough on his plate with his work and helping to take care of the health of his pack mates. He enjoyed being of service to people. It had always been important to him.

But when he'd been called to the scene last night were Barry had been fighting, part of him wanted to yell 'not it' or feign he was busy and couldn't go. He felt instantly guilty with those thoughts. But they had a significantly higher than normal number of young wolves struggling to control themselves in the last year and it had become exhausting to keep up with them all. Between young Vicki, a fifteen-year-old wolf who had changed hard and too soon and was constantly doing harm to herself because of it, Barry with his anger issues, and two other young wolves in similar situations, CJ and the other two medical personnel had their work cut out for them.

It had been an overwhelming relief when he arrived last night and found out that while the fight had done some damage, it wasn't as bad as he'd expected. That had been thanks to an Omega wolf. CJ had been pleasantly surprised by that information until he realized it had been a surprised to Darian as well. Darian was the pack Beta. That he hadn't known there was an Omega wolf with that kind of power in the area had CJ a little concerned. Not that he would say that out loud.

He liked the Omega wolf. He sensed something about her that just told him he was going to like her, that the two of them would be fast friends. CJ prided himself on having quick and accurate first impressions of people, and even though the two of them had barely spoken to each other, there was no doubt in his mind.

Then another twist in the plot came along when it had been Raelene who came to pick her up. CJ had been amused when the Omega wolf mentioned her roommate was a pack werewolf. He thought it was funny a pack werewolf managed to keep that kind of thing quiet. But when that pack werewolf turned out to be Raelene, CJ was shocked. He and Raelene had known each other for years and about a month and a half ago, he finally gotten up enough courage to ask her out on the date he had been yearning for since he first laid eyes on her. Since then, they hit it off swimmingly. It'd been a little awkward at first, just the whole getting to know people better thing. But once they got past that it'd been great. CJ could see something long-term happening. Raelene mentioned having a roommate, and that the arrangement had been relatively new. But there was nothing about the roommate being a werewolf, just a childhood friend. So he used the opportunity of giving her a rundown of Emma's health to probe a question or two.

They hadn't been dating that long, and he could understand her motives for wanting to protect her friend, but he was still surprised he missed her roommate was a wolf. He'd been to the apartment a handful of times. He should've been able to smell that two werewolves lived there and not a werewolf and a human woman.

He started his day checking in at the pack office to get an update on Vicki, who spent a record three nights in one of the pack rooms. Stopping by and seeing Raelene and Emma was what he needed this morning. Seeing the woman he cared for and a patient he was fairly certain would become his friend would be a nice pick me up after a tiring night. But then, Keegan had decided to tag along. He and Keegan were cordial enough, though they never hung out or spent time alone before. So when Keegan hit the parking lot at the same time as him and followed him all the way to Raelene's address, he'd made up his mind that he would pause in the parking lot and walk up with the other man. His wolf wanted to make sure Keegan wasn't trying to lay any moves on Raelene while the man and the medic in him didn't want him bothering his patient before he got a chance to check them out.

"So what brings you to this neck of the woods?" CJ kept his tone light as he stood at the foot of the stairs to Raelene and Emma's apartment.

Keegan pushed his sunglasses down slightly so he could look CJ in the eyes. A gesture CJ wanted to squirm under but fought not to. "I've come to talk to the Omega wolf. What are you doing here?"

Fighting to keep his voice authoritative, CJ straightened, grabbing the strap on the over the shoulder bag that held his to go medical supplies. "I'm checking on a patient. I want to see how she's doing after last night. I'd appreciate if you let me check her out before you go about questioning her."

Keegan raised one eyebrow and stared at him a beat before putting his glasses back over his eyes and giving one nod.

Taking that as an affirmative, CJ turned and headed up the stairs. So when he knocked on Raelene's door he was sure they made an awkward site with him a little hunched and Keegan, standing with his arms folded, sunglasses covering his eyes.

Raelene only opened the door a crack, her face pleasant when she looked at him then curiously a Keegan. "Yes?"

"I've come to check on your roommate to see how she's doing. I don't know what the heck he's doing here."

He watched amusement run through Raelene's eyes for a split second and he felt his own lips quirk up in response. Then Raelene looked right at Keegan, her question playing on her face.

"I've come to talk to Emma. The pack has a question for her." His voice was calm and assertive and gave nothing away.

CJ felt unease waft off of Raelene and he fought not to reach out and comfort her.

"She doesn't want to join the pack," Raelene responded angrily.

"That's not why I'm here. Darian wanted me to ask her for a favor. She's free to say no but I still have to ask." His voice was almost razor-sharp. CJ knew Keegan was used to being listened to because of his position within the pack and he bet it just dawned on him that Raelene just might not let Keegan into the apartment at all.

"Oh just let them in. The sooner they come in the sooner they can leave," came a tired voice from farther in the apartment that CJ recognized as Emma's.

Raelene's gaze flicked into the apartment and her expression turned worried before she stepped out of the way and open the door wide enough for both of them to walk in.

Once inside, CJ beeline straight for the area he knew the couches to be. It worked to his advantage that he's been in the apartment before, where Keegan would have to get his bearings for a split second. CJ went right to Emma, standing between her and the small glass coffee table. He laid his bag down on the floor and took a good look at her.

The bags under her eyes were dark. Exhaustion seemed to seep from her pores. She was curled up on one half of the couch with her legs curled under her and cradled a mug of coffee. Her long silvery hair was still in a somewhat mussed braid letting him know that must've been how she wore it to bed. Her clothes were relatively thin and light and he had the strong urge to cover her with the knit blanket thrown over the back of the couch but he fought it. He didn't know this woman well enough to decide things like her temperature or modesty for her.

"How are you feeling this morning?" Years of practice kept the worry from his voice. Patients didn't like the medical personnel looking after them to sound worried.

She looked at him and gave a small weak smile. "A lot better than I would've been if you hadn't given me those pain pills last night. Thank you for that. Between that and the exhaustion, I slept like a rock and now it just feels like a hangover. I'm actually surprised I don't feel worse, not that I want to jinx it." That last part was tacked on quickly, her eyes widening slightly as she spoke.

CJ grinned down at her before he plopped himself on the seat next to her. "I'm glad to hear that. I brought more of those pain pills so you can have them on hand in case this kind of thing happens again. Just never take more than two in a twelve-hour period. Now, if you don't mind, I would just like to take all of your vitals." He didn't touch her until he saw her arm move over so he could reach it.

He made note of her heart rate, breathing, and blood pressure. Everything seemed normal. Much like the Omega in the pack he'd grown up with, the exhaustion wasn't anything he could treat. Part of him was disappointed he couldn't do more for her but he wasn't surprised.

"I'd like to suggest that you up your intake of protein today. Oh, and water. If you consume more of both of those than you do on an average day, it might help you recover faster. I have no scientific basis for this. It's just based on the Omega I grew up with and what worked for her. If you're okay with it, I would like to do some research and reach out to several Omegas in neighboring packs and get some advice on recovery and keep records on all of this so that we can look out for you better."

It hurt his heart that she looked at him with wide-eyed surprise when he asked her permission to reach out to other Omega wolves. She was honestly surprised that someone would want to help her, look out for her. Anger swept through him. Omegas should be taken care of better than what he had a suspicion this woman was used to.

"Um, sure, if it helps. But I don't know if you want to waste your time doing that. I have no intention of joining the pack and your responsibility is to them first."

CJ knew there was a flash of anger on his face before he could catch it and put that pleasant blank expression back in its place. He also knew she saw it. "You're a wolf in my pack's territory. You did us a favor. Your health matters. I'll get back to you if anything useful comes up. You have my number to reach out if you need me. And if you follow, my advice and get more protein and water today, let me know how you're feeling in the morning. Just shoot me a text so I can write notes so that were better prepared if and when this happens again." He gave her nearest hand a little squeeze and smiled at her.

The smile she gave back at him as she squeezed his hand was hopeful, tentative, but hopeful. As he turned to look at Raelene and Keegan, he saw the affection Raelene had for him in her eyes. There was a deep appreciation for the way he was treating her roommate that made his heart pang again. He wanted more information on what warranted such strong reactions from these women but part of him was worried he wouldn't like the answers when he got them.

Keegan, sensing his cue, made his own way across the room to sit on the loveseat that sat in an L-shape with the couch he and Emma occupied. CJ didn't move. He knew it was silly to stick next to Emma just in case she needed the help, even though he was fairly certain Keegan didn't pose any kind of threat.

"I'm glad to see that you're feeling better today. I was a little concerned after last night that you might be down for the count." Keegan's deep voice floundered and for the first time CJ took a good look at the other man.

Does he look nervous? CJ asked his wolf.

Though his wolf was not dominant, CJ realized over the years that the animal was incredibly perceptive.

A little yes, his wolf responded hesitantly, coming forward in his mind as if trying to get a closer look.

Do you think what he has to ask her is going to be bad?

He could almost feel his wolf squinting. *No I don't think so. I don't think it's that kind of nervous.*

Keegan continued, unaware of how closely CJ and his wolf were watching him. "You were able to help Barry last night. And though we don't know if it'll have a lasting effect on him and his wolf, that lack of rage…" he paused, as if trying to find the right words. "Stayed with him well into the morning, when I checked in with his parents. So, my immediate superior, Darian, whom you met last night, was wondering if you might be willing to come in and help another young wolf in our pack. We cannot pay you, as we do not have any sort of official agreement with you but if you're willing, the pack will owe you a favor, a big one."

He was making unflinching eye contact with Emma and CJ couldn't help but wonder why. The other man had taken his glasses off and was looking at Emma with such open interest and curiosity he wondered whether that blatant interest was as obvious to her as it was to him.

He's interested in her as a significant other, CJ said to his wolf, amused.

Yeah, that's interesting, his wolf responded.

CJ shifted his gaze from Keegan to Emma and he fought to keep the grin off his face. She was looking at Keegan warily as if unaware of the man's open and interested body language.

I'm willing to put money on her being totally oblivious to his interest.

His wolf only snorted in response.

"What, exactly, is it you need?" Emma's voice was tired and hesitant, caution threaded heavily through her words.

"We have a young female werewolf, very young, who instead of changing gradually in her late teens seems to of finished her entire shifting process in a matter of months. She's only fifteen and is really struggling with everything being a werewolf entails. Especially, all the turmoil that those first changes bring as well as her regular hormones. She's in a bit of a tailspin and we're trying to help her as best we can. But Darian wondered whether maybe you'd be able to help calm her down a bit, even for a little while. Give her some kind reprieve."

Vicki, he's talking about poor little Vicki, CJ thought. He could think of no one in more need of the help Emma might give.

Emma was now biting her lower lip with a worried expression on her face.

"She would need it in writing. Get the agreement in writing with either Darian or Ethan's signature that this favor would gain her a favor from the pack. And that if multiple meetings are needed over a long period, a deal will be worked out to compensate her in the long term." As Raelene spoke sharply from where she still stood near the door, CJ saw Keegan jump.

The other man's attention had been so fully engrossed with Emma it was as if he'd forgotten the rest of them were there.

Keegan turned his attention from Emma but even as he turned his head it was as if it was difficult for him to rip his eyes away from the Omega wolf.

"That should be easy enough to arrange," he said blankly to Raelene.

"I don't know what I can do." Emma's almost helpless voice drew everyone's attention again, and she took a long sip from her mug. "As of right now, I still feel incredibly drained. I don't know how long it's going to take to rebuild my reserves. A minimum of a few days. And even then I don't know if I could replicate what I did with Barry. I'm just being honest. I don't want to make promises I can't keep."

Keegan watched her for several beats, the urge for the man to reach out and touch her was so loudly telegraphed CJ was baffled that Emma didn't seem to notice.

"It'll take me a couple days to get the paperwork together. How about I come by and grab you Friday night, since you don't teach on Fridays and you can come and check her out? I'll have the paperwork by then and I can get your signature once you've seen her and see if there's anything you can do to help her. That way you're under no obligation and if you do in fact need more time, you have a better understanding of the situation at hand." The man's voice was so calm and caring CJ felt his lips twitch again.

He was used to seeing Keegan sometimes joking around but mostly one of the quiet right-hand men of the pack's second in command. He was a very dominant wolf, and though not harsh, usually got his way. That he was being almost tender and delicate with Emma made CJ want to check over the other man to make sure he wasn't ill.

"Okay," Emma agreed somewhat tentatively. "Come by about four on Friday and we'll go from there."

Keegan's shoulders slumped in relief and he gave a small smile that CJ could tell was a poor imitation of the smile the man was probably holding back. "Excellent. I'll let you know in class on Wednesday if I need any information or if there are any hiccups in the process." Keegan watched her another beat before he pushed off the couch, though his eyes lingered on Emma, before leaving the apartment.

CJ turned his head to make eye contact with Raelene after the other wolf left and he raised an eyebrow.

Raelene shrugged giving him an expression of disbelief. She was just as caught off guard by Keegan's behavior as he was. Which let them know this might just be a new thing.

He turned back to Emma and waited until she was looking at him to speak. "I'll make sure I'm around on Friday when you're visiting Vicki. There isn't a lot I can do but if I can be on site to help out in any way, I want to do it. Plus if nothing else, you'll have another semi friendly face." He gave her a genuine lopsided grin and received a genuine smile in return.

"You're the one dating Raelene, aren't you?" Emma's eyes danced with mischief as she looked at him. He heard Raelene make a sound behind him but didn't dare look to see what her expression was. He felt his own eyes widen a little in surprise.

"Yes," he responded cautiously.

The laugh she let out was melodious and light, almost as if it was a carbonated sound. "I didn't recognize you last night, but sitting this close to you I recognize the scent. I've smelled you around the apartment when you come to visit, even though I haven't seen you. By the time I get off from work you're usually sequestered in Raelene's bedroom." Her lip quirked up in a smirk. "It's nice to officially meet you. And to see that you're a genuine good guy. I guess this means I don't have to threaten to kill you." She was full on grinning as she finished.

He heard Raelene scoff behind him. "As if you could take anyone. You forget I grew up training for fights with you."

Emma smiled. "But you're not taking into account my new unfair advantage." She then wiggled her fingers around her mug up near her head as if they were some kind of wave and moved them in the direction to where he knew Raelene stood.

"Okay, well on that note, I really have to get to work." Raelene snorted before he heard her moving about the room.

He took that as his own cue and gave Emma his goodbye before walking past Raelene and giving her a quick peck and confirming their dinner date for tonight before making his own way out of the apartment.

Chapter 32:
A Good Plan Takes Time

Wilson

"She is already skittish," Wilson growled. "You cannot push her into joining us. She will run directly into the arms of the pack." Wilson fought himself not to tighten his fists. Though he knew he stood stiff and the snarl on his face was clear, he didn't want to appear overly aggressive toward the group.

It hadn't been Mario that called this little meeting Thursday night. It had been Randy, which is why Wilson was so angry. Apparently, Mario had been going behind his back and feeding his insecurities about

Wilson to other members of the alliance that Wilson wasn't as tight with. Randy was one such individual. Wilson had been completely blindsided when Randy thanked everyone for coming then seceded the floor to Mario who proceeded to tell everyone how Wilson had been deceiving them about the new she-wolf.

"Honestly.... Sure, a dominant lone she-wolf is rare," Colin interjected as he folded his arms across his chest and frowned in irritation. "But who cares whether Wilson convinces her or not. There are just as many lone wolves in the territory not affiliated with us or the pack as there are in our alliance. After our initial recruitment of them for the most part we left them alone. Why is she so different?"

There were mutters of agreement and Wilson gritted his teeth. He could sense there was something different about Emma. She didn't smell or feel like a regular dominant wolf, but he couldn't quite put his finger on why. It made him wonder whether she really was an Alpha wolf who didn't particularly want to be an Alpha. Having her on his side could be to his advantage, but if she was as dominant as he suspected, she could challenge him. He didn't particularly want to think about what the challenge would look like.

It might be in your best interest, but Colin is right. If people don't see her as a big deal then they might not care as much about how long it takes to convince her to join you, Wilson's wolf commented.

Before he could make any kind of decision Mario piped up, puffing himself up as a growl threaded his voice. "If she is as dominant as she appears than she is a threat to us. She spoke to me and Wilson with no respect to our dominance and with much disdain. If she doesn't join us she is a major threat." His eyes were almost fanatical as he finished speaking. Something he did from time to time.

It was one of the reasons the pack wanted a tighter control over Mario and what he did in his fights and weightlifting competitions. The man had never fully gotten control of the aggression that came with being a dominant werewolf. There'd been more than one incident that had to be cleaned up because Mario couldn't control his temper.

Colin turned to Wilson. "Is she a threat?" The man raised one single black eyebrow.

All attention pivoted to him and Wilson heard Mario and Randy growl.

"No." A white lie could be detectable by scent, so Wilson chose his words carefully. "She has no interest in joining any kind of formal werewolf group. She doesn't seem to want to be beholden to anyone and wants to be left alone. I think that once the pack sees how dominant she is it will step in and try to control her actions. That will be the best time to convince her to join us. If we push her too much into joining us, she might be a threat but only to the end that she would become combative. She would still be one wolf against many so to that end she isn't a real threat. She can cause problems for us, maybe minor inconveniences but that's it. The plus side is that I get the impression that even if we push her, she still won't want to join the pack. I don't for see the pack, once they are aware of her, letting her live in their territory with no kind of agreement with them. I think that is the biggest threat to her joining us. If she decides to have some sort of treaty with the pack, letting her stay but not be involved with them might be the lesser of two evils compared to us, if we push her." Wilson forced his voice to slow down and smooth out all the anger. He spoke as matter-of-factly as possible to make Mario and Randy look even more outrageous by contrast.

"There we go then. This whole thing is a waste of time. If Wilson can get her to join us, great, but if he can't who cares. Mario, Randy, I don't particularly appreciate you making me waste my time to come down here over one she-wolf. I don't care how rare she is. If she is not a threat to us and I don't have to roll out a welcome wagon, then I don't need to know about it." Colin lowered his arms, rolling his attention across the entire group.

As he finished there were more than a dozen mumbles of agreement. There was a beat for Colin and twenty others made their way out of the small warehouse they were leasing as their home base. After about ten minutes the only people left were Mario,

Randy, Wilson, and his two lieutenants, Jerry and Wallace. Wilson would've put money on Jerry and Wallace only sticking around because Mario and Randy had. Both men stood on either side of Wilson, one step behind him, showing a position of solidarity. Even though the two men were much smaller than Mario, the imposing image would've still had some effect.

"If you cannot convince one lone female wolf to join us then how are you going to convince an entire pack not to revolt against us when we take out Ethan?" Randy hissed.

There was a scoff over Wilson's shoulder. He turned his head slightly toward Jerry, without taking his eyes off Randy and Mario.

"As was already stated, there are many lone wolves we don't actively pursue. Why is it that this one is a thing? And why are you so dead set on it happening urgently?" The disgust in the older man's voice was plain.

Randy glanced at Mario, it was quick, but Wilson still caught it. Showing Wilson Mario was the ringleader here. Not only that, but Randy doesn't seem fully committed or appraised of the whole situation. That could be dangerous. If Mario was amassing allies, he could be more of a threat than Wilson initially gave him credit for.

"She works with Wilson, has pack wolves in her class. That gives her ties to both us and the pack. Do you even remember the last time you met a dominant female lone wolf? One that was unattached to a lone male wolf?" Mario asked, scanning all three of them as he waited for an answer.

None of them answered. Female lone wolves were incredibly rare, at least in the United States. They were more common in northern Europe and Canada, but in the rest of the world it was almost unheard of. Most lone wolves had to have a certain level of dominance to gain and maintain their autonomy. But they were never Alpha or extremely dominant wolves because most packs would see them as too dangerous to have running around in their territory. It was possible Keegan, and by extension Ethan, didn't know how dominant of a wolf Emma was yet because Wilson would've noticed if they'd come to some kind of agreement. Not to mention their spies within the pack would've told him.

"We have bigger problems at hand." Wilson chose to change the subject instead of addressing Mario's obvious question. "We are planning to use the insider information we possess to wheedle our way into control of the pack. We only have one more in our group to put in place for everything to be set. We can't be rocking the boat amongst ourselves or causing attention to fall on us from the pack while were still trying to put every piece into place. Do you really want to be responsible for the alliance's plan failing because you got hung up on a lone female wolf?"

Good, Wilson's wolf commented. *Now the blame will shift on to Mario shoulders if things go sideways with either Emma or the plan. He'll make a good scapegoat if anything goes wrong now that he has so formally campaigned against you.*

Randy was looking warily between Wilson and Mario. Suddenly trying to decide whether he had really picked the best position for himself. Mario on the other hand hadn't seemed to have caught on to the threat in that statement the way Randy had. Instead, the larger man took one step forward, balling his hands into fists and growled.

"If this plan of yours fails, it will be because you took too long to implement it. Subtlety is not the best form of leadership. Sometimes blunt force is the only way to get things done." Mario stood still a second, purposefully looming over Wilson.

Wilson wasn't intimidated. He was fairly certain Randy wouldn't step in if a fight ensued and between Jerry, Wallace, and himself they could take Mario if he attacked. So instead he just stood there looking at Mario blankly until the other man looked away and continued to growl as he stormed out of the warehouse, Randy hot on his heels.

The three of them were silent for several minutes. They all wanted to make sure the other men were gone completely before speaking.

"He's going to be a problem," Wallace announced as he moved to stand next to Wilson instead of behind him.

"Agreed." Wilson nodded. "Can you track down just how many people agree with this assessment? I doubt Mario has a following other than Randy. We need to do some preemptive moves before he starts jeopardizing our plan at large."

Wallace inclined his head before clasping his hands. "Done." He then pivoted and headed out of the warehouse.

"What is his obsession with the female wolf? To be fair, a lone dominant female wolf would be a boon to our group and may convince several lone wolves that are on the fence to join us once they hear about it. But this aggression he's feeling doesn't add up," Jerry commented. Wilson pivoted so he could look at the other man.

"I don't get it either. Do some research on her, I've gathered enough to know that she's come from the Central Washington pack, or at least she was a lone wolf in their territory before moving here. And that's only based on the copy of her resume I could get ahold of. From what I know of Alpha Peters, I can't imagine him tolerating a lone wolf, let alone a dominant one, living in his territory. Maybe she managed to live under his radar but I don't know. Find out what you can and get back to me."

Jerry was a private investigator in his everyday life, which came in handy more than once. The older man nodded his salt and pepper head before he too left the warehouse.

Keep your focus. Don't let this intriguing she-wolf distract you, his wolf chastised. *Perhaps it's time to check in with our men positioned within the pack. See if they can't do a little snooping on a certain female lone wolf and what is known about her within the pack. With any luck there will be nothing.*

Wilson muttered his agreement with his wolf and made a mental note to reach out to the three men that hadn't been at the meeting tonight, as they were pretending to be good little pack members and they didn't want their covers blown. He would have to be discreet about it but he was sure he'd be able to get a hold of each of them before the weekend was out.

Emma would be an asset, to a point. But Colin was also right. There was no reason to waste too many resources on trying to recruit her. He would keep at it, keep being there in case she needed a friendly shoulder to lean on when Ethan and his pack came calling as Wilson knew they would. He would be there, adding to that frustrated fire he knew would grow within her once they started to meddle in her life. He would be there to stoke the flames that would be necessary to get her to join in their little rebellion.

Chapter 33:
In Over Your Head

Emma

Emma was a bundle of nerves all day Friday. Though she was feeling much better, she still wasn't at one hundred percent. She couldn't stop the little voice of doubt in the back of her mind that said even at one hundred percent there was no way she'd be able to help the young werewolf Keegan talked about.

Stop doubting our power. Just because it's new doesn't mean it's faulty. You and I can both feel the power growing within you every day. We are merely catching up for lost time. I have total faith that once you are used to using it, the pain and struggle that comes along with it will subside and the recovery time will lessen.

Emma didn't share her wolf's confidence. And it wasn't simply because she had never been a confident person, outside of the classroom, but she'd never met an Omega before. She didn't know what their powers entailed, and it seemed like the closest, straightest path to disaster to assume she could do anything.

That meant the nerves got her so much Friday that by the time Keegan was knocking at her door, Emma hadn't eaten more than some cottage cheese and a banana. Her wolf chastised her throughout the day that being low on nutrition was not going to help her get things done. But that hadn't convinced her stomach that eating was the best idea.

Giving the large bun piled on top of her head one last pat to make sure it was securely in place, Emma strode to the door and opened it. Keegan stood on the other side in dark jeans and a black fitted T-shirt. Though not a look Emma generally went for, on Keegan it was pleasantly appealing. She couldn't help the little thrill that went through her at the dark, fit image he made standing in her doorway.

He gave her a small hesitant smile, "So, you still up for this?" There was no judgment in his tone. Just the pure question.

Emma really appreciated that. She wanted to push herself to help this young girl. She asked Raelene for more information on the situation, so she wasn't walking in blind. With everything Raelene had shared, she was even more convinced that she needed to help this poor young wolf. She was pushing herself to get better all week to help this little girl.

"Let me grab my purse and I'll be ready." She made a motion for him to come in while he waited.

While inclining his head, he held the door open for himself and took a step toward her. Emma let go of the door and walked across the living room to where she dropped her large black leather purse. When she swung it over her shoulders and walked back towards Keegan, she could smell a spicy scent he must use as either a body wash or cologne.

Don't lie to me and tell me that isn't a pleasant smell. Her wolf growled happily.

Of course it is, it's ridiculously pleasant, but that doesn't mean I'm going to act on it. I don't know this guy and I'm not exactly in a situation where I should be making moves on anyone. But I don't know why I'm just now smelling it.

Because you can grow a little nose blind in a classroom full of smells. And now that he's in your domicile the difference in scent is noticeable. And I believe your senses are getting sharper along with your strengthening power.

Swallowing that information so she could investigate it later, when she wasn't trying to concentrate on helping a young girl, Emma smiled at Keegan, "Honestly, I'm not one hundred percent, but I'm as ready as I'm going to get." Taking a deep breath Emma headed out the still open door. "All right let's do this."

"What, no coat?" Keegan commented as he held the door wider so she could walk past him out into the hall.

Emma snorted as she rolled her eyes. "Look who's talking. You're not wearing one either. And it doesn't get as cold over here as it does in the other parts of the state so to me it's still a little too warm and I don't really own any light jackets."

Werewolves tended to run hot anyway, making light jackets kind of obsolete. But when you lived in an area where it snowed a lot you bought the snow jacket, even if it might be too warm, so that you'd fit in with your human neighbors. Nothing says werewolves might be real like a bunch of crazy people walking around in negative degree weather as if it was nothing.

She locked the door behind them and the two of them walked downstairs in silence. There was no talking once they got in the car and Emma could feel the silence was awkward. There was a sort of nervousness to it she didn't quite understand.

Have things gotten worse with the young girl? Had something changed?

Only one way to find out, she muttered to her wolf.

"All right, since you've become such a lively conversationalist, tell me about this girl." She'd received the basic information but in case there was something Raelene missed from CJ or something had changed, she felt it was a safer topic to broach.

"She just turned fifteen. Started making changes from human to werewolf at fourteen. There were no urges or quiet changes. It was as if the entire process hit her full on at once. She can't control when she changes. She's had to stay home from school because she'll wake up from a nightmare and be partially changed and her body can't quite figure out how to change itself back. Her wolf seems as panicked as she is. When she's in wolf form, she can't really run with the pack like the older adolescents do, even though most are between sixteen and eighteen. Her wolf is so panicked by its early changes that it doesn't know what to do.

"Other than giving her sedatives or bandaging her up we're not sure how to help her other than keep her safe until the changes balance themselves out. But it's been three months now, and she hasn't shown a single sign of improvement. To say the poor girl is depressed and fatigued is an understatement. We're hoping since you were able to calm Barry's wolf that maybe you can help this girl. Even if you can just make the changes easier or you can rationalize with her wolf, it would help. Really anything to in any way improve the situation would be great."

There was silence again, and this time it was less awkward but much sadder.

Emma herself had been a late bloomer. Her first full complete change from human to wolf had been when she was almost nineteen. It wasn't a completely unheard of age but she was the last one in her friend group to make said change. Everything had come on slow for her and then she had started dating Richard at twenty-two. She'd always figured because she was such a submissive wolf the fact that her growth seemed to halt meant she was done. Now she was believing that her wolf was right. That somehow being with Richard, or something Richard did, stunted her growth. She was in her mid-twenties and she should be a fully solidified Omega wolf, not just learning her craft. But part of her still struggled to believe that Richard knew about her abilities and bought her a necklace for the express reason of quieting her power. But she had given it a lot of thought and there was no other explanation.

Shaking her head, Emma cleared her thoughts away from herself and focused more on the poor child. It'd been rough being a late bloomer, but she understood having powers come at you all at once would be much worse. Her Omega powers had been the same way, so while she felt for the young girl from her own experience, she knew that the change from human to werewolf was much more daunting than from werewolf to Omega. What Vicki was going through was several times rougher than what Emma herself was doing.

They sat in silence another ten minutes and Emma and her wolf discussed how they could help this little girl. They were really just spit balling ideas since they wouldn't know what they would find until they met Vicki. But then her wolf brought up a good point.

We still don't know what kind of deal they're going to be offering us. What exactly they're going to give you for helping.

Honestly, I would rather help her with nothing in return. She's a young woman being tortured. If there's anything we can do, we should do it.

Her wolf growled and stepped forward from the recesses of her mind so her full large body was in view. *I understand your need to help a young pup but at the same time she is a pack wolf and without some kind of agreement about you helping them you are one step closer to joining the pack. Pack does favors for pack without compensation. Those outside the pack do it for other reasons. Unless you are prepared to officially join the Seattle Pack, I suggest you get those details out of the way first before going in to see the little girl. We don't want you to get attached to her and end up helping her before you even get the chance to sign an agreement.*

Her wolf was chastising her, and she knew it, so Emma gritted her teeth to stop herself from getting into an argument with her furry other half. *Fine. I'll ask about the agreement ahead of time.*

Her wolf nodded as if satisfied but didn't step back into the shadows of her brain. As if she didn't trust Emma to follow through on her word. That perturbed Emma a bit, but she said nothing.

"My wolf and I would like to know exactly what this agreement is before we agree to set foot in one of the pack buildings to help this little girl." It was a bit of an exaggeration but she wanted to keep up the dominant wolf persona for as long as she could.

She watched Keegan's fingers flex on the steering wheel as his brows creased slightly before smoothing out again. "My understanding is that the pack will owe you a favor of your choosing. While I don't know the details, my understanding is that they purposely made it open-ended just in case helping Vicki required more mental work than any of us anticipated."

Emma didn't like the idea of not exactly knowing what was in that agreement. It made her wonder whether they sent him for her because they had a tenuous connection more than because he had any real standing in the pack. It was an idea worth chewing on and she kept one eye on him for the rest of the drive as the two of them sat in silence watching the city streets pass by them.

Chapter 34:
Are We in Agreement?

Emma

Emma didn't know what she was expecting from the Seattle pack house but this wasn't it. The pack house in Central Washington, where Richard grew up and his parents still lived, was a mansion with the huge property and several tiny homes dotting said property so others can live on site if need be. This pack house however was a full-fledged property. They had driven out of Seattle heading southeast. They had gone on for quite a while, though she didn't know how much of that was how far they went versus the rush-hour traffic they were stuck in. They were on the road just over an hour when they approached a large gate and

Keegan gave his name, after rolling down the window. The two men in the small guardhouse pressed some button, and the gate opened. As they came up to the main building, it was distractingly large. It looked like one of those country estates she would've seen in a Victorian English movie. She could see three other buildings around it, much larger than the half a dozen tiny homes the Central pack had. There was a lot of money and wealth that went into this house and Emma knew she was gawking. She couldn't make out which part of the building was administrative in which was where the family lived. It was overwhelmingly large.

Remember every step we take. Just in case. I don't want to rely on anyone else to get us out of the building.

Her wolf's words were sobering. Instead of taking in the beauty of the surrounding view, Emma's veins ran cold. Her wolf was right. She needed to know exactly how to get out of this place, just in case. She wanted to believe Raelene wouldn't belong to a pack that would trap people, but she knew firsthand that just because those at the lower levels of the pack didn't know something was happening didn't mean it wasn't happening.

She fought to keep her face as neutral as possible now that her thoughts turned. No need to show Keegan what she was actually thinking.

"Shall we?" he asked as he pulled his keys out of the ignition.

Emma gave only a nod as a response and opened the passenger door to exit. The air was crisp and she could smell werewolves on the property but she couldn't exactly pinpoint where they were. Along with a light breeze there was a soft crispness to the air letting her know that even though the November air wasn't exactly too cold now, the kinder weather wouldn't last much longer.

She watched Keegan step around the car and wait for her. When she was in line with him, he motioned toward the front doors to the left of them on the circle drive. The two of them walked quietly, the anxiety and tension between them increasing. Emma didn't know whether she was imagining it, projecting her own tension on

Keegan, or whether he was feeling it as well. They walked up to the door and Keegan opened it for her. Inclining her head, she walked in and made a mental note that the door hadn't been locked. Apparently, the Seattle pack believed so much in their own security they didn't feel the need to lock their doors. It was weird, but she supposed if you had werewolves guarding the property you had to figure that no one that made it this far in was going to be a problem. There was a large half circle of a front room done in dark reds, golds, with wood everywhere. There were three large hallways, one leading to the left side of the building, one leading straight ahead toward a long hallway or up a staircase, and then the last to the right.

"To the left. We're going to go by the Alpha's office first." Keegan moved in front of her but was still slightly turned as if he wanted her to walk beside him instead of following.

It was weird as she was used to following behind people, but she tried not to show it. She also tried not to show her nervousness at going straight to the Alpha. Meeting the Alpha of any pack was not a little thing. Unless a pack was small, you can enter a pack's territory and be there quite a while before ever interacting with the Alpha. They were often fairly busy in larger packs so the fact that he was troubling himself to meet with her either meant that this Vicki came from a very prominent family in the pack or that he might've taken a special interest in her as an Omega wolf. Either option wasn't entirely pleasing to think about.

Well, we'll know soon enough, her wolf commented, hunkering down in the front of her mind as if getting ready to spring forward into action if Emma needed her.

It was a weird sensation to feel her wolf crouching as Emma didn't know what the wolf thought she would do if they ran into a problem. Was the wolf expecting to change? Not letting herself get too distracted, she kept track of the way they walked. They went straight, then turned right at the end of the hallway. They passed three doors before they stopped and faced the outer wall on the left and Keegan knocked.

Emma was grateful it was a fairly straightforward way they'd made through the building and she wouldn't have to duck in and out of halls and curves should she have to leave quickly. A deep growl answered the knock from inside the room. "Come on in, Keegan."

She didn't know how to feel about the fact that whoever was in the room already knew who was at the door. She supposed if they were expecting them and the guards at the front gate called over it would make sense, but that didn't stop the nervous anxiety from spiking.

Easy there. We don't know what's happening yet. Just give it a chance, her wolf responded calmly, still ready to strike.

Keegan opened the door and before he stepped in, Emma got a view of two other men already in the room. One was the pack's second in command, though she couldn't remember his name. She followed Keegan into the room, trying to maintain her composure as best she could, which became a bit harder when Keegan shut the door behind her.

Her wolf growled inwardly at being trapped with three dominant wolves.

Her eyes scanned the room but landed on the shortest man. He was bulky but not large, and she was fairly certain shorter than six feet tall. He had auburn hair and was wearing a crimson WSU hoodie and giving her a polite smile. The second in command, Darian, was his name she believed, had a slight frown.

"Ah, so you are the Omega wolf, Emma. I have heard so little about you." The short man smiled, amused, and motioned to the chair on the closest side of his desk. "Please, sit. I would like to speak with you for a few minutes before putting you in a room with one of our most vulnerable."

His words made her think of a caring Alpha and that was definitely a point in his favor. But that didn't mean he owed her any allegiance. Sitting in that chair put her farther from the door and put her at a disadvantage since the three male dominant wolves in the room were all standing. Even in her own home, Emma would not have been comfortable sitting in a room full of standing dominant wolves.

With all the strength she could muster, trying to suppress the urge to obey an Alpha, Emma gave a tightlipped smile. "No thank you. I am not about to move farther from the door and be the only one sitting in a room full of dominant wolves. I'm not about to put myself at a distinct disadvantage. So, ask whatever questions it is you want to ask so we can sign an agreement and I can get to helping your young wolf."

Her wolf growled, full of pride and satisfaction.

It'd been more courage and confidence than Emma felt but she knew she had to fake it, these people didn't know, at least she didn't think they knew, exactly how submissive a Wolf she had been before coming here. Though it was getting easier, she still had to fight all of her ingrained submissive urges. She would just have to fake it until the confidence filled itself in.

The Alpha eyed her a moment before the left side of his mouth cracked open in a smile and if Emma wasn't mistaken, he looked impressed and pleased by her response.

"Very well, standing it is then. You've already met Darian and Keegan, and I'm Ethan. I am the Alpha of this pack. I'd like to start by thanking you for coming out here in the effort to help our young Vicki. What type of abilities do you have as an Omega wolf? What do you think you can do to help Vicki?"

Her wolf snarled a bit but didn't respond beyond that.

"At this point, I don't particularly know the extent of my abilities. I was a bit of a late bloomer and my abilities are growing rather rapidly. And I won't know if I can help her or in what way until I've had a chance to meet her in person. Everyone and their wolf is different so I can't guarantee anything."

He watched her thoughtfully. Emma bet he wasn't pleased with her answer but was gauging how he felt about the level of honesty she was sharing. "All right, I can appreciate that. Tell me though, if you're not willing to join our pack, which Keegan says you are adamant about, I'd like to know why that is and why you would be willing to sign an agreement with us if you're not willing to join us. I'd also like to know under what terms you left your other pack. While I could reach out to Alpha Peters and find out, I'd like to hear your side first."

He doesn't like Alpha Peters, her wolf observed.

Yeah, I caught that in his tone as well, Emma responded.

When Ethan said Alpha Peters' name, there was the briefest snarl. It was an interesting reaction and Emma made a mental note to watch his expressions closely as he spoke. Maybe the suspicion she and the others at the lower end of the pack had that Peters wasn't on the best terms with the Seattle pack were true. If that was the case, Emma couldn't help but wonder if that would benefit her or not. Could she be a bargaining chip to strengthen their relationship? Or would Ethan feel no allegiance to Peters and therefore be more likely to help her stay in his territory unscathed?

"You are correct in your thinking that I don't wish to join the pack. It's nothing about your pack in particular. Just packs at large." Emma chose her words very, very carefully to be sure not to offend anyone since she had never been good at physical fighting. And even if she had, odds weren't in her favor in the current situation. "Suffice it to say, I didn't leave the Central Washington pack on the best of terms because they and I disagreed on how much control the Alpha should have over my life and I have a sneaking suspicion over how I should use my Omega wolf abilities."

She watched as anger flashed through Ethan's eyes before his face became that peaceful pleasant blank again. "Were the terms of your leaving openly hostile?" There was something to his tone that told Emma there was more behind that statement, part of her wanted to ask but she didn't know how much rope she was going to be given.

Tread carefully, her wolf warned.

"I was given the ultimatum to mate with the Alpha's son or... No, it really wasn't a choice. And because I didn't want to do that, I ran." She was really laying her cards out on the table and hoping Raelene was right, that Ethan was a different Alpha than Peters.

She could smell the anger flashing from all three of the men. That it was strong enough, even though the office wasn't exactly big, for her to smell it told her exactly how they felt about that arrangement.

"You weren't given a choice? At all?" Darian's voice was a low growl from where he stood across the room from her.

She slowly turned her head to him before shaking it from side to side. "Not even remotely."

She heard the man growl and she could practically see the wolf inside his head causing that sound.

"I assure you that's not how we run things here. But I can understand why you wouldn't believe me on that front." With his words, Emma's attention drew back to Ethan. "I assume that means you would prefer we not tell the Alpha of your whereabouts?"

Did saying yes put her at a disadvantage? Emma didn't know. Would that mean she owed the pack of favor if they kept her secret? Emma wasn't good at politics and wasn't used to having any kind of leverage, which she didn't really have in this situation, anyway.

"I would prefer he not know," was all she said. Stating a preference versus asking the favor.

Ethan watched her appraisingly for what felt like a full minute before he nodded and tapped the legal sized paper on his desk. "This is the agreement we would like to come to for your help with Vicki. Please read over it and sign if you agree. There are two copies and you will see that I have already signed both. One is your copy and one is ours."

Surprised by the subject change, Emma blinked a few seconds before stepping forward to lean over the desk. It meant putting her back to Keegan and moving Darian almost out of her eyesight which neither she nor her wolf liked. But she figured she had to show some sign of trust if they were going to be in some kind of agreement with each other. Hoping for the best, Emma leaned over the desk and began reading the four-page document in front of her.

Chapter 35:
Lost Little Girl

Emma

It's a prison, Emma's wolf growled as Emma looked around the sub-basement the three pack wolves led her to.

While Emma would never agree out loud, it was the only word that came to mind. At the base of the stairs, the room opened to a semi-circle with three doors on each side of a hallway that jutted back directly across from the stairs. Emma could see from where she stood that down the hallway all pretense had been given up, there were bars jutting out instead of the internal doors she could see in the semi-circle.

She must not have hidden the distaste as well as she would have liked because Keegan spoke from next to her a second later. "We do not bring our brothers and sisters down here unless there is no other choice. Please believe me when I say this is not where we would put Vicki if we could think of any other option."

Unsure of whether she could keep her thoughts to herself, Emma measured each word carefully and through gritted teeth. "Which one is she in?"

All three male wolves bristled, Emma could feel it. Her budding Omega abilities enhancing her werewolf senses. But she couldn't bring herself to care.

Caging a fifteen-year-old girl. Who does that? she hissed to her wolf as her respect for Ethan wavered.

I don't know. Maybe she is a strong wolf or naturally dominant? Even as she spoke her wolf sounded unconvinced.

Darian moved to stand in front of her, motioning to the door closed to the left of them. He then walked toward the door, pulling out a key ring. As she focused on the door Emma could see five different locks spanning the top half.

Locked in? That can't be necessary! Emma commented to her wolf.

If this appealingly well-functioning pack does this to their out of control young, what do you think Alpha Peters does? her wolf countered.

It was a thought Emma didn't want to consider. *Maybe they are not as well functioning as they appear?*

Maybe, but my point still stands, her wolf countered as she settled into a more comfortable position as both she and Emma moved their concentration to the door.

When the last lock disengaged with an audible click, Darian opened the door excruciatingly slow. He'd positioned himself directly in the doorway, as if expecting an attack and trying to make himself the target. After several beats he stepped aside, opening the door wide so the others could see the room.

The room was so unexpected, Emma blink several times before her brain processed what she was seeing. The light in the room came from one recessed bulb in the ceiling. The only furniture was a large pillow, which Emma assumed was a dog bed and a heavily cushioned folding chair. A thin, petite brunette sat in the chair looking up at them expectantly from over the e-reader she held.

Is this the girl who has so little control over her changes that she is a danger to herself? Emma asked her wolf, unsure of what she was seeing.

It appears so. We should get closer to get a better read on her though.

Despite her wolf's words Emma didn't move from where she stood outside the room. What she was seeing was so off from what she thought would be on the other side of the door that she was at a loss what to do next.

"I'm not tired yet, Darian. I think I have another hour or two before you have to take the chair away," the young girl said, her eyes not leaving the man holding the door.

"I know Vicki," Darian responded gently. "But I have that Omega wolf we talked about here with me to see if she can help you."

Emma's heart broke a little when Vicki's attention shifted to her. The girl watched her appraisingly, but there was a sliver of hope in her eyes.

I really hope we can help her, Emma commented to her wolf.

Her wolf only made a rumbling noise in agreement.

Forcing one foot in front of the other, Emma brushed passed Darian and knelt in front of the girl. Vicki watched her move warily.

"I'm going to be honest with you, Vicki. I've never tried to do this before. So I don't know how much help I'm going to be." Emma watched the young girl frown. But she continued on. "I think the best way for you and I to communicate is to be completely honest and open with each other. I don't want to lie to you and promise you some kind of miracle and let you down. I'm going to try the hardest I can to help you, though. But only if that's okay with you, I don't know how much of a choice you were given in this, but I will not do anything unless you tell me it's okay first."

Emma could feel the indignant responses from the three men behind her, but she ignored them. Vicki was who she needed to concentrate on. Even though it meant ignoring the threat the three dominant wolves could pose, something in her knew she needed to put all of her attention and focus on helping Vicki.

The younger woman looked at her more curious now as if Emma's words hadn't been something she expected. Then after a beat or two she smiled thinly. "I'm up for whatever is going to help. It'd be nice to get a good night's sleep more often than once every other week."

Emma's heart hurt again but she pushed it aside and concentrated on the young girl's words. "Is that when you have trouble? When you're sleeping?"

Vicki glanced past Emma, and she knew she was looking at the dominant wolves in her pack for permission to tell Emma whatever it was she was going to say. She must've gotten some sort of affirmation from the men behind Emma because when she looked back at her Vicki almost looked relieved. "It's worse when I'm tired. It's like I can't control it unless I can give it my full concentration. If I am at all agitated, sleepy, or upset, the wolf takes hold. And sometimes it's not a big deal but most of the time it's like my wolf is angry or scared because it lashes out at other people and things. Not to mention if I get super embarrassed at school I sometimes turn partially fuzzy, you know?"

Emma simply nodded as the young girl spoke and waited until she was sure Vicki was done before she held out her hands, palms up onto the young girl's knees. "If you put each of your hands in mine, it'll be a little bit easier for me to connect with your wolf. Once I've connected the first time, it's easier for me to connect again." Emma didn't know why she thought being able to touch Vicki's hands would help but instinctively she knew it. Whether it was because she was becoming more in tune with her powers or because she was still recovering from the incident with Barry, she didn't know.

Vicki closed the cover over the e-reader she'd been holding and slid it into the side of the chair next to her before putting her hands into Emma's, palm touching palm.

Moving all of her focus, Emma concentrated on the young girls pale blue eyes. She wasn't quite looking into the eyes themselves but passed them. She felt her abilities snake up through her palms and up Vicki's arms, much like vines connecting them together. She saw Vicki's eyes widen in surprise momentarily but the younger woman didn't remove her hands. Once those vines reached over Vicki shoulders and up her neck, there was an almost audible snap as the dark place where Vicki's wolf lived came into focus. The pale gray wolf looked malnourished and frightened out of its wits.

Are you all right? When the wolf's attention pivoted to her the cowering stopped in the hair raised across its body as it lunged and snapped at her. Emma was sure she let out an audible yelp but didn't let go of Vicki's hands.

Oh this won't do it all. Her wolf growled and an additional push of power flowed through her and into Vicki as a projection of her wolf stood in front of Vicki's growling one. Emma's wolf was larger by far and more dominant than Vicki's wolf.

Emma's wolf snarled at the young one and snapped her jaw at it several times, not lunging but making the aggressive nature of her feelings known.

The younger wolf lunged and snarled again and Emma's wolf sidestepped before lunging herself and grabbing the scruff at the back of the young wolf's neck, shaking it several times, clamping its strong jaw. Not enough to hurt but enough to warn. Vicki's wolf went limp and Emma's wolf waited several beats before dropping the young pup. The Omega took two steps back, ready to lunge again if needed, but the young wolf stayed on the floor in defeat, not moving.

You will not be attacking us again. Do you understand?

The younger wolf let out a whimper and turned its head to look at both Emma and her wolf.

Emma knew the other wolf wasn't injured but she couldn't help the pang of guilt at making the wolf submit like that.

Her wolf took several steps back and disappeared from view and Emma felt the power recede into her head again as the projection moved back into her brain. She hadn't even been aware that her wolf could jump – she could think of no other word for it – into somebody else's head but she didn't have the time to marvel at it.

Young wolf, can you tell me why you are struggling with the change so much? Emma asked in the most soothing tone she could manage.

The young wolf looked at her sorrowfully but didn't respond.

Vicki's inner monologue answered on the wolf's behalf.

She can't talk. Is she supposed to talk? The girl's voice was so distant and quiet Emma wasn't sure the girl was entirely present within the place where her wolf was.

Vicki? Keep talking to me in your head? You can talk about anything. Describe the book you're reading. I'm going to come find you. Don't worry if that doesn't make sense.

Oh, okay, um, I'm reading a book about a woman who's a soldier in the middle of a battle. She's injured and blacks out. When she comes to the entire crew is gone and her ship is on course for a planet she's never heard of. All she knows is that it's a different direction than where they're supposed to be headed.

Emma moved, drowning out Vicki's actual words.

Are you thinking there is something separating them? Emma's wolf asked quietly from inside her own head.

I don't know. I'm wondering if there's some kind of disconnect between her and her wolf that makes it impossible for them to communicate. Or at least difficult for them to do so. That lack of communication or connection might be what's causing them problems.

Emma felt herself floating out of the cave the wolf was in. Vicki's wolf didn't move from where it lay on the floor. The blue eyes that matched Vicki's watched as Emma floated up and through the ceiling of the cave. It was pitch black and though Emma could feel that she was moving somewhere in Vicki's subconscious, she couldn't see a thing but continued toward the drone of Vicki talking about the book she was reading.

Then out of nowhere, Emma let out a hiss. She wasn't sure whether she had done it inside or outside of her head. There'd been a scrape against her back and when she made herself stop moving and turn she reached out hesitantly and felt something sharp. Carefully moving around the sharp point, she felt up to what appeared to be a thorn. Beyond it felt like a plant. It felt like the blackberry bushes that had grown thick and wild on the edge of her grandmother's property growing up.

What is this? she said with awe as she continued to touch and felt a second spike a few inches away.

I honestly don't know, her wolf answered. *Try pushing against it with your abilities and see if you can make it budge.*

Unsure whether this was a good idea, Emma pushed it tentatively and while it had some give, it slid right back into place. The vine felt thick. She could wrap both of her hands around it, in between the thorns, and barely feel her fingers from the other hand on the backside. The vines seem to have grown completely over the dark cave that Vicki's wolf lived in. Emma reached her entire arm span but couldn't find the end of it.

There's an actual barrier between them. I'm surprised her wolf is surviving at all.

What if it isn't her wolf that's trapped? What if it's the girl? After all, she has less control over her body.

Her wolf's words were a frightening thought. So Emma didn't respond.

Instead, she placed both hands around one section of the barrier, curling her fingers and trying to avoid the scrape of the sharp spikes, though several thorns had gotten her while she explored. Grabbing her energy deep in her chest, she pushed the power through her hands and in to the vine-like barrier less than a foot from her face. Emma felt her hands get hot and the more she pushed at it the more she felt the vines give. Almost as if her hands were some kind of food processor and she was turning the barrier into mush, at least the branch like strand she was holding. She could almost feel the pieces melting away between her hands as she continued to push toward that barrier.

Then one of the thorns fell instead of melting and sliced across her face before hitting her shoulder and bouncing off. The pain surprised her so much Emma pushed away, scraping her other hand on the thorn next to it. But she pushed past the pain, putting her hands wider and pushed all her power into each of her hands, widening the hole she had created. Then she moved to the next branch, slowly moving her hands to not get pricked. This time she put her hands out in front of her and up so that if something fell, it wouldn't slice her face again. Now that she knew approximately what to do, she forced her power into her hands again and again there was initial pushback but eventually the plant between her hands gave way and crumbled. Emma repeated the process a dozen more times until she had created a hole big enough that she could pass through without scratching any of the plants.

    She was getting exhausted. She could feel her body draining, and though she wanted to work on getting more of that area cleared, she did not know how big the barrier was and she didn't know how far off she would have to go to find Vicki within the girl's own head. The last thing she wanted to do was use up all of her energy breaking that barrier if there were other challenges ahead of her.

She didn't have to float for much longer as Vicki's voice got louder and louder as Emma eased her way passed the barrier. Then after another minute or two she saw an image of Vicki standing on a stage, waving her arms back and forth as she described something. Emma knew the second Vicki saw her because she stopped speaking and her eyes lit up.

How did you get here? Vicki asked in amazement.

Honestly, I'm not sure.

As she stepped closer to Vicki, the young girl frowned. *You're bleeding. What happened?*

Trying not to think too much about the worry in the young girl's words, Emma reached out the hand with minor scratches to Vicki. *I need you to take my hand. I'm going to take you to your wolf.*

The young girl looked at her hand warily for almost a full minute before jumping off the stage and putting her hand in Emma's.

Emma walked them away from the stage until the area was inky black again. She wasn't entirely sure she could get back to where the wolf was, as she had been following Vicki's voice before but now she had no tether to head toward.

Wolf, I need you to howl. Howl for me and I will bring your girl to you, Emma yelled at the top of her lungs hoping the noise would resonate throughout the young girl subconscious and get the wolf's attention. She felt Vicki stiffen, but she didn't let go of her hand. Clearly the young girl trusted her enough that she would not be put in danger. There were several long quiet seconds and Emma thought she might have to navigate her way back to that barrier with no reference point but then the wolf howled.

It was quiet at first and hesitant but then it grew to a long note and Emma felt herself smile. *Good job, wolf! Keep it up until you see us,* she yelled, louder this time to be heard over the howl.

Once she finished speaking, the howl seemed to get louder as if the wolf had grown in confidence. She gave Vicki a reassuring squeeze then headed toward the sound. She moved faster this time, knowing that until they reached the barrier there wasn't a lot of things that could get in their way. Once she felt something solid hit her shoe, she stopped abruptly and turned to where she knew Vicki was, even though she couldn't see her.

There's a barrier here with thorns. I created a small hole that's big enough for us to go through side-by-side but that's about it. So we need to be careful. Squeeze my hand if you heard me.

The last bit she tacked on, not entirely sure if this oppressive darkness muffled sound. She was relieved when there was a squeeze. Emma concentrated on moving her feet slowly back and forth. It turned out that they hadn't approached the barrier exactly where the hole had been, meaning she somehow had gotten off her original path to finding Vicki. Her foot got stuck on several thorns and she considered herself lucky her shoes somehow manifested in Vicki subconscious. Without them she was sure these astral feet would hurt as well. It took several slow, painstaking minutes, but she found the edge to the hole.

Be very careful, Vicki. Grab my shoulders and go through the hole right where I'm going through it.

She waited as she felt Vicki get closer and the hand that wasn't holding hers grabbed her arm. A few inches at a time Vicki crossed her shoulders until her arms were around Emma's waist and then she wrapped her legs around Emma's waist making herself into a backpack. Normally the weight would've been too much for Emma but with the almost weightless quality to Vicki subconscious the girl couldn't have been more than five or ten pounds of extra weight.

Emma guided her feet, so she aimed for the middle of the hole. She was fairly certain with Vicki sitting on her like a backpack the two of them would fit easily but she worried some of the barrier grew back.

She went through as slowly as her astral self would go. Not stopping until she was positive both she and Vicki made it through the barrier.

All right, I think it's safe, she told Vicki, and she stopped and waited for the young girl to slowly move back to holding hands.

Moving much faster this time, Emma headed straight for the cave like structure where she knew Vicki's wolf was. It was directly below the hole so there was less navigating to do. Within moments, she and Vicki stood holding hands in front of the baying wolf.

When the wolf saw them, its front paws danced and it let out less of a howl and more of a happy sound at Vicki.

Aww. Letting go of Emma's hand, Vicki walked over to the practically prancing creature.

Is this your first time seeing each other? Emma asked, watching the girl reach up and hug the scruff around her wolf's neck.

The wolf was only a few inches shy of Vicki's own height. Making Emma wonder whether both girl and wolf were malnourished.

Yes, I've never seen her before. I didn't know I could. Is this something you did?

No, Emma responded frowning. *You should be able to communicate with your wolf just about from the get go. I don't know what that barrier was between you and your wolf but it shouldn't be there. I'm going to have to do some research to find out why. But hopefully the fact that the two of you can communicate with each other now will help. But you and I are going to have to meet like this several times so I can erode away at that barrier you have.* Emma looked up as she spoke. Even though she couldn't see the barrier from where she was, now that she was aware of it she could reach out with her power and feel that it enclosed the space. Emma was grateful that the hole she'd made didn't seem to be regrowing.

Looking back at the girl and her wolf Emma smiled, relieved that in some way she could help. *I don't know how long you can stay in this area with your wolf. But at least now you can travel back and forth and in and out of that hole I made to see each other. Just be careful of the thorns. This place where your wolf lives is deep in your subconscious and you're not made to stick around here. Visiting once in a while, sure. Reaching out to your wolf and seeing that it's here is normal, but if you stay in here too long, you'll become comatose on the outside. I need to make sure you are able to get out again before I leave and report to those on the outside.*

The girl pulled away from her little wolf looking sad before letting go and nodding to Emma. *But I'll be able to talk to her now, right?*

Yes, I believe so. You might have to talk a little loud to get through the barrier but yes. Do you remember where the hole is so you can get out again?

Vicki nodded. *I think so.*

I'll come with you and see if I can't make it a little larger. This is your subconscious, so if you can find a way to mark it somehow that would be wonderful.

Vicki looked at her in concentration, as if trying to figure out some way to edit her own inner world to get them what they needed. *Glow-in-the-dark chalk!* Vicki concentrated on her hands and in a few seconds, a large stick of glow-in-the-dark chalk appeared and Vicki grinned in triumph.

Emma wasn't sure whether that would work but since they were talking about the girl's own imagination and subconscious, she would not question it. So again the two of them floated up to where that hole was and once Emma found one edge, she grabbed the inside of the hole and concentrated her power on it, moving her hands slightly around the side in a half circle motion, melting away the edges. Since she wasn't melting a new branch but was in fact only expanding the hole it went faster this time.

The first couple of tries she pushed out farther than she'd meant to and ended up having to move herself forward just to reach the edges again. She kept working until she could feel her power depleting and a headache forming. Even then, she pushed past the headache until it turned into a full-fledged migraine before dropping her arms and moving away from the hole. She looked back to see Vicki had drawn thick lines with her glow-in-the-dark chalk, that had somehow now become something closer to a highlighter than a piece of chalk. She stood on the opposite end of the hole as Emma, tracing as Emma relaxed. The hole was now the size of an average bedroom and Emma was shocked by how much she had melted away after creating the original hole. She watched in silence as Vicki traced the hole twice over on either side of the barrier, creating thick bright lines.

Vicki smiled broadly down at Emma as she finished tracing the circle on the outside of the barrier. *Thank you! I think this is going to make a big difference. At least I hope.* She looked passed Emma, down in to the darkness where she now knew her wolf was. *I will be back to visit you later!*

Emma winced as Vicki yelled at the top of her lungs.

Okay, let's join the real world again. The sooner we get that taken care of the sooner I can get back and spend time with her.

The joy Emma heard in the young girl's voice sent a pang through Emma's chest. She couldn't imagine what it would be like to not have been able to communicate with her wolf.

We did it before, her wolf reminded her bitterly of the time she was with Richard.

But that wasn't our most formative years, Emma countered.

While her wolf didn't respond, Emma could feel her wolf's begrudging agreement.

Chapter 36:
Going Weak in the Knees

Emma

Emma watched as the young girl floated back and out of sight. She didn't sense any distress, so she wasn't concerned about anything happening to Vicki once she lost sight of her. But that left her alone, in the dark, floating above the brambles with nothing but the voice of her wolf to keep her company.

How the heck am I going to get out of here?

If I had to guess, came her wolf's calm tone, as if her furry companion was standing beside her, though Emma knew she wasn't, *I would say it's going to be much like waking from a dream. Just make yourself wake up.* Emma could practically hear a shrug in her wolf's voice.

Okay. She closed her eyes. Which made her feel a little silly since it was completely dark around them, but she wanted to focus and closing her eyes was the easiest way to do that.

Emma concentrated on remembering when she was a young girl and could wake herself up from nightmares. It had been more than a decade since she tried, unsuccessfully; she knew she was going to be rusty but there weren't any other ideas floating around so she put all her might into it and yelled in her head, *wake up.* The same time as she forced her eyes open.

As her eyes opened, she slumped her shoulders forward. She was still in the dark abyss of Vicki's mind. Letting out a frustrated growl, she tried again. She could practically hear her own heart in her head as she forced her concentration. It was doing nothing to help the migraine she felt brewing.

Wake the hell up.

This time she threw her power behind it, like when she was clearing out the brambles from Vicki's head. Now when she opened her eyes, the world swam around her as her eyes registered she was back in that cell. Nausea rolled through her and her head pounded. She let her arms drop from Vicki, who was awake and grinning at her. Emma forced her face to blank before gently smiling back at the young girl, despite the discomfort in her stiff limbs and the pain in her head.

As Vicki looked past her, Emma slowly turned her head to glance at what the young girl was watching. Ethan, Keegan, and Darian stood nervously in the doorway behind them. Clearly trying to give them as much space as possible. Turning her head made the headache worse, and the world swam some more. Emma closed her eyes and turned back to Vicki.

The little girl still looked past her. "I think, I think she fixed it. Or at least started to. But it was actually really exhausting. Is there any way, maybe, I might take a nap or sleep in one of the guest rooms upstairs?"

Emma didn't need to be an Omega to sense the uncertainty and doubt from the three men behind her. But she didn't turn her head again to confirm.

After several long seconds, Ethan answered. "Yes, of course. Darian, will you take Vicki upstairs and get her settled, please?"

Vicki let out a very young squeal before standing up and wrapping her arms around Emma for a quick hug. "Thank you. I can never thank you enough." She gave another quick squeeze that had Emma shutting her eyes to fight the vomit from rising up her throat.

Luckily, Vicki let go and was heading toward the door and didn't seem to notice Emma never hugged her back.

There were a few more seconds and Emma heard footsteps walking away from the cell and Vicki chattering about what happened inside her head. Emma didn't move. She got the distinct impression that any kind of sudden movements and she would lose the contents of her stomach.

"Keegan, go get whatever medic is on duty." This time Ethan's voice held a lot of concern and seemed closer than it had before.

There was a shuffling of feet and this time the footsteps moved away a lot faster than the first two sets head.

He's moving toward you, her wolf warned.

"Are you all right? Is this going to be an emergency? Do I need to get a full-fledged doctor?" Though his voice was soft, the questions were clipped as Ethan's long strides ate the distance between them and he came into view in front of her.

Emma forced her vision to move upward so she could focus on his face. "I honestly don't know. My body is really stiff from however long I've been sitting like this. But I have a wrenching headache and I'm trying not to hurl."

One part of her wanted to maintain a sense of decorum and pretend that she had things much more together than she actually did, but she needed the correct medical attention more.

She heard several curses under Ethan's breath as he squatted down closer to her eye level. "Both of you sat here with your eyes closed for more than an hour. Keegan even stepped in to see if either of you registered the movement and neither of you did. I can imagine your body's pretty stiff. Once a medic is in here, they can check you out and get you the appropriate painkillers. Do you want to sleep it off? You're more than welcome to use one of our guest bedrooms."

"No." It came across much sharper than Emma intended. "Sorry, no. I'd rather go home." Finally closing her eyes again, Emma raised her hands so she could rub above her eyebrows to relieve the pounding.

A few seconds later, she heard the faint sound of the door opening and two sets of shoes pounding towards them. She heard Ethan stand up and walked toward the door.

After a few more seconds, Emma heard somebody kneel in front of her.

CJ, her wolf commented. Whether that was because her wolf could sense the medic or Emma had somehow unconsciously memorized his scent, she didn't know.

"Headache worse than last time, CJ. Almost twice as bad. Trying not to puke. And I guess I've been sitting here for an hour. Everything is really sore because I'm apparently too old to be doing that." Her voice was tired and worn even to her own ears.

"Gotcha. I figured you would at least get a similar headache as last time. So I already have a mini bottle of water and the same pills I gave you last time to help with the headache." There was a cracking noise. Emma was pretty sure it was a water bottle being opened. "If you can hold out your hands, I'll put the pills in one in the water bottle in the other and we can deal with that first."

Emma did as she was told and swallowed the pills and the swig of water in one quick motion. Her stomach rolled as the contents splashed down.

"I've got a shot I can give you that will be a more instantaneous pain reliever. It's incredibly strong, can be rather addictive, and will only last about half an hour. But it will at least make you mobile again until the other painkillers have kicked in. The ones you've already taken aren't as strong as the shot, so some of the pain will come back with a vengeance, but it won't be nearly as bad as it is now. Do you want to take the shot as well? With as fast as our metabolisms are, it is relatively safe to take both." That last part was tacked on as if CJ had almost forgotten about it.

"Yeah, just do it." She sighed. Still not opening her eyes, she let her hand drop to the floor and set the water bottle next to her.

There was more rustling in front of her, and then she felt him moving her sleeve up over her shoulder with one hand and the quick sting of a needle in her upper arm. It felt much like a tetanus shot, painful and sore. But considering the other pain she was feeling, it was next to nothing.

Emma knew it was silly to expect instant relief from the pain, but she had. Three seconds went by, then five, and she felt a cooling, soothing sensation radiate out from her arm until it coated the rest of her body. Her head stopped pounding and felt soothed. She let out a long ragged breath and opened her eyes, pleased to see the world didn't spin as she looked into CJ's dark green eyes.

"Thank you," she whispered.

He gave her a pitying look. "It's my job. But I'm sorry that helping us in this way takes such a toll on you. Part of me thinks you should stop doing us any favors if this is the outcome each time. You might also want to get checked out by a werewolf doctor to make sure there are no long term affects happening. Just to be safe."

It hadn't even occurred to her there would be long term negative effects to using her power at this high level.

You're going to be fine. We're doing what we were made to do. No need to concern yourself with yet another problem, especially one that isn't an issue, snapped her wolf.

Emma wasn't sure why she trusted her wolf to be speaking the truth. It seemed silly that the wolf would have any more knowledge than she did, but her wolf's words calmed her rising panic.

"Well, the hope is that it will always get easier." She smiled a little as she responded to CJ.

He let out a gruff noise that let Emma know he didn't agree with her assessment, but wasn't going to argue.

"Do you need help to get up?" Keegan as from somewhere behind her.

Her pride wanted to say no, but if she'd been sitting in this position for over an hour and her muscles were as upset as they had felt before the shot, then she was going to need it.

She maintained eye contact with CJ. "Will you help me up?" she asked quietly.

There was a flash to his face, and he looked over her shoulder, where she was sure Ethan and Keegan stood.

"Yeah, of course. Let's get you out of here." He stood then, sliding a messenger bag over his head and twisting it behind his back. He then leaned down and put his arm for her to grip.

Reaching out, she grabbed his arms right above his elbows, leaning forward as she did. Relieved to feel that although her muscles were tense, there wasn't the same pain and discomfort as she got up. Granted, she might end up regretting that sudden movement later.

She pushed her feet out onto the floor, separating her crossed legs, bending at the knee. Once she was in place, he began to lean back, pulling her on her feet. He did so slowly and carefully and she appreciated the care CJ provided in everything he did. Once she was on her feet, he wrapped one of his arms around her waist to help hold her weight, as her legs were a little wobbly.

When she turned to see Ethan and Keegan, she was confused by the sight in front of her. Keegan was frowning at her and CJ, clearly unhappy with something. And Ethan was looking at them all, rather amused.

She wasn't sure how to process that, so she ignored it. "CJ, can you take me somewhere that I can sit down for a bit until my legs get more accustomed to walking."

"Take her up to my office," Ethan responded before CJ could.

"Okay," CJ said quickly as the two of them began moving, steering a wide berth around Keegan, who had not moved from where he stood in the middle of the room.

While there wasn't a lot of pain in her legs, they were definitely weak. Wobbly, they went up the stairs, and about halfway up Emma realized neither Ethan nor Keegan were following them.

I wonder what they have to talk about.

My guess is they're wondering just how valuable you might be. I think we have to keep our wits about us. Her wolf's response sounded distracted and Emma found herself yet again wondering if her wolf could pay attention to things that Emma herself couldn't see.

She was grateful CJ didn't feel like talking, or wasn't pushing her to talk as they made their way up to the office. She liked CJ. She innately trusted him more than any of the other new pack wolves she'd met. Emma just knew CJ was good people. Even though she was attracted to Keegan and she was willing to bet he might be attracted to her, she didn't know how much trust she had in him. The more primitive part of her wasn't sure she wanted him helping her while she was weak.

It was a strange train of thought. One Emma wasn't sure now was the best time to be exploring. But maybe at some point, she would have to think long and hard about what her actual feelings were toward Keegan.

Chapter 37:
Tired and Untrustworthy

Emma

The large visitors' chairs in Ethan's office were deceptively comfortable. Not that Emma had a lot of Alpha offices to compare this with. But at home, she supposed it wasn't home anymore, Alpha Peters' visitor's chairs were incredibly uncomfortable. She'd been told once it was to keep people on edge when they visited him, making it clear his comfort was more important than theirs. She always wondered whether that was an insecurity on Alpha Peters' part or if it was simply an Alpha wolf thing. She supposed this cozy chair was the answer to that.

Emma was exhausted, so when CJ walked her into the room, gingerly lowering her into a seat, she didn't fight him. Though it was more of a power move to be standing, she didn't have the energy. Even with the majority of the pain gone, her muscles were still stiff, and she lacked the energy to do much more than stay awake. It'd been a relief when she heard CJ plop down in the other visitor's chair. The chairs were relatively close together, and she felt better about it being CJ who was that close to her. It also made her feel better about leaning back in the chair with her eyes closed. It was a sign of weakness and trust and that was not the sort of thing Emma, or her wolf, felt she should display in front of the foreign Alpha and Keegan.

"CJ, would you be able to take me home?"

The question was out before the thought had fully formed itself in her mind. But as the words crossed her lips, her wolf approved, and Emma felt a little bit of tension seep from her body. She felt curiosity waft off of him a moment before he cleared his throat.

"Yeah, sure. I can do that. I'm fairly certain Ethan will release me early now that Vicki seems to be doing a bit better and you clearly need someone to look after you."

He trailed off with those last words and a tiny part of Emma was curious, as it didn't sound like he had completed his thought. She wondered whether he was actually going to do so, but before he had the chance to decide himself, the door to the office opened. Emma snarled before anyone could see her, and she snapped her eyes open, leaning forward a little. It took much of the energy she still had in reserves, but the fewer signs of weakness she could show, the better Emma would feel about this interaction.

Good girl, her wolf commented.

"Sorry to have kept you waiting," Ethan said as he walked around the two visitors' chairs and sat down in his own larger office chair. "But now that we've seen your gift in action, and on to the point, the toll it takes on you, we're not sure the compensation initially agreed upon is going to be good enough."

That was a surprise to Emma. She couldn't imagine a scenario where Alpha Peters would consider paying someone for their services, or paying them more if he felt they were worth it. It seemed a very unalpha like gesture. The more time she spent around Ethan, the more she wanted to believe this attitude was more the norm and Peters was the outlier. Not wanting to give away her surprise or curiosity, she watched him with what she hoped was a blank expression.

Ethan frowned at her a little, clearly not seeing what he had expected. He pushed his rolling chair forward to clasp his hands on the desk. "I would like to double the fee from the contract. I'll have the new one printed up and ready for you to sign on Monday. As it is, your payment will be given to you before you leave, the part from our initial contract, that is. Then once the second new work contract is signed, the other half of the payment will be given to you." He leaned back, unclasping his hands, and moving to the armrest. "I have to admit, though, I'm a little confused. Keegan has informed me you are dead set against joining our pack. May I ask if that opinion still stands? And if so, does that mean you intend to join the noisemakers currently living in my territory who are dead set on dethroning me?" There was a biting threat as he spoke that second part that set Emma's teeth on edge.

Her wolf snarled in her head, but Emma fought it from showing on her face. "With all due respect, Alpha, I have no interest in joining any werewolf group, official pack or loose organization. I just wish to be left alone. If that is not something you can manage, then I can find somewhere else to live. I have no problem occasionally helping those that are in need and being compensated for it. But I do not wish our association to go any further than that." Emma mentally padded herself on the back for how neutral her tone was as she spoke, because inside of her head was a mixture of anger and fear. She didn't enjoy being put on the spot, especially after doing them a favor. But she also knew she was out right challenging the Alpha, something that someone of her rank had absolutely no place doing. It was a cold hard bluff that she prayed worked.

There was a flash of rage and surprise across Ethan's face before it stilled again. "If you do not wish to join us, and you do not join them, I believe we can come to an understanding as long as you live in my pack's territory. And as long as you agree to do paid favors for the pack, we will, in turn, extend a certain amount of protection toward you, in certain circumstances, should you need it. You would not be considered one of the pack. But if you had a problem with the unruly wolves making noise in my territory, we would be willing to step in on your behalf."

It was Emma's turn to flash a surprised expression, though she was sure she didn't bury it as fast as Ethan did. She was expecting anger, even aggressive behavior. But instead, he agreed to neutrality. Not even true neutrality but offering to help her, within reason, if she needed.

Nothing is in writing. An Alpha's word should count for something, but we've known Peters long enough to know that it doesn't. Just shake his hand and don't expect anything to come of it.

Her wolf's words stung and deep down Emma still hoped, still wanted to see the good in people. But her wolf was right.

She could rely on herself and a handful of friends. But no one else.

"I believe we have an understanding," she said in a soft tone as she stretched out her hand and Ethan shook it.

As their hands parted, he looked past her and CJ, where she was fairly certain Keegan stood at the back of the room next to the door. "Keegan, if you would be so kind as to act as escort...."

Emma didn't even let him finish his sentence. She waved the hand he'd just shook in a silencing motion to get his attention. "As long as it is all right with you, CJ has agreed to take me home. That way there is someone on hand if something health related comes up. Even if it is just to give me a ride home and not stick around, it would be much appreciated."

Ethan's eyes shifted toward her as she spoke and there was a curiosity there he didn't quite hide, but he smiled and nodded briefly before turning to CJ. "That is fine by me. Call one of your compatriots to come out and watch Vicki, just in case." His eyes shifted back to Emma. "It isn't that I don't trust that you were able to help Vicki. It is just prudent planning for contingencies." His tone was a little cold.

Emma slowly nodded her response, matching his indifferent tone as she made eye contact with him. "Yes, we have that in common."

It was a kind of threat, or promise, and they both knew it. He was saying he wasn't entirely sure whatever she had done worked. And she was saying she didn't trust him either. As friendly as Ethan was, and as accommodating as he seemed to be, there was something comforting to Emma to know the distrust she was used to was still there.

They all sat in silence for several beats before CJ pushed up from his chair and held his hands out to Emma. "Well, if that's it, I'm going to get her home and to bed. As it is, we're not going to make it in time for when the shot wears off. But the closer I can get to that, the better."

"Yes, of course. Ethan stood from his chair, but didn't come around his desk. "I will send somebody to you on Monday with the new contract and extra payment." He turned to CJ. "Parker should be around the front hall by the time you get there. He should have Emma's check."

Emma was super curious whether this Parker person was a butler of some kind and how exactly that worked. But she knew better than to open her mouth and start asking questions. So instead, she pulled herself up, using CJ's arms as leverage. Clearly, he had a lot of experience yanking people up without it looking as if they were not doing it on their own strength. The two of them walked around the chairs and out of the office. Keegan was careful not to make eye contact as they walked passed. But she could feel anger simmering around him. Something must've happened before he and Ethan had come upstairs.

As they walked down the hall, CJ, thankfully, didn't start up any kind of conversation with her. It left her mind wandering and thinking about Keegan. She felt a spark there. She knew she did. But she just got out of a serious long-term relationship that had her sense of reality doing a complete one-eighty. Now was not the time to be leaning into something new, no matter how attractive he was. Plus, with his standing in the pack, she didn't want to waive any flags that might get back to Richard and his horrible father. She also didn't know who she could trust. He seemed like a gentleman, but Vicki had been locked in a cell. Something about that made her not trust him, or Ethan. Her mind kept circling around until they reached the front of the building and a man in his early fifties, with close cropped gray hair, dressed in a black button up and black slacks, stood waiting for them. When they were a mere foot or two away, he held out an envelope to her.

"Your payment." His voice was deep, and if she wasn't mistaken, had a faint British accent.

Emma mumbled a thank you, took the envelope, and she and CJ headed out the door.

"I'm going to set you down on this bench near the door. I'm parked in the side parking lot and I don't think you should walk that if you don't need to." As he spoke, CJ slowly lowered her down on a wood slatted bench. He made sure she was relatively comfortable before dashing off around the left side of the building.

Left to her own thoughts, Emma continued to wonder about the situation she found herself in. Living in isolation was looking better and better. Much less complicated than this high-wire act between Ethan and Wilson wanting a war. She couldn't be somewhere where there was attention or might be a spotlight. It was the exact opposite of hiding, which was what she was here to do. She couldn't have some males swiping at each other telling that manipulative jerk of an ex-fiancé where she was. Making up her mind, Emma told herself as soon as she was feeling back to normal again, she would update her resume and start applying for jobs in Alaska, where she would be safe.

Chapter 38:
Your Hand is Showing

Keegan

"My friend, I am not so sure she reciprocates those feelings you're displaying, so please blank your face," Ethan chided when it is clear CJ and Emma are far enough down the hall not to hear him.

Keegan whipped his head around toward his Alpha from where he had been watching the other two slowly disappear around the corner. Before he could reply, Ethan's smile widened, and he walked around the desk.

"Her choice clearly offended you to have CJ take her home when you brought her here. I'm guessing this is some of the reluctance in what I read about earlier." He held his hand up in a stopping motion as Keegan opened his mouth again. "It's all right. She's very attractive and is definitely a wolf that can keep you on your toes. I think she would actually be good for you." He said the last part with a quirk of amusement on his face.

Keegan simply frowned at his Alpha. He wanted to snap at the man, but he knew making jokes was Ethan's way of releasing the tension he felt as his interactions with Emma were also not going as he planned. Though Keegan could have told him as much, as most of his interactions with Emma didn't go as planned.

He was at a loss though. Where Emma had always been sort of open to their interactions, once she finished with Vicki it was as if a wall had come down between them and he didn't know how to fix it or why it had appeared.

Before Keegan could say anything, Darian came striding down the opposite end of the hallway and pivoted into Ethan's office, closing the door behind him.

"Well, if her abilities look as promising as what she just showed, I can see why Alpha Peters wanted to keep it hush-hush and so desperately wants her back. I can't remember the last time I saw Vicki so happy and lighthearted." While Darian's voice conveyed how impressed he was, Keegan could see he was also concerned about the ramifications whenever Peters finds out exactly where the wolf he was looking for had gone.

Frowning, Ethan folded his arms across his chest. "I agree, I'm not sure I would want people knowing I had an Omega that powerful in my back pocket, unless I was sure that's where she was. Though the way he's going about it is clearly despicable. Her powers are incredibly promising. I've only met a handful of Omegas and while her powers are quite impressive, I haven't seen one similar to this before and she is clearly not in total control of all she has to offer. Which makes me a little sick, because I'm fairly certain Peters and that spoiled son of his planned on using her as some kind of weapon. I need to decide whether it is better to tell him she is here and we have no intention of giving her up against her will, or whether it's better to stay silent and hope he never finds out where she went.

Keegan hated both options. He might not be sure why he was suddenly getting the cold shoulder from her, not that things had been particularly warm between them to begin with, but that didn't mean he believed she should be thrown to the mercy of Alpha Peters and whatever stupid plan he and his son concocted.

"Yes, I know you prefer we just let her stay here and live the way she wants to. It's written all over your face," Ethan commented, waving his hand toward Keegan before putting his attention back to Darian.

Darian glanced at Keegan and his lips twitched up into a small smile. "Looking for a challenge, are we?" he muttered before drawing his attention back to the Alpha.

Keegan rolled his eyes at both of them. He didn't think he was being obvious. He couldn't be, clearly because she hadn't noticed yet. Though Keegan wasn't sure whether that meant she was oblivious or if he was hiding his feelings for her well. He pushed that aside. He definitely didn't want to be putting in any time on that train of thought.

"I'm leaning toward telling him, once we have the updated written agreement. Telling him she is now under our protection. It's a matter of how to go about doing it. Whether I should simply say we now have an Omega or tell him we found his. We will not be letting them have her, but I don't like the idea of it being sprung on him as a surprise."

"You don't think that'll make him an enemy of ours? If we suddenly pop up with an Omega?" Darian asked.

Slowly, Ethan shook his head. "Sure it will. If we just let it slip that we have an Omega, it might help with our Wilson problem. But you saw how exhausting what she did for Vicki was for her. I'm willing to bet Peters doesn't know exactly what her skill set is. So, we might slide that under the radar, for at least a little while. We can't hide her forever. Not only is that not workable, but eventually, word will get out."

"We have to protect her. As soon as you give Alpha Peters the heads up that we might have the person he's looking for I wouldn't put it past him to come kidnap her," Keegan interjected, trying to keep the frustration from his voice but was sure he was failing.

"Maybe, but with all the pushing and shoving he's been doing lately, I'm not sure he would consider it his best move to sneak into our territory and steal someone out from under us. Especially if we've officially granted her protection. He doesn't have the might to come in and do that yet. Even if he did it somewhat sneakily, as soon as we found out about it, it would be a problem. At this point, it's just something to think about." He moved back around his desk and put his hands on the back of his chair.

"You sound like you've already decided," Darian commented.

"Basically, it's just a matter of the timeline. Keegan, your dismissed. Darian and I have other things we need to discuss this evening."

Keegan ground his teeth in frustration. He had seen the images, heard the ultimatum Peters had given her, and seen that smug face his son had pulled. He didn't want Emma thrown into that again.

Feelings aside, it wasn't right to do that to anyone. He couldn't think of the last time he questioned one of Ethan's decisions. But now, he was pretty sure the other man was relying too heavily on his own clout and not enough on Peters' megalomania.

"I said, you're dismissed." This time there was much more command in Ethan's voice. He'd even pushed the slightest bit of Alpha wolf magic behind it to emphasize his point.

Balling his hands into fists and clenching his jaw, Keegan pivoted and only opened his left hand long enough to wrench the door open and slam it behind him. Emma deserved to know what was coming for her, even if it wasn't immediately. He might get punished later for giving her a heads up, but there was no way he was going to think she could blindly trust they would take care of her. He heard rumors of the way Alpha Peters did things, and he was fairly certain as soon as he knew Emma was there, her safety would be in jeopardy. Taking a few deep breaths to get himself under control, he headed toward the pack filing room to find the phone information for

Emma's roommate. He didn't think visiting them this late at night was in anyone's best interest. Especially when Emma needed to breathe, recoup, and re-heal. But if he could call tonight to set up a meeting for tomorrow, hopefully that would be soon enough.

Chapter 39:
Too Tired to Fight

CJ

"What the hell happened to her?" Raelene asked, her tone more than slightly accusatory.

She pulled the door farther back so Emma and CJ, who was taking most of her weight, could limp their way through the door. Once through, she quickly closed and locked the door behind them before scurrying over to the couch and pushing aside all the throw blankets so CJ could ease Emma down.

"She looks white as a sheet. It's like she has pneumonia or something," Raelene whispered.

"I'm still awake. I can hear you," Emma retorted.

"I think she just overdid it. The initial pain blocker I gave her has worn off." As he spoke, CJ swung his medical travel bag onto the floor and began rooting through it.

Though her eyes are closed, Emma turned her head toward her friend. "See, it would be a heck of a lot worse if I didn't have those pain pills."

Raelene plopped down on the couch next to Emma, sliding her hand to her friend's forehead. "You're burning up. I'm calling Morris." With that, she leapt up from the couch and dashed into her bedroom, where her phone sat on the charger.

"Who the heck is Morris?" Though he asked, CJ didn't really expect a response. He had the smallest prickle of jealousy that the woman he was seeing would rely on a different man to help her with the problem that should be in his wheelhouse. "He's a friend from my old pack. His grandmother is an Omega. She has, sort of, been fielding questions as they come up." Although she lay with her head rested on the back of the couch, and her eyes closed, Emma still had a reassuring tone as if she could feel CJ's frustration.

Feeling a little embarrassed, he didn't respond. Instead he pulled out his thermometer to check Emma's temperature. Then a memory pricked in the back of his mind.

It couldn't be, could it? Wasn't that the name of the grandson of the Omega from home? CJ asked his wolf.

I honestly don't remember his name, his wolf responded curiously, stepping more to the forefront of CJ's mind.

As the thermometer beeped, he heard Raelene running back into the room.

"No, she feels boiling hot. I swear she has a fever." She looked at CJ for confirmation.

"99.7," he supplied.

"Who is that?" came a growly male voice through the speaker.

"That's CJ. He's the guy I've been seeing. He's also a pack medic and an EMT. He brought Emma home from the pack house. I don't know what happened." Her voice was frantic as she stood beside the couch, all nervous energy.

"CJ?" the voice asked.

"Yeah," he responded.

"Can you tell me exactly what happened?" There was a quick pause before CJ could speak. The voice continued, "No, hold on. This is stupid. I'm going to joint call with my grandmother. She'll have a better idea what to do. And I won't make you explain everything twice." The line went quiet.

CJ took advantage of the momentary silence by going in and grabbing one of the washcloths he knew was kept in the kitchen drawer. He got the water as cool as would be comfortable and dampened the towel. When he came back into the living room, he placed it over Emma's forehead.

She jumped, hissed, and cracked one eye open to what he assumed was supposed to be a glare. "That's super cold, man."

Luckily, she didn't remove it from her head. Anxiety with how useless he felt gnawed at CJ as he stood by the couch, waiting for the other end of the phone to click back to life.

"What has happened?" asked an older woman's voice after a few clicking noises on the phone.

CJ didn't wait for any kind of formal introduction. Instead, he launched into everything he knew that had happened between Vicki and Emma. There was silence for several moments until the older woman's voice cut through a second time.

"Emma, are you in any shape to shed more light on the situation?" Though the woman's voice was soft, CJ could hear worry threading through it.

He recognized the voice right away, a calm presence from his childhood. It was an awfully small world. He didn't know what the odds were that the Omega from his childhood, was the grandmother of this Omega's good friend. CJ wasn't one for coincidences, and he had to wonder whether this was some kind of fate stirring the pot.

"I think so," Emma croaked from the couch. "I can't explain to you how I did it, just that my wolf helped walk me through it. I climbed inside the young girl's head, and I found both her and her wolf. There was this thorny dome surrounding where the wolf was, separating the girl from her wolf. They claim to have never met before. I could use my abilities to, for lack of a better phrase, cut a hole through the vines big enough that the girl and I could get through it comfortably. I don't know if it's going to grow back or not. But moving back and forth within her mind, and destroying the vines seem to have zapped any kind of energy I have. CJ gave me a powerful painkiller. I'm nauseous, I feel like I have one of the worst hangovers of my life, and a horrible migraine. It's also really hot. But I think that goes with the fever."

There was silence again, but longer this time.

When the old woman spoke, she made a frustrated noise. "This would be much easier if you had a guardian with you. She doesn't by chance still have that brooch, does she, Morris?" The older woman's voice didn't sound hopeful about the answer to her question.

"No, I brought it back with me," the male, Morris, answered warily.

There was a heavy sigh. "Are you wearing the bracelet I had Morris give you?"

This time, there was a little more hope in her voice.

"Yeah," Emma answered warily. "Though I haven't been wearing it as often as he said you recommended."

"In this circumstance, you not following recommendations will benefit us. Morris, do you have a recent photo of Emma?"

"Um, I think so. Raelene took one of us on Emma's phone. I was afraid of having one on my phone because of the circumstances I told you about."

That sent out warning bells in CJ's head, but he knew better than to ask. He could always bring it up with Raelene later.

"Okay," the older woman sounded a little put out. "Here's what I need all of you to do. First, find that photo of the two of you and send it to Morris. Morris, you then send that to me. Or circumvent that whole thing and Morris can give you my number and you can send it straight on to me. Second, you're going to get Emma to a dark place where she can lie down. Somewhere comfortable. Then you're going to wait. I'm going to contact my guardian, Samuel and he and I are going to try something. I don't know if it'll work or not. I'm going to see if we can't give you a little of an energy boost through that bracelet of yours. If there's still enough of my imprint on it, I should be able to get through. If you would have worn at all the time, you would've imprinted on it over mine and this would be impossible. I don't have healing magic, so I can't do that for you. But maybe if I throw a little extra magic your way, it'll help your system reboot itself. It will take Samuel and me about twenty minutes to get set up. He lives about ten minutes away. Can you hold on for us, Emma?"

"Not sure I have much of a choice, since there isn't really an alternative," Emma groaned.

"Okay, if all goes well, I'll see you, and only you, in about twenty minutes. If I can't get through will do this whole phone thing again."

The phone went quiet for several beats before Morris' voice came on the phone. "Mormor?" When there was no answer, he sighed. "I guess that means she's gone. Raelene, keep me updated on what happens, please. If this doesn't work, I can hop in my car and be over there as fast as traffic will let me. Good luck to you guys. Hang in there, Emma." With that, Morris hung up as well.

"All right, you heard the lady. Let's lift you up and get you into your bedroom. We have twenty minutes so we can at least get you into more comfortable clothes," Raelene exclaimed as she practically leapt around the couch and maneuvered herself to get under Emma's right arm.

CJ scooted in and did the same on the left side. Emma let out an 'oof' as they lifted her up. Then the three of them slowly maneuvered across the living room toward Emma's bedroom.

Chapter 40:
Long Distance Relationship

Emma

Thankfully, before they left the room, Raelene had not only sent along the photo Morris' grandmother needed, but she started Emma's relaxation playlist. Sounds of rain and beach noises filled the room in soothing waves. Though Emma was in pain, she could feel her body beginning to slow down, an automatic response to the familiar noises. She kept her hands on her chest, her hand not wearing the bracelet clutched around the wrist the bracelet was on. She wasn't sure how much or how little she should touch the bracelet, but something about holding it with the other hand felt right. Closing her eyes, Emma forced her breathing to slow. It wasn't helping with the headache, but it gave her something to distract herself with.

She didn't know how long she lay there, in the dark, listening to the soothing noise, but after a while she felt a tug inside of her. It was almost as if her wolf was trying to get her attention, but this didn't feel like her wolf. Emma fought through the pain and discomfort and made her way deeper into her mind, much like she had when going to the location where her wolf lived. It was a little harder to concentrate and get there than it should've been, but she managed. Once she was there, she stood next to her wolf. Though the wolf towered about a foot and a half above her, she slid her hand down its front right leg in a mutually soothing gesture.

She then looked off to the left, where her wolf was looking, and saw what she thought was a doorway. It was large, round, and had bricks lining it around the outside. Like something from a garden. Now that she was looking at it, she knew the pull she felt was coming from that doorway. It wasn't a violent pull. She didn't feel frightened as she looked at it. But it was strong enough that it was hard to ignore.

Are we meant to go through it? she asked her wolf, not moving her eyes away from this recent addition to her own mind.

I think so. There are wolves on the other side. They don't seem unfriendly. Her wolf's voice was speculative. Neither of them were entirely sure what to make of this doorway to nowhere.

It could be Morris' grandmother, Emma commented.

Yes, it could. But since we have never met her, I don't know.

"Emma, Emma, I need you to step through the doorway and into a neutral space for this to work."

Well, that's Morris' grandmother or someone pretending to be her, Emma countered.

Shall we go through? her wolf asked gently.

Yeah, might as well. Let's just hope it doesn't disappear behind us.

Her wolf snorted as they, in unison, walked toward the brick gateway. Both hesitated for a whole beat before stepping through together.

It was a sensation Emma hadn't felt before. It was like moving from a humid exterior into a fully air-conditioned building. There was no actual temperature difference, but somehow the air felt different. It had Emma stopping as she regained her footing.

"There you are, dear. Glad to see you brought the wolf with you. She will help."

Emma craned her neck around her wolf's chest. Several yards away stood an older woman who held a vague resemblance to Morris. Next to her was a giant black wolf. On the other side was an older gentleman who looked to be a very fit seventy, and on his left was an extremely large salt-and-pepper wolf. The salt-and-pepper wolf towered over the man. It had maybe half a foot on Emma's wolf as well.

The man inclined his head toward them, as did the wolf, when they saw Emma looking in his direction.

Behind the older couple was a vague outline of a garden. There was a stone fence, with vines curling up it from several rosebushes. But it was a ghost of an image. As if she was only seeing a shadow of whatever place the two people stood in.

Morris' grandmother frowned, then turned her head to look behind them before chuckling and turning back to Emma with a grin. "Yes, that happens sometimes. Both Samuel and I are standing in my back garden. I find the garden to be very grounding. What you're seeing is my backyard. And because that is where I am grounding from, you're seeing the imprint, in how were vaguely aware of what's behind us. Just like if you look behind you, you'll see the outline of your bedroom." The older woman jutted her chin, lifting her head past Emma and her wolf.

Emma swiveled her head and sure enough, to the right over their shoulder was the wall behind Emma's back. Her collection of movie posters lined up. As well as a drawing Raelene had done when they were in high school of Raelene, Bess, and Emma, sitting in the booth at their favorite diner in Ellensburg. But all of it was vague and almost sheer the way the garden fence was.

"That's a little disconcerting," Emma commented as she turned back to the older couple.

"Yes." The woman chuckled. "Yes, it can be. But eventually, you do this enough, and you'll get used to it." She rubbed her hands together and took two large steps forward, her wolf trailing a step behind her. Samuel moved to stay in line with the wolf. His own wolf trailing behind them. Almost as if he was protecting the group at large.

It had Emma wondering if there was something they needed to be protected from, or if this was an automatic gesture.

"I'd like to apologize. You don't know my name. Which seems a little silly at this point. My name is Ida, and this is one of my guardians, the last one of my guardians, Samuel."

At the introduction, Samuel inclined his head again, lower this time.

"It's nice to meet you both, I guess. My name is Emma."

Ida smiled encouragingly. "Now, let's get down to business. Like I said on the phone, I can't heal you, but I can give you a little boost of energy. Over the decades, I've learned how to build up reserves, so you'll be able to take without us having to worry. Also, I have Samuel here to stand in as a backup battery in case you need a large amount of energy."

The older woman stopped walking about a yard away from Emma.

"It's quite nice of you guys to do this for me. Even if it doesn't help, I appreciate it. I just..." She waved her hands around vaguely in front of her trying to come up with the right words. "I'm just not used to people helping me."

Ida frowned, and Samuel did the same. His eyes shifted curiously to Ida. And whatever Morris may have told his grandmother about Emma's situation, the older woman had not passed it on to her guardian. It made Emma feel a little warm. The woman was keeping her secrets, though she didn't need to.

"Now, you and I are going to put our hands over each other's wrists." She put both her hands palm up toward Emma. And Emma saw both wrists had several large bracelets on each. "I'm then going to push energy your way. We'll start gently, as I don't know if our magic is compatible. If it's not, it might make you sick, so I'd prefer we not do that. Once we know it's compatible and you can take the energy on, I'll push more and more your way. We will see if that makes a difference in how you're feeling. Unfortunately, we won't know until after you've left your headspace again. Being this deep into our minds makes it a little hard to stay connected to what our physical bodies are doing." Ida's serene face frowned again.

    Emma didn't blame her. It seemed a critical flaw. She began raising her arms and then hesitated, just a second, before taking a deep breath and placing her arms lightly on the older woman's. It seemed weird to be able to tell that Ida's hands were soft and warm, while the bracelets seemed ice cold against Emma's skin. She grabbed the older woman's forearms just beyond the bracelets and felt Ida's fingers curl around her own forearms.

    "Close your eyes. It'll help you keep in tune with how your magic is doing. You'll know faster if it's going to make you ill or not."

"Oh, okay." Emma's voice sounded timid, even to her own ears. But she did as the older woman suggested and closed her eyes.

It was a strange sensation. Vibrant green energy tingled up her fingertips, wrists, and forearms. It was very light at first. But she could definitely see something happening. She figured it had to be Ida's energy slowly making its way through Emma's body. The green wasn't dense at first. Almost like a misting rain. It made its way up her arms and though she couldn't feel the difference, she could see with her eyes closed. Once that mist rolled into her torso, she felt her stomach lurch once and held her breath. She let go of the air, feeling her shoulders slump in relief when nausea didn't follow that initial lurch.

"How are you feeling, dear?" Ida's kind and comforting voice penetrated Emma's concentration.

"There was an initial lurch to my stomach but no nausea."

"Good, that's a relief. I'm going to push it a little more now."

As she spoke, Emma could see the density of the green getting thicker around her wrists and hands where their skin was in contact. The density was built like a thick fog. It began rolling up her arms. She felt a sliver of panic as it reached her shoulders and then cascaded down her torso.

She felt a gasp wrench from her throat and her body jerked a little with the impact.

"Are you all right?" This time it was a gruff male voice she assumed was Samuel's.

"I, I think so," Emma responded timidly. "It was just a bit of a shock."

When he didn't respond to that, she assumed they were taking her at her word.

The green energy was so thick it practically vibrated throughout all of her body. She felt as if she had too much caffeine, her system seemed to jitter. All she could see now was that bright green color. It didn't feel as if there was any more space for it to go. Yet the current kept moving, more and more energy filling up inside of her.

Ida gave her arms a squeeze. "There now. I think that's more than enough to get you by. You were pretty empty of energy.

You need to be a bit more careful with how much of your gift you're using until you have a better idea of how much energy a task takes. And yes, I understand that sort of thing is trial and error. But depleting your energy will always make you not feel quite right. And stretching your gifts will cause this all over pain and headache you're feeling. It will get easier and easier as you find the limits of your gift. But if you continue to push yourself to your limit before you have the time to recover, you're going to do permanent damage."

With that last part, Emma's eyes popped open, and she stared at the other woman who was slowly letting go of Emma's wrists and moving her arms down to her sides.

"What do you mean, permanent damage?" She couldn't curb the worry and fright in her voice.

"If you overuse your gift, especially early on, you can damage how much energy you can use. It limits the work you can do. And eventually you can burn the gift out entirely. It's important to move at an even, steady pace and not continually leap forward." Ida frowned in a motherly fashion as she finished.

"I know nothing about any of this!" Emma exclaimed. "I don't know the rules. I don't know my limitations. I don't know what I can and can't do. How am I supposed to stop myself from doing it if I don't know those things?" Her voice quaked and tears pricked at her eyes.

Her chest was so tight it became difficult to breathe.

Her wolf leaned in against her, lending her furry, warm comfort to Emma.

She is so young.

Turning toward Samuel's wolf, Emma scowled through her watery eyes. "I'm not that young. I have no control over the fact that these powers are supposedly coming late and all at once.

Samuel and his wolf exchanged glances. Though she couldn't read the wolf's expression, Samuel's brow was furrowed.

You can hear me? The wolf sounded amused this time.

"Of course I can hear you. I can hear pretty much everybody's wolf when I'm standing this close," Emma responded flippantly.

"He's using our private channel to communicate. Not even Ida can hear him. And she and I have been able to communicate mentally for decades," Samuel said aloud.

It was as if a splash of cold water hit Emma. She was hearing thoughts she wasn't supposed to hear. Was she not supposed to hear people's wolves? Should she not have told anyone about that? Or was it only in specific situations? What was the etiquette for this? She hadn't figured out how to block people's inner voices.

"I don't know any Omega that has that capability," Ida chimed in thoughtfully. "I'm gonna have to ask around. That seems like something you're going to need training for because it could get you into some sticky situations. Bare minimum, maybe someone can train you how to ignore the conversations. Otherwise, this could get exhausting as your gift grows."

Ida took a step back and instinctively reached out to pet the flank of her own wolf and seemed to get lost in her own thoughts.

"That may take me a little while. You have my number on your phone now. So reach out to me directly with questions. I'm going to stick some feelers out to the different Omegas I know and see if one of us might have some gift close enough to yours to be helpful. But until then try not to spend too much energy, all right? And yes, I say that knowing it's easier said than done when you don't know your limits. Maybe hold off on doing anything that even mildly gives you a headache."

"That's pretty much everything," Emma muttered under her breath.

Ida gave her a sympathetic smile. "We're going to head out now. Walk back through the gateway, and it will bring you straight back to wherever you are in your own mind. Give me a call if you aren't feeling better when you come back to yourself. Otherwise, I'm going to assume that this worked and go about recharging my own batteries. You take care of yourself, Emma."

There was a motherly concern to the older woman's words, and despite her frustration and anxiety about the situation, Emma found she was touched.

"Thank you again to both of you. Like I said, even if it doesn't work, I appreciate the effort."

This time, both Ida and Samuel inclined their heads. Emma waited a beat before she turned around, her wolf doing the same behind her and the two of them headed back through the brick lined gate.

Chapter 41:
A Call to the Gatekeeper

Keegan

"Hello?" came a female voice over the phone.

Keegan's gut reaction was to say he had the wrong number and hang up. But he double checked the number he entered from the pack records before hitting call. Unless the pack records were wrong, the questioning woman on the other side of the phone was Raelene.

"Hello," A light female voice answered.

"Raelene?"

"Yes..."

Once he verified it was Raelene, Keegan proceeded. "Hello, this is Keegan from the pack office." He floundered after that, unsure what to say. He didn't want to use his title because he didn't want her to think she was required to let him speak to Emma. But there was a sense of urgency where it concerned the two of them talking.

"Okay, I'm going to move past the creepiness that you somehow hunted down my number and ask what I can do for you."

Keegan felt himself slump as he exhaled. She didn't hang up on him right away. This was a good start. Not a great one, but a good one. So he rushed forward to get everything out before she changed her mind.

"I know tonight is not a good time, but I need to swing by and have a few words with Emma. Preferably where the Alpha and his second won't be within hearing distance."

Way to make that sound suspicious, his wolf quipped.

Oh, and how would you phrase it? he snapped back.

Despite the wolf being in his own head, the mutter was still low enough

Keegan didn't hear what he said. Which was probably for the best.

"I assume you want to swing by tomorrow morning?" she asked slowly, as if she was still thinking through the question as she spoke.

"That would be preferable if you say it's okay." He didn't want Raelene's opinion to matter. The dominant wolf in him wanted to show up no matter how the less dominant wolf felt about it. But the human part of him knew what a bad idea that would be. Emma already didn't trust the pack. And him barging into her home would not endear him or the pack to her.

"Is what you have to say going to endanger my friend?" There was no mistaking the protective anger that threaded her tone.

"Not directly." Keegan knew he had to step lightly here. "What I'm going to tell her will be a problem for her. But the act of me telling her, I'm hoping, will give her a heads up to a forthcoming problem."

"Does she need to run?" It was said with such dire concern his heart hurt.

Keegan knew what it was Emma would run from. What her friend was worried she would need to continue running from. But even if he hadn't seen those glimpses into her memory, that tone would've set off alarm bells.

"I don't believe so. At least not in the foreseeable future. But, I think that could change, which is why I want to talk to her."

There was a long silence on the other end of the phone and for a while Keegan worried he was going to be hung up on.

"All right, be here at ten. I'll make sure she's up and coherent by then. But if you think I'm leaving her alone to hear whatever news you're going to tell her without support, you got another thing coming."

"Understood. I'll see you in the morning." With that, Keegan hung up.

It itched, going behind his Alpha's back, but he couldn't back out now. This was information Emma deserved to have. She deserved to know she might be used for something close to a bargaining tactic. Keegan hated playing politics. It was his least favorite part of being part of a pack. It was why he never wanted to be Alpha or Beta. And why Darrin and Ethan trusted him so much. At his core, Keegan wanted to be useful and helpful to his pack. But anytime there was a power play of any kind, Keegan wanted no part of it. When Wilson started the rumors for his little rebellion, several of the members actually approached Keegan, misunderstanding his hatred of politics for hatred of the pack. He shot that down pretty quickly and reported the conversation to Darrin. That helped give Ethan a heads up when the attempted coup happened.

    This, though, this was different. This wasn't family politics, or big secrets for the good of the pack. Ethan was going to be letting Emma's abusers know where she was. He just couldn't get behind that. And while he couldn't challenge the Alpha out right, he could still do something to help the Omega wolf. Because unlike Ethan, he didn't trust Peters and the wolves of his pack to mind their own business.

Chapter 42:
Emma in Wolfland

Emma

The air was thick with mist. Emma knew this wasn't real life, even though she'd been on the ferry to Friday Harbor a handful of times in her life. But she'd never done so after dark, and there certainly was never a giant black wolf with her, like there was now. Luckily, the wolf with her was her own and not a stranger. Her surroundings in this dream were a little off, so her wolf's presence was a comfort.

We have been on this boat for a while, her wolf commented.

The ferry takes a while.

But we have seen no sight of land the entire time we've been on this boat. We didn't get on the boat, we've just been sailing on it. And if you look around, you'll see we are the boat's only inhabitants.

Dread and anxiety crept up the back of her neck at her wolf's words. Emma sensed no one else on the ferry, but it was a dream, so that wasn't entirely unheard of. But now that her wolf mentioned they were the only ones on the ferry, something about it didn't sit well with her. As if it was a scene in a horror movie, Emma slowly looked over her shoulder and fear ripped through her.

If we are alone, who the hell are they? Emma's breathing grew heavy as she saw half a dozen ragged people staring at them through the giant panes of glass. She and her wolf stood on the outside. The figures staring at them were pale, almost translucent white, their clothes ripped apart and hair matted.

What exactly do you see? her wolf asked warily as she spun around, scanning the surrounding area.

You, you don't see them? The six people staring directly at us right there? Afraid to point, Emma inclined her head toward their viewers, fear spiking within her.

Emma, I see no one. It's not possible for you to see something I don't. We are in your head, my home. I should see all that you see. Describe them to me? her wolf commanded as she took a slight step forward, as if she meant to get in between Emma and the figures she had yet to see.

I see six people, four women and two men. I can't tell you how old they are, but they are all adults. Their hair is matted black. Their eyes are just like black holes in their faces. Their lips are a dark color, but not quite black. I can't see them clearly from here. They are pale and translucent. Their clothes seem like rags, several of them have rips in the cloth. They're standing there, staring at us. Their expressions... I don't know if they're meant to be expressionless, but if they are, they're not quite pulling it off. The way they look, I could only describe it as hatred. None of them have moved since I turned around.

Can you wake yourself up? her wolf asked low, coming to lean up against her.

Do you believe leaving them here unattended is a good idea? She sounded crazy. If this was some dream, they were figments of her imagination, yet she couldn't convince herself of that.

Before the wolf could respond, the taller woman, two over from the left, took a step forward. She was uncomfortably close to the glass. Emma should've seen her breath clouding the window, but it didn't. She was so close that surely some part of her was pressed up against the wall uncomfortably. Yet the woman didn't seem phased.

One of them moved closer, Emma commented quietly, even though they were only communicating to each other. Although she wasn't speaking with her mouth, it felt as if any volume, even in her own head, would somehow tip whatever was happening in the wrong direction.

I still cannot see them or sense them. Her wolf growled. The giant beast's hackle rose. Her tail came up at attention.

The mouth of the woman against the glass stretched into a predatory grin, but there was no crinkling about her eyes. All of her front teeth were sharpened to points.

What? What? barked her wolf.

The one that stepped forward is smiling, and she has very sharp teeth.

Then the noise started. The one against the glass created something between a growl and a purr.

That I hear. The wolf was at full alert now, ears twitching and face pointed in the sound's direction.

Well, at least there's that, I guess. Emma's breathing was fast and shallow. Her heart beat so hard and quick it was as if she'd been running for miles.

Emma had some hand-to-hand combat training. Most werewolves did, but she wasn't especially good at it. And some deep part of her told her not to reach out with her Omega wolf gifts and see what was in the heads of those six beings.

The woman took another step forward, a large one, and she traveled right through the wall of the ferry and now stood on the deck with Emma and her wolf.

She moved closer. It was a statement and not a question from her wolf.

After the woman completed that step, the sound stopped abruptly, and the grin fell just as fast from her face. The woman cocked her head, birdlike, where she stood. Emma glanced away as she sensed movement. The other five beings had moved up to the glass and stared at her with that same expressionless look on their faces.

Emma felt herself shaking. Deep down in her gut, she knew these were not figments of her imagination. They were interlopers in her dream world, and she didn't know how to get them out.

The woman closest to them took a deep breath through her nose, as if pulling some scent into her lungs.

Unclear where the threat was coming from, her wolf deliberately turned herself, so she was blocking Emma from the woman.

I can't fight what I can't see, her Wolf snarled as she snapped out in front of her. She missed the woman by a good foot and the woman didn't even seem to notice how close the jaws of the giant wolf got to her.

"Wretch," the garbled hiss from the woman's mouth was startling and raw.

Emma knew her wolf heard it as the furry body stiffened.

"Bleed," the elongated word came from a different female voice. Emma could no longer see any of the beings with her wolf in the way.

The second after the word hit her ears, she doubled over in pain that erupted from everywhere. It suddenly felt as if her skin was being ripped open all over her body, but when she looked down as she doubled over, she looked the same.

Emma? Emma, what's wrong? Are they attacking you? asked her wolf, panic playing in her voice.

I don't know, I can't see them. I can just hear their words.

"Bleed." This time it was louder and more assertive.

Emma fell to her knees and began retching. But instead of vomiting, it was almost as if her own essence poured out of her. It felt as if her energy was coming out of her nose, mouth, eyes, and the imaginary rips in her skin. She screamed in pain and couldn't do anything else. Then she felt a cold skeletal hand on the top of her head, nails digging into her scalp. If this was the real world, she was sure there would be puncture wounds.

"You are a disgrace and will be dealt with as such," the first woman's voice hissed.

There was so much pain and nausea flowing through her body Emma couldn't fight back. Fear roared through her, wave after wave. She did not know where one scream ended in the next one began.

She swore she could hear her wolf talking but couldn't make out a word.

"That's it, empty that husk of an Omega wolf," the woman hissed again, her nails digging deeper and pushing Emma further toward the ground, onto her hands and knees.

It was hard to breathe through the thick mist and pain. Emma had felt nothing like it in her life. It felt as if there were no barriers between her and the environment she was in. As if every ounce of her body was pouring out of her. Her head pounded with the franticness of her heart.

Rage bubbled up inside of her and overrode the fear and the scream inside her became one of a warrior instead of a victim.

She wrenched herself up, swatting her right hand out into the air, and felt it connect with the skeletal arm holding her head in place.

Apparently, that shook the woman, because she lost her grip entirely. And though it still felt as if everything leaked out of her, the pain lessened a little in her head. The woman's head was cocked again, and she slowly leaned down until she was nose to nose with Emma. Her body was at an unnatural angle to do so. The black soulless eyes bore into her. She felt as if this woman was burrowing her way in through her eyes. And yet she couldn't close her lids. They felt held in place by some unknown force. The black eyes kept getting closer, slowly. Inch by inch. Their noses didn't bump when they should have. Instead, it was as if the woman's nose almost passed through Emma's.

Fear griped Emma again. Her wolf couldn't save her, she couldn't see what was happening. Emma was completely alone and falling into the depths of those dark eyes. In a last-ditch effort, she didn't fully understand, Emma grabbed all of her Omega power and pushed it out of her.

Sending it scattering amongst the cosmos. She didn't know what these beings wanted with her. But if it had something to do with her power, she certainly wouldn't let them get it.

Chapter 43:
Interconnected

CJ

CJ woke mid holler, sitting up in Raelene's bed. Panic coursed through him as he threw back the sheets.

"What? What's going on?" came Raelene's panicked voice from the other side of the bed.

"I don't know. I don't know how I know this, but something is wrong with Emma," he answered as he tore from the room, almost ripping the door off its hinges as he yanked it open.

He felt similar to the way he felt on a full moon, right before he changed. It felt as if the power of the werewolf was coursing through him, but at a level he never felt before. And for whatever reason, that power told him something was wrong with Emma. CJ was vaguely aware of the sound of the phone ringing behind him, but he ignored it. That wasn't his responsibility. His patient needed him.

They'd left Emma's door ajar in case she needed them, so it was nothing to slam it open. He held out his arm as it rebounded off the wall and slapped back.

Emma lay in her bed, perfectly still, looking to the world as if she was peacefully asleep. But something in CJ knew better. She needed to wake up, and it needed to be *now*. There were dire consequences if she didn't wake up this instant.

"Emma, you need to wake up." As far as commands went, it was a soft one. He jumped onto her bed and climbed on all fours, straddling her.

His words had no effect, and a new wave of panic shot through him.

"Emma, you need to wake up and you have to do it now!" It was much louder and almost right in her face. Anyone in a normal sleep would've woken up with a start. But Emma didn't.

"What do you mean 'wake Emma up'?" came Raelene's confused voice into the room.

"I don't know what to tell you, Raelene, but she needs to be awake, and it has to happen now," came Morris' voice through the phone.

CJ had a split second to wonder why both he and Morris were thinking the same thing. The next second, he twisted around and snatched the phone from Raelene's hand. She had a shocked and angry expression on her face.

"I have an idea. You're going to say it with me. Don't ask me why I think this, because it's crazy," tt came out as a rush as CJ turned back.

He grabbed one of Emma's hands and put the phone on top of it. He then grabbed her other hand. "Yell for her to wake up after I say three. Ready?" CJ didn't wait for the other man to respond. "One, two, three. Emma, wake up!"

Both men yelled in unison, and he heard Raelene chiming in from behind him.

He felt the excess power pouring through him slam into her, as if he had been holding a bucket of water and dropped it on her. He felt insane, but he swore he felt the same thing happen from the phone.

Immediately following that sensation, Emma's eyes snapped open, and she gasped, as if breathing for the first time in a long time. She looked up at him with a fear CJ had never seen in real life before. CJ's heartbeat, which had been so fast and so loud, finally slowed.

"What the hell is going on, CJ? Someone tell me what the hell is going on."

"Did it work? It felt like it worked. Did she wake up?" Morris asked.

"Yes, she woke up." Suddenly very aware he was sitting on top of her, CJ gingerly moved to the side, taking the phone with him. As he moved, he noticed how hard Emma was shaking.

"Emma, Emma, are you with us?" the other man's voice was wary as it came through the speaker.

"Yes," came the watery answer before Emma sobbed. It was so hard it wracked her shoulders.

"Dang it, dang it, Raelene? Raelene, are you in the room?" Morris called through the phone.

"Yeah, I'm here," Raelene answered as she came to stand on the opposite side of the bed CJ was on. Raelene sat down next to her friend, collecting her up in a tight hug. Emma clung to her as if she was a life preserver and continued to sob.

"I can't get there tonight. But I'm going to get there as soon as I can. I need to talk to my grandmother first. But something not right just happened." Then the line went dead as Morris hung up.

CJ slowly placed the phone on the nightstand next to the bed. Deliberately taking slow movements so as not to startle anyone and to calm his body down. When he turned back, Raelene was eyeing him over her friend's still shaking shoulder.

'What happened?' she mouth. She looked just as panicked and frightened as he felt.

"I don't know," he whispered, just loud enough for her to hear over her friend's sobs. That answer seemed to frighten Raelene further.

"Do you want CJ to get you a sedative?" Raelene's voice came out in a soothing tone she clearly didn't feel.

"No!" Emma squeaked, shaking harder. "Please don't make me sleep again. I don't know if they'll come back,"

CJ could see it was on the tip of Raelene's tongue to ask who 'they' were, but he shook his head vigorously and she shut her mouth. Whatever Emma had experienced when she was asleep, he knew it was more than a nightmare. He didn't know what it was, but it had definitely not been good. There was something at play here that he didn't understand. And somehow, whatever was happening to Emma was connected to him and Morris as well.

Guardians, his wolf commented quietly.

That one word sent a shiver through CJ. He knew what a guardian was, what their job was for an Omega. CJ was not a dominant wolf, though it would explain why he felt an instant connection with Emma, even before finding out she was Raelene's roommate, he couldn't think of anyone who would be a more unlikely guardian. Yet, as his wolf uttered the word, every fiber of CJ's being knew it was true. He just wasn't sure how he was going to explain that to Raelene.

Chapter 44:
The Stuff of Nightmares

Dante

"She needs you. Run!" his sister, Cecily's voice echoed in his ear. It was almost like a stage whisper.

But Dante knew better than to ever question his little sister. So he ran. He didn't know where he was running and whether it was to or from something, but he didn't question it. He knew better than most that even though he was in a dreamscape, the things that lurked around the corners of consciousness could still hurt you.

Soon the childhood playground he and his sister had been sitting on swings in became a murky, cloudy place. It was almost as if he was running through a damp, thick fog. If it had been in real life, his clothes would've been soaked. But he kept running. Soon he burst out onto a scene he didn't understand. There was a large salt and pepper wolf snarling and snapping blindly around a woman on her knees. And several beings that looked like something out of a horror movie were reaching for the woman. She'd poured out her power all around her as if she was draining herself dry.

"She's in Omega wolf. She needs your help. You're going to be the only one who can do it," came his sister's calm but concerned voice from next to him.

When Dante looked over at her, he saw his snowy white wolf stood on Cecily's other side, its attention on the horror movie mob in front of them.

"Take out the ones on the other side of the wolf," Dante commented to his other half before quickly striding forward and reaching his arms around the neck of the skeletal woman leaning down into the Omega's face.

"That is quite enough of that," he snapped at the woman as he wrenched her away from the Omega.

As he pulled, a feeling of dread coiled through him. Something about this scene wasn't quite right. It wasn't something Dante could put his finger on, but he really didn't have the time to put more thought into it.

The woman in his arms, who he now had a chokehold on, screeched like a bird, flailing and kicking her feet. But Dante held strong, tightening his grip.

A few seconds later he felt power, not the Omega's, but something closely tied to it, pulse through the scene around them and voices cut through the air.

"Emma, wake up!" It was two male voices infused together.

The Omega on the ground gasped loudly and then she disappeared.

Now it was him, the salt-and-pepper wolf who couldn't seem to see the surrounding figures, and his own wolf who seemed to be holding his own against the three unearthly beings attacking him. One more stood watching as if trying to decide whether to go after him or the wolf.

Dante ignored the scene around him and tightened his grip against the pale woman in his arms. Her kicking was more desperate now, and he held tighter, using his inhuman strength. After a few more seconds she stopped moving entirely, but Dante wasn't fooled. He didn't want to chance whatever this was waking up again. So he squeezed even harder and held until he was sure she was truly knocked out. He then dropped her on the deck and moved to fight with his wolf.

The last being had joined the fray and his wolf had several scratches along its muzzle where the man with talon like hands must've scratched him. As he joined the wolf, he felt a little better about their odds. The wolf had already taken out two of the attackers. One was clearly not getting back up again, as there were huge gashes in its side and blood all over the deck around it. The second was missing one leg, and one arm was barely attached.

Dante tackled the tall, thin man who was heading to slash along his wolf's back haunch. As they hit the ground, he felt his teeth rattle in his head. Luckily, he had hit the man in such a way that he at least was on top and wasn't taking the brunt of the fall. He took advantage of the man's momentarily stunned state and began repeatedly punching his head.

The man got one scratch along Dante's arm before Dante gripped the man's head and slammed it, harder than was probably necessary, onto the flooring of the boat they were still on. He waited a beat to make sure whatever this being was wouldn't be getting up again. If this was real life, the being would be dead, but Dante had a sneaking suspicion whatever they were fighting wasn't strictly human.

When he stood up, he saw his wolf throttling the last of the other beings before dropping the short woman to the ground. His wolf had a few scratches and scrapes but luckily nothing looked permanent or worrisome. He himself had scratch marks up his arm from the first woman and large gashes from the man he had just taken down. It was a fifty fifty shot on whether they would exist when he woke up. Dante just hoped they weren't bad enough that he needed to go in for stitches. It was always difficult to explain injuries one got in a dream to the emergency room staff. He lost track of the number of lies he had told over the years.

"Do we need to get rid of these things?" Dante asked his sister, keeping his voice loud enough that he knew it would reach her from the foggy area she hadn't left since they entered the space.

Cecily wasn't much of a fighter. It was what killed her two years ago. She was an Omega wolf in her own right, and she miscalculated how possessive a werewolf ex-boyfriend was. Dante had killed the wolf, but not before he had sent Cecily to the hospital into a coma before she eventually died.

"Yes, we are still in the Omega's subconscious, and I wouldn't feel right leaving whatever these things are here. I can do some clearing magic and get rid of them, provided they don't actually belong here."

"All right," Dante nodded. "Just let me know if there's something you need me to do. I'll stay out of your way until you tell me otherwise."

"Will do," Cecily responded from closer, letting him know she had moved toward them now that the fight itself was over.

Dante walked over to stand next to his wolf, who was now standing face-to-face with the salt-and-pepper wolf, both of them appraising each other from about three feet away.

When he stopped moving, the salt-and-pepper wolf shifted her gaze between him and the wolf, clearly clocking they were two halves of the same whole. The wolf then made a large deep inhale, clearly scenting both him and the wolf.

You're a Guardian.

It wasn't a question, just a matter-of-fact statement as the wolf watched both of them.

"Yes." His answer was quick and pained. He had been one of his sister's guardians, and the fact that she died left a sick twinge of guilt every time he thought about it. She had two guardians, so they had both failed her. But that didn't lessen the guilt and pain.

Dante pushed his feelings aside and forced his face not to show his emotions. His sister told him, the first time she visited him in one of his dreams, that he should expect to become a guardian for a different Omega. Dante had been outraged by her statement. He didn't want to be anyone else's guardian. He'd already failed one Omega. Why would the universe trust him with another? But as he looked at the salt-and-pepper wolf in front of him, he knew Cecily's prediction had come true. He was meant to protect this wolf and her white-haired human counterpart. The dread and fear and anxiety crept through him like tendrils raking the inside of his chest as they moved to his throat. He couldn't fail another Omega, he just couldn't.

Where's your home? his wolf asked. Though it sounded a bit like a command, his wolf softened his tone a little in an effort not to spook the Omega wolf.

Currently? Western Washington State. But I do not know for how much longer that will be the case.

Dante couldn't have been more shocked if a vat of ice water had been dumped on him. His pack was in Western Washington. He was one of the lieutenants in that pack. He took his pack ties very seriously, and he loved his home. But if this Omega left Washington, he knew he would have no choice but to follow. He would never leave his Omega alone again as long as he drew breath.

Then it clicked and his eyes widened. "Are you the Omega from Eastern Washington?"

The wolf's tail bristled as she straightened up, almost as if preparing for a fight. *Yes*. The response was short and clipped.

Your old Alpha is looking for you, his wolf responded.

I'm sure he is. The wolf growled.

For Dante, this confirmed the theory that Alpha Peters had not been treating his Omega properly when she lived under his protection. Anger and disgust replaced the anxiety that had been rippling through him.

Are you pack or are you with Wilson? the wolf asked warily.

Dante hesitated, but only for a moment, before deciding to tell the truth.

"I'm pack, but for a short while I was with Wilson, until it became clear that all the things he wanted were not in the best interest of the pack as a whole. It sometimes itches how much power the pack has over our lives, but the alternative that Wilson wants is unacceptable to me. I will not live somewhere where strength is the only way to get respect and that those without it are not taken care of."

The female wolf eyed him appraisingly. Part of him wanted to ask why, what about his words was so interesting. But he had a sneaking suspicion she wouldn't tell him, even if he asked.

"Okay, I cleared them." His sister's voice came from the other side of the wolves.

All three of them jumped at the sound of her voice before turning to her. It was almost as if they had all forgotten she was there.

Dante looked around them and sure enough, the four of them were the only ones on the ship.

Since she died, Cecily very rarely visited with her wolf. Dante had never asked why the female wolf, who seemed a twin to his own, never came with her. Part of him didn't want to know the answer. The other part of him figured the answer would probably be more upsetting to Cecily than anything else.

"However, they might be back." Though she looked between the three of them as she spoke, when she finished, she centered on the salt-and-pepper wolf.

Why?

"They are part of you, in a way. They're of the same lineage as you. I'm not sure how to explain it, but they are ancestors. But not the ghosts or spirits of ancestors. There is something more charged about them. As if they are ghosts hooked up to a battery. I do not know what angered them enough that they would attack someone of their lineage. But I did a bit of warding. That should give you a few months of peace, at least."

The female wolf bowed to his sister. *Thank you. We are in your debt for your assistance.*

Cecily chuckled and waved the wolf off. "Not at all. If we Omegas are not looking out for each other, no one is doing it."

The words stung Dante deep in his soul. He knew his sister didn't mean it as a jab at his Guardian skills. But that didn't stop it from feeling like one.

You are dead.

"Yes, but I have a very strong connection to my brother and happened to be visiting him in his dream when we sensed the attack. I merely gave him a push in the right direction and came along for the ride."

The wolf tilted her head as if listening for something. She stood like that for several long seconds before straightening up again.

I dislike that we have three guardians so quickly. We went from zero, well, one really, though he did not know it at the time. The last part the wolf said more to herself than to the group. *To three in a matter of days. I don't think we are fully prepared for what might be headed our way to require the extra protection.*

Dante looked over to see his sister frowning. "What sort of ability do you possess? I was good with protection, such as wards and force fields and the like."

The wolf bobbed her head. *I don't know the words for it. But we can go into the heads of others and assert control there.*

Cecily gasped, and Dante's own mouth dropped open.

"A mind weaver? Mind weavers are rare and can extort immense amounts of power on others. I've never met any, but the Omega that trained me met one once. She could plant ideas in people's heads. Make them think things were happening that weren't. Almost like an illusionist. The woman's power grew so terrifying she had to be put down. I don't think you should let people know about those gifts unless you trust them absolutely. Mind weavers are the second most powerful Omega abilities anyone's ever heard of. You need to be very careful." Cecily emphasized the last sentence to make sure the wolf fully understood the ramifications of what she was saying. She then looked at Dante, the worry and shock playing on her face.

Dante knew of mind weavers. He read everything he could about Omega wolves once they realized what his sister was. The power they could amass was terrifying. They had targets on their backs just by existing. And now here he was fated to protect one of the most powerful.

You should go, the female wolf said so quietly Dante barely heard it. *My human half is asking for me and I wish to give her more than just part of my attention.*

"Of course. You be careful," his sister responded, and she held her hand out for a second as if she was going to pet the wolf in a comforting gesture, but stopped mid-motion and dropped her hand. "Let's go, Dante. It's almost morning and you have to be up soon."

His sister didn't wait for him, just turned and assumed he would follow. He gave one last look at the she-wolf in front of him. But her attention was elsewhere. Either on what his sister had said, or on what was happening in the waking world. So he didn't engage her further and instead he and his wolf followed his sister back firmly into his own headspace.

Chapter 45:
About a Girl

Keegan

He knew even before knocking at the door that something wasn't right. It was a feeling and smell of unease wafting from inside the apartment. If he'd been coming for any other subject, he would've found a reason to cancel. But he wasn't entirely sure what he needed to talk to Emma about could wait, so he pushed past his own concerns and knocked.

It took several long beats before the door opened, and when it did, it was only a crack. Much to Keegan's surprise, CJ was the one who stood in the doorway.

The shorter man looked exhausted, as if he hadn't slept a wink. If Keegan wasn't mistaken, there was a hint of fear in the other man's scent.

"What the hell happened?" The words left Keegan's mouth before he could think better of them.

CJ's expression didn't change, and he didn't open the door any further for Keegan to enter. "I'm not sure I could give you a coherent answer."

That response had Keegan frowning. "Are the women okay?" Even his wolf was standing at attention, straining in wait for the answer.

"I don't, I don't actually know how to answer that," CJ sputtered.

Before Keegan could ask any more questions, Raelene's voice wafted from inside the apartment. "Is that Keegan? If so, let him in."

CJ looked for a second like he was going to question her, but then he let out a sigh and opened the door for Keegan to step inside.

Once Keegan did so, he took in the scene in front of him and dread crept through his stomach and chest. His heart rate spiked at the instinctual werewolf's need to rip something to pieces.

Raelene sat on the couch with a shawl wrapped around her. She, too, looked as if she hadn't slept. But it was Emma that had Keegan wanting to start a fight. Raelene had one hand around a large mug, and the other around her friend, rubbing Emma's left shoulder. Emma looked drained. Where CJ and Raelene looked as if they might not have slept for a few nights, Emma looked as if she hadn't slept for weeks. Her face looked this side of gaunt, her skin was pale, and the bags under her eyes were dark.

"What the hell happened?" Keegan asked again as he dashed across the room and knelt in front of Emma, who was wrapped in a thick comforter, her hands around her own large mug of what smelled like coffee.

"I don't know," Emma whispered.

"What do you mean, you don't know? You just woke up this morning like this? Or did you not sleep?"

Emma shook her head several times and then, as if noticing she was doing it, forced herself to stop. "I had a nightmare that wasn't quite a nightmare. There were these beings that were so angry with me. They were draining me of my energy and power. They would have drained me completely, but some male werewolf came in and pulled them away. And CJ and Morris forced me awake before I could see what happened. But the damage seemed to already be done. My power seems to be completely on the fritz. I can't hear any wolf but mine. All of my newfound abilities seem to be gone."

It was something Keegan never heard of.

Could an Omega lose their powers? Weren't they an innate gift they were born with?

It made little sense.

This is bad, his wolf commented.

Do you think she lost her power forever? And if she did, do you think that would make her less valuable to Peters? He couldn't help the little hope in his voice.

Something in me doubts it. His wolf's words were a cold splash of water.

"You can't do anything?" he reiterated.

Emma shook her head again.

"No one can know she can't do anything. She can't be a sitting duck for Wilson, or the pack." Raelene's words held a thin layer of panic.

He agreed with her. He didn't think it was in anyone's best interest that word get out. If she was of no use to the pack, it would be easier for Ethan to give her up to Peters, and that was not a situation Keegan wanted to put her in.

"Agreed. He won't hear it from me. But I'm afraid that's not the sum of your problems."

Both women looked at him sharply and CJ came around the couch, so he loomed behind them. It was the most dominant Keegan had ever seen the medic. It was an interesting development and Keegan wasn't sure whether it was Raelene or Emma causing this reaction.

"What exactly does that mean?" the other man growled.

Keegan took a deep breath, then walked them through the conversation he'd had with Darian and Ethan. How the Alpha considered it just a matter of time before he reported Emma's presence to Alpha Peters. He gauged Emma's reaction as he told the story and he thought no more color could've drained from her face, but it did. Her eyes grew wider before she slumped in defeat. When he finished, they all sat in silence.

"I'm going to have to run again." The comment was barely above a whisper, and he was pretty sure Emma meant to be talking to herself and not the rest of them.

He watched Raelene's hand grip her friend tighter when he looked at the other woman's face. He saw Raelene agreed with Emma.

"I won't let him give you up to Alpha Peters. Not after knowing what you went through to get here. And I don't think I'm alone in that. If you run, you might always have to run. You won't have the support against Peters that you have here."

That seemed to shock Emma. She looked at Keegan as if she had never seen him before and her eyes teared up a bit.

"I'll stand between you as well," added CJ.

Emma began blinking furiously. "I can't be putting other people in that position. I'm a sitting duck. I can't do anything. What little worth I had in this crazy game is nonexistent at the moment, maybe forever. I can't ask people to go out on a limb for me. Especially people that I've just met."

"You don't have to have known someone a long time to do the right thing," CJ answered, full of resolve.

"He hasn't contacted Peters yet. I think you should give yourself a chance to rest and recoup before you worry about going on the run. Going on the run wounded will only make things harder for you," Keegan softened his voice so he didn't sound too pushy.

He didn't want Emma to leave. A bit of him panicked at the thought. But he wasn't sure how best to convince her to stay.

"He does actually have a point there," Raelene said, frowning. "You need more strength in order to get a fair use out of whatever head start you're given."

Emma looked between Keegan and Raelene several times before turning and looking at CJ as well.

"Besides, Morris is headed this way. You and I both know he'll be pissed if you leave before he can see you." This time, Raelene's tone was a little teasing.

Emma let out a tired chuckle. "Yeah, that's a good point. Okay, I'll give it a week and see where I'm at then go from there."

Keegan was sure his relief was visible. "Glad to hear it. Let's get your mind off of this. You need to get out of your own headspace and think about something that won't stress you out. Let me take you to dinner tomorrow night. Just rest and sleep through today and meet me at Beth's Café tomorrow at seven. It's a very fun atmosphere in the local area. You can get lost in the crowd and not worry about werewolf politics."

He could see her opening her mouth to argue, and he held up his hand to stop her.

"I won't keep you out late. I think you just need to clear your head and do something that's not related to work or wolves. And you won't have to worry about being out and vulnerable because I'm actually quite an accomplished fighter." He tacked on the last bit in hopes it would push her over the edge.

She blushed a little before opening and closing her mouth before finally sighing. "I've actually been wanting to check Beth's out. And I think you might be right. I need to do something that is not werewolf related. So sure." There was a soft smile on her face as she finished speaking.

Hope bloomed through Keegan. He wouldn't get ahead of himself. It's not like one date would convince her to stay. But she agreed to a date, nonetheless. It was something he had been trying to gear up to do for months. And it happened. He fought back the huge grin forming on his face.

"Great, and I'll let all of you know if I hear anything else about Ethan and Alpha Peters."

He got up to leave and looked at the skeptical faces of CJ and Raelene. CJ was sizing him up as a threat, which was new and interesting. Raelene looked more curious, but still protective. Actually, it made him feel a little retroactively embarrassed. He was glad he hadn't looked at them while he was asking her out. He probably would've lost his nerve.

When he got to the door, he turned back around, giving a soft smile. "You need to sleep today. Like most of the day. Of course, let me know if you're too exhausted for dinner. But do what you need to do to get rest. You getting back to fighting shape is more important than anything else." Then Keegan waved to the group of them. "You all have a good day." With that, he walked out of the apartment.

As he headed to his car, he found himself torn between the guilt for basically betraying his Alpha, the worry for Emma, and the anticipation of their date.

Chapter 46:
Rat in a Cage

Emma

"Are you sure you're up for this?" Raelene asked as Emma stood in the open doorway.

Emma had her doubts, and she was no more in control of her abilities than she was the night before. But she thought Keegan was right. Getting her mind off of her loss of power would be good for her. So she forced a smile at her childhood friend.

"Yes, I'm going to be fine. I won't be out long. So if I get exhausted, I'll come right home. It's just dinner, not a full night out or anything." Her stomach did a little flip-flop as she made that last statement, but she ignored it. It was way too soon in her opinion to be thinking about stuff like that.

Emma took a deep breath of the cool, fresh air outside. And found it calming to ground herself for a moment. Slowly, she made her way down the apartment steps to the parking lot. Once she unlocked her car, she stood there a second longer, her hand on the door and took another breath.

Once she was in and started the engine, she set the GPS on her phone to give her directions to Beth's Café. She had a vague recollection of where it was, as she had passed it a time or two while headed other places. So her mind wandered as she exited the parking lot. She was so envious of herself from three or four months ago. Even though her relationship had been a lie, she'd been happy. Contented in a job that she was fairly certain was going in a direction that would get her tenure. She had a wonderful apartment, and what she had thought, had been a wonderful boyfriend. Everything in her life had been going so smoothly. She was so happy. And now life was anxiety, pain, and an ability she didn't really understand. And while it was a comfort to have her wolf with her for the first time in a long time, it didn't quite balance out all the stress she was living under. All she wanted was a peaceful existence left to her own devices, but it seemed fate had other ideas.

Her mind wandered the entire drive to Beth's. Her GPS had startled her two or three times, ripping her from her thought process. When she reached the destination it took her another five minutes to find a parking spot. She heard rumors Beth's was quite a popular destination, but she hadn't assumed it would simply be street parking they would all be duking it out for.

As she stepped out of the car, Emma slid her phone into her back pocket and began striding toward the café. She hadn't gotten more than a dozen steps before her wolf shouted in her head.

Wolf. Threat.

Before Emma could do anything beyond register her wolf's words, she heard heavy breathing and loud fast steps. Then there was chloroform, or at least what she assumed was chloroform, over her mouth and nose. She wrenched her arms up to fight, as an arm braced around her elbows, rendering her arms useless. Panic shot through her. She could hear her heart in her ears and she fought against her body not to breathe faster. Lifting her legs, counting on her attacker to be taking all of her weight, Emma kicked back with all of her might. She had been wrong though. Her attacker was taking none of her weight. So she went to the ground, crashing to her knees. The pain blistered through her and she could feel herself losing consciousness. Though her arms were now free, she couldn't make them move to defend herself.

She swore she heard a male voice over her shoulder cursing to someone else. Then a second voice growling back.

So there are multiple wolves... Then she felt the world fade to black around her.

Chapter 47:
Cleared Schedule

Keegan

After a half hour past Keegan and Emma's supposed meeting time, Keegan's concern that maybe she wasn't feeling up to it turned into a sense of dread. Anxiousness coiled its way up his chest. Finally, deciding he had been getting enough glares for holding a table, he paid for his coffee and the pancakes he ordered about fifteen minutes ago, so he didn't look ridiculous sitting at an empty table. He threw down what he figured the bill would be, plus a hefty tip for the server, who'd come by several times asking if he was okay and if there was any news on his companion.

If any other date, established as a date or otherwise, stood Keegan up by thirty minutes, he would be angry and dismissive. But he couldn't feel that way about Emma. There were too many other factors to rule out. The server saw him standing and stepped over. Keegan took the bills off the table and handed them to her, thanking her with a nod. He then strode out of the café, past the line of people waiting to get a table. Halfway down the block, Keegan pulled out his phone and dialed the number he saved for Raelene.

The woman picked up after two rings. "Keegan? Is everything okay? Did something happen to Emma? Is she okay?" Her questions came out in a quick, breathy rush.

The dread coiling through him flared like fire, engulfing all of him.

"You mean she's not with you? She never made it to Beth's."

Panicked cursing came through the phone and he could hear Raelene yelling for CJ in the background.

"She left just over an hour ago. She should definitely be there. Hold on, I'm running down to the parking lot to see if her car is here." There were a few long seconds of silence. Not true silence, as he could hear Raelene's panicked breaths through the phone.

"She's not in her spot." There was more cursing, and she was clearly talking to CJ.

If he'd been paying attention, Keegan could've heard what she was saying, but his mind was reeling so he didn't catch the words.

"What type of car does she drive?"

Maybe, just maybe, she had gotten here early and fallen asleep in the driver's seat. The thought was so absurd Keegan could hear his wolf growling in the back of his mind.

"Um, it's a red Honda Fit. I don't know the license plate number." There was more rustling over the phone.

"Okay, I'm going to do a jog of the neighboring two or three blocks and see if I can find it. Because that seems like a pretty easy to distinguish vehicle."

Keegan jogged as fast as he dared. Werewolves could naturally run faster than human beings and for longer, as their stamina was better. But he didn't want to draw attention to himself by running faster than seemed humanly possible.

"Okay, we're getting in the car and heading your way. CJ's driving. Let me know if you find her."

Making a grunt of agreement, Keegan went a little faster, pushing as fast as he dared. He went two blocks, scanning each side of the street before he found a red car. Pivoting, so he could turn left, he jogged up to it.

"I found a red Honda Fit," he said into the phone as he glanced at the little logo on the back.

He could tell she wasn't in the car. He scanned around him for people before he put his face against the driver's side window and sniffed as hard as he could. Filling his lungs with the air to get some sort of hint of Emma. Then it came through loud and clear. "This is her car. She's not in it."

"Okay, okay, and you would've noticed her if you passed her on the way from the restaurant. Can you follow her scent on the street?" Raelene's tone conveyed barely controlled panic.

Shaking his head, Keegan pivoted, bending over to get closer to the sidewalk. He could smell Emma, but it was faint. It had been a bit and people had been walking up and down the busy street. It wouldn't be easy to follow her. He didn't have the best werewolf sense of smell, and though werewolves had a better sense of smell than humans, he couldn't pick one scent out of dozens.

"Kind of. But it's not very strong. If I caught it maybe twenty-five minutes earlier, before it was walked over, I could've traced it. But I'm only getting it about another two car lengths away from her car."

"Crap, do you think Ethan would help us? Because while Ethan has done some things that I may question from time to time, I can't see him kidnapping Emma against her will."

"He might help us. I can't see the value in him kidnapping her. I'm going to hang up with you. I'm about two blocks down from the restaurant and one block to the left. If I don't call you back by the time you get here, I should be in the area."

He didn't bother to say goodbye. Instead he hung up, scrolled, and clicked Ethan's name.

"Keegan, to what do I owe the pleasure?" Ethan's tone was jovial, which struck Keegan, even though there was no way for Ethan to know what was going on.

"I had dinner plans with Emma. We were supposed to meet at seven at Beth's. She never arrived. I called her roommate, and she told me Emma left about an hour ago. I jogged around until I found her car. So she was clearly here but never made it to the restaurant. I'm going to re-walk the surrounding blocks. But I think she's been taken, Alpha."

"What?" The shock in Ethan's tone was palpable. "Who would dare take a wolf from the middle of our territory?"

"Do you think Peters or his son would?" They were the first culprits Keegan could think of.

"I've no word of Peters making a move, and it would be an act of war to abduct a wolf from inside my territory." There was a long pause and when he spoke again, Ethan's tone was gravelly. "Though he might see it as simply taking his own wolf from my property. In which case, unless she's there to deny being his wolf, it's a bit of a gray area. I'll send some wolves to scour with you. Including some of our tracers. If none of you locate her, head to the pack house. We'll try to come up with a more solid plan. Text me and keep me informed of what's going on. I'll head to the pack house now and make my phone calls along the way. Don't worry, Keegan. We'll find her." There was a pause, then his phone went quiet.

    Keegan texted the update to Raelene and then began jogging a several block radii of the restaurant. Even going as far as searching the dumpster and alleys behind the restaurant. His gut knew it was a long shot. That she was long gone. But until there was more information, Keegan wasn't sure what else he could do.

Chapter 48: Introductions All Around

Morris

Something told Morris his meeting with Darian was not the reason for the unease he smelled on the air and the rather large number of wolves he saw bee-lining into the pack house when security flagged him through the gate.

When it became clear to Morris that Emma was doing better in Seattle and that he was one of her guardians, he started looking for work at several Seattle colleges. He had a job interview early next week, and scheduled a meeting with the second in command of the pack to introduce himself. He wasn't sure whether he wanted to join the pack. If Emma had, Morris would've done it without giving it a thought. But since she hadn't, as far as he knew, he settled for introducing himself as one of the Omega's guardians. Even though he hadn't had the conversation with Emma about what that meant, the second-in-command of the Seattle pack would know.

    Steering his car to the side to park behind several vehicles, Morris took in the people he saw standing around. It graded him to be on pack grounds, for a pack he didn't belong to, surrounded by wolves he didn't know. Wolves who had no loyalty to him and for who hospitality rules were the only things standing between him and whatever they saw fit to do. Morris was a very dominant wolf. And he could more than hold his own in a fight. But he saw at least a dozen, mostly armed, werewolves walking around. He couldn't take them all.

    Slowly, he walked toward the main entrance, getting weird glances here and there. His concern ticked up a notch when he finally recognized one wolf standing outside the front door.

"Raelene?" he called, concern clear in his voice as he looked at Emma's visibly worried friend.

The woman's head swiveled to him and her eyes widened as she stepped towards him without visibly thinking about it.

"Morris? What are you doing here? Has Emma talked to you?"

Oh, this is bad, Morris commented to his wolf.

I don't sense Emma near here, his wolf responded.

"Raelene, what happened?" There was more authority in his voice than he meant to throw the woman's way, but he didn't try to negate the effect.

If Raelene noticed the dominant power, she didn't show it.

"Emma was meeting one of the pack wolves for dinner." She gestured toward one of the two male wolves she had been standing with on the front porch.

Morris eyed him and quickly calculated he could take the other man in a fight if he needed to. Both he and the blond man standing at the front of the house were looking at Morris and Raelene with frowns on their faces.

"She never showed up. So, about a half-hour later, he goes looking for her and finds her car totally abandoned several blocks away. He couldn't find her. Neither can any of the pack trackers. Did Peters mention anything about finding Emma?"

Worry and concern vied for his attention. He knew how bad things would be for Emma if Peters knew where she was. He had been questioned multiple times, bordering on aggressive. But Peters didn't cross the line and Morris was pretty sure it was because the other man didn't know how strong Morris actually was. He would not be surprised to learn Peters, or Richard for that matter, kidnapped Emma. But Richard couldn't keep a secret. Morris was pretty sure, since he been paying attention of late, he would've heard something.

"Not that I know of, but Peters doesn't keep me as a confidant. You're sure she was taken, that she didn't leave?"

He knew he'd given too much away when Raelene's worried face went to a sad shock.

We might be the only ones aware of how serious she was considering leaving, his wolf commented.

"I don't know how she could. We found her car. And all her stuff is still at the apartment." Her voice was higher now, laced with panic.

That seemed to trigger the blond man on the steps as he, frowning, moved toward Raelene and himself. The black-haired man was only a step behind him.

"Who is this?" snapped the black-haired man when he reached them.

Morris copied the other man's dominant gesture. "Morris, Emma's friend from her old pack. One of two."

The man with black hair seemed to process that information, then his eyes lit up as if remembering something Emma might've told him. Morris wondered how close she was to this man that she would've been bringing up Morris.

"I see. And how did you find us here? This time, his tone was calm but still on guard.

Morris really didn't feel he owed the man an explanation but weighing pros and cons of keeping the secret if Emma was indeed missing, Morris let out a sigh. "I have a meeting with Darian scheduled in about ten minutes from now."

The black-haired man raised an eyebrow. "A little late for a meeting, isn't it?"

Morris bristled. "Maybe for you."

"Either way, it's going to have to wait," the blond man, he was pretty sure was CJ, interrupted, clearly trying to keep the peace.

That voice had Morris turn his attention to the blond man. He wasn't outright ignoring the dark haired man, but he recognized the blond man's voice. He felt his head tilt as his wolf's attention was drawn to him as well. "You're CJ, the other guardian?"

The blond man straightened and clearly tried to ignore the look the black-haired man gave him. Apparently, this wasn't common knowledge yet. Morris didn't know how long the blond man planned on keeping this secret.

"Yes."

"Were you with her when she was taken?"

"Of course not." He looked indignant.

"We don't have time for all of this. I'm going to introduce you to Ethan and Darian. I assume you're okay delaying whatever your meeting is about to help us search for Emma?" Raelene was clearly put out by the entire conversation.

"Yes." He gave her a soft smile. "And if you give me and this gentleman," he pointed his thumb at CJ, "a quiet space, we can probably point you in the right direction of where she happens to be.

"We can?" CJ questioned.

"How?" the darker haired man asked, sounding much more dubious and untrusting than CJ.

"We can, as her guardians, track her, for lack of a better word, based on our connection with her. It's one of the perks of being a guardian and being in the general vicinity of your charge. It doesn't work if she is more than fifty or sixty miles away. So if they traveled outside of the vicinity, it might be of no help. But if they haven't, we can find her.

"Then what the hell are we standing around here for? Let's get you introduced." Raelene grabbed his arm and practically dragged him through the front doors. It wasn't exactly what Morris expected for his first impression, but finding Emma was way more important than any sense of decorum or werewolf manners.

Chapter 49:
Take No for an Answer

Emma

Emma came to with a throbbing headache. Her initial response was to roll over and try to go back to sleep, hoping she could sleep it off. Then she realized she wasn't in her bed. She was on the floor somewhere. Before she could attempt to scramble to her feet, her memory came flooding back to her. At least two male werewolves had kidnapped her.

Stay still. Pretend you're still out, commanded her wolf.

I don't know if I've already moved.

A little, but you could've just been moving in your sleep. Just stay still and listen. I've smelled at least four werewolves around us. I don't recognize any of them.

Emma wasn't sure if she was more frightened or relieved her wolf didn't recognize her kidnappers. On the one hand, it probably meant it wasn't any one from her childhood pack. But seeing as she hadn't met the entire Seattle pack, that didn't rule them out.

"Exactly how much chloroform did you put on that rag?" growled an angry voice from somewhere to her left.

"I doused it! She's a dominant wolf. I wasn't gonna take chances," responded another, deeper voice from the same direction.

"We need to wake her up. Eventually people are going to be looking for her and then we'll have a problem."

"What do you think we should do? Slap her awake?" came a third voice from somewhere to her right.

They didn't even tie you up, murmured her wolf.

That's kind of insulting.

Her wolf chuffed, but didn't respond.

"Well, you slap her then," commented the second voice.

"Why the hell do I have to do it?" whined the third voice.

"Because we were the ones who went and got her," barked the second voice. Emma figured he might be the one in charge.

There was grumbling and the shuffling of shoes as he got closer to her. She knew she would only have a moment to take advantage of her prone position. She could kick his legs out from under him and do her best to jump up. The problem was, she didn't know how drowsy and out of it her body was. And she probably wouldn't know until she tried some kind of movement. Werewolf metabolism was great, but she didn't know how much she was burning with her powers on the fritz.

She heard the footsteps stop and braced herself. As he leaned down Emma made her move, pushing at the floor with her arm as she kicked out, swiping into the side of his leg. She couldn't quite get enough momentum to knock out both legs. But she opened her eyes to see him toppling, not expecting to lose his balance.

Jumping to her feet, still a little wobbly, Emma stood in a fighting stance and kicked out his other leg, causing the shorter man to fall to the ground. She then spotted an exit past the two other men and cursed before making a break straight for the wall across from her. Planning to pivot as soon as the other men chased. All she could do was hope she was faster than the large bulky man and the guy that stood beside him.

"Oh no you don't," growled the larger man. "Tackle her."

It was then the fourth man her wolf warned her about sprinted for the exit. He was closer than Emma and had an advantage since she couldn't see any other way out of the building. All she could hope for was bowling him over.

Just as she tried to pivot again, to throw the fourth man off course, she felt a larger body tackle her from behind. She'd no other option but to roll with it, or risk doing a lot of damage. Damage she couldn't afford with the scenario she found herself in.

They both landed with a whoosh of air exiting their lungs. But Emma rolled them so he landed first, taking the brunt of the hit. She tried to get away while he was stunned, but he tripped her, tangling his legs with her, so she fell down on all fours. The second fall gave the fourth man enough time to come up and grab her by the arm.

"Gotcha." His grin was predatory and triumphant.

This is not a good time to not have access to your Omega abilities.

Emma ignored her wolf. "Let me go. What the hell are you doing? And who the hell are you?" She began tugging at her arm in earnest, but the man wouldn't let go as he practically dragged her over to where the bulky man stood.

"Believe it or not, we just want to be friends." The bulky man smiled down at her as he spoke.

In that moment, recognition dawned. This was the man who'd gotten out of the backseat of Wilson's car. So this was the consequences of denying Wilson? He seemed only a little pushy. She never thought he would resort to kidnapping her.

But she supposed she didn't really know the man.

"Wilson's been trying for months, the nice way, to get you to join us. And yet you refuse. So now we're going to do things my way. You will be a useful ally for us against the pack. And you're not leaving here until you agree to join our group and our cause to take down Ethan and his underlings." There was a fanatical zeal as he spoke. And Emma wasn't sure which part of his little rant he was most excited about. The one thing she knew for sure, he was dangerous and, most likely, unstable.

"I told Wilson and I'm going to tell you, I don't want to join your little group, and I don't want to join the pack. I just want to be left alone."

The huge man stepped forward, so he stood in her personal space and made her crane to look up at him. "That's not an option for you anymore. You either side with us or I take you out of the equation."

A new bolt of adrenaline rocketed through her. They were going to kill her. This was their version of my way or the highway. And she didn't have enough magic to get herself out of it.

Quickly, she scanned the room. There were only the four of them and she couldn't hear anyone outside. So, she worked off a hunch. "And what do you think Wilson's going to say when he finds out you kidnapped me and threatened to kill me?"

There it was, just for a moment, a flicker of concern in the other man's eyes before he smiled at her again.

"What does it matter? You're going to be on our side."

She refrained from commenting that even if she agreed to work with them, it didn't mean she had to. They couldn't force her and not make it obvious. Mainly because this man didn't seem smart, she didn't want to give him that information if it hadn't already occurred to him.

Her mind began whirling. She had to think of something, some way to stall or get out of this. But nothing was coming to mind.

Emma? Morris' voice echoed in her head.

It startled her enough that she physically stiffened. She did not know what the men who kidnapped her thought the reasoning for that motion was, but she wasn't about to volunteer it.

Yeah, I'm here. She pushed the statement out as hard as she could. But she felt her headache get worse, and she wasn't sure she had enough power to reach him.

You're really faint. I've been trying to reach you. Do you know where you are? He sounded so frantic, yet excited.

No, it looks like it's a warehouse. That's all I know.

We're trying to track you. Are you an immediate danger?

She didn't know how to answer that. She didn't know if this man was bluffing about killing her or if he meant it.

I don't know, she responded slowly.

We'll get there as soon as we can. I'm in Seattle, with the pack.

She wanted to feel relief that help could be on the way. But since she didn't know exactly where she was, she didn't know how long it would take them to get to her.

"Hey, I'm talking to you!" a bulky man barked at her as the man holding her shook her several times.

"I don't want to join your alliance. I don't want to join anyone. If the only way to avoid sides is for me to leave the Seattle area, I can do that. I can disappear to parts unknown." She hoped giving a third option to this predicament would be good enough for him, though she doubted it would.

"No, my pal here," he motioned his arm to the one who tackled her earlier, "has been working in the pack offices and he tells me you're an Omega. And that makes you far more valuable than just a run-of-the-mill dominant wolf. Whoever has that power on their side is going to win this little skirmish. And I want to make sure it's us."

Her mind began whirling. Somehow it became common knowledge in the pack she was an Omega, and now this one weird alliance knew about it too. She was not safe here. Even if the pack could protect her for a little while, Richard and his father would find her sooner rather than later. She needed to get out of here and flee. Or she needed to join the Seattle pack officially. It was nowhere near the top of her priority list, but they could protect her, according to werewolf laws, from Richard and his dad.

Her stomach churned wave after wave and nausea rolled through her. She had no desire for any of this. She just wanted to be left alone. She felt tears prick at her eyes.

"Fine then, hard way it is." The bulky man cracked his knuckles dramatically before making a fist and pulling it back. Emma closed her eyes, flinching and tucking her body as much as she could, waiting for the impact.

"What the hell are you doing?" boomed a dominant werewolf voice. There was dominant wolf power behind it and she felt everyone pause and turn toward the voice.

She knew without looking it was Wilson. She'd spoken to him enough that she recognized the voice, even if it sounded slightly different when he used his power behind it.

"You were taking too long, so I took matters into my own hands," barked the bulky man, but he almost sounded like a petulant child.

"And what part of beating her up do you think is going to endear her to our cause?" Wilson cocked an eyebrow as he spoke. But there was a razor thin edge to his voice that told Emma even though he looked calm as he strode toward them, he was angry.

"I've given her a choice. Join us or join the afterlife."

"You're an idiot," muttered Wilson under his breath. Then he turned to the man holding her. "Let her go."

The man holding her looked at Wilson and the bulky man. Clearly unsure of who he should take orders from.

"You don't understand, Wilson..."

"Don't go telling me what I don't understand. You numbskulls kidnapped a powerful wolf and thought you could somehow convince her to join us. You are what, going to beat her to death if she didn't? You realize she lives with a member of the pack, right? They'll notice she was missing. And that is assuming they haven't already. It won't take them much time to figure out we're behind it. So far, they've left us alone, mostly. You're putting a large target on all our backs." He wasn't hiding his anger now.

The bulky man had taken a step back while Wilson spoke and was now looking at Wilson, confused. He was angry because Wilson interrupted his plan. But he also seemed to be processing the information Wilson gave him, as if none of that occurred to him before. Clearly, this was not a man who thought out any of his actions.

"She's an Omega wolf! That's something we need to have on our side," chimed in the man behind her, walking up to stand next to the bulky man.

Wilson's eyes went wide and his gaze shot to her quickly before going back to the men who supposedly worked under him.

"You thought kidnapping an Omega wolf was a good idea? Are you aware there are laws punishable by death for maiming or killing an Omega wolf? You beat an Omega wolf to death and they find you. The sentence is to beat you twice as bad as you beat the Omega wolf before killing you, you absolute imbeciles!" Toward the end, he was over-pronouncing every word at a shout.

The man who had been holding her arm released her and stepped away. In fact, all of them but Wilson and the bulky man took several steps back.

"Yeah, didn't really think that through, did you?" He pointed to the man who announced what she was. "You've been spying in the pack. You should be more aware of the pack rules than we are. Was it your idea to take her?"

The man looked panicked and began vigorously shaking his head while stepping back further.

"No, it was mine!" the bulky man responded. He almost seemed angry his idea was being attributed to someone else.

Wilson cursed vigorously before turning his attention back to Emma. "I would appreciate it if you'd let me handle this. I'm going to drive you back into town. Please don't judge the entire group by these four idiots' actions. I would consider it a personal favor if you wouldn't mention to the pack that members of our group tried to kill you."

He paused then, tilting his head and giving the smallest of smiles. "But if you decide to tell them, please give a very detailed description so they'll take out the right ones. Now if you come with me, we'll get out of here." He reached out his hand as if he expected Emma to take it.

Which she absolutely was not about to do. But she gave the bulky man a wide berth before moving to stand next to Wilson. She didn't know why, but in that moment she trusted Wilson not to hurt her and stick to his word.

When she stood next to him, his attention drifted back to his four colleagues. "I'll deal with you four later. You almost ruined our entire plan. Years' worth of work with one spontaneous, idiotic idea." He glared at them a moment longer before turning to Emma and motioning that she should go in front of him.

That worried her. He didn't want those men at Emma's back without him standing between them. She somehow instinctively knew it wasn't a 'lady's first' gesture. Perhaps things were not as stable in Wilson's little group as she thought. Or as he thought, apparently.

When they got out of the warehouse, she saw Wilson's car halfway across the gravel parking area.

"How did you know we were here?" she whispered. She didn't want the men to hear her.

"They tried to recruit someone else into the scheme this same way. He turned them down, claiming to be busy. Then called me and filled me in. Unlike these morons, he understood the ramifications of kidnapping a wolf with connections to the pack. Even if those connections aren't official. Though I am surprised to find out you're an Omega. But it certainly explains a few things." He gestured vaguely as he unlocked his car. "I assume they didn't take your phone or your wallet or anything from you?"

Emma patted her pockets and Wilson's hunch proved to be correct.

He's right. This was pretty idiotic. And to leave you with your phone, her wolf commented in disgust.

When she pulled out her phone and waved it at him, Wilson rolled his eyes. "Of course not. When we get closer to town, you might want to call and have someone pick you up. I won't drop you off somewhere close to pack territory, as I don't have a death wish. If I'm lucky, they won't know you've been taken."

"They know," she said simply.

"Dang it," letting out a sigh, Wilson started the car. "Okay, where did they take you from? I'll drop you off near there."

"Beth's Café in Seattle. A few blocks away."

He muttered something to himself. Quiet enough she didn't hear it. She figured he was probably talking to his wolf, just out loud. He was shaking his head so she figured it was yet another thing wrong with their plan.

"Thank you for saving me," she said after sitting in silence for about ten minutes.

Wilson let out a weary breath, followed by a chuckle. "I'll admit, part of it had to do with you. But I don't want them to put me on a hit list before I'm ready to make a move on the pack simply because some of my colleagues are not so good at thinking.

He's purposely not saying any of their names.

Yeah, I noticed that.

He's showing loyalty to them when they could've caused him a death sentence.

I'm still surprised they all listened to him.

He wasn't exaggerating. There is quite the hefty punishment for going after an Omega wolf. I think he just caught them by surprise.

With her wolf mentioning that unhappy thought, Emma sat in silence. And Wilson didn't engage her the rest of the car ride back into Seattle.

Chapter 50:
Phone a Friend

Alpha Peters

"Hello?" Alpha Peters answered his phone questioningly. The screen had shown a number with no note underneath, stating it might be a spam risk. Though his phone number wasn't exactly a secret, it wasn't public knowledge either.

"Is this Alpha Peters of the Central Washington pack?" asked the deep male voice. Even though it was a question, the tone was bland as if the answer didn't particularly matter.

"This is he," Alpha Peters matched the caller's tone.

"I have some information that may interest you."

Peters knew this was meant to intrigue him in some way, but it had the opposite effect. He was irritated someone would waste his time.

"If it's so interesting, then get on with it. I do have matters to attend to."

There was a pause and Peters smirked to himself. He managed to throw off whoever was calling him with such vague nonsense.

"I know where you're missing Omega wolf is." The smugness in his tone overruled the calm the caller was trying to portray.

But that piqued his interest. He had been sending feelers out looking for Emma. But he had done so under the guise of it being his son's fiancée. He hadn't mentioned to anyone at all that she was an Omega wolf. Whoever this was had more information than Peters was comfortable with. Which meant the price was going to be steep.

"What makes you think I'm looking for an Omega wolf?" He purposely kept his tone smooth, as if they were discussing groceries.

"Don't pretend with me. I know your son's so-called fiancée is an Omega wolf. I know you're looking for her and that she doesn't want to be found."

Peters' mind went in several directions. He tried to calculate what exactly it would cost him for such information.

"And what are you asking for in exchange for the information on my dear, sweet, future daughter-in-law?" He didn't have it in him to syrup his tone as he gave the endearment.

"I know you're making moves, building alliances, trying to take over more territory under the radar."

That set off a few alarm bells. Peters had been careful to keep his deals and agreements as quiet as possible. If word was getting out, he needed to be more careful. Odds were against this being a wolf from one of the territories he had agreements with. They'd all promised that should Emma appear in their pack territories, they would report it to him at once.

"That does not answer my question." This time his tone was a little sharp and

Peters ground his teeth together, trying to force himself to push his anger down.

"All I ask in return is that you leave the pack's territory she's in alone in this takeover scheme of yours."

Now that intrigued him. An Alpha was trading his own power and position for the location of an Omega wolf. That must mean the Alpha tried to get Emma to swear, and she refused. Otherwise, he didn't know why somebody would be willing to give up an Omega in their territory.

"I'll give you my word that I will leave your territory alone, as long as you do not hinder me and my son picking up my daughter-in-law."

"Good, I will hold you to that." There was a self-satisfied quality in his delivery.

Peters wanted to rip into the other man, but he knew he needed to bide his time.

He'll promise this Alpha he won't invade their territory. And he won't, at first. But eventually the Alpha would have no witness to Peters' promise, and it would be nothing to go back on.

"She's hiding in Western Washington pack territory. In Seattle. Living with a member of the pack who I believe used to be one of yours."

A grin spread across his face. So this was Ethan. It wouldn't take much to find out who that little friend was and hunt down her current address. Then the next step of his plan, that he was holding off on since Emma disappeared, could be set into motion.

"From one Alpha to another, I thank you for your help in finding my wayward pack member."

"An Alpha does have to do what's best for their pack," the voice responded.

"Indeed." With that, Peters hung up.

Smiling, he began tapping his phone against the desk. The plan could now finally come together. With an Omega wolf at his disposal, one who could read minds no less, no one would dare oppose him. And those who did would be taken down quick. He would control the West Coast in no time.

"Richard!" he yelled at the top of his lungs, knowing that if Richard wasn't in hearing distance, somebody else would get him.

Sure enough, the office door cracked open and one of the mid-level wolves bobbed his head up and down as he bent through the doorway.

"He's in another part of the house, Alpha. He asked not to be disturbed."

Peters rolled his eyes. His son could be a conniving plotter with the best of them, but screwing she-wolves was his downfall.

"I don't care what he said. Interrupt him. Tell him his Alpha has found his fiancée."

The wolf's eyes widened, and he bobbed his head again. "Yes, Alpha. Right away, Alpha."

Once the door was shut again, he started calling his lieutenants. Richard would need some reinforcements, and they would need a place to keep their wayward Omega once she was retrieved.

Chapter 51:
Return of the Man

Morris

"How is she not here yet?" Raelene asked, exasperated.

"She didn't exactly give me a roadmap on where she was coming from," responded Morris agitatedly.

They were in a pack lounge room with Raelene, CJ, Keegan, the Alpha, his second in command, Darian, and a lieutenant whose name Morris couldn't remember. Everyone else had been dismissed when Emma called, letting him know she was safe and heading home. At the same time, she had communicated to him mentally, letting him know she assumed she was safe, but the person she was with was iffy. And she would explain everything when she got there.

He let her know they were all at the pack headquarters and she promised to get there as soon as she picked up her car. When he commented they could meet her at her car, she refused adamantly and said she needed some time by herself to collect her thoughts before reporting back to him and who knew who else.

That had been over an hour ago. Morris reached out to her twice since then. Both times, she reassured him she was fine. The last time she'd even mentioned being in her car by herself. She added she would go a long route to get to the pack house because she didn't know if she was being followed and didn't particularly feel like being kidnapped again.

Every guardian instinct within him crawled at the thought of leaving her by herself. But he trusted Emma when she said she was fine, so he hadn't pushed the issue. But if she wasn't there in another half an hour, he was going to go out looking for her instead of being cramped in the space with everyone climbing the walls.

"We should go looking for her," Keegan piped in.

"And where exactly would we look? Sure, Morris can track her. But by the time we all get organized and figure out a way to follow her, she could already be here. Besides, it's kind of like going on a wild goose chase. Her abilities are really weak. There's no guarantee we could pinpoint her location."

Morris appreciated CJ's direct approach to things. The shorter man was blunt but caring. He was going to make a very good guardian.

There was a knock at the door of the lounge.

"Enter," Ethan called.

A she-wolf, barely five feet tall, popped her head in before sliding through the door and closing it behind her. She looked embarrassed and concerned.

"What's wrong, Agatha?" Darian asked as he walked towards the smaller woman.

"A wolf just walked through the door. He, well, he claims to be Emma's fiancé."

All eyes in the room swiveled to Morris.

He held up his hands in a stopping gesture and shook his head. "I sure as hell didn't tell him."

"All right, Agatha. Darian," the Alpha turned his attention to his second in command, "will you take Richard down to my office and have him wait for me? I've been waiting for this to happen. I just didn't think it would be this fast."

Morris didn't like the sound of that. He looked at Raelene, but her expression gave nothing away. He didn't want to think the Seattle Alpha had made an agreement with Peters, but he didn't know the man.

Darian nodded once, and with his hand at the small of Agatha's back, the two of them left the lounge, closing the door behind them.

Ethan took in the entire room. "Dante, Keegan, you're with me. Raelene, CJ, Morris, you lot stay here. I don't want him knowing you're here, Morris. And I don't want him thinking that we're concerned for any reason."

Ethan didn't wait to see if anyone would argue. He just slowly strode from the room and the two lieutenants followed him.

Once the door closed again, Morris exchanged looks with the other two. "It feels suspicious to me that we're being left out of the loop."

CJ grunted and Raelene bit her lip. The three of them clearly itched to follow down the hallway, but none of them did. Because Ethan had a point. Best not let Richard and his father know exactly what was going on.

There was another knock at the door and all three of them swiveled as it opened and there stood Agatha again.

She gave them all a nervous smile. "You three are to follow me. I'm taking you to the observation room." She was outwardly less nervous this time, but the nerves were still clear in her voice.

As the three of them started walking, Morris stepped in line with CJ. "Observation room?"

CJ nodded. "Yeah, I've heard rumors about these. Supposedly, there are small observation rooms attached to the higher level pack offices. They're all locked and only a few people have keys. I thought it was a paranoid rumor."

It was an interesting development. One Morris knew he had to set aside for now. Finding out what Richard was doing here took precedent over multiple hidden rooms within the pack house.

The four of them headed down several hallways before Agatha stopped next to a nondescript door that looked like a broom closet. She took out a little key and unlocked it, opening the door wide so they could walk through, but she stayed out in the hall.

"It locks from the inside, so while others are locked out, you're not locked in." She gave them that nervous smile again before slowly shutting the door.

The lights were already on and Morris could hear a conversation in progress in the next room. They were only covering pleasantries, the sort of benign chit chat that etiquette stated high-ranking wolves do in their meetings. But there was a strain on the situation since Richard had come uninvited and without asking for permission.

"I'm glad to hear your father is well. Are you here on business for him or on your own accord?" Ethan asked politely, getting straight to the point quicker than was customary.

"Well, you see, first and foremost, I would like to thank you. I want you to know how much my father and I appreciate you keeping my fiancée safe and alerting us to her presence here in your territory."

Shock flooded Morris. And from the squeak he heard Raelene make next to him, she was feeling the same way.

"I can't believe it. Ethan told them she was here?" CJ sounded so surprised his tone was almost too breathy to make out the words.

"I take care of all the wolves in my care," Ethan said carefully.

Morris felt Raelene grip his arm, her nails digging into his skin. When he turned to look at her, her mouth and eyes were wide. "You have to warn her, Morris. You have to warn her not to come here!"

Chapter 52:
No Good Sides

Emma

"I take care of all the wolves in my care."

Ethan's words echoed through Emma's head. A few minutes earlier, she heard a conversation in her head. It sounded like Richard and Ethan. And if she wasn't mistaken, she heard Darian's voice, too. It'd been so disorientating that it impacted her driving. Luckily, there was an empty parking lot she could pull into.

It was similar to when Morris spoke to her, or her wolf, except this was like a radio. Like someone was playing her a conversation that was happening. It was surreal.

"Ah, so you're saying she is officially in your care?" came Richard's smug voice. It made her skin crawl after hearing it again. It reminded her of all the lies he told her over the years.

There was a pause, and Emma wasn't sure whether she lost the connection or if no one was talking. Then, when she heard Ethan again, he had a bit of a false start before speaking.

"Well, not exactly. We have a signed agreement that she will help the pack and be compensated for her efforts."

"So that is a no. You have to know her agreement with my father's pack was never truly voided, since she didn't join yours. That means she is technically one of my father's wolves and he is requesting she be returned to us."

She felt a wave of anger from whoever was projecting this conversation to her.

The wave was matched with one of her own, except hers was panic. Ethan told Richard and his father where to find her. She didn't think he would do such a thing, but maybe he figured their agreement was enough. Emma didn't know enough about those sorts of pack rules to say one way or the other. But he let them know where to find her and Richard had come running. It was only a matter of time before Ethan handed her over or they figured out where she was living and snatched her. She didn't have a choice. She had to leave, and she had to do it now.

She heard from talking to Morris that Raelene was there with him, as were CJ and Keegan. So that meant all her allies were in the pack house. And she knew instinctively it wasn't Morris sending her these messages. While she didn't know who was helping her by giving her the heads up, not a bone in her body doubted the audio's validity.

Thank you, she thought hard in the direction the connection was coming from. *I will take your warning and react appropriately.* She then pushed away the connection. At least she was fairly certain she did. She didn't exactly have practice with this kind of thing. But it was too exhausting to live in the moment and listen to the pack betray her.

She knew she only had a bit of time before she would be found. So instead of heading to the pack house, she turned around and headed toward her apartment. She would gather up everything, or at least everything she could quickly fit in her car and leave.

Emma. This time, she recognized Morris' voice. It was faint. *Emma, Richard is here looking for you. It looks like Ethan let them know where to find you. The pack house isn't safe. You need to go somewhere else. Head to the apartment and Raelene and I will get there as soon as we can.*

Emma sent along her agreement and part of her felt bad for lying to her friend. She would not be a sitting duck. She didn't know if Richard or somebody helping him would follow them to her destination. Or if Ethan would just give him the address. It was in her best interest to get ready and get out. She would leave them a note, letting them know she was fine but not letting them know where she was headed. The less information they had, the safer they would be. Because now it wasn't just Peters she had to hide from. It was the Seattle pack as well.

Fighting the tears that stung her eyes, she did something she never would've expected herself to do. She scrolled through her phone and called Wilson as she headed back out onto the street.

"Emma? This is...unexpected."

Emma knew her voice would be watery, shaky, but there was nothing she could do about it now. "I've been found by the people I was hiding from. It turns out the Alpha of the Seattle pack gave me away. I need to leave town, and fast."

There was a long pause before Wilson took a deep breath. "Okay, give me your address. I'll meet you there. I have several bug-out bags and a contact that can get you a new ID. You can pay me back when you get settled wherever you go."

She didn't know why she was trusting Wilson to help her. Maybe it was the fact that he just saved her. Maybe it was because she didn't know who else to trust. But her gut was sure he would help her.

"Thank you," she whispered as she rattled off her address.

"A piece of advice. Don't pack more than you can stow in your trunk. That's maybe a suitcase, a duffel bag, maybe a backpack. Don't take more than that. Not only do you not have the time to pack, but you don't know when you'll have to stow your car. I'll see you as soon as I can get there."

With that done, Emma fought the tears that began streaming down her face all the way to the apartment she had been calling home.

Chapter 53:
Line in the sand

Morris

"She agreed to meet us at the apartment. She sounded faint, though. So I don't know if what little power she had stored is draining or if both of our emotions are impeding the connection. But I got through and she agreed to stay put there."

He could see Raelene's relief at his words.

"Is that safe?" CJ asked. "The pack knows Raelene's address."

Morris gave one confident nod of his head. "Yes, but they'd have to go look up Raelene's address. And if they do that, we can beat them to the apartment and warn her. But the only person outside of this room that knows where the apartment is off the top of his head is Keegan. And I can't see him giving them that information. Just look at his face. He's trying to hide it, but he is livid."

"Yeah, he's not doing a great job of hiding that," Raelene murmured.

"So, if you could just point me toward my fiancée so I may go pick her up, I would appreciate it." Richard smiled, a cat that got the Canary grin, as he spoke.

It made Morris want to punch him in the face.

"Excuse me, I'm getting a call I absolutely have to take," interrupted the lieutenant, Dante. Before anyone could respond to his statement, he was out of the office door, closing it behind him.

It irritated Morris, during a time that was so important, at least important for Emma, that Dante would be so flippant about a phone call. But for all he knew, there was some other disaster happening to the pack. He knew the world didn't revolve around them and their problems. But that didn't stop the irritation from bubbling up inside of him.

"Let me get this straight," Ethan replied as he slowly pulled out his desk chair and sat down. "Your fiancée leaves your territory without telling you, moves to an entirely different territory, presumably to escape you. And you want me to tell you exactly where she is?"

The words shocked Morris. He and Raelene exchanged confused glances before looking back into the room.

Richard bristled. "Yes, but she was not trying to escape me, as you put it. We had a misunderstanding. Nothing we can't clear up and get back to normal."

Ethan leaned forward, steepling his hands on the desk. "Even if I knew exactly where she was staying, that feels like a violation of trust. If she wanted you to know where she was living, I think she would tell you."

Richard growled, not the best move politically when facing off against an Alpha of a different pack.

"You will watch your tone," interjected Darian, his own growl lacing his voice.

Richard straightened and though his hands balled into fists, the growling stopped. "Why on earth would you tell my father she was here if you're not willing to give me her address?"

That seemed to take Ethan back, as he blinked several times. "The hell do you mean? I haven't spoken to your father in weeks."

"There's no reason to lie, Alpha. You spoke to him earlier this evening and told him that if he agreed to leave your pack territory alone, you would divulge where Emma was staying."

Ethan leaned back, the disbelief so genuine on his face that Morris believed him.

"I did no such thing. I don't know who told your father that Emma was here, but it was not me."

Snarling, Richard leaned in, somehow ignoring the other two werewolves in the room. "This is bull. You had the conversation with him. Just tell me where she is."

Ethan stood faster than he sat and leaned across his desk. Even though he was shorter than Richard by a good amount, his presence seemed twice the size of the taller man.

"I would never make that kind of agreement with your father. I would not give up someone's safety like that. I also have no doubt that should your father choose to try to take over our territory, he would fail. Run back home to your daddy, little pup. You'll be getting no help from us here."

Richard was seething. Morris was sure if they had been in the Central Washington pack house, he would be throwing things and screaming. This was the most restraint Morris had ever seen Richard exhibit.

"I will let my father know you have gone back on your deal and we will move accordingly." Once he finished, Richard stormed from the room, slamming the office door behind him.

"What the hell was that?" Keegan asked loudly.

"I don't know, but I'm going to find out." The Alpha turned to the mirror as if looking directly at Morris, CJ, and Raelene. "You have my word. I had no such conversation with Alpha Peters. Before Keegan's phone call, I was at my nephew's birthday party. Was there all afternoon. There are witnesses should you need them." He then gave one last meaningful look, as if willing them to believe him, before pulling out his phone and exiting his office.

"This is bad, this is terrible. If Ethan's telling the truth, and I think he is, there's someone in the pack who called Peters pretending to be him. We don't know who we can trust." CJ looked between Raelene and Morris as he spoke. "Can you reach her still?"

Morris reached out, pushing his power down the connection he shared with Emma. But it just kept going. Where he should've found Emma at the other end, there was nothing. He didn't know how that could be. His grandmother had mentioned nothing like that. Panic began to set in.

"No, I can't."

"We need to get to the apartment. Now!" Raelene responded as she ripped the door open and dashed out into the hallway.

"Be calm, Raelene," CJ hissed after her. "We don't want Richard to see you. Even if he didn't bring reinforcements, if he sees you, he'll follow you back to find Emma."

When Morris joined them in the hallway, Raelene was biting her lip and fighting back tears. Her hands were shaking fists. We need to warn her."

She grabbed her back pocket and yanked out her phone. Her hands were shaking as she scrolled to what Morris presumed was Emma's number. After several seconds, she started cursing. "She's not answering!" She began tapping the screen. "I'm just going to text her. But we need to find a way out of here so Richard doesn't see us. There's no telling if whoever pretended to be Ethan won't slip Richard my address. I can't believe this is happening."

Morris couldn't either. For good measure, he tried calling Emma. But again, she didn't pick up. So he also fired off a text warning her about what was happening and how they were heading to the apartment as soon as they could.

Carefully, the three of them headed down the hallway, ears straining for Richard's voice.

"I'm going on ahead," CJ finally commented after a minute or two. "He doesn't know what I look like or anything about me. Seeing another wolf won't throw him off. I'll let you know when he's left the parking lot." Not waiting for a response, CJ jogged the rest of the way down the hall.

"How long is she going to have to run and hide for, Morris?"

When Morris looked down at Raelene, he could tell she wanted an answer, and she wanted a comforting one. But he didn't have that to give her.

"I don't know, Raelene. I don't know."

Chapter 54:
Won't Take No for an Answer

Emma
Later that night

She could never repay Wilson. The go bag he brought her had three grand in cash, a burner phone, as well as a first aid kit and various other things someone might need while on the run. It also had a notecard with the name and number of a very discreet person who could make her a new ID. He also instructed her to use cash whenever possible. That it would behoove her to pull out as much cash as possible before she left the Seattle area so they couldn't track her credit or debit cards.

It made her queasy. All the steps she would have to take to disappear. She was also curious why Wilson knew all this information. But it wasn't as if she had time to ask.

When she left the apartment for the last time, she left her phone sitting on the kitchen table, as well as the apartment key. And a note for her friends letting them know she was safe and protecting them by not giving them any information. She also emailed work, putting in her immediate notice. Which was fairly easy since she wasn't set to teach any courses this quarter.

As they were leaving, she asked him one thing. "Why did you agree to help me?"

Wilson pressed his lips together as if considering his answer before speaking. "I'm a firm believer that other people should not choose your life for you. That was the whole point of the lone wolf alliance, at least to begin with. I don't think an Alpha should be in charge of speaking for other people. This situation is a prime example of why. They're more worried about politics than you. Plus, I think I owe you one, since in a way I'm at least partially responsible for you getting abducted." He gave her a humorless smile with that last part.

"Well, thank you. I'll figure out a way to pay you back."

Wilson shrugged and opened his car door. "There's no rush, and you won't be able to do it soon. Between gas and food and paying for a new ID, you got some expenses coming up. Good luck, Emma." He gave her one last look before getting into his car and starting it.

Emma watched him leave the parking lot before getting into her own vehicle. Only the trunk was packed, just as Wilson suggested. She felt weird leaving all her stuff. She was mad about leaving it all behind. Emma felt bad. She was basically saddling Raelene with it. On the note, she mentioned Raelene could bring the stuff back to Emma's parents' house. They have room in their garage for it, but she also prepared herself for her possessions getting sold off or given away. But there are more important things to worry about, so she started her own car and began driving north.

— — — — — — — — — — — — —

Emma had been on the road for over an hour before she pulled over. There was a little coffee stand next to the gas station she was at and Emma made the decision to grab herself something just as soon as her car was filled. She would drive as far as her body would let her, and the caffeine would help after the adrenaline wore off. She had taken Wilson's advice and removed as much money as she could from an ATM before leaving Seattle. It wasn't a lot, but if she was careful, it would last her until she could get the new ID and a new job.

As she heard the gas pump click that her tank was full, an engine roared up behind her car. She glanced over to see a motorcycle pulling into the empty lot, stopping at the pump immediately behind her. The rider got off the motorcycle and instead of going to the pump, began walking toward her. Emma froze, almost certain she hadn't been followed. But prepared to run for her car if she needed to.

The rider put their hands out in a placating gesture and said something muffled under the helmet. A second later, he took the helmet off, and Emma blinked several times.

"You, I know you." But she could not quite put together how.

Even still, the man in front of her looked so familiar.

He's the man who saved us in that ferry dream, her wolf supplied.

"Yes, that was me." Though he was answering her wolf, he spoke out loud.

Startled, Emma took a step back, almost dropping the gas hose in her hand. Not moving her eyes off the man, she returned it to the cradle.

I'm one of your guardians. I tracked you. I'm the one who shared with you what was happening at the pack house. Told you Richard was there.

"Why are you here?" Her gut said to believe him. But she still needed to know.

He tilted his head inquisitively. "I know you can hear me. Why are you speaking verbally?"

"It's a long story. Suffice it to say, I pretty much drained my power and am not really able to use it easily."

Surprised worry filled his expression. "That's not good."

"Yeah, does this mean Morris is going to track me, too?" While she loved her friend, she didn't want him endangering himself. Or convincing her that her plan was stupid.

He smiled and shook his head. "No, I've erected a sort of barrier." He looked a little sheepish then. "I can explain it in more detail later, but until you're out of range, I figured it was better if he couldn't hunt you down and take you back to pack territory."

"I'm sorry. Who are you? What, what is your name?" He was incredibly handsome, scruffy, and muscular, with an air of roughness about him.

His smile grew, and he bowed toward her. "Dante, one of your guardians. At your service. I had a hunch after your comment to me that you were going on the run. So I went home, grabbed my go bag and tracked you using our connection. I may have sped a bit to catch up with you."

"Does everyone but me have a go bag?" Emma exclaimed.

That may Dante chuckle.

"While I appreciate you taking your guardian duties seriously, you should turn around. I don't know what it is you have as a day job, but you can't be throwing that away to protect me. You have a life. Just go live it and pretend we never ran into each other."

The smile dropped from his face. "That's not an option. I've lost one Omega before and under no circumstances will I lose a second. It is not in me to let you go, wherever you're planning to go, unprotected. Especially now that I know you don't have your powers to help you." He turned away from her and began tapping the screen to pump his own gas. "Now, you can drive away if you want. But know I'll continue tracking you. I'll follow you wherever you're headed. So, I think it's best if we do this together instead of me stalking you for hundreds of miles."

Emma found comfort in that. She really didn't want to be alone. She didn't know the wolf in front of her, but she trusted him, her wolf trusted him. She knew the moment he said he was one of her guardians.

Letting out a sigh of defeat and a release of stress, Emma closed her gas tank cover. "I hope you got a passport, because we're headed to Alaska."

Still not facing her, he nodded. "Yeah, I'm all set."

"All right. I'll wait for you to finish and we'll get on the road together."

"Sounds like a plan," he responded, sliding a card through the reader.

Emma got into the car and started it, pulling away from the pumps but not leaving the lot.

Well, this is certainly an interesting turn, her wolf commented.

It is, is it bad that I'm a little relieved?

Her wolf appeared out of the shadows she usually lived in. *No, Omegas have guardians for a reason. They're some of the longest lasting relationships Omegas have. I'm glad we won't be alone.*

Me too, me too.

The End, For Now.

About the Author

Gretchen spawned in the Puget Sound region. After some wandering she returned there and now lives with her husband and the daintiest Rottweiler on the planet. When not drowning herself in coffee, as is custom in the Greater Seattle Area, Gretchen can be found at her day job or sitting at her desk in the home office, flailing her arms as she dictates to her computer.

If you enjoyed this book, please feel free to leave a review on the site of a retailer of your choice. Reviews are always appreciated.

You can find Gretchen at:

Gretchens.b.author@gmail.com
Gretchensb.com
www.tiktok.com/@gretchensb
Facebook.com/authorGretchenSB
www.instagram.com/authorgretchensb

Turn the page to find out more about Gretchen's other series.

Night World Series

These paranormal romances take place in a world with warriors, werecreatures, immortals, and magical practitioners. A rebellious plot may be coming to North America but that isn't stopping fate from putting the Night World inhabitants in the paths of their mates.

Each book has different main characters, though the members of the community keep popping up in other books.

Trigger Warnings: Some light fight scenes, kidnapping, consensual adult scenes.

Lady of the Dead
Viking Sensitivity
A Wolf in Cop's Clothing
Hidden Shifter
Visions Across the Veil

Berman's Wolves Trilogy

While in college an experiment goes horribly wrong and hundreds of students are turned into werewolves. Now years later these werewolves struggle to survive on their own as strange scientists try to take them for experimentation one by one. The more they dig into those scientists, the bigger their problems seem to be. Even their own are keeping secrets and could change everything.

Trigger Warnings: Some mild fight scene.

Berman's Wolves
Berman's Chosen
Berman's Secret
Berman's Origin *(A companion Novella)*

Anthony Hollownton Series

Anthony Hollownton is a workaholic homicide detective. When a case has him stumbling into the supernatural world, he finds it hard to believe. Even when he finds familiar faces. He wants no part of it and they don't want him there either. Yet case after case he's pulled back in.

Trigger Warnings: Some light fight scenes, graphic crime scenes.

Hollownton Homicide
Hollownton Outsiders
Hollownton Legacy
Hollownton Case File *(A companion Novella)*

Jas Bond Series

Jas owns a supernatural antique store he inherited from his mother. Though as a magicless son of the witch he doesn't always have a lot in common with his customers. All Jas wants is to live a quiet life with Bailey his goofy Rottweiler and run the store. But the characters who come into his shop keep yanking him back into trouble.

Trigger Warnings: Some light fight scenes.

Green Goo Goblin
Spectacle Stealing Supernatural
Book Burgling Blood Magic
Antique Absconding Arsonist
Property Pilfering Pariah

Lantern Lake Series

The holiday season is a big one for lantern Lake. Though the lake is surrounded by three small towns their holiday festival is something people come to see from all over the state. Not only does winter bring that holiday festival but it usually brings love along with it.

Each book has different main characters, though the members of the community keep popping up in other books. The heat level is low, with usually just kissing.

Pizza Pockets and Puppy Love
A flurry of Feelings
Teacher's Crush
Pugs and Peppermint Sticks
Moving Home for the Holidays
Mayor May Not
Building a Holiday Miracle

Scent of Home Series

A werewolf knows their mate when they smell them. The smell is said to be like coming home. And though that means something different to everyone it's always unmistakable. While finding one's mate might be easy keeping them is another story.

Each book has different main characters, though the members of the community keep popping up in other books. The heat level is low, with usually just kissing, with more happening off-page.

(Coming 2024)

Alpha's Magical Mate
Girl Meets Wolf